MEMORY

AND

DESIRE

Also by Philip Caputo

Hunter's Moon (2019)
Some Rise by Sin (2017)
The Longest Road (2013)
Crossers (2009)
Acts of Faith (2005)
10,000 Days of Thunder (2005)
13 Seconds: A Look Back at the Kent State Shootings (2005)
In the Shadows of the Morning (2002)
Ghosts of Tsavo (2002)
The Voyage (1999)
Exiles (1997)
Equation for Evil (1996)
Means of Escape (1991)
Indian Country (1987)
DelCorso's Gallery (1983)
Horn of Africa (1980)
A Rumor of War (1977)

MEMORY
AND
DESIRE

A NOVEL

PHILIP CAPUTO

Arcade Publishing • New York

April is the cruellest month, breeding
Lilacs out of the dead land, mixing
Memory and desire, stirring
Dull roots with spring rain.

—T. S. Eliot, *The Waste Land*

Author's Note

Persons familiar with the recent histories of South Florida and the Florida Keys will observe certain anachronisms in this narrative. They are not mistakes; I placed them there deliberately to tell the story in the way I wished to tell it. Likewise, some of the characters, while inspired by real people living and dead, are not intended to represent them.

PART ONE

1

In the hour before dawn, a full two hours before the sun threw its first punch of the day, Gunny assembled his derelict squad on the sidewalk in front of the Red Doors Inn. He'd collected them from under palm trees, where they'd slept unmindful of falling coconuts; from benches in Bayview Park, where the apostle of Cuban liberty offered the remains of his heart to the people of Key West; and from doorways and beaches and the White Street Pier, piercing the still, black, venereal sea.

From the upper deck of Mike Conway's house, across from the Red Doors, Luke could see the squad in the streetlights, standing at attention in a rank of five. At attention more or less, more less than more, their bellies sagging, shoulders slumped—postures that would have inspired epics of profanity were Gunny still the gunnery sergeant he'd been twelve years and a bad-conduct discharge ago. Now, he had no choice but to overlook their unsoldierly bearing and unshaven faces, their slovenly outfits: dirty T-shirts, grubby shorts, baseball caps rimed with dried sweat.

—*Lissen up, maggots! Rye-e! et face!* Gunny commanded.

A spastic comedy as one or two managed to face right while the others made clumsy pirouettes to the left or remained in place, twitching their arms and legs like marionettes on strings pulled by a palsied puppeteer.

—*Faw-wad 'arch!*

Luke leaned out over the gingerbread rail and watched men ruined by their addictions, men down on their luck, madmen insufficiently mad to warrant commitment shuffle and shamble down Caroline toward Garland's grocery, their feet ungoverned by Gunny's cadence: *wantup-threepfoyolefhadalefhadalefryelef.* That they were woefully, ridiculously out of step did not faze him, did not stop him from singing his measured tune. Luke suspected that Gunny, in his own wine-fogged mind, was not herding homeless wrecks down a cracked street in Key West; he was on a drill field at Parris Island, marching sharp recruits in stern formation—three straight files precisely an arm's length apart, precisely thirty inches back to breast, boot heels striking pavement in perfect unison.

—*Dee-tail, halt! Fall out! Lamp is lit. Smoke 'em if you got 'em.*

Matches and Bic lighters flared, and the winos flopped down at curbside to wait for Garland's to open, when they would pool meager resources for their daily ration of Night Train or Mad Dog. They seemed content to Luke. He thought them content with Gunny's predawn ceremony, in which they participated willingly; it conferred some measure of regularity on their inchoate lives. Out of the corner of his eye, he made out a geometry of long, thin, drooping triangles—shrimpers' nets hung out to dry from long poles in Singleton's yards; in the harbor beyond, where dock lights won a partial victory over the darkness, shrimp boats rafted up gunwale to gunwale, their raised trawl booms rocking gently on an incoming tide like giant metronomes. Workers were pulling into Singleton's parking lot to begin their shift in the packing and processing house. Hard, monotonous labor, standing by a conveyor belt in puddles of smelly brine, decapitating and packing shrimp by the millions, the wages low, but the plant provided a place to be, the job a thing to do. Start at six, quit at two—a fixed bracket of time in the day. It was important to have a place you had to be and something definite to do, Luke thought. If you did not, you risked becoming like Gunny's derelicts, rudderless and adrift; yet even they had a need for order. That was why, whenever Gunny pedaled up on his one-speed Conch Cruiser during his early-morning roundups, they willingly rose from their beds under the palms or from the benches in Bayview Park to answer his call: *Reveille! Off your asses and on your feet! Fall in at the Red Doors!*

"You're awake." It was Mike, already dressed in his fishing togs: loose shirt with vents in the back, khaki shorts, a long-billed cap. Luke, still in his underwear, hadn't heard him come up the stairs. "Sleep okay? Everything in Casa Conway to your satisfaction?"

Luke often stayed with the Conways on his fishing getaways to Key West. He said he'd slept well, despite being frazzled after the drive from Miami.

"Did that asshole's parade roust you?"

"Nope. Been up since five thirty."

"He marches those bums up and down, waking up the whole neighborhood. Day before yesterday, I called the cops but the battalion had retreated by the time our finest got here."

"Soon come summer, mon," Luke said, falling into a parody of island patois. "The winos will be flying north with the sober snowbirds."

"Turdbirds. More of 'em now than ever. There oughta be a law."

"You're the county mayor. Pass one."

"In a few months, former mayor."

"Still and all, the *Citizen* said you and Manny are the two most powerful men in Monroe County."

"Yeah. Every now and then that rag gets something right." Mike bared his slightly irregular teeth in a smile that bordered on the roguish. He liked to think of himself as a rogue, Michael Liam Conway, an unorthodox but effective politician respected by men, an Irish devil irresistible to women. "Suit up, m'boy. We've got fish to catch."

They drove in Mike's car to the M-and-M Café on White Street, picked up café con leches and the greasy sandwiches Mike called "coronary specials"—eggs, cheese, and bacon on buttered Cuban bread—and headed toward the marina on Stock Island by way of A1A. Condominiums and motels barricaded the highway's west side except for a half-mile stretch of salt ponds, their shimmer winking through the chaotic mangroves. On the opposite side, the clear green Atlantic reached to cloud mountains ranged on the horizon and tinted lava-red by the new sun. Luke never tired of that view: the expanse of infinite ocean, promising fresh possibilities, made him happy and hopeful.

"Ah, would you look at that artful slut," said Mike, taking one hand from the wheel to point at a woman running along the jogging and bicycle path on A1A's sea side.

Luke glimpsed bare arms, bare legs tanned and shiny, the bounce and swing of a blond ponytail.

"Am I missing something?" he asked, with a glance at the woman's retreating figure in the sideview mirror. "I don't see what's slutty about her. Or artful."

"That's Clarice. The hostess at Louie's? You didn't see how she came on to me last night? She was coming on, all right, and strong. I'll tell the world."

"Couldn't have been for your looks." Mike's vanity often amused, but sometimes annoyed Luke. Actually, at six feet, with a slender nose and lips set off by an Alec Guinness mustache, he wasn't a bad-looking man, just not as devastatingly handsome as he thought. "Okay, exactly how did this Clarice come on to you?"

"Christ, you're supposed to be a trained observer. You didn't notice the smile she threw me when I asked for our table? The twinkle in her eyes? Man, oh, man, those eyes. Blue as mine but positively Nilotic. Cleopatra probably had eyes like that."

"You're Marc Antony now?"

They passed Houseboat Row, a kind of maritime slum, and then the tidy grounds and white buildings of the naval hospital.

"She knows I'm married," Mike said. "Hell, she knows Liz. Liz wines and dines customers at Louie's, but that didn't stop her from flirting." That seemed to suffice as an explanation for Clarice's sluttish-ness, if not her artfulness. "It's power, not looks. Henry Kissinger said that, and he oughta know, married to that goddess, what's her name."

"Nancy Maginnes."

"She's six feet barefoot and he's a pudge lucky to make five eight with a good wind under him. It's power that does it," Mike went on, as if there were an equivalency between the power wielded by a for-mer secretary of state and the mayor of a county that consisted of the Everglades and a chain of islands dribbling off Florida's nose.

They crossed Vaca channel onto Stock Island, split by US 1, the groomed fairways and contrived roughs of the Key West golf course on the left, and on the right a clutter of bait-and-tackle shops, liquor stores, fish wholesalers, boatyards, and trailer parks inhabited by people more likely to smoke crack than golf for recreation. Mike turned onto Maloney toward their destination, Oceanside Marina. A sheriff's car was parked near a dented double-wide on concrete blocks. Probably responding to a domestic, Luke surmised, possibly a minor drug bust. Two ragged men wearing prophet's beards and flip-flops weaved down the street.

"Not too long from now, you won't see dirtbags like that around here," Mike said. "This rathole is going to be cleaned up. Ah-dee-fuckin'-os to the winos, crackheads, and all the refugees from the sixties."

"And how is this going to happen?"

"The ordinance! What's wrong with you? It was in the Keys sec-tion, front page of the Keys section of your own newspaper last week."

Mike's most recent achievement, the one he was most proud of: the Comprehensive Plan, a growth-management ordinance he'd shepherded through the county commission. No easy thing; from the Georgia line down to the Keys, the affection between politicians and real estate moguls ran deep in Florida's DNA. The ordinance curbed unrestrained development in Monroe County, but—the quo for the quid—permitted the gentrification of neighborhoods like Stock Island.

Mike himself had been a contractor, renovating old houses, and had gone into politics because he craved applause. It also provided a way to reconcile the altruist in his nature with the rogue. He relished the arm-twisting, cutting deals on the inside to cut ribbons on the outside: power exercised for the public good. Achieving worthy ends sometimes required a hand from characters whose ethics were questionable, even by Florida's subbasement standards. Chief among these were a Tallahassee fixer and influence peddler, Roy Stovall, who drove a black Corvette with a front license plate displaying his nom de guerre—DVLSDCPL—and Manuel Higgs, a half Cuban, half Anglo lawyer skilled in navigating the tricky reefs between the legitimate and its opposite. He also served, pro bono, as the Monroe County attorney, Mike's go-to guy for making things happen. It was Higgs who'd connected him to Stovall, who in turn guided him to the right people to green-light appropriations for his pet projects. Mike had often regaled Luke with tales about their shenanigans. Growing up in South Boston, one of three kids abandoned by their father and raised by a mother prone to fits of religious delirium, Mike had run the streets with delinquents who would later run with Whitey Bulger. Something in him was drawn to clever miscreants who got away with bending—or breaking—the rules. He lived vicariously through them. No harm in that, Luke believed, so long as the living remained vicarious.

At the marina, fishing guides were loading tackle into their charter boats, or putting them in the water; engines kicked into life; a forklift rumbled out of the enormous storage shed with a skiff on its prongs. The bustle and the white-hulled boats and the sun kindling the flat green sea stirred the old anticipation in Luke. He loved to fish for the hope it aroused, even if the hope often went unfulfilled. Cardenas was at the fuel dock, gassing up his vessel, a twenty-five-foot center-console with twin 150 Yamahas, its name—*Marekrishna*—and his—*Capt. Dustin Cardenas*—painted on its sides in black script.

"Well, here they are, my celebrities," he said, pulled the hose from the fuel-fill, and screwed the cap down tight. "Good morning, Mister Mayor, good morning, Mister Pulitzer Prize."

Luke had never won the Pulitzer; he'd only been nominated, fifteen years ago, for his coverage of the civil war in El Salvador.

"We expect to be shown due deference," Mike said, passing the grease-spotted sandwich bag to the guide.

"I'd show it to you, but you're"—Cardenas looked at his watch, a Rolex one of his megabuck clients had given him for Christmas—"more than ten minutes late. If you've gotta piss, piss now, if not, hop in. We've got a long run out to Tail End, and I want to be first one there."

Luke and Mike tossed their con leches in a trash bin and jumped onboard after wiping their feet on a dockside mat—a purely ceremonial gesture. *Marekrishna* was no gleaming sportsman's yacht. A working boat, her deck was permanently discolored from dried fish blood and slime, her hull scuffed from hard use. Her captain's appearance matched hers: a filthy baseball cap bearing a tackle company's logo, a T-shirt with a hole under one armpit, faded pants and deck shoes whose stitching was coming undone at the toes. Cardenas, considered to be one of the three or four top guides in South Florida, could have been mistaken for a homeless man, a recruit for Gunny's raggle-taggle army, if not for the Rolex.

He started the engines, Luke freed the bow and stern lines, and *Marekrishna* chugged through a no-wake zone toward open water.

"So what's at Tail End?" asked Mike.

"Blackfins, tons of 'em. We'll see if they're there. Not there, we can always run to the Marquesas and look for tarpon in the channels."

Cardenas throttled up. They raced to the reef, crossed it, and turned west past Sand Key light, the boat skipping like a coin over the sea swells. The Gulf Stream had meandered close in to the reef; the water was now a deep blue, almost purple, and speckled with archipelagos of brass-colored sargassum weed. Luke gripped the handrail on the console, his scarred knees flexing to the vessel's rises and falls.

The traumatic osteoarthritis in them and in his upper calves sent brief jolts of pain up his leg; yet he gloried in the wind, in the salt spray that smacked his face when the bow slewed into the trough of a long swell. A joy to be out here, under an open sky in an open boat, cutting across the unbounded circle of the sea.

Maureen would be getting ready for Mass right about now. If he were home in Coral Gables, she would also be nudging him to go with her, and he probably would—more for her sake than for the good of his soul. It bothered her to enter the church alone, when other women were accompanied by their husbands, so yes, he probably would go to make her happy. Keeping her happy wasn't always easy, and when her demons took control it became impossible.

Cormorants robed in black plumage roosted atop the light on Cosgrove Shoal, falling astern; ahead, Tail End Buoy, marking the western limit of the bar, bobbed on swirling currents. Cardenas throttled back to idle, shifted to neutral, then switched off the engine. The boat drifted in a silence that felt eerie after the noise of the twin outboards. These were wild waters, no land in sight, the Marquesas ten miles to the north, invisible below the horizon; so too the Dry Tortugas, fifty miles westward and nothing beyond them but more water until you reached the Mexican coast, four hundred miles away.

Cardenas looked up at a cloud of frigatebirds hanging well above the bar, dark wings moving just enough to hold them stationary. It looked as though every frigate within a hundred miles had decided to hover over this one patch of ocean. They were large, with long, forked tails and wingspans exceeding six feet, yet they weighed only half as much as the smaller pelican, their bones as light as balsa wood.

"Keep your eyes on 'em," Cardenas said. "They'll tell us when something's about to happen."

"Birds as prophets!" said Mike, a smile breaking beneath his Tunes-of-Glory mustache. "We have regressed to ancient times. Let's shoot one and read its entrails!"

Accustomed to Mike's occasional silly outbursts, Cardenas paid no attention, watching the birds floating, not soaring; floating on the air like tethered kites.

"Any second now," he said, alerted by some change in the frigates' movements too subtle for Luke to notice. He pulled two stout spinning rods racked alongside the console and handed them to his anglers. Luke went forward to the casting deck and braced a leg against a bow rail stanchion for stability.

A collective shiver rippled through the frigates and Cardenas yelled, "It's on!" as schools of balao shot out of the sea; it looked as if some submerged and profligate madman were flinging silver dollars into the air, thousands of them. Behind these brilliant showers flashed the arched backs of lunging tuna. The water was dark with them, dark with sparks of gold. They crashed into the panicked baitfish and slashed and tore and beat their tailfins, whipping the serene sea into a froth while the frigates dove on the wounded, scooping them up in their long, hooked bills. Stabbing beaks, snapping jaws, balao leaping into the alien air to escape the tuna only to be struck from above by the birds—the placidness of only seconds ago had become a frenzied mayhem, a kind of riot.

"Cast right into 'em, no finesse required," Cardenas said.

Luke pitched a white, feathered jig into the slaughter. The strike was shocking. In half of a half of a half of a second, monofilament line was tearing off the reel as the tuna streaked away like a torpedo. Fishing brings an intimacy with one's quarry. Line and rod transmitted the fish's power and tenacity of life into Luke's core; line and rod connected him to the blitzing tuna and, indirectly, to the swooping birds. He was not an observer in the audience but on the stage, a dancer in the anarchic ballet of predator and prey. Maureen was far from his thoughts now; so was a meeting he had to attend tomorrow with the Ritters, owners of the chain that owned the *Miami Examiner*, its flagship newspaper.

He wasn't thinking about anything except catching the damn fish.

It didn't stop its run till it had torn off better than two hundred yards of line, which Luke began to recover yard by yard, each yard fiercely contested. Mike had also hooked up, but to a much smaller and more docile fish. He had it boatside in no time, and Cardenas released it. Luke's reel hand ached, his forearm trembled as he raised the rod tip to keep pressure on his blackfin. After some ten minutes of struggle, its resistance grew weaker, its will to survive surrendering to exhaustion. It was still a good fifty yards out, the taut line slicing through the water in quick zigzags.

"Looks like you've got you a real keeper there," said Cardenas. He grabbed a gaff from a rack under the gunwale. "I can smell tuna steaks grillin' on the grill, damn if I can't taste 'em!"

Lower the rod and crank the reel, raise the rod, thumbing the spool to apply maximum pressure without breaking the line. At last, the fish was subdued, twitching some but definitely whipped, alongside the boat now and about two fathoms below. Leaning over the gunwale, careful not to throw slack in the line, Luke saw through the royal blue water what resembled a football, a yard long and half again as wide.

"A keeper, all right," said Cardenas. "He'll go thirty plus, easy."

With sweat stinging his eyes, Luke began to haul the tuna up to within range of Cardenas's gaff. He felt as if he were trying to raise an anchor with a spinning rod. And then he wasn't. A bright, silvery flash, like sunlight glinting off a chrome bumper, blood billowing green beneath the surface, and the heaviness was gone. Luke reeled up a head and a few inches of body, cleanly sliced, as if by a whetted cleaver.

"Ah, but life is nasty, brutish, and short on the Florida reef," commented Mike.

Cardenas pulled the hook out of the tuna's mouth and tossed the head overboard. "That might have been the biggest goddamn barracuda I've ever seen. Five foot if he was an inch."

"That's what it was, a barracuda?" asked Luke, stunned by the ferocity and speed of the attack. All he'd seen was the flash.

"Five feet of him, yeah. Must've had jaws like a gator's."

"I'm sorry for your loss," Mike quipped.

"No need for condolences," Luke said. "I can see the sorrow on your face."

Serenity had been restored to the sea as the school of migrating tuna moved on to wherever it was bound. The frigates resumed their vigil aloft, waiting for the next flotilla to swim through. The three men munched their sandwiches and waited with the birds, the boat rocking gently at anchor. The *Marekrishna* lacked a bimini top or any form of shelter from the sun, its reflection off the dazzling water doubling the force of its blows. The scorching brightness promised skin cancer as confidently as extreme cold forecasts frostbite. Luke greased his face and hands with sunblock; Mike rubbed a paste-white goo onto his lips and nose. Cardenas dipped into the ice chest below the forward seat and passed around bottles of cold water. Mike drank only a few sips from his and, removing his baseball cap, poured the rest over his head.

"Mary mother of God, your scalp could burn out here right through your hat. Oh, it will be good to get to Ireland. Clouds, cool rain, Guinness at the pub."

"Ireland?" Luke said.

"I'm buying a house there," Mike declared. It was the first Luke had heard of it. "The house my mother was born in. It's in County Mayo, near Leenane. It's a shambles now, so I'm getting it for a song, for a pittance, m'boy, for the price of a used Toyota Corolla. Well, maybe a new one. The house and five acres of sheep pasture."

"You're going to raise sheep?" asked Luke.

"Hell no. That's what my grandfather did. Why do you suppose he put the whole family and himself on a boat for the States? I'm going to renovate it. It'll be the kind of house my mother wished she'd been born in."

Setting things to rights again, Luke thought while Mike gazed off into the vacancy of ocean and sky—a blank canvas on which he made a verbal sketch of what the dilapidated place would look like when he was done.

"The local micks will walk by," he said. "And they'll say, 'D'yuh see that fine house there? Would you believe that's Liam Hughes's old house? It's Liam's daughter, Bridget. It's her son, Michael Conway, who made that miracle. An American, he is.'" Mike injected a brogue into the invented commentary. "When it's finished, I'll bring the old lady over, if she's still with us—Christ, she'll be eighty-six this year—and I'll sit her down in it and tell her, 'This is the house you lived in when you were a kid, Ma. Bet you don't recognize it.'"

The affection in his voice struck Luke's ears as strange. The whole time they'd known each other, he'd rarely heard his friend speak a kind word about his mother. When Mike was twelve, she'd caught him masturbating and dragged him to the church down the block to confess to their parish priest, face to face. That and other humiliations had made an enduring impression on her son's psyche. Whenever he came to breakfast in a sour, snappish mood, his wife, Liz, would ask, "Another bad night with Mom, darling?"

"It's going to be our summer place when I'm done with politics," Mike carried on. "There's a river not far from it, the Erriff, and a waterfall, Aasleagh Falls. Nice salmon in it. You'll be welcome anytime, Luke. Dustin, you too. We'll fish it and then stop off at the pub and knock back a couple of pints. The closing is set for middle of June, and—"

"We'll be in Ireland then, Maureen and me," Luke interrupted.

Mike's eyebrows arched. "What's taking you there?"

"The Bloomsday festivities. That's on the sixteenth. Maureen's been asked to give some kind of lecture."

"Bloomsday?"

"What kind of Irishman are you? It's this big celebration about Joyce's *Ulysses*. Held every June sixteenth, the day the novel takes place."

"Guess I'm a half-assed Irishman. Never read it myself."

"I wouldn't have either if I wasn't married to a Joycean expert. The lecture's a big deal for Maureen. A feather in her bonnet."

"The sixteenth, you said. Guess we'll miss each other, then."

"We're taking a week to tour the countryside. Maureen wants to see the ancestral lands. Maybe we could swing by your village."

Mike applied more goo to his lips. "Uh-huh. We'll see. Closings can get complicated, especially when you're dealing with another country's way of doing things."

"Sure," said Luke. His wife wasn't one of Mike's favorite people. Still, he would have liked a more enthusiastic response, an invitation to get together while they were both over there.

"Yo! World travelers, we're gonna do some traveling," Cardenas said. He motioned at the frigates breaking formation, soaring away. "Looks like the tuna blitz is over for the day."

They motored northeastward. What appeared as a haze on the horizon took on shape and substance, as if smoke were transforming itself into a solid. Soon, the Marquesas Keys, a broken ring of unpeopled islands around a shallow basin, rose out of the sea. The tide was nearing the bottom of the ebb, its fall exposing the parts of the flats girdling the islands. The golden-brown patches resembled mown wheat fields from a distance, and upon them, egrets and great white herons stalked on spindly legs.

Cardenas headed off to starboard, entering a narrow channel that formed an emerald-green serpent through the paler greens and whites of the flats.

"Look for rollers," he said after he'd dropped anchor and readied two big-game flyrods. Rollers meant tarpon surfacing to gulp air. "So who's first in the batter's box?"

Mike pointed at Luke. "And it's okay by me if he takes second, too. You know me, Dustin. I don't fish for what I can't eat."

"Yeah. I thought you might have had a change of heart," said Cardenas as he handed a rod to Luke.

"Not a chance. If you can't put it on the stove or sell it in a market, leave it in the water."

"The intention is to release them."

"I meant leave the fish alone. Blame my deprived childhood if you want. Fishing purely for sport is the pointless pastime of aristocrats."

Returning to the bow, Luke stripped fifty feet of flyline from the reel and laid it in loose coils on the casting deck. Mike's aversion to fishing for amusement, he guessed, was a way of not betraying his blue-collar roots. As for Luke himself, his background—an army brat, son of a retired master sergeant from the Kentucky coal fields and the daughter of a cannery foreman—barred him from membership in any aristocracy; nevertheless, he had no objections to catching the inedible. Pointless? Sure. The pointlessness was what appealed to him. Too much of his life, practically all of it, had a point, from the missions, large and small, the master sergeant assigned him in his boyhood to those he continued to assign himself. With the rod in his right hand, thumb and two fingers of his left pinching the fly to prevent it from trailing in the water, he scanned the channel for fins and silvered backs breaking the surface.

Cardenas, sitting behind him on a gunwale, poked the back of his knee. "Hey, Luke, can you make out what that is on the beach? That red thing?"

"What red thing?" asked Luke. All he saw were the leaning palms, the strip of sand bordering sea oats, and mangrove jungle.

"Look right. Those two palm trees way off at the tip of the island. Come about a fist left of them."

Swinging his gaze in the required direction, he spotted a large, boxy object. It was at least a mile off, so he could make out nothing beyond its anomalous color.

"A dinghy maybe?" he said, squinting against the late morning glare. "Or some big piece of junk that washed ashore?"

"I'd swear it's a car."

"Dustin, do I need to remind you that we're more than twenty miles at sea?"

"Unless I'm hallucinating, it's a goddamn automobile," Cardenas said, enunciating each syllable. *Aw-toe-mo-beel.*

"What are they asking for it?" Mike asked.

"We can always count on Mister Mayor for a laugh." Moving aft, the guide pulled a pair of binoculars from a drawer under the console and trained them on the mystery object. "And all of a sudden it might not be so funny. It *is* a car. A red car on some kinda raft, and it looks like two people laying down next to it and they're not moving."

"A chug?" Mike said, turning serious.

"What else? We'd better check it out."

"Chug" was slang for the jury-rigged vessels in which Cubans fled Fidel Castro's Communist paradise. A handful, piloted by people familiar with the sea, made the ninety-mile voyage successfully. Likewise those who were plain lucky. The rest—no one knew how many—provided easy meals for hammerheads and tiger sharks.

Once again, the *Marekrishna* weighed anchor. Cardenas steered her along the edge of the flats until she was almost abeam of the coconut palms that lent a South Sea aspect to the island. Then, pressing a button to raise the engines and keep the props from hitting bottom, he nudged her as far onto the flat as was prudent. The depth could not have been more than two feet. Luke tossed the anchor and snubbed the line to the bow cleat. The flukes dug in and the boat swung to, bow pointing landward, two hundred yards away across thin water growing thinner as the tide continued to fall.

Cardenas hopped up on the casting deck and scoped the scene ashore.

"I'm not liking this," he said. "It's two people for sure. One of 'em is a woman, and if they're not dead, they're the next thing to it. This is one for the Coast Guard."

He went aft to make the call, passing the binoculars to Luke. To the naked eye, the two prostrate figures might have appeared as an island-hopping couple asleep on the beach. The eight-by-fifties revealed a very different picture. The man was lying face down in the sand, his feet splayed; the woman was on her back, a tattered dress twisted around her knees; one of her arms was flung out wide, the other thrown across her chest. Neither twitched a muscle.

"Coast Guard Key West, Coast Guard Key West," Cardenas intoned over the VHF radio. "This is the motor vessel *Marekrishna*. How do you read? Over."

Luke shifted his gaze to the beached chug. "Contraption" didn't describe it. The rusted chassis of a 1950s-era sedan was roped to planks fastened in some way to fifty-gallon drums. The platform resembled a swimmer's raft, except for the metal plate attached to its back end as a makeshift rudder.

"Coast Guard Key West," Cardenas repeated with more urgency. "This is the motor vessel *Marekrishna* calling Coast Guard Key West. Come in, please."

Luke was about to hand the glasses to Mike when he saw a third figure emerge from the shadows cast by the palm trees: a boy of perhaps fourteen or fifteen who had spotted the boat. Staggering toward the water's edge, yelling unintelligibly, he looked like a cartoon castaway: barefoot, pants torn, a shirt with one sleeve ripped and flapping as he frantically waved his arms. Then he collapsed to all fours.

Cardenas dropped the radio handset, snatched two plastic water jugs from the ice chest, and said, "Can't wait for the Coasties. Let's go!"

They all three jumped into the water. It was as warm as the air. A bonnethead shark about two feet long cruised past with lazy sweeps of its tail. The marl bottom crunched underfoot as they slogged knee-deep toward what they knew was a tragedy. The only question now was how tragic it would turn out to be. The boy had got back to his feet and yelled again. *Ayúdanos! Por favor ayuda!* The water shallowed to their ankles and they began to run. Luke, carrying one of the plastic jugs, was the first ashore.

2

Maureen was in the Florida room, gazing through the open jalousies at the royal poinciana in the backyard, a tree she much admired when its scarlet flowers bloomed in late spring. The morning light fell on her in stripes as she sat on the sofa—the old one with frayed bindings on its bamboo arms—her bare feet propped on an ottoman, ankles crossed. She had brushed her shining auburn hair, put on lipstick and blush, and dressed in tan shorts and a dark green blouse printed with white orchids. Luke, standing in the doorway to the living room, felt the tightness in his chest relax, the tightness that had gripped him moments ago when he opened his eyes to find her side of the bed empty at six in the morning. Maureen was completely put together, completely composed. She hadn't been up all night, whirling about the house, rearranging chairs or pictures, or tearing weeds out of the flower garden in her nightgown; she'd merely woken up earlier than usual.

"You're up with the birds," he said.

She turned toward him, lavishing him with a brilliant smile.

"Thought I'd get a head start," she said, patting a stack of papers beside her. "My undergrads' term papers."

At the University of Miami, she taught an undergraduate English

course in addition to two graduate-level seminars: one on Irish literature, the other devoted exclusively to her specialty, James Joyce.

"Sleep well?" Luke asked, to confirm that his impression of her
serenity was correct.

"But of course. Like a dead buffalo."

He chuckled. "As opposed to what? A dead horse? A dead cow? A
dead armadillo?"

"There is something deader about a dead buffalo than the other
megafauna you mentioned."

"An armadillo doesn't make it as megafauna."

"Got me there," she said in a sing-song.

He was silent, unable to think of a way to keep the badinage going.

She asked, "What time did you get in last night?"

It was a simple inquiry, not an accusation in a question's clothing.

"Maybe half past eleven." He leaned against the doorframe, fingers plucking the loose threads in the pockets of his robe—the white
terrycloth she'd given him for his fiftieth birthday. "Got through with
the TV types at seven or so, right before I called you, but the traffic on
US 1 was thick as an LA freeway's." A simple inquiry, yes, but he felt a
need to explain the lateness of his arrival home. "I could've left by three
or four, but with all the TV people down there, I thought I'd give Mike
and Dustin a hand till the last dog died."

"Is that some new ruralism of yours?"

"President Clinton's. I've adopted it."

"Saw you three on the news, and it didn't look to me like Mike
needed a hand. He hogged the cameras, upstaged you and the other
one, what's his name."

"Dustin," Luke repeated. "A camera is catnip to a politician.
Anyway, it didn't feel quite right, me being part of a story, so I kind
of hung back. But listen, a man is dead, a woman is in the ICU, and a
teenage kid in Krome will be an orphan if she dies." Krome was the
detention center where foreign refugees, mostly Haitians and Cubans,

were held till somebody could figure out what to do with them. "That's the issue here, not who got the most airtime."

The last statement came out harsher than intended.

"Darling, I certainly didn't mean it was," she said, curling her lower lip out into a girlish pout. "The reporter said that the man was the kid's grandfather, the woman his daughter, and that he died of exposure."

"Heat stroke, dehydration, they'd run out of water," he elaborated. "He was dead when we found him. He probably died that morning. The body wasn't stiff yet."

"Oh, it must have been awful."

"I've seen worse."

"Yes. But you expect that in a war."

"TV doesn't have what the *Examiner* does," Luke said, shifting the subject slightly. He had no wish to get into what he'd seen in Vietnam or the Golan Heights or El Salvador. "I called our Keys bureau soon as we got back to Key West, and Kristen hopped to and found out that the guy had been a boat mechanic in Cuba. That's how he knew how to rig a car with a marine shaft with a prop in place of a drive shaft."

"She found that out from a dead man?"

"She interviewed the kid, Emilio Cortazar, before they shipped him to Krome. She speaks fluent Spanish," Luke answered. "Took the old man two years to build the thing in secret. Weird looking, but it worked. Crossed ninety miles of ocean in a forty-year-old car, a '59 Mercury to be exact. Incredible."

"Unfair is what I'd call it. All that effort, all that risk, and he makes it here and dies."

"Fairness had nothing to do with it. Wouldn't your church say that it was providential? That the Almighty called him to heaven for the Almighty's own inscrutable purposes?"

She shut her eyes and turned her face toward the ceiling, signaling strained forbearance. "As usual, I find your sarcasm tiresome, not to mention wholly unoriginal. Coddled eggs for breakfast—okay with you?"

"I was hoping for something more original."

"Oh, piss off," she said cheerfully. It was an expression she preferred over "fuck off."

By the time Luke finished shaving, showering, and dressing—in his new suit, a light gray poplin with blue pinstripes—breakfast was ready, the table in the Florida room set as if a photographer from some lifestyle magazine was expected at any moment. An egg coddler sat on each sparkling dish, hugged by slices of buttered toast cut into precise halves; and in the middle of the glass-topped table a silver carafe of coffee stood beside a bowl filled with oranges and mangoes. The breakfast table looked like this almost every morning. Maureen was Boston Irish, like Mike; unlike him, she was the laciest of lace-curtain Irish, on the same social plane as the WASPified Kennedys. She'd grown up in a household where proper etiquette and good taste were so natural as to be reflex. Her father, Ted Carrington, had held high rank in the State Department; her mother, Thelma, a concert pianist—albeit a failed one—had graduated from Miss Porter's School, whose most famous alumna was Jacqueline Bouvier. Thus, Maureen's decorous breakfasts, her classy dinners, and the chic cocktail parties she threw for the faculty were attempts to reproduce, as best she could without the full-time staff employed by her parents, a way of life that had been extinct since at least the 1960s. Ritual, rules, and routines were her three R's. Breakfast was always taken between 7:30 and 7:45 a.m. and always in the Florida room, except on the rare winter mornings when a cold front came through; dinner was served between 7:00 and 7:15 p.m., by candlelight in the dining room. A color-coded calendar hung above the desk in the master bedroom—yellow marked her class days, red social events, green shopping days, blue birthdays. Instructions for Adriana Montoya, the Venezuelan cleaning lady who came in twice a week, were posted, in Spanish, on a white board in the kitchen. Maureen attended the same Mass—the ten o'clock high Mass—at the same church—Our Lady of Sorrows—every Sunday.

She had a mind much like Florida itself—flooded in brilliant light but periodically ravaged by gales, against whose destructive surges the three R's served as a seawall. More than that, like her daily lithium doses, they helped prevent those mental cyclones from forming in the first place. Unexpected events upset her; serious disruptions could literally drive her insane. That was the big difference between Maureen and any other highly organized person. Luke had learned to tread cautiously in her presence, as if she were made of some fragile, volatile explosive. Wary of upsetting her even in minor ways, he submitted to the strict regime by which she managed her life—and therefore his. Raised on military bases till he was eighteen, a veteran himself of four years in the army, he had long ago gotten his fill of regimentation, but in the event she went mad again, he did not want to be the cause. His spousal mission was to help her maintain her equilibrium—for his own sake as much as for hers. He was afraid of her.

"The suit I picked out for you!" she exclaimed as he sat down, her sea-green eyes signaling approval. "What's up? Your usual outfit is a sport jacket with shiny elbows and no tie."

"Big pow-wow today with the Ritters." Luke unscrewed the top to the coddler cup, revealing mushy steamed egg, and yearned for two over easy with bacon and hash browns. "I expect to hear a lot of babble about *transitioning to the twenty-first century* and *meeting the challenges of digital media.* Then we'll be told to cut costs, meaning thin out the newsroom herd even more than we have already."

The pout formed again on her lips, red and full. "I know how you hate having to fire people."

"Yup. I'm the hire-and-fire guy. Me and Nick." Nicholas Ortega was the executive editor, Luke's boss.

Maureen had collected the morning paper. It lay open on an empty chair. She held it up like a flash card, front page facing him. "There you are."

Luke scanned the story, the headline and subhead spread across the front page below the fold:

CUBANS FOUND STRANDED IN FLA KEYS, ONE DEAD.
EXAMINER EDITOR AIDS IN RESCUE OF SURVIVORS
By Kristen Bernal

Key West, May 6—Three Cuban refugees, stranded in the remote Marquesas Keys after a harrowing voyage . . . Marred by tragic death of . . . made their desperate bid for freedom in a vintage automobile mounted on . . . The makeshift vessel was spotted by a Key West charter captain guiding Lucas Blackburn, this newspaper's managing editor, and Monroe County mayor Michael Conway . . .

It was weird to see his name displaced from its usual spot on the editorial page masthead. "I saw Kristen's raw copy before I left last night," he said, looking up.

"I'm surprised you let the clichés slip past. 'Harrowing voyage' . . . 'Desperate bid for freedom' . . . 'Marred by the tragic death.' Argh."

Ah, Professor Carrington was speaking now.

"Jesus, Maureen. It's a news story. It's not supposed to be deathless prose."

"It succeeded as far as that goes."

Professor Carrington was noted for the acidic comments she scratched in the margins of her students' essays and theses.

"Okay. It's not James Joyce, but at least it's intelligible," he said, returning fire.

"Chuckle, chortle, chuckle. You read *Dubliners*, so you know that Joyce was perfectly capable of writing intelligible prose."

"So . . . Speaking of Dublin, we'll be there in six weeks," he offered, with somewhat artificial enthusiasm. He wasn't looking forward to spending a couple of days among Joycean scholars and aficionados, with whom he had as much in common as he did with nuclear physicists. "How's your speech coming?"

She paused, gazing over his shoulder at the royal poinciana. "How I love that tree. The flame of the islands. It isn't a speech like I'm running for office."

"Lecture?"

She frowned. "I'll be more like a master of ceremonies. I choose excerpts from Molly Bloom's soliloquy, the actress recites them, and I shed light on what Joyce was getting at." She got up from the table and pulled a FedEx envelope from under the stack of student papers. "This came yesterday."

From the envelope, she removed a slick, four-page brochure, its title page reading BLOOMSDAY, DUBLIN, 1999, and gave it to him. Maureen's photograph and the actress's appeared on the third page, with a short description of the event to be staged at the Samuel Beckett Theatre at Trinity College. Fiona Powell was a TV star in Ireland and the UK. Maureen was tagged as "the distinguished American scholar, Dr. Maureen Carrington."

"She'll be on a bed, in a nightgown. In the novel, the scene takes place while Molly is in bed, remember?"

He did not. Maureen had assigned *Ulysses* to Luke after he'd read *Dubliners*. He'd found it incomprehensible, could not fathom why it was considered one of the greatest novels ever written, and skimmed vast sections, right up through the final episode, the now famed, once-infamous soliloquy.

Maureen said, "She's quite beautiful, isn't she, Fiona?"

"So are you. And a distinguished scholar. Says so right here."

"But she's younger. Quite a bit younger."

Wishing to avert a drift into her insecurities, he announced, "Mike is going to be in Ireland while we're there."

Maureen raised the carafe. He covered his cup with his hand.

"He'll be in Dublin?" she asked, her voice dipping several degrees.

"No. In a small town somewhere. I forget the name. Begins with an 'L' and it's not Limerick."

They finished their eggs and toast. Rising, Maureen gathered the plates and flatware and placed them on the butler's cart parked beside the table. "What's taking him there? Holiday?"

"He's buying a house. The house his mother was born in. He's going to renovate it, and I guess live there part of the year after he leaves office."

"How nice. Return of the native. The native's grandson, anyway."

Luke opened the French doors that led inside and followed her as she rolled the cart through the living and dining rooms into the kitchen, the spacious kitchen they spent a fortune updating shortly after they bought the house.

"Since we're going to be touring around, I thought we could spend a day or two with him and Liz," Luke ventured, striving to sound neither tentative nor assertive.

In her usual tidy fashion, stacking knives and forks in the bin with handles down, lining up plates like little round soldiers, Maureen loaded the dishwasher—a Bosch that did almost everything but mix drinks.

"Mike said there's a salmon stream nearby. He and I could fish while you and Liz . . ."

"You're sure she'll be there?"

"I imagine so. She should be. They're buying a house."

"Could you find out? A day or two with just Mike Conway in an Irish village—not my idea of a relaxing time."

"Y'know, I wish you would—" He cut himself short, dropping his gaze to the floor. Its tiles needed to be polished. They were the only thing he and Maureen kept before they renovated the kitchen:

sky-blue squares inlaid with white, geometric patterns that looked vaguely Islamic. Imported from Havana, the realtor had told them.

"You wish I'd learn to like him," Maureen said.

He nodded.

"It would help if he warmed up to me. Even then, it wouldn't be easy. Your fishing buddy suffers from *folie de grandeur*. The way he struts around, like being the mayor of a string of mangrove islands makes him somebody."

Recalling Mike's theory that power bestows sexual advantages, drawing a parallel between himself and Henry Kissinger, Luke could not disagree with this portrait. But he withheld his assent. Mike was more than a fishing buddy—he was a confidant, the brother Luke wished he had.

"Anyway, I want a cat," Maureen said. McKinley, their orange tom, had also been afflicted with delusions of grandeur, paying for them with his life after he'd picked a fight with a raccoon. "I'm going to the shelter today and buy a cat."

Put on his back foot by the abrupt change in topic, Luke looked at her, taking in her dimpled chin, her radiant russet hair, and her figure, kept in trim by half-mile swims thrice weekly in the gym pool (she'd swum on the medley relay team when she was at Wellesley). She was forty-nine, and there were thirty-year-olds who would trade their bodies for hers.

"No classes today, I have the time," Maureen said into his silence. "The shelter had an ad on TV last night. There was one adorable kitten . . ."

She cocked her chin, turning her head slightly aside while never taking her eyes from him. It was a gesture he was familiar with—she was daring him to object.

He said, "You ought to wait till we're back from Ireland. Why get a cat when we'll have to board him or find a pet sitter in only six weeks?"

It wasn't much as objections went. Maureen appeared to be disappointed.

"It could be a female, you know."

"Right. Him *or her*."

"If it is a male, let's make sure to get him fixed." she said. "That's what got McKinley in trouble. All that feline testosterone. I wonder if in his wanderings around the neighborhood, McKinley—"

Luke stood and kissed her cool forehead. "You want a cat, it's yours."

3

Aplace to go, a thing to do.

Piloting his Land Cruiser carefully through the Gables' narrow streets—designed to accommodate Model A's and T's, not super-size SUVs—Luke was happy that the *Examiner* provided him with both, in addition to a six-figure income and work that he loved. The newsroom was also a refuge from Maureen—or, more to the point, from his responsibilities for her, the same responsibilities he would have were she plagued with Parkinson's or MS, or any other crippling physical disease. In fact, as he'd been told by her shrink, hers *was* physical, at least in part. Of the episodes she'd suffered during the twenty-one years she'd been married to Luke, three had been total breakdowns. The last one, in the aftermath of a meteorological storm—Hurricane Andrew—had been the worst, landing her in the psychiatric ward at Jackson Memorial for sixteen days.

She'd been the soul of competence and efficiency as Andrew approached landfall, stocking up on water, canned goods, and flashlight batteries; she gave Luke a hand installing hurricane shutters, then evacuated herself to a shelter, where she rode out the monster's tree-leveling, roof-ripping passage through Dade County while Luke hunkered down in the *Examiner*'s newsroom, deploying his staff to cover the disaster.

Their house had sustained only minor damage, Coral Gables having been spared the worst. Luke—he had just been promoted to assistant managing editor—put in twelve-hour days, directing coverage of the recovery effort, so it was left to Maureen to hire crews to clean up fallen branches and replace broken roof tiles. The strain of it all—supervising the repairs, cooking by lantern light over a Coleman stove till power was restored, rearranging her ruptured class schedules—had no effect on her until things returned more or less to normal. Then, liberated from the need to take action, she went crazy. Crazier than Luke had ever seen her, or anyone for that matter.

One night, at around two in the morning, she got out of bed and began to roam the house, wracked by fits of weeping. When he went to comfort her, she turned on him, hurling insults in language that would have shocked her if she'd been able to hear herself. Dangerous objects—two solid brass bookends—flew as well. Her transformation from a very controlled woman into one utterly out of control had been terrifying, and was the origin of his understanding why people in the Middle Ages believed the mentally ill were possessed. Hours later, after two burly attendants hustled her into the ward at Jackson and slammed a steel door behind them, Luke thought he would never see her lucid again.

She came under the care of a prominent psychiatrist, Nathan Pearle, who restored her to sanity in a little over two weeks. Luke considered it the nearest thing to a miracle he would ever witness. Following her release, he met with Pearle in his offices in a medical building with windows like a fortress's firing slits. Luke had a conventional image of a shrink, which Pearle did not fit. Dressed in khakis and a polo shirt, he was thin and athletic, with a fisherman's tan: circles around his eyes two shades lighter than his cheeks from wearing polarized sunglasses. A bull dolphin hung on one wall, a tarpon on another. He and Luke hit it off fairly well; they talked fishing for a while before moving on to Maureen's case. Pearle assured Luke he had her permission to discuss it with him. He opened a folder containing her medical history: her previous episodes, one in 1981, the next two years later, had been diagnosed as postpartum reactions to miscarriages in the first trimester. The second attack had required hospitalization in St. Elizabeth's. (At the time, they'd been living in Washington, where Luke was covering the State Department for the Associated Press.)

"The doctor there told us to think twice about getting pregnant again," Luke said, feeling compelled to elaborate. "He had her on some medication that didn't work well with birth control pills, so he recommended an IUD or good old-fashioned condoms, but I . . . I decided not to take any chances. IUDs slip, condoms can break. I had a vasectomy." He paused while Pearle made notes. "I thought that if she just didn't get pregnant, she'd be all right, but . . ."

"There was no pregnancy, no miscarriage involved this time," the psychiatrist said.

"That's what blindsided me. It was like she was . . . like demons had taken hold of her."

Pearle indulged the supernatural simile with a professional smile, then offered his diagnosis. Postpartum had been the trigger in her earlier episodes for an underlying illness—Bipolar I, once known as manic depression. What Luke described as her "demons" were drastic malfunctions in her brain's electrochemistry, often but by no means always caused by stress.

Pearle expanded on his theme: There was a chemical in every human being, 5-hydroxytryptamine, alias serotonin, that carried messages via the nervous system to receptors in the brain. In some people, the messages got scrambled or were misdelivered, for reasons no one had yet figured out, and their brains went haywire, calling for the introduction of another chemical, Li_2CO_3, aka lithium carbonate, a simple salt that, also for unknown reasons, unscrambled the messages or redirected them to correct addresses in cases of errant deliveries. That, anyway, was how Luke understood the etiology.

As the conversation went on, Pearle donned the mantle of marriage counselor, advising Luke to avoid conflating his wife with her illness. In the throes of an episode, she was not herself, no more responsible for her words and actions than a cancer patient was for the renegade cells devouring her body. Luke would find it useful to remember that, for his own peace of mind as well as for the health of his marriage. He promised he would, though he wasn't convinced; he couldn't help but think that the real, true Maureen had been set free by her post-Andrew collapse; far from not being herself, she'd been fully herself, and meant every vile word she'd spoken to him. *In insaniam veritas.*

He loved her nevertheless, though not in the way he once did— "cared for her" described his feelings better. He shivered when he imagined what might have become of her if she'd been alone after Andrew. Possibly what he needed to escape wasn't her, or her affliction, so much as his reactions to it. They'd become instinctive. His alarm this morning, when he woke to find her out of bed at an early hour, had been as automatic as an eye-blink. His sensory apparatus was constantly tuned for bad signs: flashes of irritability or excessive giddiness, outbursts of unprovoked temper, too-rapid speech, quick, illogical leaps in thought. There had been flickers of madness in the past seven years, none severe. Still, he was determined not to be caught off guard again. He was a kind of weatherman, his eye fixed on her emotional barometer for ominous drops in pressure. The ceaseless, unconscious vigilance wore on his own nerves.

A place to go, a thing to do. Yes, he was only too happy to have a place to go, a thing to do. For him, work was a sort of daily vacation.

He and the two cars in front of him proceeded at cortege speed up Granada, under the live oak and ficus that made the street a shadowy arcade, lined by houses with clay-tile roofs, exteriors painted in approved colors. The Gables was a carefully managed enclave in Dade County's promiscuous sprawl, an artifact from an older, more genteel

Florida. Its imitation Spanish villas and Italian palazzos, most of which dated back to the twenties and thirties, threw off the formaldehyde scent of historic preservation.

A turn onto the multiple-named Eighth Street (Calle Ocho, the Tamiami Trail, also US 41) brought him into present-day Miami, the street gagging on traffic, heat shimmers already rising off the pavement. Eighth was a stop-start-stop mess all the way into Little Havana, where old men in guayabera shirts played dominos in Garcia Park and reminisced about the Bay of Pigs while dreaming futile dreams of liberating the homeland. Luke cranked up the AC a notch, popped a Tito Puente into the CD player, and crawled into downtown, arriving at the *Examiner*'s parking lot half an hour before the 9:00 a.m. meeting with the Ritters.

His reserved space had some shade from a royal palm; he blocked the windshield with a stiff paper curtain anyway. He locked the car and, in air as gummy as Saigon's, crossed the lot into the lobby, a marble-faced cavern, greeted the security guard, and rode the elevator to the fourth-floor newsroom. His first job in the newspaper business had been between his junior and senior years at Sierra Vista High School: a summer internship as a copy boy with the *Arizona Daily Star* in Tucson. It had been his gateway drug into a lifelong addiction. He remembered a city room that could have been a set for *Front Page* or *Deadline-U.S.A.*: reporters who talked fast and typed faster on their manual Underwoods; telexes hammering dispatches from far-flung places; deskmen yelling to copy boys like himself; the whole cacophonous carnival tented by a haze of cigar and cigarette smoke. Now, with the noise subdued, smoking banned, and reporters penned in cubicles behind desktop screens, newsrooms like the *Examiner*'s were as sedate as insurance offices. Not all the romance was gone. Looking out across the vast space where 427 reporters and editors toiled to produce Florida's largest and most influential newspaper gave Luke deep pleasure. He felt the completeness that comes when the thing you have found to do is the thing you were born to do. He was, down to the marrow, a *newspaperman*—a term with more red-blooded swagger in it than the anemic *journalist*. What he and everyone else in this room did for a living wasn't a job or a profession; a calling, rather. Information, *accurate* information, was light, and facts were the photons that carried the light into the dark places, dispelling ignorance, exposing the corrupt and the criminal, speaking truth to power.

He strode down a long aisle toward his office. Two or three staffers peeked out from their cubicles, giving him thumbs up for his rescue feat; Edith Buchmayr, the paper's senior investigative reporter, went a step further. Crossing her hands over her heart, fluttering her eyelashes, she mouthed the words "Our hero," then said aloud, "You're looking très Palm Beach in that suit. Well, maybe West Palm." Long ago, when he was fairly new to the *Examiner*, he'd worked with her on a political scandal. She considered them equals, even though he was now her boss. Luke flipped her the bird and strode into his office and shut the door.

The *Examiner* building's entire east side, a wall of windows five floors high and half a city block long, facing Biscayne Bay, gave the newsroom a view reputed to be the finest in journalism. Luke's share of it framed the MacArthur Causeway, spanning the scintillant water and the white towers of Miami Beach beyond. His office's opposite wall was solid plate glass, allowing the staff to see him and him to see them. He took off his suit jacket and draped it over his desk chair—to avoid wrinkling it—and then phoned Mercy Hospital for an update on the rescued woman's condition. Eleana Cortazar was stable, came the answer. He then checked his voicemail and email for anything that might demand immediate attention, but it was all routine stuff. One unhappy reader, apparently mistaking Luke for the opinion page editor, had sent a screed objecting to the paper's Sunday editorial calling on US Sugar to stop dumping waste water into the Everglades. He suspected that the disgruntled citizen was an industry lobbyist. He heard a tap on the glass, saw that it was Edith, and waved her in. With two long strides, she crossed the room, grabbed a chair, dragged it in front of Luke's desk, and sat down.

"Please, take a seat," he said dryly.

Edith was a woman of sixty-one, never married but reputed to have had a string of lovers. An inch or two above average height and slim edging on scrawny, she made no attempt to powder over the crags at the corners of her mouth and canny blue eyes; flaunted her gray hair, wearing it long and loose; and in contrast to young staffers, who favored the studied T-shirt and jeans sloppiness popularized by tech entrepreneurs, always came to work smartly dressed. Today's outfit was a dark blue suit, a white blouse, and high heels. She was a newsroom legend, the last *Examiner* reporter to stop using a typewriter. For months after computers took over the newsroom, her manual Royal could be heard clattering—a sound as anachronistic as horses' hooves on cobblestones—until she was compelled to surrender it. She'd given it a burial at sea, tossing it into Biscayne Bay.

"I know I should go through the chain of command but thought I'd save a step," she said.

"Whatever it is, you've got five minutes."

"I'll do it in four," she responded. He liked her directness.

"Did you get into a bar fight over the weekend?" he asked, noticing a round, flesh-colored bandage plastered on her left cheek.

"Too much of the only thing that's free in the Sunshine State," she answered. Her accent carried traces of her Florida panhandle roots. "A basal cell. Had it cut out last Friday. We've just used up thirty seconds of my four minutes."

With a twirl of his hand, he signaled her to go ahead. She crossed her legs—shapely by anyone's standards but especially so for a woman born before Pearl Harbor—and clasped her hands over her knees.

"I know there've been reductions in travel budgets, but I'm going to the Caymans and I'd appreciate it if you had my back in case the bean-counters howl."

"You're asking permission?"

"I never ask for permission, only for forgiveness."

"I assume this won't be a vacation," he said.

"Let's not waste my four minutes on cheesy humor," she replied. "I'm looking into an outfit called Oceanaire Properties, Limited. Incorporated on Grand Cayman. It's supposed to be a real estate investment firm. My source says maybe that and more. The Caymans—there's a red flag."

"What's the Florida angle?"

"TBI Development Corp. Ring a bell?"

After thinking for a moment, Luke heard it, loud and clear. "Thomas B. Incroce. Astoria Island."

"Thirty acres of prime undeveloped land within pissing distance of Key West," Edith said, to refresh his memory of the details.

Named for a Havana-bound ferry that had run aground in 1920, Astoria was a spoil island formed when the US Navy dredged Key West Harbor during the Spanish–American War. The navy had planned to build a coaling station on the heap of sand and limestone rock; after diesel replaced steam, it was going to be a fuel depot. Those and other projects never got past the blueprint stage, and in time nature collaborated with man to create a tropical wilderness: red mangrove colonized the island's shores, white mangrove, buttonwood, and casuarina its interior. In recent years, it had become a playground for graying hippies, a campground for homeless people able to hitch a boat ride, and a battleground. The combatants: Thomas Incroce, who wanted to turn it into a luxury resort, environmentalists who wanted to preserve it, and the United States government, which claimed to own it. Incroce had inherited the island from his father, Thomas Incroce Sr., who had won it in a high-stakes poker game from Samuel Lowe, a state senator and flamboyant crook, who'd bought it from the state of Florida back in the 1950s. There had been a problem with that transaction in that the island wasn't the state's to sell; it was the property of the federal government. By means that remained a mystery to the present day, the deal had gone through; Florida conveyed Astoria to Lowe through a quit-claim deed. But clear title wasn't passed to Lowe, nor to Incroce Sr. and so nor to Incroce Jr. The title was, as Edith had written in one story, "as murky as the waters in the Miami canal." To clear it and thus get the green light to proceed with his development, Junior sued in federal court. He lost, the judge ruling that the island was now and had been since its beginning the federal government's. He then appealed the decision. The case was going to be heard soon in the Eleventh Circuit Court of Appeals.

"A new twist to the saga," Edith said. "TBI has acquired a partner, a silent partner, Oceanaire Properties. According to my source, they've got money coming out of every orifice. The question is, Where does the money come from?"

"Any ideas?"

Edith answered with a shrug that could have meant anything.

"You're usually not this vague," Luke said. "Who's your source?"

"My very own Deep Throat."

"You're not going to tell me."

"He wants nobody but me to know that, for now, anyway," she said, leaning forward, tilting her jaw. "*Cui bono*, he told me. Who benefits? His way of saying follow the money. That's why I'm starting where it does, in the Caymans."

"Okay. But keep the expenses in bounds. No four-star hotel."

"No problem. I'm just a simple farm girl. There's one other thing." She hesitated, gazing at the display of *Examiner* historical front pages on the wall behind him. "I feel funny mentioning this. You and Mike Conway have been best buds since way before he took office—"

"Mike?" Luke interrupted, stiffening. "What—?"

An imperious wave of her hand stopped him from finishing the question. "Has he ever mentioned anything to you about Astoria or Incroce?"

"Nope."

"In case he does, I'd appreciate it if you clued me in on what."

"You'll be the first to know. But I doubt he will—he's retiring from politics. Besides, the flap is between Incroce and the federal government. Monroe County isn't a player."

"Right. But can I ask you to keep this under your hat?"

Bristling, Luke thought that was a pretty cheeky request to make of one's managing editor, even if the woman making it was an institution in her own right.

"I'll be the very *essence* of discretion."

There was another tap on the glass. It was Nick Ortega, summoning him to the meeting.

"Time's up," he said to Edith. "Keep me updated, and watch your skinny butt down there."

Compared with nationwide media empires like Gannett or McClatchy, Ritter Communications was a modestly sized dukedom. The *Examiner* was its most important province; otherwise, it consisted of fifteen small- to mid-market newspapers and an equal number of regional TV and radio stations in the Southeast. Its corulers were Owen and Gloria Ritter, a brother-sister team who'd inherited the chain from their father, Calvin Ritter, a good old boy from Walton County. He started the company in 1949, buying two small dailies, one in Florida, one in Alabama. Twenty years later, Ritter owned twice as many media outlets as it did now; in 1993, his children had sold half of them to raise capital to purchase the *Examiner* and borrowed the rest. Gloria was the duo's brains, Owen the brawn—a rough, profane character from whose mouth F-bombs dropped like iron bombs from a B-52.

The meeting, attended by managers from the advertising, production, and circulation departments in addition to four editors from the news division, took place in a wainscoted conference room on the fifth floor—Ritter's corporate headquarters. Gloria, a plump, middle-aged woman who wore her hair yanked back in a severe bun, turned down the lights and led off with a PowerPoint: pie charts, bar charts, and graphs projected onto a wall screen, followed by columns of statistics showing a gradual but dismaying decline in revenues and circulation over the previous five years. She spoke in a soothing monotone, sprinkling her presentation with standard corporate-speak idioms—branding, change agent, etc.—and added a few, the interpretation of which would have challenged a Harvard MBA. *In fiscal year 2000, we will undertake strategic initiatives company-wide to facilitate cross-functional synergy between platforms and institute data-driven procedures aimed at increasing impactful digital content.* She then launched into a disquisition comparing digital advertising revenues and production costs to print's (ad revenues much lower for digital, production costs much higher for print).

She brightened the lights. Her brother pitched forward in his seat at the head of the table, braced his elbows on the polished walnut, rapped his knuckles against each other, and silently scanned the faces of the thirteen people seated around him. With his sleek, black hair and blunt, rugged features, Owen resembled a younger Anthony Quinn.

"The message is this, gents," he began, ignoring the fact that three attendees, not including his sister, were female. "Print is fucked. You wanna know where print is right now? It's where illuminated manuscripts were when Gutenberg invented the printing press. You heard Gloria—digital media is the future, and Ritter Communications is not gonna get caught with its ass stuck in the past. Adapt or die! Adapt is what the dinosaurs didn't do, and they fucking died."

Three or four wordless seconds went by.

"We'll be doubling down on improving the online editions we launched a year ago," Owen resumed, directing a glance at Sarah Gordon, the online editor. "The website is gonna be redesigned top to bottom. You'll be hearing more about that in the near future. But I'll give you a sneak preview. Gloria mentioned cross-functional synergy across platforms. Here's what that means (*Thank you!* Luke thought).

Content providers in the print end of things are gonna do more than post their stories in the online editions. Video! Audio! In the next five years or so, they're gonna make videos of every fucking story they cover—"

"Excuse me," Ortega interrupted. "By content providers, you mean reporters, correct?"

His attempt to keep the sarcasm out of his tone hadn't altogether succeeded, and Owen glared at him.

"What the fuck do you think I meant?" A thick, liquid sound had come into Owen's voice, as if he were gargling as he spoke. "There'll be links on our online editions. There's more—we expect our reporters—is that better, Nick? *Reporters?*—to start blogging. Blogs with zip and zing. Any questions so far?"

Luke ventured one: If staffers were going to be blogging and making videos in addition to writing stories, how about offering them raises?

"The answer is no," Owen snapped. "We're going to be doing more with less. We're gonna trim the fat."

Ortega scribbled on a notepad and slid it toward Luke: *Here it comes.*

"Every department is going to have to lighten up on personnel," Owen went on. "Our estimate is that we need at least a 10 percent reduction in labor costs by year end, and more by the end of fiscal 2000." Luke glanced sidelong at Ortega. The executive editor's face, long and narrow with deep-set eyes and sunken cheeks, had a naturally grave expression; now he looked mournful. "HR is drawing up compensation packages as we speak," Owen was saying. "You know what to do—you've got people nearing retirement, offer 'em golden parachutes. Actually, silver parachutes should do. Whatever, we want to see every fucking department and division start Y2K lean and mean."

Luke pictured himself offering Edith Buchmayr a parachute to soften an early-retirement landing. Odds were she'd reject it, saying something like, "You want me gone, you'll have to fire me," knowing he would do no such thing. Half accidentally, half deliberately, he flipped his pencil like a cigarette butt; it rolled across the table almost into Sarah Gordon's lap.

"You've got a comment?" Owen asked, with a sharpness that indicated he didn't care to hear it.

"Yes, sir, I do," Luke answered, figuring the "sir" might make Owen more receptive. "Editorial has shed sixty-four people over the last four years. Better than half of those on my watch as the ME. It's one thing to sack somebody who's lazy or incompetent, another thing to tell people who are good at what they do to clean out their desks."

"Well, that's part of what an ME does," Owen barked. "What's your comment?"

"If we let another thirty, forty go, the newsroom staff will be under four hundred. We'll be lean, all right, but not mean. I don't see how we can keep doing our job, the kind of quality job we have been—six Pulitzers in the last twelve years."

"I don't give a flying fuck about Pulitzers. To me, prizes are—"

Owen's sister laid a palm on his arm, restraining him from further blasphemies.

"Luke, we're aware that print is our core business," she said, and paused for a beat. "*For the present time.* You've seen the numbers. The print editions aren't selling like they used to, and they'll be selling less in the not-too-distant future. And the future is . . ."

She flipped a switch on the projector and pointed at the screen, across which bold, black letters spelled **DRUDGE REPORT**.

A few low moans and sighs rose from around the table. Ortega laughed and said, "If that's the future, God save us all."

"Oh? Who broke the Monica Lewinsky scandal?" Gloria asked rhetorically. "That's not bad journalism. And pretty good from the business angle."

She rattled on, now with the fervor of a televangelist. Only four years out from inception and Drudge had one-third as many monthly page views as the *New York Times*! Its worth was estimated at between one hundred and two hundred million, and it was growing exponentially! One guy, Matt Drudge, with a desktop!

"And Drudge is only the beginning," she said, winding up. "Plans are in the works all over the country for entire online news companies, generating their own stories, with their own staffs but stripped down from typical mainstream staffs, and without the legacy costs. That's what we're up against."

Yes, Drudge had broken the Lewinsky scandal, Luke thought. But a blowjob in the Oval Office was a traffic citation compared with a true felony like, say, Watergate. That story would have overwhelmed the one guy with his desktop. But he knew that deploying the powers and glories of the printed word against Gloria Ritter's remorseless analytics would be like trying to shoot down a guided missile with a rifle.

He silently rejoiced as the meeting drew to a close.

"Can't stop progress, I guess," Nick said as they took the elevator down to the newsroom.

"Progress is change, but change isn't always progress," replied Luke philosophically. He thought of the Luddites, smashing textile machines in Britain a hundred and fifty years ago. They'd failed to stop progress, but it must have felt good to take sledgehammers to the machinery that would transform them from craftsmen into wage slaves. He wouldn't mind breaking computers into pieces. He was as dejected as he'd been buoyed when he walked into the newsroom two hours ago. He gazed over the warrens of desks and cubicles and wondered which would be empty in a few weeks, which of his crew he would have to push out of the plane, with or without parachutes. Returning to his office, he sat down to look at the story budget for today's editions.

PART TWO

4

He'd picked the Triggerfish Saloon and Grill for the rendezvous with Corinne. *Rendezvous.* The word carried a whiff of the illicit. Not that meeting her would be. Still, he'd wanted a place where people he knew in Key West would be unlikely to see him with a strange woman. The Triggerfish, in a district of ramshackle boatyards, marine repair shops, and grungy commercial docks at the tip of Stock Island, filled the bill. It lacked air-conditioning, relying on paddle fans and a front open to the sea to spare its patrons from suffocation: a mix of boat bums, diesel mechanics, lobstermen, and tourists soaking up local color.

Luke sat on the deck outside, at a pitted metal table shaded by a beach umbrella. A brisk sea wind, pushed by a Bermuda high, cooled him while he enjoyed a chilled Bombay martini and munched conch fritters. He seldom drank anything stronger than a beer at lunch, but he needed the martini to settle his nerves and the fritters to soak up the gin and thus prevent his brain from going walkabout.

He had not seen Corinne for thirty years, nor she him—in person, that is. She had caught his appearance on television a month ago, and two weeks later that had prompted her to write him, in care of the *Examiner*. When he'd plucked her letter from his newsroom mailbox, he immediately recognized her cramped backhand. He went into his office, eager to open the envelope and afraid to at the same time, as if it might contain a letter-bomb. In a way, it had.

In shock after reading the two lined pages, he stashed them in his desk drawer. Out of sight but most definitely not out of mind. He reread them again and again in the following days. Finally, he could think of no way out—he penned an answer that was cool and businesslike: "Needless to say, hearing from you after all this time knocked me for a loop. I'll be in Key West the weekend after Memorial Day. We need to talk about this face to face. Let's say the Triggerfish on Stock Island at 1:00 on Sunday, the 4th. Let me know if that's okay with you. If you have access to email, my address is lblackburn@examiner. com." Corinne did not have email; she responded with a terse, handwritten note: "I will see you then."

He'd come half an hour in advance so he could compose himself. It was entirely possible that he didn't need to arrive early. She would most likely be late, unless she'd changed her haphazard ways in the past three decades. She was how old now? Forty-nine? Hard to picture Corinne as middle-aged.

She is marching with the Art Academy krewe in the Mardi Gras parade, a girl of just nineteen, slender and lithe, costumed as the Queen of Mars in a crown of bobbing green antennae, green fishnets sheathing the longest legs Luke has ever seen on a woman. But her outfit isn't what captures his attention; it's the way she moves. It can't be called marching or even walking—she flows down Bourbon Street, languid as a bayou.

He is on a three-day pass from Fort Polk with Jim Fertel, his army buddy and a New Orleans native. He will later reckon it as destiny that when Jim gets them invited to a post-parade party in the Garden District, the Martian queen is there, towering in spike heels over her lady-in-waiting and an assembly of male subjects. Her complexion is fair and luminescent, but she isn't conventionally pretty—a wide, sloping forehead, a prominent nose, a long chin, and tightly curled black hair hanging over her shoulders like a scarf woven out of black lamb's wool. Yet she throws off an erotic charge that he can feel across the room.

"I've got to meet that one," Luke says. He will also reckon it as destiny that his friend happens to know the lady-in-waiting, a coppery blonde dressed as a Star Trek character. Jim makes a path through the crowd of courtiers and whispers to the blonde, whose name is Marie-Carol. She gives Luke a once-over and waves him over, saying with mock formality, "Luke, may I introduce you to Her Royal Majesty, Corinne Terrebonne."

Majestic she is, despite the ridiculous crown. In those heels, she is three inches taller than Luke's five-eleven. He has to raise his eyes to meet hers, lustrous as her skin and dark as her hair. There is something in their expression, something he cannot identify, that unsettles him.

"You must bow in the presence of royalty," instructs Marie-Carol.

He plays along and makes an exaggerated bow, the gesture not entirely an act. Corinne's sexual magnetism, as natural and unselfconscious as the markings on a butterfly's wings, commands submission. When he stands straight again, she, in a parody of granting knighthood, lays a hand on each of his shoulders. Then she pauses, and a little shudder goes through him as she brushes his biceps with a forefinger, her touch light as a current of air. "Mister Luke, honey, are you an athlete?" she asks, putting on a flirty Southern belle accent. Was, he stammered. On the wrestling team in high school. "You have the most beautiful arms," she continues, now in her natural voice—low, rich, captivating. Her accent is pure New Orleans: a gumbo of bayou Cajun and Deep South mixed, oddly enough, with an undertone of Brooklynese. "Why, Michelangelo himself could not have improved on them."

Luke wants to return the compliment, offer clever words of admiration for her slim figure, and how she seems to be in sinuous movement even when standing still. But he is speechless, a warm prickling in his face rising. Beads of sweat pop from his forehead. A blush spreads over Corinne's cheeks as well. Maybe she thinks she's embarrassed herself, flirting with him, telling him he has beautiful arms ten seconds after meeting him.

But no, he thinks. It's not embarrassment. She's feeling what he feels. He's sure of it, and no less sure that he can now read the expression in her eyes. It's one of challenge and surrender, as if she's daring him to carry her off right then, promising that she'll offer no resistance, will in fact welcome it. Everyone in the room fades into the background, their voices falling into an unintelligible murmur. The young man and the young woman might as well be alone, in thrall to the overpowering and instantaneous attraction that people commonly call love at first sight, the benign triteness domesticating its thrilling terror. Luke knows—and knows that Corinne does, too—that their lives can no longer be separate, nor be completely their own, and there is nothing they can do about it.

Luke reached into his back pocket for the letter, smoothing the creases with his palm as he laid the pages on the table, and then reread them for, what was it now? The fifth time? The sixth?

808 Ashe St.
Key West, FL 33040
May 18, 1999

Dear Luke,

I've argued with myself for days and days if I should write you. Guess the ayes have it. I hardly know where to begin, I'm still blown away from seeing you on the TV news a couple of weeks ago. Almost fell out of my chair! (You're aging well, by the way.) That must have been some experience, finding those stranded people. Weird thing is, I hardly ever watch the news. I just happened to be surfing channels and there you were on the screen! Let me say I'm happy you made it back from Vietnam in one piece. I had no idea you were here in Florida. As you can see, so am I. Moved to K.W. from Texas six months ago. Fate? Coincidence?

Better get to the reason I'm writing before I lose the nerve. I'll try to be concise. I've been in touch with Ian off and on the past few years. I even got to meet him. It was okay with his parents. You probably don't know this, but the laws and rules about adopted children making contact with their birth parents were loosened up some time ago. That's how we were able to get in touch.

Now for the hard parts. First, his parents died a while back, his mother of cancer, his father of a stroke around two years later. Second, he's in jail in Arizona. Drug charges. So far, he's served two years of a three-year sentence and will be up for early release this summer. He's requested to do his parole in another state. To do that, he has to have a sponsor. I've volunteered because I feel it's the right thing for me to step into the shoes I vacated so long ago. He's going to live with me for the time he's on parole. Third hard part. Ian has asked me a couple of times about his birth father. I told him—honestly—that I knew nothing about where he was or even if he was living or dead. All I knew was his name and I couldn't reveal that without permission.

Ian might ask me again, might not. I don't want to lie to him if he does, but I can't tell him about you without your consent. So I'm asking if you're willing to give it. Believe me, if the answer is no, I'll honor that. I sure don't want to cause you any trouble, and I probably have some nerve, asking in the first place. But maybe you've wondered about him all these many, many years. Please let me know whenever you can one way or the other.

XOXO

She signed it, as she had the letters she'd sent him when he was in the army, with an outline of a cat sitting on its haunches. It stood for her initials: C.A.T., Corinne Anne Terrebonne.

Ian. Ian what? Locked up on drug charges, Jesus H. Christ. Corinne's words stirred in Luke an emotional brawl as fierce as when he'd read them the first time. Regret, shame, longing, sorrow, excitement, nostalgia, and terror—all took swings at him. One line, "the right thing for me to step into the shoes I vacated so long ago," struck the hardest. If Corinne had not written it, he might well not be here now, waiting for her.

Mr. Hayakawa lives across Jones Street in a stucco-faced townhouse as unblemished as desert bone. Looking out the front window, Luke watches him back a Mercedes sedan out of the garage, park it in the driveway, then remove a long-handled brush from the trunk and whisk the car's exterior with the care of a conscientious maid dusting a treasured heirloom. Luke has never met the man and doesn't know his real name. He calls him Mr. Hayakawa because, with his Asian features, black mustache, and trim black hair, he resembles Sessue Hayakawa as Colonel Saito in The Bridge on the River Kwai. *He is wearing snug leather gloves, although it isn't cold, and goes over the entire car, roof to rocker panels. When he's done, he cleans the brush with his hands, returns it to the trunk, and drives off toward the intersection of Jones and Jackson Streets. This routine takes place every morning, invariably between 7:30 and 7:45, when fog still cloaks the city below and shrouded ships in San Francisco Bay converse in a cryptic language of shrill whistle blasts and the diaphonic groans of foghorns.*

An early riser, Luke first noticed his neighbor the day after he and Corinne moved into the second-floor studio on a short-term lease. The man caught his attention because cleaning the car was completely unnecessary: the pale yellow sedan was showroom spotless. Corinne—who goes at life freestyle, making it up as she does her paintings, without a plan, following her whims and instincts, which are, in Luke's opinion, not always reliable—has called him an "obsessive-compulsive, a guy with a stick up his ass." He doesn't think Mr. Hayakawa has a stick up his ass. No, he's an apostle of order. His punctuality, dependable as sunrise, the methodical strokes of the brush as it passes over the Mercedes' shining skin are a silent gospel preaching that there is a fitness to things. Luke has made a ritual of watching Mr. Hayakawa's ritual for the past month; it calms him, fortifies him to face what he knows is coming.

The memory calmed him now. The inner quiet didn't last long. When a pink taxi with FIVE 6's stenciled on its door stopped across the street and Corinne stepped out, wearing large sunglasses and a sleeveless, canary-yellow caftan that swirled around her ankles and knees, he felt a fluttering in his chest. Quarter past one. Prompt by her standards. She climbed the stairs to the deck. He stood and waved to her. The caftan was slit up one side, showing a lot of leg as she came to him with the fluid, hip-swinging glissade of a runway model. Two tattooed bubbas several tables away turned to gawk, their heads snapping as if yanked by a string. Middle age, it appeared, hadn't diminished her power to affect men from fifty feet away.

They regarded each other, both speechless, for several seconds.

"My God. Hello, Luke," she said in her deep, thrilling voice. With a strained smile, she extended her hand. As he clasped it, she startled him by leaning over the table to kiss his cheek. He caught her scent, a strong but not unpleasant odor of humid flesh mingled with the smells of oil paint and turpentine. "It's been a while."

"Thirty years does qualify as a while," he said coolly, and sat down. *We're two old friends, seeing each other for the first time in a long time*, Luke told himself. The waitress stopped by and asked if he wanted a refill on the martini. He declined—he had to drive to Miami this afternoon. Corinne ordered a mojito.

"You look like a guy trying to look like a drug dealer," she said brightly to break the ice. Luke was wearing a straw fedora, Ray-Bans, and a red Hawaiian shirt printed with white blossoms.

"I'm missing the requisite gold chain."

"But my impression from the TV is confirmed—you are aging well, Mr. Blackburn."

Luke willed his pulse rate to slow. The skinny girl he'd seen swaying down Bourbon Street had put on weight, but it became her. So did her hair, cut short, no longer draping shawl-like over her shoulders, though still charcoal black, a few gray tips excepted. Lines like chicken scratches ran across her forehead, and two creases hooking around the corners of her lips lent a downturned look to her mouth. Otherwise, he would have recognized her in an instant.

"And you, too, Ms. Terrebonne."

"That's not my name. I sign my work with my maiden name, and I signed the letter with the cat to avoid confusing you."

"Your work? You're still painting?"

"More than ever."

"So your name is . . ."

"Ollerton. My second ex. Before that it was Fitzgerald. You're married?"

"The same woman for twenty-one years. Maureen. She's a professor at the University of Miami."

"A professor! Whoo! Kids?"

"No," he answered, with a flatness that told her not to pursue that line of inquiry.

"For me"—she spread her middle and index fingers in a V. "Girls. Theresa and Kate. Terry by number one, Kate by number two."

He checked an impulse to ask about her former husbands, particularly the first, Fitzgerald. When had she married him? Was that why she'd stopped writing while Luke was in Vietnam? Too ashamed to confess that she'd thrown him over for someone else? There had been a period, while he was trying to evict her from his memory, that he'd hated her. Hatred cooled to a bitterness, which in time melted into forgetfulness. But he wasn't as sure as he'd like to be that the resentment was beyond reviving.

"A few minutes ago, just before you got here, I was thinking about Mr. Hayakawa," he said, after a brief, awkward silence.

"Who?"

"The Japanese guy who lived on Jones, across from us. The one who dusted off his car every morning? You could set your watch by him."

Knitting her brow, Corinne turned slightly to stare across a glassy channel alongside the deck toward a dock on which lobster traps were piled like building blocks. She used to claim, without evidence, that her frizzy hair and obsidian eyes were legacies of a Black ancestor. She'd been in love with the notion that she was an octoroon. Her pearl-white complexion testified otherwise, while her high cheekbones and aquiline nose, in profile, suggested that if she was mixed race, some Choctaw or Houma had coupled with a white predecessor.

"Oh, yeah, I remember now," she said, returning her gaze to Luke. "He had a fancy car."

"A Mercedes."

"You used to watch him every morning."

"You were giving me a refresher in the Cajun waltz when I pointed him out."

"No. It was way later than that. I was giving you the dance lesson on our . . . on the day before you shipped out. But maybe this isn't the time to take a drive down memory lane?" Corinne said, and after Luke nodded his agreement, "Was it bad over there? Were you, y'know . . ."

"Wounded? Yeah. Shrapnel in my knees. Like that Indian battle in the Wild West, Wounded Knee. A million-dollar wound—it got me sent home two months early. That's far enough down that particular memory lane, okay?"

"Sure. Do you get to Key West often?"

"About one weekend a month."

"Funny we haven't run into each other."

"Travel in different circles, I guess. I go fishing with a buddy of mine. You must have seen him on the TV segment."

"The guy with the mustache?"

"Mike Conway. Sometimes I come down to check in with our Keys correspondent."

She removed her sunglasses and looked at him with a directness that reminded him of what Jim Fertel had said about her: *That voodoo swamp witch, she's cast a spell on you.*

"I was wondering why you wanted to see me. You could have dropped me a line with your answer," she said.

He hesitated, feeling a thrum of panic. "Maybe I wanted to see you for no other reason than I wanted to see you. Maybe I thought it would be better to hash this out in person. Maybe I wanted to hear from you why you want to fill the shoes you vacated."

"Whoo-hoo, a lot of maybes. You want to hear why, okay—it's not every day you get a chance to make up for what you did in the past. Terry and Kate thought it was a bad idea to sponsor Ian. So did my friends. But since when did I ever listen to anybody's advice?"

He let out a sour laugh. "That never was one of your long suits."

"So . . . ? Can I tell him about you?"

Luke contemplated his empty martini glass and wished he had ordered a second. Another blast of gin might blow the dam in his mind, the one blocking him from expressing his thoughts aloud. He wasn't a fatalist, yet he saw a connection to events that appeared fateful: If, a month ago, he and Mike and Dustin had not turned toward the Marquesas, they would not have discovered the shipwrecked refugees and made the news; if Corrine had not moved to Key West from Texas, and if she had not happened to see him on the broadcast, purely by chance (if it was by chance), then he would not now be considering if he, too, had been summoned to step into his own pair of empty shoes.

"I . . . I can't right now. Can't say to go ahead. I have to talk to Maureen first."

"You haven't?"

"She doesn't know that I'm here, with you. She thinks I'm fishing. I never told her about you, never told her I had a kid from before I met her, never told her any of it."

Corinne's eyes widened. "Don't you think you should have? That's one hell of a big secret to keep from your wife."

"I kept it a secret from everybody, my parents, my friends. Hell, I kept it a secret from myself!" Luke said vehemently. "You remember what it was like, how we weren't allowed to know anything about the people adopting him and them anything about you or me. The kid couldn't know about us, either. Top secret. I didn't even know his name was Ian till you wrote me last month. So I'd just put him out of my mind, and after your letters stopped coming and mine got returned, 'Not at this address'—you'd just disappeared, not so much as a Dear John—after all that I put *you* out of my mind." Luke was lancing an abscess he thought had healed. "Vietnam helped. Trying to remember things from before I went there was like trying to remember stuff I'd done in grade school. It never even occurred to me to tell her. It was like it never happened, so don't go righteous on me about what I should have done."

Corinne flinched, then recovered from the verbal flurry. "Okay, I get it. But now you do know. It wouldn't be fair to keep her in the dark." She spread her hands and bowed. "Apologies if that sounds righteous."

"Did you tell your exes before you married them?"

"I did, yes."

"And how did that work out?"

She took a healthy slug of the mojito. "Don't be an asshole, Luke. That's not the reason we split up."

"It's complicated," he said.

"Where are we now?"

"Why I'm going to have a tough time coming out with this to Maureen."

"Sure. She'll be pissed off. I'm a woman, I know how I'd feel. That your silence was one long lie."

"Yeah, you ought to know about silence if anybody does."

She clasped her hands on the table, her body stiffening. "Just what do you mean by that?"

"Nothing," he replied, troubled to feel the fossilized bitterness stirring back to life. "I could use another drink. I'll get into it after I've had another drink."

"It's Ian Campbell," she said after he placed his order. "I could swear I'd written you his name right after he was born."

"Not the kind of thing I'd forget," he said.

"I found it out by accident. I was in the lawyer's office, the one who handled the adoption, to sign some final papers. This was about six weeks after, and I was a mess. I was supposed to sign the top page, and I broke down when I saw it. So the lawyer said, 'Do you need a minute?' and I said I did and he went out. While he was gone, I looked under the page and saw the names Winslow and Justine Campbell and under that, Ian." Her voice had thickened; a sheen had come into her eyes. "I repeated it to myself over and over till the lawyer came back. Ian. Ian. Ian."

A nineteen-year-old kid. He needed to remember, when old wounds throbbed again, that she'd been a nineteen-year-old kid. Luke reached to place his hands on hers, but she slipped them off the table and into her lap.

"It's how I was able to find him, after they relaxed all those tight-ass rules and laws. I heard about agencies that helped adopted kids get in touch with their biological parents, and vice versa. I registered with a whole bunch of them, gave them my consent to release my identity in case he was looking for me. Well, he was. He'd registered, too. He was living in Arizona, in Phoenix, and I went out there and we got together."

"What was it like?"

She shrugged. "Kind of okay. Awkward at first, but then okay. That's when he asked the first time if I could tell him anything about his father. It's only natural that he'd want to know. Don't we all want to know who we came from?"

The martini arrived with a second order of conch fritters. He gestured to her to help herself, which she did, biting into a fritter delicately.

"You've got your drink. You were going to tell me what you meant, about me knowing something."

"I wasn't referring to that."

"Well, shoot for Christ's sake at whatever you were aiming at."

He was quiet for a moment, trying to assemble his thoughts while he looked at—or pretended to—a pelican that had stationed itself on a piling. He rolled the icy glass across his forehead; then he said:

"Maureen miscarried twice. Both times she had a kind of postpartum reaction, and the second one was pretty bad. The doctor warned us not to get pregnant again, and I had a vasectomy."

Corinne did not say anything. She polished her sunglasses with a napkin and put them back on.

"I thought pregnancy was the cause, whether she miscarried or went full term, whatever," Luke continued. "I found out later, way later, that I was wrong. She's bipolar, okay? But I'm not going into that."

"You don't need to."

"So my point is . . ."

"Is that you had a kid but not with her, and you don't know how you're going to break that news," Corinne said. "Besides the fact that you've kept it from her all this time."

He pursed his lips and nodded. Why had he confided in her like this? "I don't know how she'll react. That's the thing about bipolars. You never know what will set them off. She's perfectly normal for months, years, then, like that"—he snapped his fingers—"she's not."

"Oh, Luke, Luke. I'm sorry. If I'd known this, I wouldn't have put you in this situation."

"Well, the genie's out of the bottle," he said sharply. "Let's shift gears. Tell me how he landed in jail. Drug charges, you said."

She didn't know all the details. He'd been arrested for dealing meth, and there was something about an assault as well.

"What do you mean, 'something about an assault?'" he interrupted, the reporter in him coming out. "He attacked somebody? With a weapon?'"

She couldn't answer. The assault charge had been reduced to intimidation. Either way, she'd been shocked, because Ian hadn't seemed to be a violent person. And his parents had been good, decent people, his father a software engineer, his mother a hospital administrator. They had adopted two other kids, who'd turned out all right.

"I think their dying screwed him up," she said. "Left a big hole in his life, and he fell into it. But, y'know, I felt kind of . . . kind of disappointed when I heard what happened. I didn't have any right to feel that way, but I did anyway. When . . . When I . . . When I gave him up, my thought was, 'Okay, this hurts, but they'll give him a better life than I can.' And they did. So it was like he didn't have the usual excuses for taking a wrong turn."

Meth. Assault. Prison. *A loser*, Luke thought.

"I guess I was pretty out of control when I was young," Corinne went on. "There were, there are, some not-so-respectable people in my family. Hot-tempered men and wayward girls, like I was. And that makes me wonder if I passed something on, y'know, the bad seed idea."

"My mother used to put her thumb on the nature side of the nature-nurture scale," said Luke. "'Blood tells, it always tells,' she'd say. My Dad's side had a few unrespectables—my uncle did time for second-degree murder. So maybe I contributed a bad seed or two myself. When does Ian get out?"

"He goes before the parole board in late July. They give him their seal of approval, he's a free man."

Luke said nothing. His eyes slipped sideways to the pelican, still roosted atop the piling, its long, yellow bill tucked against its belly.

"So . . . we're done?" Corinne asked.

"For now. I'll give you a lift home," he said.

"Not necessary. I'll call a cab."

"I got you out here, only fair that I get you back."

Because the tourist season in the Keys was now year-round, traffic on US 1 and Truman Avenue rivaled Miami's. In the stop-and-go, Corinne tossed out snippets about her life. She'd been living in Texas, in Austin, since she was twenty-five, touring around in her early years there with country-rock bands—"kind of a USO girl for rock 'n' roll," she said, raising in Luke's mind an image of her screwing the talent.

"Of course, I couldn't keep that up for long, so I went back to art school and got a fine arts degree. How about that, Luke? From a community college, but still . . . first one in my family to get a college degree!"

She did not mention, even obliquely, anything about the years between the last letter she'd written from San Francisco and her move to Austin. Nor did he ask. He didn't want to hear.

"How did you end up here?" he inquired.

"Long story." She flipped an AC vent to blow directly on her and sank into her seat in a languorous slouch. "Short of it is, I heard from a friend of a friend that the Mel Fisher Museum was looking to hire an artist to do illustrations of the stuff they salvaged from the *Atocha*. I didn't know anything about the *Atocha* then, but the friend of the friend filled me in. Sunken treasure from a Spanish galleon, I mean, *cher*, who could resist that? So I packed up and headed for F-L-A. My day job and only part time, but it helps pay the rent and leaves me free to do my own work. A gallery on Duval shows it. Check it out. The Compass Rose gallery."

He said he would.

"It's different from most of the crap that calls itself art down here. Mine, it might be crap, too, but at least it's not the same old, same old crap. Seascapes. Street scenes. Tropical flowers. Rothko said, 'Do something new,' and I'm trying to."

Luke turned down White, then into the shady precincts of Old Town. Shotgun houses and conch cottages, some undergoing renovations, some exuding an air of decrepit romance, lined the streets and narrow lanes.

"I do paint the sea," Corinne went on, "but not the sea as sea. You could say it's the sea as I see it. Pun intended."

Luke offered nothing more about his own life beyond what he'd presented earlier. For the time being, the less she knew about him the better. He did not yet completely trust her. She'd been a true child of the sixties, romantic, exciting, free-spirited, but the spontaneity that had so charmed him, he remembered, sometimes morphed into feck- lessness. He wasn't confident, her decision to step into the vacated shoes notwithstanding, that she'd left all of her younger self behind.

"There's my place, on the right."

It was a two-story frame, with gingerbread rails on the porches upstairs and down, cockeyed shutters, and blistered paint. Unkempt bougainvillea dripped over a fence with crooked pickets. The sort of house a realtor would say needed TLC.

"It's yours?"

"Are you kidding? A garage in this town goes for what a house would anywhere else. I rent the second floor. It's got a skylight on the backside."

He pulled to the curb.

"Luke, what I did to you, disappearing the way I did . . . I'm ashamed of it. Do you think you ever could, you know . . . Oh, hell, I'll wait to hear from you. Like I said—"

"Got it. You'll honor my wishes, whatever they are."

She hesitated. "Did you ever write that novel you said you were going to write? Just curious."

Jesus, why was she bringing that up? He shook his head.

"It was the whole reason you volunteered to go over there. You were going to be the, who was it? The James Jones or the Norman Mailer of the Vietnam War?"

"It was Jones," he said, blushing at the recollection. Only a twenty- one-year-old full of himself would have made such an idiotic comment. "But that wasn't the reason I went. Writing press releases from Fort Polk, Louisiana, bored me to tears. I needed to do some real journalism."

"Whatever reason you had, it made me nuts. Guys were doing anything and everything to stay out of that war, pretending they were lunatics, pretending they were gay, even chopping off a finger or a toe, and you'd volunteered. We got into a big fight over it, on the phone."

"Cost me a fistful of quarters," he said with a faint smile.

"A big old phone fight and we broke up. But it wasn't for long. A month maybe."

And, he recalled, it was less than a month later that she sent him the letter that changed everything.

"I still have that poem you wrote to me," she said. "Do you remember it?"

"No. Except that it's the only poem I ever wrote and that it wasn't very good."

She was quiet, looking at him, her lips slightly parted. She seemed to be prolonging her departure, and he worried that she was going to invite him in to show him the poem. He worried because he was fairly sure he would accept. But she opened the car door and fluttered her hand in goodbye. Watching her walk up the steps to her front door, he felt as if he'd had a close call.

5

Luke was partway over the Seven Mile Bridge, re-playing the conversation, when he caught himself in a lie, or at least a half-truth. The true part: Circumstances had compelled him, for his own emotional health if for no other reason, to forget Corinne and the birth of their love child. The untruth: saying that the self-induced amnesia had been so scorched-earth thorough that it was as if their love had never been and their child had never drawn breath, and so he'd never even thought to tell Maureen. He *had* thought to, of course he had—fathering a child out of wedlock wasn't something you entirely erased from memory.

Twenty-two years ago, while he and Maureen were crossing another bridge—the Longfellow between Boston and Cambridge—the child he'd never seen, whose name he did not then know, broke out of a lockbox in Luke's mind and prodded him to make a full confession. The moment seemed right, though it possibly could not have been more wrong: he was taking her to a snug Italian place on the North End, where he intended to ask her to marry him. An engagement ring was in his jacket pocket. The Associated Press had sent him to Harvard for a year on a Neiman Fellowship, a reward for his coverage of the October War in 1973 and the fall of Saigon two years later. Maureen, after a stint teaching high school English in Amherst, was at BU, studying for her master's. They'd met at a party, begun dating, and fallen in love, she the diplomat's daughter, he the master sergeant's son, she the Phi Beta Kappa from Wellesley, he the University of Arizona dropout. What their backgrounds shared was rootlessness, the disrupted childhoods of military and State Department brats, forced to make new friends every two or three years, always living as strangers in strange places, Luke raised on army bases from Baumholden, Germany to Fort Huachuca, Arizona, Maureen in Rome, Paris, and Geneva before she was packed off to Wellesley.

She dazzled him. She was gorgeous, incandescent, and smart, fluent in three languages, capable of reciting from memory Yeats's longer poems and entire passages of Shakespeare and Beckett without stumbling over a word. The social circles she moved in sprinkled on additional glitter. During the winter break, she'd invited him to meet her family in DC, where Ted Carrington was serving as Under Secretary of State for European Affairs. Luke would discover later that the Carringtons were not a happy family, thanks to the tensions among Maureen's vain older brother, Don, her gay younger brother, Stuart, and her toxic mother, but they put on a good performance of harmony at a dinner party in their Georgetown townhouse on the second night of Luke's visit. The guests—the British and Italian ambassadors and a famous columnist from the *Washington Post*—were interested in his views about the Middle East and Southeast Asia. He was careful not to say anything controversial or stupid, and also to use the right forks at dinner. He was seated between the UK ambassador and his wife, and across from the famous columnist. Luke worried that they regarded him, the roughneck war correspondent, as a curiosity, like some exotic tribal chieftain. In truth, recalling his parents' backyard barbecues in Sierra Vista, old noncoms swilling Budweisers, he began to feel like an imposter. In response to a question from the columnist, he said that he was now "on a Neiman at

Harvard." The columnist knew what a Neiman was, but the others might have gotten the impression that he was a full-fledged grad student. Maureen was meanwhile chatting with the Italian ambassador—in Italian. Luke wasn't the sort she'd been raised to marry, the polished preppy destined for an investment bank or a white-shoe law firm. She might have fallen for him in reaction to her upbringing. A mild rebellion. Her mother did not then believe she was serious about him; her daughter was having a fling. Thelma, an imposing woman, reminded him of his place as the party was breaking up. She took him aside and whispered, "You're not really *at* Harvard, now are you, Luke?"

That remark and the tone in which she'd made it was on his mind as he drove across the Longfellow bridge. Winning Maureen's love struck him as an undeserved good fortune that could be withdrawn at any moment. And so he squelched the inner voice prompting him to come clean about his past. The revelation could be a deal-breaker.

But what about now?

His thoughts tumbled as he and a multitude of tourists returning to the mainland crawled through the Matecumbes, Islamorada, Tavernier. On Key Largo, he left US 1 for the Card Sound Road. The lightly trafficked route took him into the national crocodile refuge, a semi-wilderness whose forests of gumbo limbo and mahogany and lignum vitae fenced the two-lane asphalt. The detour would add a good half an hour to the drive, but that was okay; he needed time to formulate what he would say to Maureen and how he would say it. He admired the late sunlight illuminating the treetops while he gave tryouts to opening lines. *Maureen, I have something to tell you, you'd better sit down.* . . . That wasn't quite right. *Maureen, there's something I need to talk over with you.* . . . *It's something I should have told you before we got married.* . . . *I'm not sure why I didn't, or why I've kept it from you for all this time.* . . . Once again, not quite right. She would demand an explanation, and he could not think of one other than the one he was unwilling to give. It would be a blow to her self-esteem to say that he'd withheld the truth from fear for her mental stability. Also, not entirely honest.

Near the tip of North Key Largo, the road hooked left and bridged the sound for which it was named. From fifty feet up, Luke watched a sailboat northing toward Biscayne Bay and wished he were aboard it. He watched a flight of white ibis and wished he were a bird. Beyond the bridge, the Card Sound passed through mangroves cut by slow, dark channels and eventually led him back to US 1 into Florida City, where he picked up the Turnpike. The whole past week at work had been miserable; the massacre had begun. He'd had to tell three veteran staffers, one reporter, and two copy editors to clean out their desks. HR recommended—mandated, actually—the quick and ruthless approach to terminations. Luke didn't do ruthless very well, and the scenes had been messy, scenes that would be repeated over and over in the coming weeks. Newsroom morale was in a sinkhole, everyone dreading to hear the summons, "Mr. Blackburn wants to see you." Now he had to deal with *this*. Goddamn Corinne. Not a word from her for three decades, and then she springs *this* on him. He should have written back straightaway, "I don't want him to know who I am or where I am, I don't owe him anything, it was all a really, really long time ago."

On the other, hand, maybe he did owe Ian something.

It was six thirty, still early, when he swung off the Turnpike and followed US 1 into the Gables. He did not feel ready to face Maureen. Pulling his BlackBerry from the glove compartment, he pressed speed dial.

She picked up after two rings. "Hi, honey."

"Hi. You sound chipper."

"Chipper? A word that's faded from common use, but, yes, I'm chipper. Where are you in relation to here?"

"Close, but I might be a little late," he said.

"Everything okay?"

"Uh-huh. Traffic, as usual."

The lies were piling up. To Corinne. To Maureen. To Mike. Luke had told him he couldn't fish today because he had a meeting with his Keys correspondent, then lied, again to Maureen, telling her he was fishing with Mike.

"Give me an ETA," she said. "I'll keep dinner warm."

"Eight. Let's make it eight, no later."

He went to Matheson Beach, parked in a nearly empty lot, and strolled along one of two sandy, palm-shaded arms embracing a shallow lagoon. It lay flat, perfectly reflecting peach-colored clouds, the trees, and two people wading. A small boy with his mother walked the beach. Otherwise, Luke was alone. He flopped down under a coconut palm and stared out to the darkening sea. The cirrus streaking the sky had deepened in color from yellow to tangerine. *If you see Corrina, tell her to hurry home. . . .* The old blues tune wormed into his ear. *I ain't had no true love since Corrina been gone.* The lines tethering him to the present slipped and set him adrift into the past. He remembered the studio on Jones Street, saw himself standing by the window as Mr. Hayakawa finished the ritual cleaning of his car, drove off, and . . .

He's wishing he could share in the predictable life of Mr. Hayakawa. There is only one thing he can predict: by tomorrow morning he will be on a bus headed for Travis Air Force Base, where he and some two hundred other replacements will be herded onto a chartered airliner and flown to Saigon. He won't see Corinne for at least a year. Although as a US Army correspondent he won't be a combatant, he can't dismiss the possibility that he'll never see her, or anything, again, and it's absolutely certain he'll never set eyes on their child. If souls have cells like bodies, then every cell in Luke's yearns for none of this to happen. All this past month he's hoped for a miracle—an announcement from the Paris peace talks that the war is over, or a change in his orders that will keep him in San Francisco till the baby's born. It seems strange, it seems unfair that Corinne will be alone and that he'll be at the bus station when Mr. Hayakawa performs his ritual at the appointed time tomorrow, before the fog lifts, as if nothing has changed. But then, nothing will have changed for him, so it's really not so strange, nor unfair.

Now, Luke turns from the window and glances at her, asleep on her side of the sofa-bed, strands of her black hair smudging a pale cheek. She tosses and turns at night, trying to get comfortable, and the bedsheet, twisted as if by someone improvising a rope, is coiled around her naked body. He tiptoes into the studio's dim, windowless kitchen, brews coffee, and brings two cups out to the living room. Corinne is awake, sitting up. He hands a cup to her, sits beside her, and rests his palm on her stomach, a taut dome through which he feels a movement, a rippling that lasts only a moment.

"That's him," Corinne says.

"It could be a girl, you know."

"Uh-uh. A boy. He's turning over, little by little. Pretty soon, he'll be upside down, ready to dive head first into the world." She rubs the burrow in whose darkness the he or she is turning over little by little. "The doctor told me his eyes are open now. If you pressed a bright, bright spotlight on my tummy, he'd turn toward the light. God, how I'm going to miss you, Luke."

A woman, calling loudly to her child in the lagoon, "Luis! *Ven aca! Estamos yendo a casa!*" returned Luke to June 6, 1999. It had grown late—seven forty by his watch—and the park was closing for the night. A solitary star or planet glimmered high above the ocean's horizon in a violet sky. He stood, brushed the sand off the seat of his pants, and went to his car. He'd been lost to the present for half an hour, but he would be home by eight, as promised. That he felt relieved, like a high school kid making curfew, annoyed him.

He switched on the ignition and turned the air conditioner to full blast. It came back to him then, as if blown in by the AC, except it was warm—her scent. That smell of damp skin, paints, turpentine. She must have been working on a canvas and lost track of time and dressed quickly without showering before meeting him. He unlocked the glove compartment, took out his cell, and tapped four-one-one.

He asked the operator for the number for a Corinne Ollerton at 808 Ashe Street in Key West.

"I have a C.A. Ollerton at eight-oh-eight Ashe."

Like most women living alone, Corinne avoided revealing her sex in the phone book, hence the initials. "That's it," Luke said.

The phone rang ten times before switching to an answering machine. A prerecorded, robotic voice gave the standard message.

"Hey, Corinne," Luke said after the tone. "I thought things through on the drive. Go ahead. Tell Ian. Guess I've got a pair of empty shoes to fill, too. But some ground rules—no phone calls, no emails, snail-mail only, in care of the *Examiner*."

He wanted to say more, much more. The things he wanted to say frightened him. He disconnected and started for home and Maureen.

6

The Samuel Beckett Theatre stood across a sunny rugby pitch, an architectural anomaly amid the gray Gothic buildings of Trinity College. A tall, wooden, box-like structure on wood pillars, it reminded Luke of a beach house, though it lacked windows as well as a beach. Actually, it was a kind of multiplex for the legitimate stage, housing three theaters. Maureen and Fiona Powell, the actress portraying Molly Bloom, were performing in the largest. It was no Carnegie Hall, having perhaps two hundred seats, but it pleased Luke deeply, and it must have pleased Maureen more deeply still, to see not one seat empty and people jammed shoulder to shoulder at the entrance doors in the rear. Some, fresh from the Bloomsday festivities, were wearing period fashions, men in flannel sport jackets and shirts with celluloid collars, women in long Edwardian skirts. Fiona, as alluring in person as in the photograph Luke had seen a couple of weeks ago, was a celebrity in Ireland, so it was safe to assume, without detracting from his wife's looks or her status as a "distinguished American scholar," that the SRO crowd had been pulled in by Fiona's star power.

In a white cotton nightgown, crow's wing hair brushing her pale shoulders, she was kneeling on a bed while Maureen stood behind a

lectern at one side of the stage and guided the audience through the
labyrinth of Molly Bloom's jumbled thoughts:

". . . an adulteress, as we know, dissatisfied with her aging husband,"
Maureen was saying. "But Joyce doesn't present her judgmentally. . . .
That would violate Joyce's artistic creed—true art, true beauty, as
Aquinas taught, is static, it doesn't move us to desire. . . . We accept
Molly for what she is as she reminisces about her lover, Blazes Boylan."

Maureen half turned toward Fiona. A blue stage light fell on the
actress, who put on a haughty, sexy expression and picked up the soliloquy in mid-flow, her voice bold, brassy:

*. . . when I lit the lamp yes because he must have come 3 or 4 times with that
tremendous big red brute of a thing he has I thought the vein or whatever the dickens
they call it was going to burst . . . he must have eaten oysters I think a few dozen . . . no
I never in all my life felt anyone had one the size of that to make you feel full up . . .
what's the idea making us like that with a big hole in the middle of us like a Stallion
driving it up into you . . .*

"Easy to see why Joyce caused a scandal in 1919," Maureen said
after Fiona finished. "'Big red brute of a thing' is pretty raunchy stuff
even today." She fluttered her eyebrows with comic wickedness, drawing a smattering of low laughter. "Hers is the feminine mind off the
leash, so to speak, bawdy, raw, uninhibited. I mentioned a moment ago
that Joyce asks us to accept Molly Bloom for what she is, and what is
she? An Earth goddess, Gaia, yet fully herself."

Luke, sitting in the front row with a delegation from the University
of Miami—the dean of the graduate school, a couple of PhD candidates—cast quick sidelong glances and noticed, with spousal pride,
heads nodding sagely in approval of Maureen's observations.

She and Fiona resumed their dialogue, a call-and-response.

"Our Molly's interior monologue can be seen as an erotic fantasia
as she reflects on her earliest lovers on Gibraltar."

*I wish some man or other would take me sometime when he's there and kiss me
in his arms there's nothing like a kiss long and hot down to your soul . . .*

Fiona's black hair and creamy skin. Kneeling on a bed in a white nightie. An image of Corinne flitted through Luke's memory. It flitted out when Maureen detached the lectern microphone and began to pace the stage. Wearing gray pumps, gray slacks, and an emerald-colored blouse—emerald for Ireland and to accent her flaming hair—she looked commanding as she strode back and forth, like a megachurch preacher.

"She thinks wistfully of her first love, a naval officer, Lieutenant Mulvey, on their last day together before his ship leaves Gibraltar."

. . . I could see his chest pink he wanted to touch mine with his for a moment but I wouldn't let him he was awfully put out first for fear you never know consumption or leave me with a child embarazada that old servant Ines told me that one drop even if it got into you at all . . .

"It is significant that Lieutenant Mulvey's ship is called HMS *Calypso*, for if Gaia is the first person of the Trinity that is Molly, Calypso is the second. She's a raven-haired siren who has, in a manner of speaking, captured her Odysseus, her husband, Leopold Bloom."

Luke was semiconsciously monitoring his wife's gestures, the pitch and tone of her voice, listening, watching for any signal of excessive excitement. Ten days ago, following his reverie at Matheson beach, he'd gone home determined to come clean about Corinne and Ian; his resolution did not survive contact with Maureen. She'd been rehearsing her speech and seemed to vibrate with tension. At dinner, she read it to him, then asked for his thoughts. Although he couldn't quite follow it, he didn't say so, replying that it was brilliant. She remained keyed up the entire week before their departure, excited to have a prominent role in the Bloomsday festivities, afraid that she would fail to meet expectations, and intimidated by the youthful glamour of her costar. Odd, that insecurity. She wasn't going to be in a beauty contest, after all. Whatever the reason for her nervousness, the time wasn't right to make a startling revelation. It would be like throwing a stone at someone walking a tightrope. He would wait till they returned from Ireland.

He'd held his secret for two decades; two more weeks couldn't make any difference.

That had been the right decision, because . . .

"The third person of her Trinity is, of course, Penelope, the embodiment of the faithful wife. Although Molly is not faithful in one sense, she is in another."

Striding the stage one side to the other, Maureen was in full control of the performance, of her audience, of herself.

"Not once in her interior ramblings does she think about divorcing her husband or running off with Boylan. Although her thoughts appear, at first reading, to be chaotic and capricious, they keep revolving back to Leopold Bloom."

It's all his own fault if I'm an adulteress as the thing in the gallery said O much about if that's all the harm we ever did in this vale of tears God knows . . . I suppose He wouldn't have made us the way He did so attractive to men. . . .

For which man had Corinne left him? The one named Fitzgerald? Or had there been some interim dalliance? Her desertion then ought not to trouble him now, but it did. *Mother of my child, my only one.* Corinne had dropped him a note after his phone call last month: she'd had second thoughts about disclosing Luke's identity to Ian. Luke himself should do that. She sent him Ian's prison number, his address in the minimum security block of the Arizona State Prison at Tucson. Luke had yet to write him—that, too, would have to wait.

. . . then if he wants to kiss my bottom I'll drag open my drawers and bulge it right out in his face as large as life he can stick his tongue 7 miles up my hole as he's there my brown part then . . . I'll tell him I want to buy underclothes . . .

Luke was momentarily pulled out of his own head as Maureen crossed the stage back to the lectern and placed the mike in its holder. She presented the audience with a devilish smile. "I warned you she was raunchy."

Laughter.

The grad school dean—his name was Babowitz—whispered to Luke,

"You can see why her student evals are off the charts, she's awfully good." Babowitz was a paunchy man with a bunged-up manner. While Maureen and Fiona rehearsed their act, Luke had spent much of the day touring the Dublin localities where *Ulysses* takes place with the dean, the two doctoral candidates—talkative young women who educated him about the sites, like Mr. and Mrs. Bloom's flat at Number 7 Eccles Street—and hordes of pub-crawling revelers.

"Molly is faithful, in her own way. Her lovers, past and present, have been mere playthings. Bloom is hers, she his. There is one word that directs the course of her seemingly muddled musings. They begin and end with that word—Yes. Yes occurs no less than thirty-five times in the soliloquy. It reaches a crescendo in the famed concluding passage, as Molly recalls when Bloom proposed to her on Gibraltar sixteen years earlier. It is a climax of affirmation and love—the love of Nature for her creatures, of Molly for her husband, a spring-song of the Earth."

Maureen canted her head to cue Fiona. Once again, the stage light dropped over the actress, encasing her in a transparent blue cylinder.

I love flowers I'd love to have the whole place swimming in roses God of heaven there's nothing like nature the wild mountains . . . Fiona carried on at a fevered pitch. . . . *my God after that long kiss I near lost my breath yes he said I was a flower of the mountain yes so we are flowers all a woman's body yes* . . . And on and on, and though Luke could barely make sense of the rushing words, he didn't care, carried along by their lyric beauty, his eye first on Fiona, then on Maureen, his mind's eye conjuring visions of Corinne . . . . *A flower of the mountain yes* . . . *and how he kissed me under the Moorish wall and I thought as well him as another* . . . *and then he asked me would I yes to say yes my mountain flower and I put my arms around him yes and drew down to me so he could feel my breasts all perfume yes and his heart was going like mad and yes I said yes I will Yes.*

7

After the performance, in the long summer daylight, they made their way to the Westbury for dinner—Luke and Maureen; Fiona and a boyfriend, Sean, a handsome guy built like a rugby player; Babowitz and the PhD hopefuls; two faculty members from Trinity. The festival was still in full swing, the streets swarming with tourists, many of them drunk or working hard to get that way, and with James Joyce look-alikes, balladeers crooning Celtic melodies, orators reading passages from *Ulysses* aloud. Dodging through the crowds, he overheard one baffled visitor say to his girlfriend—they were listening to a recitation from a man wearing a derby and a striped shirt with sleeve garters—"Whatever this is, it isn't English." Luke's sentiments exactly; he didn't express them to avoid being thought of as a philistine.

They passed a doorway in which someone had placed a toilet and hung a sign: LEOPOLD BLOOM'S OUTHOUSE. Babowitz clued Luke in—there was a scene in the novel depicting Bloom relieving himself in an outhouse. Fiona, apparently still in character, hiked her skirt past her knees and sat on the commode and gave Sean a racy wink as he took her picture. Maureen jumped in for the next shot, throwing an arm around Fiona, tipping at a rakish angle the straw hat she'd put on to pay homage to the styles of 1904. She stuck out her tongue at Sean, and Fiona made a reference to Molly Bloom's scatological musing: "Ah, it will never reach seven miles, dear girl." Maureen laughed. She was on a high, she and Fiona having received a standing ovation at the theater, and her laugh lasted longer than it needed to, rising to a shriek.

The merry band arrived at the Westbury, Luke and Maureen's hotel. Weeks ago, the U of M had reserved rooms for them at a much more reasonable establishment, but Maureen had canceled the reservation and booked them into the Westbury: a "deluxe king" with a breathtaking daily rate. "Jesus H! They don't charge that much at the Biltmore," Luke had objected. "We are not going to stay at some el cheapo youth hostel," Maureen retorted, as if that were the only alternative to a five-star. "No worries, darling, it's on me," she'd added, meaning she would pay the expense out of her trust fund's monthly dividend.

Dinner was to be on her, too. She announced that after the maître d' at Wilde, the Westbury's formal dining room, showed the nine of them to their table.

"I want that settled right now, and I will brook no arguments," she declared with feigned sternness. "To avoid one of those ridiculous scenes, everybody reaching for his credit card and asking the waiter to do long division."

Babowitz offered a token protest, so did Fiona, so did one of the Trinity profs, a long-jawed woman who wore the severe expression of a tough mother superior. Sean presented a vacant smile, which led Luke to peg him as a stage-door Johnny, a kept man.

Wilde affected an Art Moderne look, and the white-jacketed staff went with the decor. Their waiter, whose fine features and tidy haircut recalled Robert Redford portraying Jay Gatsby, dealt out menus, then took drink orders. Maureen beckoned him with a crooked finger to lower his ear so she could whisper into it. He mumbled, "Very good choice, madam," went off, and returned bearing a bottle of Bollinger

Special Cuvée in a silver ice bucket. As he circled the round table filling champagne glasses, Luke flipped his menu to the Drinks and Cocktails page. The Bollinger's price tag was an eye-popper. He reckoned that the dinner tab alone would reach into the four figures. His early-warning system flicked an amber alert.

Maureen clinked her glass with a fork, then stood and raised it on high.

"Oscar Wilde, for whom this restaurant is named, once observed that pleasure without champagne is artificial." The crackling in her voice reminded Luke of the sound made by a faulty fluorescent tube. "So here's to the *real* pleasure of your company and to James Joyce and to Fiona Powell"—tilting her head toward the actress—"for her marvelous performance!"

"And to you for—" Fiona began, but didn't finish as Maureen drove on at full throttle.

"—it really was mah-vah-lus, dahling, as Bette Davis would say. But you're too young to have heard of Bette Davis, so I will just say . . . You know, it might have been Tallulah Bankhead I was thinking of. But you're too young to have heard of her—"

"Oh, no, I—" Fiona ventured, to no effect; the Maureen Express rolled right over her.

"—that what was so marvelous was memorizing Molly's stream of consciousness word for word. Stream, did I say stream? A *river* of consciousness, the Nile! The Mississippi! The . . . What? So many rivers in the world, aren't there? So here's to you, Ms. Powell, and here's to all of you for . . . For being here! You are all marvelous people and I am thrilled to have you, all of you, in my life, as I'm sure Fiona is as well . . ."

Everyone, with glasses in hand, waited for the cue to toast. A rictus had formed on Babowitz's lips and on those of the mother superior. The pair of grad students stared at Dr. Carrington, their faculty adviser, with studied neutrality; Fiona's plucked eyebrows fluttered, as if she were signaling someone.

"... thrilled and grateful, I might add. You saw that crowd. Standing room only! So, so grateful. I love you all, and most of all ..." The words were flying from her now. She cut her eyes to Luke. He could see the craziness flooding into them, a hard gleam, like varnish. A natal panic kicked inside his chest. "... my husband, Luke, my very own Bloom and Blazes all rolled into one ... He is amazing, magical—"

"I'll drink to that!" Luke boomed, rose, and hoisted his glass. He had to check her now. "What guy wouldn't? Cheers, everyone."

A muted chorus of "cheers" from his dining companions. Maureen stretched her mouth into what was either a broad grin or a baring of teeth. "Yes! Yes! Cheers!"

She took a sip and sat down just as the waiter arrived to recite the evening's specials. The litany of grilled this and pan-fried that, delivered in a pleasing Irish lilt, drew a couple of overly enthusiastic oohs and ahhs from her, but she appeared to have regained control of herself—for the moment.

The moment did not last long. After everyone had ordered. Maureen requested four bottles of wine—two of a pricey St. Emilion, two of an equally exorbitant Montrachet—and then began talking and hardly stopped for a breath. No one could follow what she was saying; her words, like her thoughts, veered in flight. Luke had learned from the ever-informative Dr. Pearle that "pressure of speech" was the medical term for these verbal tsunamis; like her prodigality, they were an advisory of manic weather ahead. The only question in Luke's mind was, would it be a passing squall or a full gale? His hopes for a squall got a boost when the bill arrived; the shock of it quieted her down.

She was brushing her teeth before bed when he took a pill bottle from her toiletries bag and plunked it, loudly, on the cabinet.

She spat into the sink and gargled mouthwash and, picking up the bottle, gave it an assayer's squint.

"Ambien. Dr. Blackburn, I presume? Or might you be Nurse Ratched?"

"It's a four-hour drive to Leenane. We should leave no later than eight. You'll need—"

"My sleep. Christ, do you have to treat me like I'm an invalid?"

She popped one of the tablets into her mouth and, bending over, gulped straight from the tap.

"You were pretty cranked up at dinner. You hardly ate, you didn't stop talking, and you were rubbing Babowitz's leg with your foot."

She laughed unpleasantly. "Really? Was I?"

"Yeah, really."

"Did you spy on me under the table?"

"He told me in the men's room. He asked if you might be a little drunk and I asked why he was asking, and then he told me. Poor guy was embarrassed as hell."

"Because he's gay. Did you know he's gay?"

Luke nodded.

"So what harm was there in it, playing footsies with a gay guy? No harm, no foul."

She turned and went into the bedroom—their 375-euros-per-night deluxe king, with matching red-velvet armchairs. That would come to about 400 USD. At checkout tomorrow Maureen's monthly draw would be overdrawn, with a full two weeks till the next deposit. Well, it was her money, she could do as she pleased with it.

"I don't think you're an invalid," he declared, going into the room after he'd peed and brushed his teeth.

She was sitting upright on the bed, her satin nightgown clinging to her hips. An open magazine lay in her lap.

"Invalid," she said. "In-valid. One becomes in-valid. This woman is no longer valid, like an expired coupon."

He sat in an armchair. The velvet upholstery, he supposed, was to make guests feel they'd gotten something special for their four hundred bucks.

"Come on, expired," he scoffed. "You were terrific. You ran the show like an emcee, not like a college professor."

"What about Fiona?"

"She was terrific, too."

"She's an airhead. A beautiful airhead. She has an impressive memory, that's all, she can remember her lines even if she hasn't a clue what they mean, and she knows how to project. Otherwise, there is only oxygen, nitrogen, and a smattering of inert elements like argon in her head. That guy she was with, Shane——"

"Sean."

"Sean. Shane. Pshaw. He's perfect for her. His face——it's the kind of face you might see on a billboard plugging shaving cream. Did you hear the way she name-dropped? First names of movie stars. Brad and Matt and Jack as in Nicholson and Bob as in Redford, and she's never been in a movie with a single one of them."

Luke heard in this screed echoes of Thelma's cut and slash. "But you said that she was marvelous."

"Mah-vah-lus, dahling. I think she may have had a two-second walk-on in a Bob-as-in-Redford film. I can't bear people who refer to celebrities by their first names. But I meant what I said about you." She puckered her lips and blew him an air kiss. "Poldy and Blazes Boylan rolled into one." Suddenly, she tossed the magazine across the room, the pages flapping like the wings of a many-winged bird. "Big red brute of a thing . . ." She palmed her nightgown, sliding it up to her waist, exposing her thighs and the russet tangle between them in a whorish display at once arousing and frightening; frightening because sexual aggression was one more telltale——usually she was demure, a good Catholic girl who left it to her man to initiate sex.

"C'mon, Luke. C'mon . . ."

His apprehensions were not strong enough to annul his natural, physical reactions. Besides, she was teetering on an edge, and he thought that if he failed to respond to her invitation——her demand——she would fall off and be lost to him, lost to herself. His lovemaking was violent, fear and lust commingling to produce anger, not at her but at the demons capering under all her wild red hair. He would drive them out of her. Sex as exorcism.

He was tender in the aftermath, embracing her, stroking her cheek with his fingertips.

"*Ancora? Quando?*" she said after ten or fifteen minutes had passed.

He didn't know Italian, but the meaning was clear enough. "I'm not thirty anymore," he said.

"A kiss, then?"

Her voice had thickened; the Ambien was going to work.

"Shhhh. Let's get some sleep."

"A kiss, long and hot down to the soul."

"Shhhh. Quiet, Maureen. Let's get some sleep. Shhhh."

He was speaking to the distinguished scholar as if he were lulling an agitated child; but then, that was what she became when the devils danced.

Finally, she was asleep. Luke switched off the bedside light. He lay there in the dark, his mind leaping erratically from Maureen to the people he was going to have to fire when he returned to work, to Ian and Corinne, then to tomorrow's trip to Leenane and meeting up with Mike and Liz Conway, then back to Maureen and the Thorazine he'd packed in his dopp kit in case of a dire emergency. Whom the gods would destroy they first make mad. What had she, this bright woman, ever done to earn their enmity? Not one damn thing. The gods, like impulsive tyrants, were capricious in choosing whom they would destroy.

The nascent panic he'd felt earlier swelled into a full-blown attack. The pain rocketing through his chest mimicked a coronary, which heightened the panic, which sharpened the pain. He got out of bed, looked out the window at the street, three floors below. The weather had changed—a light rain was falling and the streetlights and neon signs shone in the wet pavement. He paced the room, doing deep-breathing exercises to settle his nerves. He had no appetite to do any of the things he was supposed to do. He felt that his life was in danger of spinning out of his control, assuming it was in his control. Like a shroud, dread dropped over him. It wasn't like the dread he'd experienced in the war; that had had a definite object. This had none. It was just a sense of some impending yet unclear calamity. *Jesus loving Christ,* he thought, *her craziness is driving me crazy*. He shuffled into the bathroom, fumbled in her bag, and took one of her sleeping pills.

8

Maureen's high had not reached extreme altitude, so the low that followed the next day did not plumb the depths. Melancholy described it better than depression, the blues as opposed to the blacks. Luke, recovered from his own bout of heebie-jeebies, compared the rise and fall in her mood to the countryside through which they drove, in soft, intermittent showers, toward Leenane: rounded green hills of modest height dipped into shallow valleys. Sitting with the seat in the rented Volvo tilted fully back, she gazed at the landscape with quiet indifference except to remark now and then on the quaintness of some village, or on a charming sight, like the sheep herd pouring whitely over a hill crest, the dogs scampering alongside, the shepherd trudging behind in high rubber boots.

They arrived at a few minutes past three, three hours behind schedule, having got off to a late start thanks to the Ambien. Luke's cautious driving—he wasn't used to the left side of the road—added an hour to the trip. Mike had booked them into the hotel where he and Liz were staying. It faced Killary Harbour, and was a lot cheaper than the Westbury.

They barely had time to unpack before the Conways called them down to the lobby and, following handshakes and hugs, ferried them through the village to Mike's mother's birthplace. Under the low, leaden sky, it looked thoroughly depressing: a one-story stone cottage overlooked by a treeless hill, with a broken-down sheep pen out back and a semi-detached barn alongside, its once-smooth walls chipped and cracked, its roof bowed in the middle.

"Our now-derelict-soon-to-be-romantic summer getaway," Liz said.

"You won't believe what we got it for, m'boy," said Mike. He was costumed as a country squire in a tweed cap and a waxed Barbour jacket. "It and those five acres you see right there," gesturing at the hillside.

"If I remember right, less than the price of a used Corolla."

"A little more, but I made out pretty well."

He unlocked the door and led them into an interior musty, dim, and damp, the walls bare, the rooms empty, save for a woodburning stove squatting in the parlor fireplace and a rust-pitted 1930s gas range in the kitchen. The low ceilings, with their age-darkened beams, induced claustrophobia; the doorways required anyone over six feet to duck.

"Those drop ceilings helped keep things warm in the winter, but they're going to be knocked out, knocked right out," Mike said. "Cathedral ceilings. Skylights. It'll be beautiful."

"I can't wait for the renovations to get done so I can start decorating, fix this little old place up," Liz added.

"Little old" came out as one word, *lilole*. Her drawl, so pronounced it sounded like a parody, elicited a wince from Maureen. Luke knew it struck her ear and Back Bay sensibilities like fingernails on a chalkboard.

Ten years younger than Mike, Liz was a honey-tongued, honey-haired, buxom woman of fifty who owned a successful interior design business in Key West. She'd migrated to the island from Arkansas with her second husband, Clive Daniels, scion of a once-prominent Hot Springs family whose impoverishment had pushed him into a life of crime. Daniels got his start in the drug trade scavenging square groupers, moved up to importing boatloads, and prospered until he began smuggling cocaine and crossed some very serious Colombians, who made Liz a widow. Although she'd never been directly mixed up in her husband's enterprises, her shop was launched with some of its proceeds: Daniels had gifted her a mink coat, quite useless in the tropics, except for the rolls of hundred-dollar notes stuffed into its pockets and sewn into its lining. After his death, taking full advantage of Key West's gentrification, she acquired clients renovating old conch houses, among whom was one Michael Conway.

Mike continued his house tour, taking them into the other rooms—there were only two—and then through a gloomy passageway to the gloomier barn. Dried-up bits of fleece scattered on the floor indicated that it had been a shearing shed.

"And this is going to be the guest cottage," he said, twirling, arms outspread. "Ah, it'll be a little jewel of a place, I'll tell the world. My mother was six when she left here, and when she sees it, she'll want to move back in. Not that I'm going to invite her to."

"Let's hope not," said Liz. "There's enough of Mom in your head without her being under the same roof."

Maureen let out a laugh, sharp and shrill, a false laugh. She knew, as well as Mike did, what it was like to have a mother occupying your head.

"I've got a couple of contractors bidding for the renovations," Mike said. "They're in Galway. And I let 'em know I used to be in the business, so no funny stuff, no trying to bullshit Michael Conway with inflated estimates. It'll all get done at a bargain. So what do you say?"

"I say that living in hovels like this one, it's no wonder the Irish drink so much," Maureen commented, with a rigid, humorless smile.

Mike returned it. "And all this time I thought you were a diplomat's daughter."

She snickered, the rebuke bouncing off the chainmail woven by her breeding and her money.

*

The weather cleared the next day. Under a benign blue sky, Liz and Maureen went on a seaside hike, which was to be followed by a shopping and sightseeing excursion to Westport, a town farther up the coast. Mike took Luke fishing on the River Erriff. He'd reserved a prime two-rod beat downstream of Aasleagh Falls and hired a gillie named Patrick Brennan, a ruddy-cheeked man who spoke in a musical West Country brogue.

"Erriff's been fishin' right well, she has," he said as they tramped a well-worn path to the river. "You'll see, sure enough. Three days past, I had two gents on beat seven, and one caught a seven-pounder and the other a nine."

His optimistic chatter was belied by the morose look that appeared to be his permanent facial expression. He wore a vest bulging with fly boxes and carried a long-handled net; Luke and Mike carried Spey rods fourteen feet in length. Despite the warm weather, Mike had garbed himself as a sporting gentleman: tattersall shirt, checkered pants tucked into knee-high Wellingtons, a tweed jacket with suede elbow patches to go with his tweed cap. His British-officer's mustache was the perfect accessory to this getup. Luke was also wearing Wellies; otherwise, in a baseball cap and jeans, he presented as an American redneck.

The path crossed a meadow and dropped down to the Erriff, running in swift, shining braids through its glacial valley. Brennan led them along a rocky bar to a wide pool in whose depths Luke caught the flash of salmon finning in the current.

Brennan sat down, opened a fly box, and studied the colorful flies, arranged in tidy rows.

"Let's see . . . A Silver Doctor, no. A Hairy Mary then? A Garry Dog? Hairy Mary Garry," he murmured to himself, sounding like one of those passages from Joyce. "Don't think so. . . . Ah, here's the one for Mister Blackburn. A Willie Gunn." He pulled out a yellow, orange, and black hair-wing and tied it to Luke's tippet with a riffle hitch. "And for Mister Conway, what will it be? A Blue Charm. It's the Blue Charm for him, works like a charm, it does."

He knotted the fly to Mike's tippet, then positioned him at the tail end of the pool, Luke at the head. On the far side, a riffle bounced beneath a garage-size boulder. Brennan told him to cast upstream at a forty-five-degree angle and allow the fly to skim the riffle's surface until it was at a forty-five downstream, then give it a few short, sharp strips. The gillie turned and went to give Mike his instructions. Luke stood in ankle-deep shallows and watched the river tumble, dancing and sparkling, through a natural spillway into the pool. The back of a salmon arched out of the riffle and Luke made a cast. He knew the fish would not strike, and it didn't. Neither the sight of it, nor the scenery, could dispel his pessimism, whose sources were his worries and preoccupations.

The never-ending worries about Maureen. She'd woken up this morning bitchy and irritable, then withdrawn into a sullenness, which morphed into a fragile excitability—all before breakfast. Once again, Luke couldn't determine if these rapid fluctuations were as bad as things would get, or if they were the outer bands of an oncoming maelstrom.

His preoccupation was with a question. What did it mean to be *a* father? Was it the guy who played catch with you in the backyard, made sure you finished your homework, taught you to drive? A father provided for his children, he protected them, he loved them, loved them above all else. Luke's father had never been affectionate or attentive; nor had he been cruel or neglectful, just absent much of the time, away on maneuvers and deployments. When at home, he imitated that movie character, the Great Santini, running his household like an army outfit, shagging Luke out of bed with commands almost identical to the Gunny's when he rousted his Key West derelicts. *Reveille, boy! Outta the rack and on your feet!* What had Ian's father been like? Winslow Campbell, the software engineer? He must have been devoted, to have adopted three children. In Corinne's telling, his death, following his wife's so closely, had left a big hole in Ian's life, a hole he'd fallen into until he struck bottom in the Arizona State Prison.

Luke made another cast, and another and another, without interesting a fish. Brennan changed flies twice, with the same results. Mike had also been skunked.

They moved on, past a rapids, to the next lie. Wading out onto a bar, they could see in the clear water salmon holding by the redds, females poised to expel roe, males to squirt milt over the eggs. *Each will father dozens of progeny, not one will do a thing to raise them,* Luke thought, as he had never provided for Ian, nor protected him, nor loved him. The only thing he'd done was to plant a seed in a womb; that is, he'd fathered him, and there was all the difference in the world between the verb and the noun.

"Fish on!" Mike shouted.

Line peeled off his reel, the rod bowed, and the salmon leaped, shaking in midair, droplets flying like crystalline spray. Several minutes and three more jumps later, he fought it to within range of Brennan's net. The fish thrashed the surface with all the ferocity that had driven it to swim across miles and miles of open sea into this river, then upstream to the very spot where it had been born. Brennan lunged and netted it, and it lay bent in the webbing, still writhing, a silver ingot infused with life.

"Oh, he's a fine one!" the gillie exclaimed. "If he don't go eight or nine, I'm a bloody liar." He slogged ashore, brained the salmon with a short club, and hooked it by the mouth to a handheld scale. "I ain't a liar, by Christ. Eight and a quarter!"

"We'll eat well tonight!" Mike shouted. "Oh, this is how I'm going to live every summer till I run out of summers!"

He pulled a mini-Canon from his jacket pocket, gave it to Luke and, clutching the salmon in both hands, struck a grip-and-grin pose. Luke took three frames, pleased by his absence of envy.

Brennan threaded a stringer through the gills, tied the fish to a low-hanging branch, and laid it in the water near the bank to keep it fresh.

"And now it's your turn, Mister Blackburn," he said.

"Until I get a tweed coat and hat, you can drop the Mister. Luke is okay with me."

Soon, Mike caught and released a grilse—a one-year salmon—but Luke's turn did not come, though they fished well into the afternoon. Disappointment seemed fitting; it seemed a fitting thing for a man who so far had not gathered the moral courage to tell his wife that he'd been living a lie for years. Who so far had failed to reveal who and where he was to the son he'd fathered.

He reeled in and said, "I'm about done in. This rod, it feels like I'm casting a telephone pole."

"Ah, stay at it now," Brennan urged. "Low light is the best time. And you know what they say about the salmon—it's the fish of a thousand casts."

"I've done a thousand and then some."

"Hey, it's Conway two, Blackburn zee-ro," Mike crowed. "Aren't you gonna try to tie me?"

"Fishing isn't a competitive sport," Luke said. "I'm done."

"Suit yourselves," said Brennan sullenly. He untied the stringer, slung the fish over his shoulder, and they trekked back to the car.

Maureen was not in the room. Her absence, Luke reluctantly admitted to himself, was welcome. He kicked off his boots and sat at the desk, scanning the *International Herald Tribune*—a UN peacekeeping force deployed in Kosovo . . . South Africa's new president settling in . . . worldwide demonstrations against the forthcoming G8 summit—then checked telex messages sent up from the front desk, one from the foreign editor and one each from his two assistant managing editors about routine stuff. Another came from Edith Buchmayr, apprising him of the progress in her investigation into Oceanaire Properties. It had a numbered account in a Grand Cayman bank: "Trusted sources told me it's in the eight figures. All signs point to a laundry. Hope to have more when you're back in harness." A final message, from Dustin Cardenas, had been made to his office phone and relayed to him by an assistant editor: Emilio Cortazar, the boy rescued in the Marquesas, had moved with his mother to Key West, where she had relatives. Dustin had hired the kid as his boat cleaner and was teaching him how to fish and tie flies.

Luke was finishing his replies when Maureen burst through the door bearing gifts from her jaunt to Westport; so many gifts that she required a bellboy to wheel them into the hotel room on a luggage cart. After he left, grateful for an overly liberal tip, she showed the haul to Luke: blouses, women's slacks, and pullovers for herself and her mother; hand-knit sweaters for her brothers; for Luke, a bottle of a premium Irish whiskey and a wool Norfolk jacket destined never to be worn in South Florida; for her father, a set of golf clubs destined never to be swung, because at seventy-seven he'd quit playing; and finally, a handsome leather suitcase to carry the booty, excepting the clubs, which came with their own padded travel bag. While she displayed these items, she delivered a commentary about her day. The hike on the coastal trail—Fabulous! Such wild beauty! Westport—Wonderful! A seaside village on the Irish Riviera. And the Westport House, a manor built by an eighteenth-century pirate queen, Grace O'Malley. Stunning! Stunning! The words, spilling promiscuously from her mouth, corroborated the hard evidence supplied by the reckless shopping spree. He'd suspected for days that she'd stopped her lithium, probably to gear herself up for the Bloomsday performance. He hadn't said anything, wary of provoking her, but he did now.

"Doctor Blackburn again," she said.

Luke swiveled the desk chair to look at her directly. "C'mon, Maureen. Did Pearle give you the okay, or did you all on your own?"

She didn't answer, which was as good as an answer, and began to refold the clothes and pack them in the exquisite suitcase. He noticed she'd had it embossed with her initials in gold.

"Do you have them with you?" he asked.

"Yes," she snapped, empty boxes stacked in her arms. "Yes, I have them and yes I stopped a couple of weeks ago and yes I started again and since I know, I just know, your next question will be—When? Yesterday." She dumped the boxes on the floor, stomped into the bathroom, and came out holding a prescription bottle, which she tossed into his lap. "You see the quantity on the label? If you care to, you can count them and you'll see there's less in the bottle. Does a successful wife make you insecure? Is that why you're always trying to stifle me?"

He placed the pills on the desk. The drug, he remembered, could take a couple of weeks before it had any effect. "I'm not trying to stifle you."

He stood and embraced her. She stiffened at first, then yielded, briefly yielded before she spun out of his arms, picked up the boxes, restacked them, and set the pile next to the waste basket.

"It just feels so great," she said, throwing herself into the armchair. "Like I did when I was a girl and my parents took us to the top of the Eiffel Tower and there was all of Paris at my feet and I wanted to launch myself into the air and fly over it, like Peter Pan. There was the tingling in my whole body. I was invulnerable, indestructible. It felt that way when I stepped out onto the stage in front of all those people. Knew I would have them in the palm of my hand, that I could do anything. Miss Gorgeous Airhead was a big help, but she wouldn't have been if I hadn't rehearsed her and written the program. It was so exciting, and that woman from Trinity? The one we had dinner with? The one with the long face? Heather Taylor. Heather is editing a collection of essays on Irish literature. Twentieth century. Irish lit in the twentieth century and she's including my essay on *Finnegan's Wake*. I showed it to her, and it knocked her out! 'Mr. Finnegan is Fine Again: Disintegration and Reintegration in *Finnegan's Wake*.' The book comes out next year.

Oxford University Press. I finished the essay before we left, those nights when I couldn't sleep? Couldn't have done it and written the performance and got ready for the trip if I was feeling all quiet and normal inside. It feels so great, so, so great . . ."

Until it doesn't, Luke thought.

"The cat. It's like the cat."

"The cat?"

"Stifling me. You insisted, insisted, insisted that we not buy the cat until after the trip."

"I don't recall that I *insisted*. Suggested."

"Insisted, and I played Little Miss Obedient Wifey, so now the one I wanted is gone and I'll have to look for another."

"You'll find one," he said. "A lot of cats in the world. Let's not quarrel about a cat, okay? I'm going to jump in the shower. We're meeting Mike and Liz in the bar at six, then for dinner."

"News to me. Liz didn't say anything about that."

"Mike and I decided. He caught a salmon this afternoon. The kitchen will do it for us for dinner. We thought we'd knock back a drink first."

"Must we? I spent all day with her."

"Thought you liked her."

"I do, but all day is enough. Listening to that hillbilly accent. But I'll play good Little Wifey again and go along."

Luke stepped into the bathroom, stripped, and turned the shower head to pulse. The hot water pounding his shoulders and the back of his neck felt like a massage. Maureen's last remark, and the accusation that he was stifling her, had confirmed another of his suppositions: she had had at least one extended phone conversation with her mother before leaving for Ireland, and it had been as responsible for her present state as going off the meds. He didn't know what had been said, and didn't need to; Thelma, with her sharp, critical tongue, could almost always be counted on to stir up the particles of disharmony in her daughter's mind. She'd objected to the marriage, though not entirely for the reasons Luke had first thought. True, he wasn't the blue-blazered preppy Maureen had been groomed to marry, but the root of Thelma's disapproval was a conviction that he would thwart Maureen's career, as her own marriage, she believed, had thwarted hers. (Maureen's doctoral degree, her successes in academia, failed to alter this opinion.) A respectable concert pianist, Thelma had persuaded herself that she would have been a great one if her genius had not been smothered, traipsing the world with her diplomat husband while bearing three children. She'd found fault with all three throughout their lives, and it never occurred to her that they would one day requite her resentment of them. Don and Stuart had been estranged from her for years; her husband finally divorced her five years ago, telling Luke, "My only regret is that I didn't do it twenty years ago." Maureen alone never quite made the break, secretly loathing Thelma while publicly expressing affection for her, forgiving her tactless cruelties. Maureen confessed to Luke that after her second miscarriage, Thelma had said, "There is probably something the matter with his . . . you know, but listen to me, dear. I know it hurts you now but believe me, you'll see that this was the best thing that could have happened." She was a malignant force of nature, Thelma was, waging a brainwashing campaign to convince Maureen that Luke was to blame for her postpartum breakdowns.

They took a table at a window looking out to the harbor and Killary Fjord, a gray-blue blade pointing at the sea beyond. Two men occupied the table nearest theirs, Brits by their accents, anglers by their neckties, decorated with likenesses of fishing flies. A turf fire burned in the bar's fireplace and two harpists—ethereal-looking sisters in lacy gowns—filled the room with plaintive Celtic ballads. Luke and Maureen had ordered martinis—gin for him, vodka for her. Mike was drinking a Guinness, while Liz, sipping a white wine, praised the hotel's seaweed baths. She'd taken one in lieu of a shower.

"They cut the seaweed every day, fresh as can be," she said in what

Maureen had termed her "hillbilly accent." "It looks real ugly in the tub, all this green slimy stuff swimming in hot salt water, and when you get in, you look like the Creature from the Black Lagoon. But, Lord, it was wonderful after all that walking and shopping. So relaxing." Her gaze flicked to Maureen. "You should try one before bed tonight, honey."

Maureen smiled without warmth or malice, a blank smile. She was overdressed in black pumps, a black cocktail dress, pearls, and diamond earrings. When she'd walked in, every man in the place gawked at her. They didn't gawk the way men did at Corinne. Maureen's beauty was cool and static. Like a statue's, it generated admiration rather than heat.

"You told me you have trouble sleeping sometimes, well, a seaweed bath will fix you right up," Liz went on. "I found out so much interesting stuff. Like some kind of, oh, I can't remember the word for what bathing in seaweed is called, some kind of therapy on account of its therapeutic effect."

Professor Carrington helped her out. "Thalassotherapy. It refers to bathing in salt water, with or without seaweed."

Her undertone of condescension had been faint but not faint enough. Mike gave her a hard look. Luke, seeking to quench any fireworks between his wife and his friend before they started, recounted Mike's tussle with the salmon they were to eat for dinner.

"I told the chef to keep it simple," Mike said. "You don't want a fresh salmon swimming in goop. He'll bake the fillets in white butter."

"Beurre blanc," said Maureen, then repeated the phrase, making fun of herself with an exaggerated roll of the *r*'s. *Bee-yurrrrre blahnc.* She raised her martini glass to her lips and held it there without drinking as she stared at Mike over the rim; stared with such flirtatiousness that he squirmed. And it wasn't easy to make Michael Conway squirm. Luke pushed his chair back and glanced, quickly and anxiously, under the table to see if she was applying the footsie treatment. She wasn't.

Mike took a stab at congeniality, asking how the conference had gone. It wasn't a conference, Maureen corrected. A celebration, rather, of Joyce's genius.

"One of the stories in *Dubliners*, "Araby," it's considered the finest short story ever written," said Mike.

"Considered by whom?"

"Critics, scholars, I suppose."

"Which ones? Cite your sources. Come now, defend your assertion."

She seemed determined to be argumentative even as she played the coquette; there was a kind of vicious trill in her voice. Luke gave her a gentle poke in the ribs. She lowered her glass, and her eyes with it. Mike turned his attention to the harpists, strumming and singing what sounded like a dirge in Gaelic.

"All their wars are merry and all their songs are sad," he observed. "That's what's said about the Irish."

"Their last one wasn't so merry, was it?" said Maureen.

"My grandfather, the one who owned the house here, Liam Hughes, was in the Easter Rebellion in 1916."

"I was talking about the Troubles in Belfast."

"I know."

"My father had a hand in the peace agreement," Maureen's voice quavered, as it often did when she spoke about her father. "He was on George Mitchell's team, an adviser for Mitchell when Mitchell was special envoy. He was called out of retirement."

"Because he's Irish?" Liz asked, innocently.

"No! Because he was a foreign service officer. He isn't Irish."

"I meant Irish descent, honey. Carrington's an Irish name, isn't it? Mine was Moore, and I was told that's Irish. Protestant Irish, but still and all, Irish."

"Potato famine Irish? My father was once assistant secretary of state for European affairs. A wonderful, wonderful man."

Liz had taken the potato famine jibe with good grace. "I'm sure I did not intend to impugn your father," she said, mispronouncing impugn.

Maureen flinched and said, "Did you hear what you just said? Impunj? It's *impyoon.*" Liz's simple mistake was the catalyst that accelerated the mixture of vodka and volatile agents in her brain. Luke could almost hear the noise inside it, could almost see her neurotransmitters flickering and flashing, delivering the wrong messages, or the right ones to the wrong places.

"My father isn't . . . no . . . did you ever hear of Robert Carrington, Captain Robert Carrington, came to America in 1740, fought in the French and Indian War and then in . . . I could have been in the DAR, you, know." She was talking faster and faster. "My mother wanted me to join but I said, 'No, thank you.' . . . Because Robert served in the Revolution, a colonel by then, at Bunker Hill, but why would anyone who can't pronounce impugn—*impyoon,* honey—why would anyone like that know one thing about history. . . . You think I'm a snob, well why would I be if I didn't join the DAR when I could have if I wanted to . . . ?"

Mike was aware of Maureen's condition; Luke had confided it to him, and he must have mentioned it to his wife, but this was the first time they had seen and heard it in action, and they were dumbstruck, beholding Maureen in a state of appalled wonderment. Luke should have been prepared, yet he was as stunned as if he'd been sucker-punched in the back of the head.

Recovering, he grasped Maureen under the arm. "Hey, hey. Take it easy," he pleaded, forcing himself to sound collected. "Do you want to go up to the room for a little while?"

"Good idea. You need a little rest, I'd say." Liz spoke with an equanimity he found impressive, considering that she'd been verbally slapped twice. "Then we can all have a pleasant dinner."

"It's Nurse Ratshit! Dr. Blackburn's assistant!" Maureen howled, drawing stares from the Englishmen at the neighboring table.

Mortified, Luke broke out in a sweat and tightened his grip on her arm. "Get a hold of yourself!"

Every patron in the room—it wasn't large—had turned toward the disturbance, but the harpists, with the perseverance of rock musicians accustomed to rowdy venues, continued to strum and sing.

"Blazes Blackburn, Blazes Boylan Blackburn, Boylan's got blazin' boils! Think you can manhandle me because of your big red brute of a thing. . . . Let me go!"

Maureen's elbow narrowly missed his chin as she twisted free. Some of his old wrestling reflexes woke up as he clutched her wrist, put her arm around his shoulders, grasped her waist, and hauled her to her feet, all in under five seconds. Muttering, "Sorry, everyone, sorry," he hustled her out through the door, like a trainer leading an injured player off the field. Or was it more like leading a drunk to bed? Yes, more like that, for what was happening to her mimicked extreme intoxication. At the elevator, as he released her to press the button, she made a break for the front entrance, her heels clattering on the tile floor; then, as she pushed the door open, she fell, tumbling onto the pavement outside in a graceless heap. Luke ran to her, the front desk clerk beside him.

"Sir—" the clerk began.

"I've got her," said Luke. He was breathless. "It's all right, a little too much to drink, y'know?"

A half moon had risen over the harbor, its indifferent light drawing a dull stripe on the still water. Maureen sat with her legs splayed and gazed dumbly at her feet. Her pumps had come off in the fall. The clerk took one arm, Luke the other, and they picked her up. She did not resist; the spill had knocked the wild fury out of her. The clerk fetched her shoes and followed the couple inside. Luke took the shoes, summoned the elevator and, with his arm once again circling her waist, brought her to the room. She leaned against him, as limp and exhausted as if she'd run a race. He sat her down in the armchair and held her there, both hands on her shoulders.

"Can I trust you to stay here for five minutes? I'm going to see if I can find a doctor."

Silent, she looked up at him.

"Maureen, can I trust you to stay in the room?"

"The song those girls were singing," she said languidly. "So sad. All their songs are sad. I can hear it in my head, but I can't understand the words. I'm not crazy. I—am—not—fucking—crazy."

"Yes, you are. You're crazy now, but you won't be in a little while."

She worked her face into an expression he couldn't quite fathom; it looked like hatred.

"I lost them. Lost them because of you. I think there's something wrong with your big red brute of a thing. A natural abortifacient in your spunk. I wanted us to try again. Just one more time, but I couldn't. You saw to that, didn't you, boilin' blazes bastard?"

In insaniam veritas.

"I'm going to find a doctor."

The local health clinic was closed for the day. The desk clerk—after Luke pleaded, falsely, that Maureen had been injured—phoned the doctor at home. He agreed to make a house call; he was the hotel's doctor as well. Luke met him in the lobby, and on the elevator ride to the third floor, he presented a very brief summary of Maureen's medical history. The doctor, a thin young man who could not have graduated med school much more than two years ago, said that emotional and mental illnesses were far beyond his competence. There was a mental health clinic in Galway, an hour's drive away, but he advised Luke to bring her home if at all possible.

They entered the room and found a somewhat subdued Maureen seated in the armchair in regal pose—ankles crossed, arms on the chair's arms.

"And who the hell are you, sonny boy?"

'Doctor Flynn," answered Doctor Flynn. "Your husband asked for me. I'm going to give you something to help you sleep."

He opened his bag and went through the motions, taking her pulse, her blood pressure, asking what medications she was on, and if was she allergic to any others. She clammed up, so Luke answered for her. When Flynn attempted to listen to her heart, she slapped the stethoscope aside.

"Hands off my tits. The trouble isn't there. It's up here." Pressing her palms to her temples. "Those blond angels downstairs were singing some tune and it's stuck up here. In Gaelic, they were singing in Gaelic, and I won't be able to sleep until I find out what the words were in English and what it was about. Stuck like records used to get stuck on turntables. An ear worm, isn't that what it's called, an ear worm?"

The doctor replied that he thought so, and promised that he would stop the song from playing so she could sleep. He removed a syringe from his bag.

Maureen stared at it for a few seconds, then said, in something resembling a normal voice, "Let me change first."

Luke was encouraged; rationality had not been totally eclipsed.

While she got undressed in the bathroom, Flynn wrote out a prescription for a tranquilizer.

"The chemist opens at eight," he said. "If you fly back to America, you'll need to keep her stable. Don't want her freaking out midway over the pond."

"I've got some Thorazine."

"The chemical straitjacket. These will be better, less severe side effects."

Once Maureen was asleep, Luke went downstairs and enlisted the concierge's help in changing their plane reservations. In less time than he'd expected, they were booked on an Aer Lingus nonstop to Miami, departing Dublin the next afternoon at three thirty. Returning to the room, he began to pack. Her things first, then his. He considered abandoning the golf clubs, but decided against it. Might upset her. Maybe he would take up golf. He packed quickly but methodically, lining up the luggage in the entry space by the door. Order. Order was essential.

Pick up the tranqs at eight sharp, he thought. *On the road no later than half past. Four-hour drive to the airport. Turn in the rental car. That will take us to one thirty. Two hours in the departure lounge. Phone Dr. Pearle from there. Nine hours in the air. Sixteen hours altogether, here to Miami International, assuming no flight delay. Please, please, no delay. Figure a half hour cab ride to Coral Gables. So make it eighteen hours just to be sure.* With the tranquilizers, he would need to keep her together for eighteen hours. He would need to keep himself together. So far, he'd handled this emergency pretty well. Congratulations, Luke. She looked so peaceful now, under the covers. He leaned over the bed and kissed her cheek, lightly, so as not to wake her. It wasn't late, only nine fifteen, twilight lingering in the summer sky and the half moon at zenith. He grabbed the bottle of the fifteen-year-old whiskey and took the stairs one flight down and knocked on Mike's and Liz's door. Liz, in bathrobe and pajamas, opened it.

"Hope I'm not barging in," he said. "I came to apologize."

"You don't have anything to apologize for."

"For Maureen. I'm apologizing for her." He held the bottle in the air. "And I need a drink and somebody to drink with."

Mike said he would join him. He was also in a robe and stretched out on the bed, watching a soccer match. He muted the TV as his wife fetched two glasses from the bathroom. Luke measured out a finger in each and sat in the desk chair, the only chair in the room. The Conways were as price conscious as Maureen was the opposite and had booked into a budget double.

"You missed a fine feed," said Mike. "The chef did a terrific job. Just the right amount of beurre blank. I mean, *bee-yurrrrre blahnc.* How is she?"

"Sleeping. The hotel doctor shot her up with a sedative." Luke took a swig of the whiskey, smooth and warm, liquid satin. "I'm glad we didn't spoil your dinner."

"Nothing could have. I would have eaten that damn fish if there'd been an earthquake."

"But I'm sorry as hell, and Maureen will be, too, when she's herself again."

Liz got onto the bed next to her husband and regarded Luke, her expression cool and fixed, like an ice sculpture's.

"She wasn't always like this," Luke pleaded. "When I first met her. when we got married, she was . . . exciting. Fun. She was witty and fun and then these spells . . ."

"Okay, so . . ." Liz said.

"When she has one of those spells, she's oblivious. Like a drunk. Doesn't know what she's saying and how it affects other people."

"Uh-huh," Liz said.

"She didn't mean to insult you."

"Uh-huh."

"She may not even remember how she behaved, just like a drunk wouldn't remember. A blackout, kind of. But if she does remember, she'll be embarrassed, ashamed, and as sorry as I am."

"Uh-huh."

"We're cutting the trip short. Flying back to Miami tomorrow. She'll see her shrink as soon as—"

Liz waved him into silence. "People say things when they're drunk they wouldn't say when they're sober, but, y'know, that doesn't mean they don't mean them."

In insaniam veritas.

"She didn't, believe me—" Luke began.

"I know how to pronounce impugn. *Impyoon.* I just got tongue-tied for a second. And I do know history. I'm not some ignorant shitkicker, which is what she seems to think. And it wasn't only what she said, but how. Like she hated me."

Lost them because of you.

"And then there's the crack she made about the house yesterday," Mike interjected. "Did she not know what she was saying then?"

Luke drank his glass dry and poured two fingers more.

"Here's my opinion, for what it's worth," his friend went on. "She uses this—whatever she's got—to control you."

"Not fair, not true," Luke shot back, resentful. Yet he thought there might be some validity in the statement. After all these years, she should have known better than to go off the meds, should have recognized the signs of a mental unraveling and taken steps to forestall it. "She can't help being the way she is."

"Sure about that, are you? I've seen you when you come down and you've got to get back to Miami and you practically give yourself an ulcer, worried you'll be late. Sometimes people can choose to be sick for what it can get them. In her case, control. It's something I got familiar with a long time ago."

"Mom again," Liz said, rolling her eyes. "Luke, you're welcome in our house anytime just like always, but if I never see Maureen again it won't bring tears to my eyes. She can go ahead and say she's sorry, but I'd have a real hard time believing her. Real hard time believing that she doesn't think I'm an ignorant shitkicker who talks funny."

Rolling the glass between his palms, he murmured, "I don't know what to do. I don't know what the hell I should do."

"You're doing as much as you can," Liz said, sympathetically.

"Not that. Not *only* that, it's . . ."

It came over him quickly, unexpectedly, like the return of an old grief. Luke rambled on for ten minutes about Corinne and Ian and withholding the truth from Maureen, aware that making his friends party to his secret was unfair to them, yet he was unable to stop himself.

"I was going to tell her after this trip, but I don't see how I can now. It would be too much."

There was a prolonged silence before Liz asked, "Too much on her or on you?"

"Too much on me because too much on her."

He glanced at Mike, who was studying the whiskey in his glass.

"Wish I could give you some advice, but I can't, m'boy."

That fatherly "m'boy" got on Luke's nerves at times. Mike was only three years older.

"I wasn't looking for any, just getting it off my chest," he said.

But later on in his room, as he lay in the dark beside Maureen, he did not feel the lightness that comes from unburdening oneself. He felt that he might have made a mistake, that perhaps he ought to have left the burden on his chest.

9

THE MIAMI EXAMINER
1630 N. BAYSHORE DR.
MIAMI, FL 33132
LUCAS BLACKBURN, MANAGING EDITOR

June 29, 1999

Arizona State Prison Complex
Santa Rita Unit
Ian Campbell, ADC# 1945041
POB 24401
Tucson, AZ 85734

Dear Ian,

  The only way I know how to begin this letter is to say that I don't know how to begin it. So, I'll be direct. I'm the ~~guy~~ person in the letterhead above, and I'm your ~~father~~ biological father . . .

Lifting his eyes from the page, Luke stared out the wall-size window across Biscayne Bay to Miami Beach, its hotels and condos a jumble of white and pastel rectangles, the bayside shore forming the base of a rough triangle, its legs the 15th Street Bridge and the MacArthur Causeway. Order had been restored to Maureen's mind. She'd dozed through most of the flight from Dublin—the Thorazine substitute had proved its worth. Upon the next day's visit to Dr. Pearle, Luke was overjoyed to hear that she would not require another hospitalization. Pearle diagnosed her state as hypomanic, in contrast to the hypermania of previous episodes, but prescribed an increased lithium dosage after he'd taken her levels. The chemical sorcery had done its work. Like the Mr. Finnegan in her essay, Maureen was fine again in only ten days, swimming laps at the Venetian pool or at the university gym, polishing a syllabus for a summer course she would start teaching next month.

Shifting his gaze slightly southward, Luke watched a cruise ship bigger than an aircraft carrier steaming out of the port of Miami, bound for one Caribbean playground or another. A yearning for escape flared up within him, and not just for a holiday with a boatload of overfed tourists. What he had in mind was self-exile to some remote backwater where he could never be found. French Guiana, once home to Devil's Island, would be a good bet. When was the last time anyone had heard or read a word about French Guiana?

He returned to the letter in his Olivetti portable, which he'd brought out of mothballs. It seemed a better instrument than his office computer for composing so personal a communication, as if the keys transmitted some part of himself into the words they hammered into the linen bond paper. He resumed:

> I have no idea how you will react to my news, but let me explain why I'm writing to you. About six weeks ago, your birth mother contacted me, by letter, after she'd seen my name in the newspaper I work for. She told me ~~about the trouble you're in~~, that you and she had been reunited a

few years ago, and about the trouble you're in, and that she's going to sponsor you on your parole. Needless to say, I was shocked—I ~~didn't even know your name~~ hadn't seen her or heard from her in thirty years, and didn't even know your name until she gave it to me. When you were adopted, as she probably told you, the identities of the child and his adoptive parents were kept secret from his biological parents.

We met face to face a little while later in Key West. It was the first time I'd laid eyes on Corinne since the day I shipped out for Vietnam~~, thirty years ago~~. We talked for more than an hour. She said that you, naturally, wanted to know who your father was—your biological father, that is—but that she could not reveal it without my permission. One of the things she said in her letter has stuck with me—that she's sponsoring you because "it's the right thing for me to step into the shoes I vacated a long time ago."

I had given her the okay to tell you who I am, but she later sent ~~me~~ a note saying that I ought to be the one to do that. And so I am. Stepping into my own pair of vacated shoes, you might say. Corinne also told me that you lost your parents. Allow me to express my sympathies. I lost mine, my father in 1978, my mother in 1990, so I know how it feels. You probably have a lot of questions. You may write me at the above address. I have to ask you, for reasons I can't go into now, to keep all this between you, me, and Corinne. I hope that one day we'll get to see each other.

Sincerely yours,

"What's that sound? What is that sound I hear? Clickety-clack, tap tap tap."

Luke swiveled his chair and faced Edith Buchmayr standing in the doorway, a hand cupping her ear.

"It comes to me like a sweet refrain from days gone by. Play it again, Sam."

"Didn't your mama teach you that closed doors are meant to be knocked on?" he said.

"They're meant to be opened, kicked open if necessary," Edith volleyed back, and stepped inside. She was smartly dressed, as usual: a beige tropical-weight pantsuit, butterscotch slip-ons, a jaunty silk scarf. Taking two more steps forward, she stretched out an arm, wiggling her thin fingers at the Olivetti. "To quote myself the first time I saw a boy with a hard-on, Can I touch it?"

Luke quickly pulled the letter from the carriage and laid it face down on the desk. Edith, with a look of mock ecstasy, reached over his shoulder and passed her fingertips over the keys.

"I do so miss my Royal."

"What do you want?" Luke asked, not hiding his irritation.

"Lunch. Joe's. On me. Thought you might have a yen for stone crabs."

"Stone crab season closed last month."

"They've put out their new summer menu. Fresh mahi-mahi, and the old standby, fried chicken. Also, I want to bring you up to speed on Oceanaire Properties and Astoria."

He slipped the letter into a desk drawer; he would type a finished copy later.

"Can you guarantee that we'll be back on time for me to make the two o'clock meeting?"

"It's early, always good to get to Joe's early, so, yeah, guaran-godamnteed."

They drove to Miami Beach in Edith's car, an unpretentious Ford Taurus, which she turned over to the valet to avoid the hunt for a parking spot. Edith loved the place more for its colorful history than its food, excellent as it was. Joe's was a Beach icon, in business for nearly ninety years, the choice dining spot for long-dead celebrities. Gloria

Swanson had eaten there with her lover, Joe Kennedy; so had the Duke and Duchess of Windsor, Will Rogers, Damon Runyon, and Walter Winchell. Also, Al Capone (under the alias of Al Brown). Edith couldn't name any living notables but thought that Madonna might have cracked a stone crab claw or two in Joe's since buying a place on South Beach.

Their arrival at 11:30 spared them a long wait—Joe's did not take reservations—and Edith, a beloved regular who tipped well, reduced the wait time to zero by shaking hands with the maître d', who deftly transferred the ten in her palm to his pants pocket. He escorted them down an aisle, its buffed terrazzo floor reflecting the overhead lights in a single bright bar, as a flat sea reflects a rising or setting sun, to a secluded table. Having dispensed with small talk and office gossip in the car, she got down to business as soon as the waiter recited the specials and took their orders.

"Okey-dokey, I followed the money and it leads to Colombia," she said in a low voice. "Oceanaire Properties is a registered company that's poured tens of millions in illegitimate money into casinos and resorts all over the Caribbean. Here's the delicious part. Its CEO, so to speak, is José Dominguez, formerly of Cali, Colombia, now resident in the Caymans. Four years ago, before the Orejuela brothers were busted, Dominguez was a middle man for the Cali cartel. Arranged sales of Colombian coke to a Mexican organization. Presently, he runs Oceanaire as a laundromat for the Orejuelas' successors."

"And now Oceanaire wants to develop Astoria?" Luke asked.

"No, Thomas Incroce does, with help from his Colombian friends. The big problem is the judge's decision that he doesn't own it."

"Which he's appealing."

"Case to be heard next week. While you were away, I flew up to DC and did some research in the National Archives. You'd be proud of me for what I dug up."

"I'm always proud of you."

"I'm proud of myself, you want to know the truth." She reached down and pulled a notebook from her shoulder bag, a Coach. Luke would have expected nothing less. Her sense of fashion, her always-well-turned-out appearance, gave the impression that she was superficial, masking her intelligence and formidable competence.

"In 1924, President Calvin Coolidge signed an executive order reserving Astoria for exclusive use by the US Navy. We now fast forward to 1953"—Edith pressed a button on an imaginary tape recorder—"when the Navy filed an official objection to Florida's sale of the island. Attached to that file is a finding by the then state attorney general that even though the sale was completed, the buyer—Senator Sam Lowe, aka the King of the Keys—knew that title was disputed. 'Under a cloud' is how the AG put it. Okay so far?"

Luke nodded, although only half his brain was engaged; the other half was on the letter to Ian. He wasn't pleased with it. There should be more warmth in it, but then, how could there be? Ian Campbell, blood of his blood, loin of his loins, was a stranger.

"So while you were away, I filed a piece about the Coolidge letter, the AG's opinion," said Edith as the waiter delivered salads and drinks—a pinot noir for her, fizzy water for him. He needed to be alert for the two o'clock meeting, when he and the two assistant managing editors would make up the next edition's front page. "And Incroce went ballistic. Called me, said that I and the *Examiner* were prejudicing his appeal in favor of the federal government."

"This is all real interesting. Is it leading to something?"

Edith chomped down on a forkful of lettuce and croutons. "Who put Incroce in touch with those Oceanaire people? If he needed financing, why did he go to a laundry and not a legit bank?"

The arrival of lunch interrupted her. They'd both ordered the mahi-mahi, otherwise known as dolphin. The Hawaiian name for the fish made it palatable by assuring diners they were not eating Flipper.

"Dee-lish," Edith said. "Sure beats a sandwich at the desk."

Luke gestured an agreement. "So, do you have answers?"

"As to question two, his company, TBI Corp., is in shoal water financially, on bad paper with major banks. As to question one, I aim to find out. Just to muddy things a little more, for zoning and building purposes, Astoria is under Monroe County jurisdiction—"

"I'm bewitched, bothered, and befuddled," said Luke. "If the feds own the island, the county's zoning laws shouldn't apply, correct?"

"Except that they do. Muddy waters, like I said. Anyhow, since the court's decision, the county has stopped processing TBI's development applications. My source—"

"This is your personal Deep Throat?"

"Yup."

"When do I found out who it is? Woodward and Bernstein, you know, told Ben Bradlee about the original Deep Throat."

"I will when I get a few things nailed down, okay? My source informs me that Incroce has fired his lawyer and hired Manny Higgs."

"A Keys intrigue wouldn't be complete without him," said Luke, with a snort.

Edith savored a chunk of mahi-mahi and licked her lips. "This sauce! Heavenly. What did the waiter say it is?"

"Clam and corn butter."

"Got to get the recipe. Manny wouldn't take on the government of the United States if he didn't think he had at least an even chance of winning. So we can safely assume he's got a rabbit somewhere in his hat, an ace up his slippery sleeve, pick your metaphor."

Luke was silent, mulling what she'd told him.

"Since Incroce went to court, this story is public property, with one big, fat exception—the connection to major-league drug money," Edith continued. "That's my exclusive. Bear market for coke now, but Colombians must still be raking it in. My guy says that almost all the two hundred fifty mill Incroce needs is going to come from Oceanaire."

"Can you develop that angle more?" he said. "Without it, this is just one more Florida real estate swindle."

"I *know* that, Luke," Edith said, peevishly. She gazed sharply around the room, twitching her lips in time with the movement of her eyes. In some ways, Luke and she were like an old married couple, literate in each other's tics and facial expressions: she had more to say and was debating whether to say it; then, focusing again on him, she ended the argument with herself. "What we have so far is a financially troubled developer cozying up to a drug cartel laundry for the money to build a huge development on an island he probably doesn't own. A very South Florida tale, no? But it could be the tip of the proverbial iceberg. It seems that the FBI has been looking into this deal, a major investigation, really, and there are rumblings—no more than that at the moment—rumblings that the Feebies have some heavy hitters in their crosshairs, in the Keys and in Miami, maybe Tallahassee, too. I don't know who yet, but I should find out fairly soon."

"Feebies" was Edith's nickname for the FBI.

"Is Higgs one of them?" asked Luke.

She shrugged. "Wouldn't surprise me."

"So are we done?"

"For now, yeah," she replied, and demonstrated her status at Joe's by summoning the waiter for the check with just a tilt of her chin. A lesser being would have had to employ a more emphatic gesture.

The lunch had a salubrious effect on Luke, taking his mind off his personal preoccupations. The reprieve wouldn't last, he knew that, but even a temporary one was welcome. Seeking to prolong it, he took a more active part than usual at the editorial meeting and in the two that followed at three and four. Normally, his role at these sessions—they were held daily in the glassed-in conference room at the back of the newsroom—was largely ceremonial. He was like a constitutional monarch, while the assistant managing editors, the metro, fashion, lifestyle, sports, photo, and foreign editors, could be compared to a parliament, whose decisions Luke either ratified or disapproved. Mostly, it was the former. But this afternoon, he plunged into the reviews of the day's story budget, the discussions about which stories would make the front page, which would go inside and where and how many column inches should be allocated to each. He was happy to be in the fray.

Around five, as he retyped the letter to Ian in his office, he sensed a vibration rippling through the floor. The moment when the presses in the printing plant, a windowless block six stories high at the north end of the *Examiner* building, began to roll out the first edition never ceased to move him. It felt as if he were on a great ship, trembling as she got underway.

Thunderheads mounted over the ocean and swept landward; the afternoon downpour, a regular event in the summer, lashed his window and stopped half an hour later. He finished his rewrite, addressed and stamped the envelope, and hand-carried it to the mailroom rather than ask a copyboy to perform the task. He was being overly cautious, perhaps ridiculously so, but he didn't want to take the tiniest risk of anyone discovering that he had a relationship with Ian Campbell, #1945041, residing at the Arizona State Prison.

His and Corinne's rediscovery of each other had resulted from an accident. Sending the letter marked another turning point, but it followed from his own deliberate and conscious choice. He'd committed himself to a course of action with an uncertain outcome, consequences he could only guess at. And yet, returning to the newsroom, he felt at peace with himself.

As he passed the center desk—the editorial department's nerve center—Alicia Reyes caught his attention with a wave of her pencil. Another artifact—the pencil. It had survived into the present day, in contrast to the typewriter, the slug-rack, and the Linotype operator.

"See you in private?" Alicia said, arching her dense, dark eyebrows.

One of Luke's assistant managing editors, she was the daughter of Cuban émigrés, a sturdy woman, broad-shouldered, broad-hipped, and brusque to the point of rudeness.

They marched into his office. He shut the door and sank into his chair, his spirits sinking at the same time. He knew why Alicia wanted to see him.

"Here it is," Alicia said, leaning aggressively forward, her knuckles on his desk.

"It" was a roster of people targeted for the next round of what were euphemistically termed "staff reductions." There were eight names on the printout, two each from metro, sports, and features, one from the foreign desk, another from the business section. Of the two metro names, one seemed to jump off the page into Luke's face. He snapped his fingers against the paper, producing a sharp crack.

"What the hell is Buchmayr doing here?" he said savagely.

Startled, Alicia drew back.

"I'm thinking back to what you told us—first to go are the people nearing retirement. Edith will be sixty-two pretty soon. *That's* what she's doing there."

"She just might be the best investigative reporter between here and New York. Far as I'm concerned, she can work for this paper till she's carried out feet first."

"Hey, Luke, you asked us for recommendations. That's all these are. Recommendations, you know? Cross her off, makes no difference to me."

Which was what Luke did, neatly blacking out her name with a felt-tip pen. It looked like a redaction in a classified document.

"Edith is off-limits," he said, his voice flat and stern. "Consider her an untouchable."

Alicia raised her hands, as if she were being held at gunpoint, and walked out. Luke then folded the list, stuffed it in his pants pocket, and went to see Ortega, his coconspirator in adding to the ranks of unemployed journalists.

Driving home on I-395, he was for once grateful for the awful traffic. It gave him time to listen to a new McCoy Tyner CD and to settle his agitation at seeing Edith's name on the list. He suspected that more than her age was the reason. Her feisty temperament had made her unpopular in the newsroom; she tended to treat editors, Luke and Nick excepted, as meddlesome fools who mangled her prose and too often failed to give her stories the play she thought they deserved. Her jousts with Alicia—another strong-minded woman deficient in what sociologists called interpersonal skills—were legendary.

Filament-like clouds were turning peach when he arrived. He pulled into the garage and, passing through the Spanish-style courtyard, entered the house by way of the side door. He called out to Maureen; she didn't answer. Peeking into the dining room, he got a surprise: paper plates in wicker holders and a box from Pizza Hut sat on the cherrywood table instead of the customary over-nice place settings. He went into the Florida room and spotted her through the jalousies: in a straw hat, down on her knees, she was weeding her flower garden. He strolled into the backyard, his suit jacket slung over his shoulder. She was unaware of his presence. He watched her pulling the weeds with quick movements, like someone plucking candles from a birthday cake. Two Maureens occupied the same body, the sane and the sick. He was husband to the former, nurse to the latter. The dual roles required him to keep the two Maureens separate in his own mind; he had to guard against penalizing the sane one for fouls committed by the sick one. Each saw him in radically different ways. In that sense, there were two of *him* in her eyes, the one loved and respected, the other despised. An insight had come to him on the flight across the Atlantic two weeks ago: he treasured her respect more than he treasured her love, and dreaded losing it. While she'd slept beside him in a tranquilizer haze, he'd reflected on the idea Thelma had planted in her daughter's mind years ago. It had flourished there, in subconscious darkness, had taken root and grown to become Maureen's own. Lucid, she dared not speak it; mad, she could and did. *I lost them because of you.* So it wasn't shame alone, nor fear of her illness alone, that restrained him from telling her the truth; to some degree, those were diversions from a deeper fear that the revelation would fuse the twin Maureens. The sane woman then would see him in the same jaundiced light as the sick woman, and scorn and scourge him with her undying contempt.

"Hey, I'm home," he said.

She started, hopping to her feet and turning to face him. "You shouldn't sneak up on me like that, I could react with deadly force."

Fine again. He laughed. "You're at it late."

"It was too hot earlier, too, too hot." She removed the hat and shook out her lustrous hair, then, leaning forward, kissed his cheek. "Look at those verbena, aren't they gorgeous?" Waving a dirt-smeared hand at a scarlet clump.

"*Verbena Peruviana.* Notoriously hard to germinate, you're doing well to get forty percent. I've done better than fifty."

The declaration demanded a positive response, and he gave it: "Good for you!"

"I got a surprise today that I need to talk over with you. Been on the phone half the afternoon and didn't have time to make anything for dinner. We're having pizza tonight."

"I saw. That's the surprise?"

She gave his shoulder a gentle push. "No, silly. At dinner, after I've showered."

Lights lowered on a dimmer switch supplanted the usual candles, paper napkins cloth, but a high-end Montepulciano lived up to her standards. Dressed for a picnic in cargo shorts, T-shirt, and sandals, Luke felt out of place in the formal dining room with its polished table, the gilt-framed portraits and prints on its walls. Scrubbed and shining, changed into linen pants and a white blouse, Maureen sat across from him and dished out pizza slices from the foil-lined carton.

"I checked my office mail today," she began, her tone upbeat. "And there was a letter from Heather Taylor. You remember, the Trinity prof we had dinner with in Dublin."

"The one with the long jaw and stringy hair?"

"That's not a charitable description, but yes, her. She's running a summer program this year. It's about literary modernism, and"—her voice rose half an octave—"she wants me to be a guest lecturer."

"What?"

"Modernism. The break with traditional modes of expression. T. S. Eliot, Ezra Pound, and Joyce. Of course, Joyce."

The brief tutorial, freighted with the assumption that he needed tutoring, irked him. As he felt misplaced in this room, so did he sometimes feel misplaced with her, accidental husband of a woman twice as erudite as he.

"My meaning was, how can you? You're teaching a summer course here."

"Not a problem. I checked with Babowitz. I can get a grad assistant to take my place." She sipped the Montepulciano and hummed her approval. "The course would run about a month, from late July till late August."

"She gave you pretty short notice."

"She apologized for that," Maureen said. "It was an impulsive thing. She'd reread my essay and knew I'd be the best one for the job. 'A perfect fit' is how she put it. I'd get a stipend, not much but something, plus free room and board. Babowitz is all for it. He thinks it would reflect well on the U to have a faculty member lecturing abroad. Trinity isn't Oxford, but it's not nothing." She drew in a breath, deeply enough to raise her shoulders halfway to her ears. "And I talked it over with Nathan."

"He's all for it, too?"

"He thinks it would be good for me, as long as I make sure to take my brain vitamins. He can give me the name of a doctor in Dublin in case, you know . . ." She trailed off for a couple of seconds. "Oh, Luke, I want to do this, but if you don't think it's a good idea, if it would be too much trouble managing things on your own for a month . . ."

"I'm pretty sure I'll get by."

It was the right thing to say, and he'd said it in the right way, with a clear note of reluctant assent.

"You won't be lonely?"

He almost shook his head but checked himself. "Sure, but I can stand it. I'm happy for you."

Which he was. Genuinely happy for her; happier still for himself. He would be getting a break, well earned in his opinion, from monitoring her moods, from making sure she took her meds, from the whole wearing effort to provide her with as stress-free a domestic life as was within his power. Buoying him still further was the fact that Ian was to arrive in Key West sometime in late July, assuming the parole board ruled in his favor. Luke would be free to go down there and see him, his son, without having to fabricate a cover story.

Maureen blew him a kiss from across the table. "I knew you'd be for it. It's one of the things I love about you, you're easy to manage." She put her hand to her mouth. "That came out all wrong, sorry. I mean you're supportive."

But it was the first utterance that lodged in his mind and bled some air out of his elation. A housebroken male, easily managed, did not fit his self-image. He recalled Mike's theory that she used her illness as an instrument of control, like the shock-collars employed by dog trainers.

"When do you think you'll leave?" he asked.

PART THREE

10

When she was seventeen and a senior at DeLasalle High, Corinne's ambition had been to become a woman with a past. She wanted that more than she wanted success, a husband, children, or any of the things young women of her time and place were told they should want. The caprice—it was more that than a true ambition—had entered her head one day while she rode the bus up St. Charles Avenue to begin another boring day in class. It was vague, the product of a teenager's romantic imagination; its vagueness was what made it enticing, as the morning mists in the Atchafalaya endowed the swamp with a magical enchantment. One thing she knew was that her past would be tragic; not soul-crushing, just tragic enough to wreathe her in an aura of mystery and an ennobling sadness that would be veiled by an outward gaiety. She pictured herself at, say, forty, wearing a look like Jeanne Moreau's or Anna Magnani's; that is, not conventionally attractive (for Corinne loathed convention) but possessing a ruined beauty that would fascinate men and women alike. She succeeded, after a fashion: by the time she did reach forty, she owned a bigger past than most people do at seventy. What she lacked, as a result, was a future. Twice married, twice divorced, a child born out of wedlock and given up for adoption, another aborted, a long string of bad decisions that bred more bad decisions and ended with her living in an Austin trailer park with daughters Terry and Kate, waitressing in a sports bar to pay the rent. She had a talent with sketch pencil and paint brush; she'd squandered it. Luke Blackburn had loved her; she'd thrown him over to waste what remained of her love on two worthless men and discovered, too late, that a woman with a history like hers—abject rather than tragic—was nothing like Jeanne Moreau or Anna Magnani, worldly, seasoned, intriguing; such a woman was pathetic at best, a lowlife at worst. Corrine felt she'd become a prisoner of her past, trapped in a tenement of squalid yesterdays.

She knew she had to break the lease on it when she returned from work one evening to find Kate sprawled on the floor of their double-wide, unconscious. The doctor at the ER confirmed a heroin overdose. *Please, please, don't let me lose her, oh, God, please.* Kate was only sixteen. *I'm sorry for screwing up, I'll change, I promise, if you'll only let her live.* Such foxhole pledges seldom come to anything once the crisis is past, but Corinne honored hers. Kate survived, went into rehab, and Corinne amended her life, enrolling in art classes at a community college. Working days, going to school nights, she completed the two-year course for an associate's degree. A few weeks later, she landed a decent-paying job at a gallery in downtown Austin and moved out of the trailer park into an apartment. Kate stayed clean, got her GED, and was accepted to Texas State, just down the road in San Marcos. Terry was farther away, newly married to a computer specialist who worked for the army at Fort Bliss.

It was during this transformative period that a letter arrived from the National Reunion Registry, one of the private agencies to which she'd given her consent to release her identity, should her illegitimate child wish to contact her. The registry had found a match: Ian Campbell, born San Francisco, California, March 24, 1969, residing in Phoenix, Arizona. She wrote back, reaffirming her consent, and gave her phone number. A week passed before he called and said, "I guess we've found each other." Corrine had a fear of flying. She took the Texas Eagle to

San Antonio, where she transferred to the Sunset Limited to Phoenix; it was as if she were reliving the rail journey she'd made more than twenty years before from New Orleans to San Francisco. She was excited and a little frightened. What if he resented her? What if she turned out to be not what he expected, or he not what she expected? What did she expect? Riding in the observation car through the West Texas deserts, she remembered holding him after he was born. St. Francis, the Catholic hospital, prohibited unwed mothers from embracing their infants, but she'd persuaded the nuns to relent and was allowed to cradle him in her arms for a few minutes; then he was taken from her, whisked away like a gift proffered and withdrawn. The most wrenching experience of her life; it felt as if he'd been ripped out of her rather than from her, a kind of brutal Cesarean section.

In its quarterly newsletter, the Registry published stories about joyous reunions between adoptees and their natural parents. Uplifting photos illustrated the uplifting tales, everyone smiling and kissing and hugging. It wasn't like that between her and Ian when she got off the train at the spare, dreary Amtrak station in Maricopa at nine in the morning. She was tired after riding overnight in a coach-class seat, and her weariness aggravated the discomfort she felt in his presence; she, the woman who'd given him birth but could not by any stretch be considered his mother. They embraced stiffly, hesitantly, unsure of each other. Then she took a step backward in a let's-have-a-look-at-you pose. He was wearing cowboy boots and jeans and a bomber jacket. The tiny thing she'd held in the hospital had grown to over six feet and was strongly built, like Luke. He had Luke's long-lashed, sexy blue-green eyes and her black hair, but it was straight instead of curly and tumbled down to his shoulders. He'd also inherited her prominent nose, unfortunately.

The station was out in the sticks, near an Indian reservation, thirty miles from Phoenix. Ian apologized for the condition of his van, reeking of cigarette smoke, cluttered with odd bits of musical paraphernalia, sheet music, a broken drum stick, wires. He played guitar in a rock band, the Other Brothers, and they shared use of the van. Trading snatches of stilted conversation, they rode through subdivisions patched with cactus desert and cotton fields. He didn't care for Phoenix—all freeways and malls and sprawl—"LA without Hollywood and an ocean." He let out a snorty laugh that reminded her of Luke's. But maybe she was just imagining.

The motel was near Sky Harbor airport. She needed a nap, and so did Ian—his band had finished a casino gig at one that morning. He rang her room at five. He took her on a driving tour of the city's downtown, then brought her to his favorite Mexican place for dinner. She refrained from telling him that she didn't like Mexican food. They were more at ease now, drinking margaritas. Ian said that he and the band's drummer were renting an apartment in a suburb, Tempe. It wasn't far from his parents' house. He spoke glowingly about them, Winslow and Justine, about his siblings, Andrea and Robert, and his childhood in San Bruno, before Winslow changed jobs and moved the family to Phoenix. A happy childhood, Corinne gathered, though she caught hints that he was presenting a somewhat airbrushed picture. His Dad, more comfortable with numbers and binary codes than with people, might not have been the warmest guy in the world. Ian described himself as a "wild child," without offering any details, and she said that he'd probably got that from her, prompting him to ask about her background.

"Well, we're Cajuns, coonasses," she said, laughing. "From back o' the bayou in Louisiana."

Ian slitted his eyes. "Coonasses?"

"The story is, we got called that because Cajuns ate raccoons in the swamp. It's not a nice word. It's like the N-word. One Cajun can call another coonass, but don't let a non-Cajun even think about it."

The lesson in ethnic slurs and folk etymology was a diversion. She didn't want to get into her history just yet, but he pressed her.

"Okay, my father's name was Etienne, that's French for Steve, and

my mother's Irene. He was a welder at Avondale, the shipyards near
New Orleans, and let me tell you he had a temper as hot as his torches.
I was afraid of him. He's gone now. I've got two sisters, Celeste and
Jeanette. But I haven't seen them, haven't had much contact with my
family in a long time." She paused and stirred her margarita. "I'm the
black sheep, sort of, the daughter gone wrong."

"Because of me?"

"That and a lot of other things."

"So how did I end up born in San Francisco?"

"A long story," she said.

"We've got the time."

"I was an unmarried Catholic girl who got pregnant. A bigger deal
then than it is now. My father would have . . . I don't know what, but
it wouldn't have been pretty. I was taking art classes in New Orleans,
and a friend of mine there—her name was Marie-Carol Landry—had
followed a boyfriend out to San Francisco. I was in my third, maybe
fourth month, and starting to show. I called Marie-Carol, and she set
things up. Her boyfriend was an antiwar activist, and a friend of his in
the movement was a lawyer who sometimes arranged adoptions with
Catholic Charities. The lawyer knew a priest who helped girls like me
get placed with families so we didn't have to go into a home for unwed
mothers. I took the train to San Francisco. Two days and nights. I wore
a pawnshop ring to avoid embarrassing questions. And, well, in a nutshell that's how you ended up born in San Francisco."

They ate without talking for two or three minutes. She was having
trouble with her chicken fajita. Ian very sweetly reached over the table,
scooped the chicken slices and vegetable onto a flour tortilla, added
some sour cream, and rolled the tortilla into a cylinder, tucking in the
ends to prevent the mixture from spilling out. She giggled at her inept-
ness and thanked him.

"Why did you give me up?" he asked abruptly but without rancor.

She'd prepared for the question. "I was nineteen, didn't have a job, no way to support myself, let alone a child. And your father, birth father, was in the army, and he went to Vietnam, and we thought it would be best for you if some stable couple adopted you."

She wasn't pleased with her explanation; it sounded canned, probably because it was.

"He was in Vietnam?" Ian inquired, obviously impressed that the man responsible for his existence had been to war.

"Yes."

"Did he make it back?"

"I . . ." She felt like she was going to choke. "I don't know. I'm pretty sure he did. I'd met an army nurse in San Francisco after you were born. She was stationed at the Presidio. I asked her to let me know if she ever saw his name on the casualty lists. She never called, but then I left the city, so I don't really know for sure." Corinne cleared her throat with a swig from the margarita. "He stayed with me about a month before you came into the world. Catholic Charities had placed me with this family in San Bruno, and I was their unpaid servant. Hated every minute I was there. He was going to be flown to Vietnam out of an Air Force base near San Francisco. Travis. He took a month's leave and rented us an apartment in the city, and we lived together till he had to go. I remember looking out the window when he got in a cab to take him to Travis, and that was the last I saw him. We wrote for a while, but then . . . I don't think I can go on with this right now."

"Hey, sure. Sure. He stopped writing, he just kind of disappeared?"

She was on tricky terrain now and needed to be careful where she stepped. "No. I did. I stopped writing to him. I jilted him, guess that's the way to put it. I married a guy I was working with."

She studied his face, searching for his reaction. Did he think she was fickle or frivolous or worse?

"I'm being honest with you, Ian. I had my reasons for doing what I did. When I look back, they don't seem like good reasons. I couldn't think straight. I didn't love Bob—that was my husband, Bob Fitzgerald.

I was still in love with Luke—" She flushed. "I shouldn't have said his name, slip of the tongue."

"And you don't know where he is or anything?"

"I don't, like I said. Even if I did, it wouldn't be right to tell you."

"Yeah. Mutual consent. The registry briefed me on that."

Changing the subject, she asked if he'd had any college, what his career plans were. She thought those questions were, well, the sort a mother-figure ought to ask. No college, he answered. Scraped through high school. Music was his calling, the guitar. Heavy metal, punk rock, classic rock, whatever the gig demanded.

"It's a real tough business," she said, hiding her displeasure. Fresh in her memory, though she'd been divorced for quite a while, was Ollerton, playing in bars from Amarillo to El Paso where "counting the teeth in the customers' heads would give you a full set," as he phrased it.

"Tell me about it," said Ian. He grinned, and her heart jumped; she'd been searching his face for expressions she recognized; his grin was her father's, thin, wolfish. "But we've got a contract with the USO to back up acts overseas. Military bases overseas. Italy, Germany. We leave in a month."

"Sounds wonderful."

"We're playing the casino again tomorrow night. Why don't you come, meet the guys. Would you like that?"

"Very much," Corinne said.

She returned to Austin happy that the reunion had turned out well, but with a nagging dissatisfaction. She had anticipated a resolution, a closing of an open emotional circuit, and the beginning of a real relationship. None of that came about. Ian sent postcards from his USO tour abroad; otherwise, she did not hear from him for nearly two years, when he mailed her a clipping of his mother's obituary with a short note stating that he and his siblings were devastated—she'd died of breast cancer, only fifty years old. Later came news of his father's death from a stroke due to his diabetes. Corinne phoned him immediately and got an automated voice informing her that the number was no longer in service. She dashed off a condolence letter and, figuring that the phone had been disconnected because he'd moved, scrawled "please forward" on the envelope. Weeks passed before he answered, only five or six lines thanking her for her sentiments and confirming that, yes, he'd moved. He gave her his new address and phone number. His voice, when she called, disturbed her; it was listless and flat, which was normal, considering that he'd lost both parents within a short time, but there was an undertone that wasn't normal, a coldness, a kind of frozen anger. Things weren't going well, he said. He'd hoped the USO tour would launch a musical career. It hadn't. He was playing pick-up gigs in bars and at weddings, working construction part-time to pay the bills, and a relationship with a young woman had ended badly. He didn't go into details, and Corinne didn't ask. The parallels with her own earlier life were depressingly obvious. She wanted to make his better but couldn't think how, and her helplessness was more depressing still.

Another two years went by. She left Austin for Key West, towing her belongings and canvases and art supplies in a U-Haul. She sold her dented 1987 Datsun to raise cash—a bike was all she needed on an eight-square-mile island—and settled into her job illustrating treasures recovered from the sunken Spanish galleon, *Nuestra Señora de Atocha*, and placed on display in the Mel Fisher Museum. The drawings were to ornament the pages of three books, for which she would receive a share of royalties: a children's tale about the wreck and Fisher's quest to salvage it, an adult coffee-table book, and a scholarly work, *An Archeology Report on Florida Shipwrecks*. There were no men in her life, which suited her just fine. Men had been the cause of nothing but sorrow and pain—with Fitzgerald the pain had been physical.

On a windy, mid-April afternoon soon after her arrival in Key West, she pedaled from the museum to the post office on Whitehead Street to pick up her mail. Terry and Kate stayed in touch by phone but never wrote; Corinne's PO box was usually empty except for junk mail and the occasional bill. So she was intrigued to find, among the flyers and Winn-Dixie coupon circulars, an envelope with the return address, Pima County, Office of the Public Defender, and a forwarding sticker pasted over her old Austin address. She read the letter, signed by one Stephen Wilcox, Esq., right there in the post office. Her chest constricted—a literal heartache. She biked to her Ashe Street apartment in a distracted state and was almost struck by a carload of spring-breakers when she ran a red light. She locked her one-speed to the rack in the backyard, climbed the exterior stairs to her studio, and, throwing herself on the bed, reread what Stephen Wilcox, Esq., had to say.

Convicted July, 1997 . . . Possession of a controlled substance with intent to distribute, Class 3 aggravated assault reduced to intimidating . . . Exemplary prisoner, goes before the parole board this coming July . . . A fixed address and a sponsor required . . . Ian has no one else to turn to . . . Younger sister in nursing school, older brother serving in the Navy . . . Has given me your name . . . I am appealing to you, on Ian's behalf. A prompt reply would be appreciated. My postal and email addresses are . . . Should you wish to speak to me, please call my direct line at . . .

The words "assault" and "intimidating" rang loudly in Corinne's head. They described what her first husband had done to her, whenever he needed to release pressure from his reservoir of violence. In one of his rages, he'd broken her right eardrum.

Screwing up her nerve, she went to the wall phone in her Pullman kitchen and called the lawyer. She got his voicemail. After leaving a message, she leaned against the kitchen counter, looking with dismay at the dirty dishes piled in the sink. The whole place was a mess, as usual: an unmade bed, half-finished canvases stacked helter-skelter in the living-room-slash-studio, a pair of jeans dripping from a dresser drawer closed in haste, dust bunnies on the floor, their sparkle in the bright square formed by the skylight a reproach. Ollerton had called her "the worst slob I've ever seen!" She'd fired back, "Well, life isn't good house-keeping." But maybe housekeeping would do some good right now. She set about in a whirl of domesticity to keep busy and with the notion that straightening up her surroundings would straighten out her cluttered thoughts and mixed-up emotions. She began with the bed, moved on to the dishes, and was sweeping the floor when the phone rang. It was Wilcox, returning her call. Following a brief exchange of greetings, she inquired what Ian had done and what exactly he, Wilcox, was asking of her.

"He was dealing meth, Ms. Ollerton—"

"Corinne. Corinne will do."

"Okay, Corinne. He was dealing methamphetamine, using, too."

Ian, Wilcox went on as she paced back and forth, stretching the coiled phone cord, had been living in Phoenix with a woman named Janice, five years older than he. This Janice had a boy from a previous relationship, fourteen years old. She was more than Ian's girlfriend—she was his drug-dealing partner as well. One night, the lawyer contin-ued, the couple got into a heated argument—over what didn't matter now—and Ian struck her. The boy leaped in to protect his mother. Ian seized him by the collar, slammed him against a wall, and threatened to beat the hell out of him. People in the neighboring apartment heard the commotion and called the police. The cops arrived and found five grams of "ice" in Ian and Janice's place, along with paraphernalia, namely balances and scales.

"That made it a class two felony, Corinne," said Wilcox. He did not speak with a western accent; but then, Phoenix was no more the West than Miami was the South. "Possession with intent to distribute. That alone can carry five years in prison."

Wilcox had worked out a plea bargain. If Ian pled guilty to the drug charges, assault would be reduced to intimidating and his sentence to three years, eligible for parole in two.

"The prosecution gave its okay. It was Ian's first offense. I can send you more details, if you wish."

Corinne breathed long and loud into the phone. "I've heard enough," she said, pressing her forehead against the wall. The tale was a chapter straight out of the annals of white trash degeneracy. She had no right to feel as she did, yet she had hoped, a very long time ago, that surrendering Ian would give him a decent shot in life, enabling him to draw on a treasury of love and caring that she could not have provided. He'd had all that as far as she knew, the love and caring and support. He'd thrown it away, like a prodigal squandering an inheritance.

"You wrote that Ian needed a parole sponsor, what's that?" she inquired.

"A parolee is out of jail, but he isn't a free man, not completely," replied Wilcox. "He needs to be paroled to someplace where a parole officer can keep tabs on him. To someplace and to someone. That can be a family member, but like I told you, the only person who can fill those shoes is you. We would have to work things out for an interstate transfer if you agree. The area code you gave me, that's in Florida, isn't it?"

"I moved here from Texas. Your letter was forwarded. So I would do what? Supervise him till he's . . ."

"No, no." Corinne heard a chuckle. "The parole officer does the supervising. The only requirements for a sponsor are to maintain a home free of drugs and alcohol, and to not have a criminal record. You haven't been convicted of any felonies, have you, Corinne? You don't use drugs? You're not a drinker?"

Now she laughed. "I raised some hell when I was young, but no. No felonies. No misdemeanors, either."

"You should be aware that your history will be checked out by the supervising authorities. They'll be looking for a criminal history."

"I told you I don't have one."

"I can take your word for it, they can't," Wilcox said. "One other thing—the police could search your home without a warrant to make sure you're in compliance."

That last warning gave her pause. Cops rifling through her cabinets and drawers wasn't appealing.

"Give it some thought," Wilcox advised. "There's time."

She asked if Ian was violent; she'd been a victim of domestic abuse. Wilcox answered that he wasn't by nature; it was the meth that had changed his personality. But he was clean now, had gone to rehab sessions in prison.

"I'll do it," she said, suddenly.

"You agree to this arrangement?"

"Yes."

"I'm pleased to hear that, and Ian will be, too," the lawyer said. "There'll be some minor paperwork for you to fill out. The parole supervisor will contact you. What's your email address?"

"I don't have email, I'm pretty much computer illiterate," Corinne answered, embarrassed.

"Uh-huh. What's your mailing address?"

She relayed it, and Wilcox ended the call.

Corinne's style was to make decisions on impulse, and only later to reflect on the reasons justifying it. That was what she did as she resumed her house cleaning. The dejection she'd felt minutes ago had lifted. Sweeping the floors, folding the laundry, she hummed tunelessly to herself. That old Simon and Garfunkel number, "Bridge Over Troubled Waters." She would be the bridge over Ian's. Her own life was on track—a job she liked, her paintings displayed at the gallery on Duval Street (one had sold for $400), Terry happily married, Kate graduated from Texas State, gainfully employed as a social worker. Reuniting with Ian, providing him with a chance to transition back into society, would brighten the one dark passage in this otherwise upbeat story. Wilcox's words buzzed through her mind. "The only one who can fill those shoes is you." *Step into the shoes*

I vacated, Corinne thought. Through no merit of her own, through a kind of grace, a chance had been presented to her as well: to revise her past, to reconcile and make amends, to be the mother she might have been.

11

There days after Luke dropped Maureen off at Miami International for her flight to Dublin, a short letter from Ian arrived in the office mail: he was immensely grateful for Luke's letter to him, had read it three or four times over; the parole board had ruled in his favor, he was due for release on Monday, July 26, and expected to arrive in Key West, by Greyhound bus, on the 29th. That was next Thursday, less than a week away. Luke did not deliberate with himself. He immediately phoned Corrine. He was coming down, he would be with her when Ian got there.

"I haven't heard from you since we saw each other," she responded. "I'm stunned . . . In a good way . . . I can't wait to . . Oh, never mind. Call me when you get in."

The following Monday, as Ian, two thousand miles away, was walking out of the Arizona State Prison at Tucson, Luke packed clothes and fishing tackle, armed the burglar alarm, locked the house, and headed south down US 1. He was due a month's vacation and was taking it all. It would provide, besides the opportunity to meet his blood son without doing so on the sneak, a respite from his role as office executioner. After Alicia Reyes had presented the latest roster of those to be sacked, he and Nick Ortega had shared the miserable task of sacking them. All but one took the news stoically; the exception made a scene, shrieking how was she, a single mom with two teenage boys on her hands, going to make ends meet on her ex's paltry child-support checks? When she snatched a ceramic paperweight from off Luke's desk and pitched it at a wall, he had to summon security to escort her out. He wasn't angry or upset with her. His rage, all the warmer for the need to suppress it, was aimed squarely at the Ritters and their accountants and MBA toadies—the whole bloodless, soulless, bottom-line wrecking crew for whom a newspaper was a mere investment and the people it employed fungible parts in a machine that generated pluses and minuses on a P & L statement.

Weekend traffic stretched the three-hour drive to five. He crossed the Vaca Key bridge in late afternoon and wound his way through Old Town to the cottage he'd rented on Catholic Lane from a friend of a friend. It was a white frame with blue shutters, a safe distance from the tourist swarms on Duval. The city cemetery, across the street, assured quiet neighbors. He found space for his outsize Land Cruiser between a rust-afflicted sedan and a hippie van plastered with bumper stickers promoting various social and environmental causes. Climbing out, he took a minute to massage his throbbing left knee. Five hours behind the wheel had aggravated the traumatic osteoarthritis resulting from the wound that had gotten him out of Vietnam two months early. A million-dollar wound that did not, in moments like the present, feel like a million. When the ache subsided, he unlatched the picket fence gate, hauled his things to the front porch, and fiddled in the mailbox for the house key, deposited there by the owner, an island denizen who went by his nickname, Biker Bob.

It was stifling inside. Luke immediately switched on the central air and got the ceiling fans spinning at high speed. Biker Bob had renovated the cottage, a cigar maker's shack dating back to the day when Cuban émigrés rolled robustos and presidentes in Key West's factories. Despite his outlaw appearance—plentiful tattoos, skull a shaved parabola—he had good taste and avoided the fussy touches that made for preciousness: Dade County pine walls sanded down to bare wood and left that way, lots of bamboo and rattan furniture, track lighting, a well-supplied kitchen. Luke stacked his rod cases in a corner of the bedroom, then unpacked, pleased with the snugness of the place—the cottage roofed an area a fraction of his Coral Gables house—and just as pleased that all the clothes he would need for the next month fit into two dresser drawers and on four hangers in the closet. A welcome minimalism. He then took his beloved Olivetti out of its case, and from his shoulder bag a ream of typing paper; fourteen pocket-size spiral notebooks with worn black covers, each emblazoned with a white star in a circle and the words "US Army"; a folder containing yellowed clippings from *Stars and Stripes*; and his journal, the one he'd started on the day he left the States: February 14, 1969. All these had spent the last thirty years in an army-issue footlocker, buried under his old uniforms. He placed them and the typewriter on a tabletop desk in the living room. Corinne's question—"Did you ever write that novel?"—had been skittering around his consciousness for the past two months. Enough books about Vietnam had been written to keep the Library of Congress busy looking for shelf space for weeks. Could Lucas Blackburn possibly add anything to the pile? The only way to find out would be to read through his notes, type them up, and mine them for fresh material. Maybe he would discover that he had something to say, maybe not, but he was free, for the time being, to give it a try.

Free.

He went to the kitchen and opened a cabinet that, Biker Bob had said, contained left-over liquor from previous tenants. A bottle of Barbancourt, about a third full, presented itself. The refrigerator offered a six-pack of Coca Cola and fresh limes and lemons. A thoughtful host was Biker Bob. Luke sliced a lime and mixed himself a rum-and-Coke *en la roca*. Sipping the drink, he gazed out the kitchen window at the tiny backyard, where a Malabar almond cast quivering shadows over a golden allamanda bush. His thoughts tumbled to Maureen's flower garden, then to Ian. Tumbling, tumbling, like the colored crystals in a kaleidoscope. Luke thought of himself as a sort of parolee, though his liberation was a limited one. More like a leave of absence, but in any event he was a free man for the next thirty days. It would be the longest time he and Maureen had been apart, save for when he'd been gone on foreign assignments early in their marriage. He smiled to himself. Then, the crystals shifting into a different pattern, the smile faded. He was happy to be away from her and feeling guilty because he was happy.

12

He stood on the battery at the West Martello Tower and watched Corrine, painting on the beach below. In tan shorts and a white blouse, she sat on a camp school under an umbrella, a shield against the sun. It was a little past noon, the sea still in the still air—a mosaic of emerald, jade, and turquoise that reached out several hundred yards until, the sea bottom falling away, it turned a uniform shade of mossy green. Sweating through his shirt, Luke wanted to dive in for a swim. Behind him, tourists strolled in the lush shade cast by ficus and palm. He recalled the Martello tower in Dublin, residence of Joyce's hero, Stephen Daedalus. This tower's fame was historical and botanical rather than literary. A Union fort in the Civil War (Key West having been the only Southern city to remain in Northern hands), it had been reclaimed from ruin by the Key West Garden Club. In the courtyard where visitors now sauntered through manicured jungles of tropical trees and flowers, blue-coated troopers had mustered; they'd stood watching for Confederate blockade runners where Luke now stood watching Corinne.

She gazed seaward, made a few quick brushstrokes on her canvas, and gazed contemplatively again. In her own world, she appeared oblivious to the oiled sunbathers broiling themselves on the sands that looked white as salt beds in the glare. Ten or twelve feet above the beach, wearing polarized sunglasses, Luke spotted a torpedo-shaped shadow some fifty yards from shore. A cruising tarpon. Corinne could not see it, or ignored it if she did, maintaining her focus, her rhythm. Look. Paint. Look. Paint. Observing her without her knowing he was, Luke felt the stalker's shameful excitement. Or was he more like a secret agent, checking out a contact before a rendezvous? That seemed a more apt comparison: he was embarked on a clandestine mission, and while Corinne was unaware that he was spying on her at the moment, she did know he was on the island. He'd phoned her day before yesterday; they'd agreed to meet for lunch this afternoon, her day off from the museum.

He went down the battery stairs, passed through the garden and out the main entrance, and after circling the tower's red brick walls, he crossed the beach toward where she sat, her back to him.

"Lunchtime," he said.

She turned in her chair, started to rise, checking an impulse to jump up and hug him. "Twelve thirty," she said, looking at her watch. "You always were depressingly punctual."

"Like you were always maddeningly late? I was raised by a career army sergeant. What's your excuse?"

"Give me a minute and I'll think of one."

She wiped a brush with a spattered rag, then got up, ducking under the umbrella, a rental from a nearby concession.

"Wonderful to see you again, Luke," she said, with a hesitant smile. "I'm so glad you could come down, grateful, you want to know the truth."

He shrugged as if to say it was nothing, although it was considerably more: a very big something.

"He phoned right after you this morning. From the Greyhound station in Dallas. If the bus doesn't get a flat, he'll be here day after tomorrow, right on schedule. Ten a.m., he said." Corinne swiped the sweat beading above her upper lip with a finger. "Weird, I've been thinking about this for weeks and weeks, and the closer it gets, the more nervous I get."

"Makes two of us." Actually, what Luke felt, as Ian's arrival approached, wasn't nerves; it was more a fearful exhilaration.

"It's been so long since I've laid eyes on him," Corinne said. "What's he like now, after two years behind bars? It's that domestic violence that's got me jumpy. How is this all going to turn out? I think I'd be a wreck if I had to do this alone."

Luke warmed to the confession; she needed him.

"All right, lunch," he said. "Any place in mind?"

"Do you know Pepe's? The café on Caroline?"

He did. It was a few doors away from Garland's, the grocery where Gunny's derelicts ended their morning parades.

Corinne returned the umbrella, then packed up her easel, paints, and brushes. Luke brought them to his car while she carried her wet canvas, holding it by two edges, and laid it carefully in the Land Cruiser's cargo compartment behind the rear seat. He looked at the painting—greens and blues in swirls, streaks, dripping blots. Except for the colors, which she'd rendered beautifully, it bore no resemblance to the waters she'd been studying with such attention.

"Do you like it?" she asked, uncertain if his frown signaled puzzlement or criticism.

"Uh . . . sure . . . But what . . . It's a seascape?"

"Not the sea as sea. The sea as I see it, pardon the pun."

"You said that last time I saw you. But the pun was intended and you didn't apologize for it."

"So now I did. I've got two pieces done. This one's the third in a series. The same scene at different times of day, in different light. Dawn. Midday. Late afternoon. Kind of like, you know, Monet's haystacks."

He didn't know but refrained from saying so, much as he did when Maureen rattled on about a novel he hadn't read.

"I'm submitting them to a show the gallery is doing on maritime art. You can bet that nine out of ten submissions will be the usual gunk. Clipper ships in storms, third-rate Winslow Homer imitations."

"When's the show?"

"The seventh next month, a week from Saturday. Invitation only. You can come as my guest if you'd like."

"That's an invitation?"

"Sounded like one to me." She looked away, toward a bait fisherman casting a net from the White Street Pier. When she returned her gaze to Luke, a hot light flared in her eyes and shimmered, corona-like, around her black pupils. What his old army buddy called her voodoo-swamp-witch look. "Wanna know the truth," she said, "I'd love it if you were there."

Feeling a lurch in the pit of his stomach, he said he would love it too.

They got into the car. The air inside was all but unbreathable. For the thinnest slice of time, they stared out the windshield at the empty tennis courts across the street. Then, without a word, they leaned toward each other and, yielding to the inevitable, kissed. A long, ardent kiss, followed by another, Corinne's hands clasped around the back of Luke's neck, his arm around her shoulders. She pulled away and said, very softly, "I'm not really hungry."

"Me neither," he said.

The secret was in the roux. The roux was key. No way you gonna make a good gumbo without you make a good roux first. Corinne's ass— no longer the skinny one of the Miss Six O'Clock she'd been when Luke first saw her, marching down Bourbon as the Queen of Mars, but broad and round, appropriate to a woman forty-nine years old— switched back and forth as she stirred flour and butter in a stockpot bubbling on the stove. The roux got to be thick, cher, thick thick thick, like chocolate it, like mud.

Luke loved the way she pronounced "cher," the "r" silent: *Sha*. He came up behind her and rubbed her rear end.

"Not now!" she cried, dropping the mimicked Cajun. She cocked her head sideways at the cutting board, knife, and vegetables arrayed on the kitchen counter. "You want something to do, chop the veggies—a rough chop—and slice the sausage."

"So now I'm your sous-chef?"

"Get to work."

After the kiss, they had driven here to his place on Catholic Lane in something like a trance, and went inside and tore at one another's clothes and fell naked to the floor, still without a word, each aware that even one would shatter the spell, and made love, frenzied and quick. The young Corinne had been an eager but demure lover; the midlife Corinne, the twice-married woman, was lewd and abandoned. She thumped her heels into the small of Luke's back and screamed when she came.

They'd lain together without talking. Spent. Exhausted. Then Luke rolled off of her onto the hardwood floor, his knees raised, an arm flung across Corinne's fleshy midriff, with its stretch marks from bearing three children. He found them attractive—they testified to hard experience, like the scars on a warrior's body, his a spider web of sickly white skin across his knees.

"Can I ask how you got those?" she'd inquired in a drowsy, post-coital voice.

"Didn't I tell you the last time we saw each other?"

"All you said was that you'd been wounded."

"Shell fragments. A one-twenty-two rocket. I was covering an op in the Central Highlands for *Stars and Stripes*. That's all I'm going to say about it."

"Understood." She turned onto her side and stroked the scars with the bottom of her foot. She'd colored her toenails the same aquamarine shade as in her painting. "I knew this was going to happen," she'd said. "Right from the second I saw you in May. I've been fighting against it ever since, pushing it, pushing you to the back of my mind. Maybe I wanted it to happen, but a little while ago, it was like . . . like it had to happen."

"Same here. This is the first time I've ever—" He stopped.

"Cheated on her?"

"Yes."

"I'm not sure how I should feel about that. About myself, I mean. You? Regrets? Remorse?"

"No. The only thing I feel guilty about is not feeling guilty."

Corinne raised herself on her elbows and gave him a long, grave look. "You haven't told her yet, have you? About Ian?"

You're easy to manage.

"And I don't intend to," Luke replied, with a harshness that caused her to blink.

"It's not fair to her, you know."

"Neither is what we just did."

She said nothing.

"Maureen went a little crazy when we were in Ireland last month," he went on, feeling a need to justify himself. "And for no reason. I don't care to think what she might do if she had one. That wouldn't be fair or right, would it? And . . ." He paused, considering how to say what he wanted to say.

"And what?"

"If I were to tell her about Ian, eventually I would now have to tell her about you. Us. I'd have to make a full confession. Half truths wouldn't cut it. Either the whole truth and nothing but, or keep quiet about everything."

"So what she doesn't know won't hurt her?"

He nodded.

"I don't want to talk about this anymore." Corinne got to her feet, picked her clothes from off the floor, and dressed. "What I want to do is eat, 'cause now I'm hungry."

It had been her idea to eat in—an early dinner to be cooked by her. A gumbo like gram-ma-maw used to make. This required a pilgrimage to two different supermarkets for the best ingredients, a visit to the shrimp docks for fresh shrimp, and for okra, a trip to a grocery in what had once been called Africa Town, now redubbed Bahama Village by real estate promoters eager to gentrify the island's only Black neighborhood by making it too expensive for Black people to live in. It was almost five by the time they returned. The early dinner would not be so early: the gumbo would take two hours.

It tasted as good as it looked, and it looked wonderful—strips of red bell pepper floating with celery slices, shrimp and sausage in a chocolate-colored roux. The AC was on full blast and a ceiling fan spun at high speed; but the cayenne and filé squeezed sweat from Luke's forehead. He wiped it with his napkin.

"Too hot for the white boy?" Corinne said, laughing.

He swigged a Côtes du Rhône he'd bought for the occasion and shook his head. There was an easy familiarity between them. They had made love, shopped together, cooked together, and now they were eating dinner together. It was as if the chasm of three decades apart had shrunk to a fissure, which they'd stepped over in less than a day.

"Do you remember that friend of yours? The one who introduced us?" he asked. "Whatever became of her?"

"Marie-Carol? We're still in touch, talk on the phone a couple times a month. She did damn well for herself. She's art director at an ad agency in New York, married to a guy with bucks, sells million-dollar condos in Manhattan. I love Marie, but she makes me feel like such a loser."

"She flings all that success in your face?"

"Do you think I'd speak to her if she did? No, she doesn't do anything except *be*. I compare my life to hers, mine doesn't look so great."

He skewered a fat shrimp and an andouille slice and savored their tang. "What you're saying is, you make yourself feel like a loser."

"*Tout pareil*, like gram-ma-maw would say. All the same."

"No, it's not. For the record, I don't think you're a loser."

Corinne puckered her lips and blew him an air kiss.

"That boyfriend of Marie-Carol's," he began. "Radical Ron."

"She dumped him and went back to New Orleans," she said, and sighed. "That was a couple of weeks before Ian was born. You gone, Marie-Carol gone, I didn't know a soul in San Francisco. I'd never been so lonely. The kind of loneliness you think you'll die of." She hugged herself and shuddered at the recollection. "After was even worse." A wistfulness entered her voice. "I stayed in that apartment until I couldn't stand it anymore. It felt haunted. By the ghost of us being together in it. By what we might have had if we could have stayed together."

Luke finished the gumbo and sopped up the roux remaining in his bowl with a chunk of French bread.

"I felt bad because you'd paid three months in advance, and more than a month of that was left. But I just had to get out of there," Corinne said. "Seconds?"

He shook his head.

"Well, how was it? Compliments to the chef?"

'Definitely," he replied, then cleared the table and brought the dishes into the kitchen. As he rinsed them and placed them in the dishwasher, an old question stole from the back of his mind into the front. He returned from the kitchen to find her standing by the desk, reading the sheet of paper in his Olivetti.

"I'm typing up the notes I took when I was in Vietnam," he said. "To see if there's a book in them."

She turned to face him and leaned against the desk, her ankles crossed, her head tilted coyly to one side. "Excuse me for snooping."

"That's okay. If there is a book there and if I do write one, it'll be because you asked me about it. I hadn't given it a thought for years and years until then."

"I was your muse? Should I be flattered?"

He didn't answer, momentarily distracted by her beckoning black eyes, her long legs, trim and tanned almost to the shade of her khaki shorts. It wasn't that she was trying to look enticing; she didn't need to try.

"I do hope you write it, Luke," she said. "It's why you went over there."

"I thought I'd made it clear that it wasn't the reason."

"But it was *a* reason."

He wasn't going to get a better opening. "Do you remember when we got together with Marie-Carol and her boyfriend at that coffee house? The one near the City Lights bookstore?"

"Kind of, yeah."

"And Radical Ron said he and his underground buddies could smuggle me into Canada. And you could come with me. You wouldn't have to give up the baby. They had contacts in Vancouver."

"I remember that, sure. And that you were really pissed off. Because he wasn't talking draft dodging, he was talking desertion. And you could never do that. Your dad was a career army man. You told Ron to go to hell and that he was lucky you didn't break his jaw."

"Did you resent me for turning him down?"

"Resent you?" she said, frowning. "Hell, no. My memory's a little foggy, but I seem to remember that I told you so, way back then. I resented the whole screwed-up situation we'd got ourselves into, but not you."

He reached for the wine bottle and refilled their glasses and set them on the coffee table in front of the sofa. He sat down; patting one of the floral-and-palm-leaf print cushions, he invited her to sit next to him. She did, looking perplexed.

"I need to know why you stopped writing," Luke said. "Why you disappeared without at least a goodbye and married someone else."

Corinne let out a long breath. "Oh, Luke. It was thirty years ago. What difference would it make now?"

"I don't know, only that it does."

"It was the worst, the most humiliating part of my life. Just thinking about it makes me ashamed. It's a Pandora's Box."

"Open it," he said sternly. Then, in a more imploring tone: "I was transferred to the Presidio after I got patched up. Six months left to my enlistment. I'd been wounded badly enough to be evacced from Vietnam, not badly enough for early discharge. I was in the Public Affairs Office, just like I'd been at Fort Polk. There I was, back in San Francisco. Whenever I could get a pass, I'd go into the city and look for you. Sometimes, if I saw a tall, dark-haired woman, I'd follow her to see if it might be you. Felt like a creep doing that, but I couldn't help it. I checked around, I staked out the apartment building on Jones once or twice, I called the adoption agency, and they wouldn't give me the time of day. I even tried hiring a private eye, but he was too expensive. It hurt, it hurt like hell. After a while, I was more mad than sad, pissed off and bitter and . . ."

He silenced himself. Had he come off as self-pitying? He'd been a soldier and a soldier's son, and the soldier son of soldier did not open himself up the way he just had.

"I'm sorry, Luke," Corrine said. "So, so sorry. I didn't mean to hurt you—I didn't think I could . . . Oh, shit."

"I didn't go home when I got out of the army," he said. "Took off, hitchhiked to Tijuana, then down to Mazatlan, then all the way to Oaxaca. Trying to get my head straight, trying to forget you. I must have fucked a dozen whores, don't know how I didn't get the clap. Three months on the road before I made it back to Arizona. Looking back, I think I was mad at myself. I'd lost you because I wouldn't go over the hill to Vancouver and take you with me. I'd think what our life might have been like."

"So did I," she said, bobbing her head. "I cooked up daydreams." She gave a short, sarcastic laugh. "The expatriate couple, the bohemian twosome. The unlived life."

"And I asked myself," Luke went on as if he hadn't heard her, "Was she pissed off at me? Way down deep, no matter that she'd said she wasn't. Did she resent me? Is that why she vanished like smoke?"

"It wasn't."

"All right. I opened my Pandora's Box. Open yours."

She took a drink of wine and put some distance between them, sliding to the middle of the sofa. "You're not going to like what you're going to hear."

13

"No one at the hospital warned me about postpartum. I just thought I was nuts, so deep down into nuts I felt like jumping out a window," Corinne began, fingers winding her curls, her gaze not on Luke but on the wall across from them. "Wondered about the baby and would he be okay and what kind of a woman was I to give him up. Wondered about you. I never looked at the newspapers or magazines or listened to the news on the radio or watched it on TV. Couldn't have watched even if I'd wanted to. No TV. I remembered seeing a copy of *Life* in the doctor's office, those war photos and feeling sick from . . . from . . . I don't know. Premonition? That you were going to get killed. Nuts. Nuts. Nuts."

After she'd moved out of the apartment on Jones, she found a cheap flat in the seedy Tenderloin district and landed a job as a cocktail waitress in a topless nightclub in North Beach, the Blue Orchid. She did not go topless, none of the waitresses did, only the dancers.

"It was like an indoor amusement park, a fun place," she went on. "There was a bumper-car arena and games like balloon darts and a shooting gallery where, if a customer hit the target, a naked lady—well, almost naked—would fall out of a bed. That was her whole job, to fall out of bed. I'd been there a few weeks when the owner found out I was an artist, and he came up with a gimmick. I would sketch a nude on stage—completely nude, it was okay for her to be wearing not one stitch as long as she didn't move—and a camera behind me projected my sketch onto a big screen. A really bizarre job, but I could say— ha!—that I was a working artist."

The editor in Luke was impatient with these extraneous details, but he did not interrupt.

"Sometimes me and a few other people who worked there would go out after hours or to Sausalito or the beach or wherever on our days off. One of them was Bob Fitzgerald. He was the barker at the naked-lady-falls-out-of-bed game, a carnival barker, like. Ten years older than me and said he'd been in the army before the war and then a bartender here and there, and he was always trying to talk to me, asking me to go out for breakfast. He came off as a pretty good guy—at first. Like when I told him about you and that I wasn't interested in dating, he said, 'Hey, no problem, just want to be friends.'"

"Then you married him?" asked Luke, his patience wearing through. "That's why I stopped hearing from you?"

"Not exactly."

"Exactly what, then?"

"I was coming to that."

Well, get to it, he thought, unkindly, but once more, he restrained himself.

"Later on, I told him about Ian," Corinne resumed. "And he said he'd been married and divorced and that his ex wouldn't allow him any contact with his son, she was a real bitch, and so he understood a little how I felt. And he said that if it had been him in your place, he would have married me before he left, marched me right to a justice of the peace and married me. It was probably what I wanted to hear. So a few weeks later—"

Luke raised a hand to stop her. "If I'm remembering right—I'm pretty sure I am—you didn't believe in marriage. It was against your hippie principles. So how come all of a sudden it was what you wanted to hear?"

She drew back. "You sound like you're on cross-examination."

"It wasn't intentional."

"The answer is, I don't know how come. We started to go out, mostly to after-hours places. It wasn't serious at first, nothing happened until something did. We ended up at Bob's place and one thing led to another. Same thing a week later. I wasn't in love with him. I was just lonely. It was a help-me-make-it-through-the-night kind of thing. Two months went by and I knew I was pregnant again."

Luke started to speak, but stifled his tongue when Corinne gave him an abashed look. "Yeah, I know," she said. "Why wasn't I on the pill? Hadn't I learned my lesson? What was I thinking? Even now I can't figure out what was the matter with me. One of the girls at the club gave me the number of a doctor who did abortions. She was from Portland and that's where he was. She said it would cost, and the plane fare besides. More than I could afford. I told Bob that I wanted an abortion and could he help pay for it. 'No way,' he said. 'No fucking way.'"

One night—it was the night the Blue Orchid's employees got paid—she and Fitzgerald went out drinking. She brought him to her apartment. When he fell asleep, drugged on alcohol and sex, she took his wallet from his pants pocket, stole his cash, and fled.

Luke cringed.

"I warned you that you wouldn't like it," she said, noticing his expression. "I went to the airport and flew to Portland—scared sick but flying was the only way—and phoned the doctor's office." Again twirling her fingers through her hair, she spoke without emotion or inflection, as if describing the actions of someone other than herself. "The doctor was an old guy. Anyway, he looked old to me. It was over in ten, fifteen minutes, but it was horrible and scary. He kept me for an hour to make sure I recovered okay. Then I hopped another taxi to the YWCA and got a room overnight and flew back to San Francisco the next day. This was the summer of '69. That's when I stopped writing to you. How could I after what I'd done?"

Luke remained silent for a while. He'd wanted an answer, he'd gotten one and then some. The news that she'd found someone else merely confirmed what he'd assumed all along; besides, too much time had passed for it to hurt now anything like it had then. Nor could he fault her for never telling him. She'd been lonely and confused and had gone through more than a nineteen-year-old should. And who was he to fault anyone for harboring a secret? It was the last part that troubled him. Waiting till payday to lure Fitzgerald into her bed, then plundering his wallet while he slept to fly off to have an abortion. That wasn't the act of a muddled post-adolescent; it took forethought and cool nerve.

"You were okay with that?" he asked.

"I wasn't going to have another kid out of wedlock," she answered, stiffening.

"Not the abortion. I get that. Stealing from him."

Corinne hesitated. She reached for her wine glass, then thought better of it and withdrew her hand. "I did what I had to do."

The survivor's amorality, Luke thought.

"I'm not like that anymore," she pleaded. "I'm nothing like the way I used to be. You don't need to judge me. I've judged myself enough."

"I'm not judging you. But after all that, you married the guy?"

She pursed her lips and nodded. "He told everybody at the Orchid that I'd murdered his baby. I went up to him and said, 'Why did you do that? What do you want from me?' And he said, 'I want to marry you.' He kind of hinted that I owed it to him. And I said, 'Okay, fine.' The owner arranged for us to go to Reno the next day, a regular wedding party, and we did. I felt powerless, unable to direct myself or do anything. I had to get drunk to marry him. And the weird thing was, I told myself that I would be with him only until you came home—"

Luke cut her off.

"You'd convinced yourself that I wasn't coming home except in a box, but then you counted on me coming back in one piece, and you were going to do what? Divorce this guy you had to get blitzed to marry?"

"It's how crazy people think and I was crazy."

He shook his head, not to deny that that was how crazy people thought but to signal his confusion.

"It lasted two years, and what came out of it was my older daughter. Terry. And a few bruises and a broken eardrum, but that's a whole other story that you wouldn't want to hear."

14

His sandals squeaked as he scuffed along the buckled sidewalk toward Pepe's, the destination he and Corinne had failed to reach yesterday. The dense air smelled of night-blooming jasmine and cat piss and clung to his skin like Saran Wrap. Roosters crowed in the predawn dark—descendants of the gamecocks Cubans had brought to Key West a hundred years ago, along with strong coffee and good cigars.

Luke had decided to establish a daily routine for himself for the next month. He thought he needed one, even though he often chafed against Maureen's rigorous schedules. So many unknowns lay ahead—what would Ian be like, would they get along, not to mention the fact that he and Corinne had launched an extramarital affair: his introduction to a story as old as marriage itself. He'd asked her to stay the night, which she declined—she had to finish her painting in the morning before going to work. The invitation had flown out of his mouth, seemingly of its own will. He sensed that his hold on himself was slipping. Having set things to do each day might keep him from losing it entirely.

His alarm had rousted him out of bed at five thirty. He made coffee, did some stretching exercises and calisthenics, then dressed and set off on foot for breakfast. He'd resolved to take a walk every morning and an ocean swim every afternoon, except when he went fishing. He would have to reserve a couple of afternoons each week for fishing, and take Ian with him. They would get to know each other. If it turned out that he had no interest in the sport, Luke would have to come up with another activity, snorkeling, say; at any rate, something healthy and wholesome, with plenty of fresh air for a man who'd been locked up for two years. As for the remainder of each day, he planned to spend at least an hour transcribing his notes; then he would check in with Alicia Reyes, acting managing editor in his absence.

He rounded a corner and headed down Grinnell, trying to process what Corrine had told him and what had passed between them. It had been so natural; it was as though they'd picked up where they'd left off, half a lifetime ago. Corinne was the whirlwind. She had blown into his life, blown out, and now had blown back in, threatening to blow it apart. Or, rather, their passion for each other threatened. It was as strong as ever, and it scared him. There were few powers as effective at creating emotional entropy as the human heart. And yet, an irresistible thrill was bound up with the terror, producing a sensation akin to running a rapids without oars or a rudder. The frightening elation that comes from submitting yourself to a destiny whose end you cannot see.

Turning left onto Caroline, under a brightening sky, he entertained the possibility that yesterday had been nothing more than a screw for old times' sake. He did not honestly believe that, nor did it quiet the agitation in his blood, for when he thought about Corinne's two husbands, particularly the first, he felt flashes of what might be termed retrograde jealousy. He shared in the common opinion that jealousy is an ugly emotion, and he sought to banish it, not least because it stirred, like a poker in a fireplace, the embers of his mistrust.

Ahead, in the gray dawn, he saw Gunny sitting on the curb with two members of his squad. His battered Conch Cruiser leaned against the wall of Garland's grocery. Bloodshot eyes squinting, he tossed Luke a shaky salute while his left hand clutched a pint of something alcoholic in a brown paper bag. "G'morning, L.T." Luke had never been an officer, but Gunny called him "L.T." regardless.

Luke returned the salute. Gunny motioned at his comrades, who sat staring between their upraised knees, as if there was something of great interest in the gutter. "All present and accounted for. We're a little understrength today, but it's another bee-yoo-tee-ful day in paradise."

"Roger that," said Luke. "Carry on, Gunnery Sergeant."

"What else am I gonna do?"

Luke was Pepe's first customer of the day. He took a table in the outside seating area, roofed by translucent slabs of fiberglass, and ordered a bacon-and-cheese omelette, whole wheat toast, and coffee from a waitress sporting a butterfly tattoo on each upper arm. Right after she delivered the coffee, he felt his BlackBerry vibrate in the side pocket of his cargo shorts.

"You show up in town and don't even let me know?" Mike Conway said before Luke could get out a hello.

"I was going to. How'd you know I was here?"

"No secrets on an island that's a gob of spit in God's big blue ocean. Liz saw you in Winn-Dixie yesterday."

There was a flutter in the center of Luke's chest—if she saw him, then she saw who he was with. Mike was gracious enough to omit mention of that.

"So where are you staying?"

Luke told him.

"You're always welcome here, y'know."

"That would be a welcome I'd wear out. I'm down for the next month. Maureen's teaching a summer course back in the old sod, at Trinity. So I thought I'd take the month off."

"Ah-hah. Taking care of that . . . What? That problem you told Liz and me about?"

Luke hesitated for a moment before replying. "I'm going to meet him day after tomorrow."

"Good luck."

"We'll see how it goes."

"Well, hell, let's wet lines this weekend. We'll take Dustin's old boat, save ourselves charter fees."

"He's got a new one?"

"Brand new. Picked it up day before yesterday," said Mike, betraying his Southy origins by pronouncing it "yeahstiday." "Twenty-eight foot Yellowfin with all the bells and whistles. He's offered to sell me the *Marekrishna* at a bargain. I was going to take it for a test drive on Saturday. Join me."

The waitress brought his breakfast. He bit into the omelette and took a slug of coffee.

"If I can't make it, rain check?"

"No problem," said Mike.

"So you're buying a boat? Aren't you retiring to your romantic shack in Ireland this fall?"

"The shack won't be ready by then. The contractor can't get to it till September and it'll take him three, four months to romanticize it. I was never going to spend all year in Ireland anyway. Plus, I've made a big change in my career plans," Mike continued. He paused. Luke heard him breathing into the phone, took another bite, and waited to hear what had changed. "No secrets on a little island, but I'm going to ask you to keep one," Mike said. "DeMette has decided not to run for reelection next year. I'm going to run for his state senate seat. That's not, I repeat, *not* for publication in your or any other newspaper. Not till I'm ready to declare, and then I'll give the *Examiner* an exclusive. Deal?"

"Deal. I'll be damned. So will I have to call you Senator Conway?"

"Only after I win," Mike joked. Then he added, not joking: "And I'm going to. Nice ring to it. *Senator* Conway."

15

Corinne sat on the floor studying the three abstract seascapes, lined up on a shelf beneath the skylight. She felt an indistinct but persistent dissatisfaction and tried to figure out what was missing from them. That something was she had no doubt; her instincts about her work, as opposed to her life, were always spot-on. She'd titled the series *Sea Triptych*. Dawn. Midday. Dusk. The quality of light for each time of day seemed right, the colors and shapes as well. Still, there was a lack of . . . What? *I paint the sea I see and not the sea as sea.* The wordplay stuttered in her head while thoughts of Luke and Ian flitted in and out. The cleaning woman she'd hired to get her apartment ready for Ian further distracted her. Corinne wanted the place spotless, to make a good impression, but didn't have time to do the work herself—nor, she'd be the first to admit, the disposition. The woman, an East European named Lena, was in the kitchen, washing the mismatched plastic dishware and glassware, scrubbing the floor. In the small apartment, Corinne could hear every clatter and thump, accompanied by Lena's incessant, tuneless humming. She was charging sixty dollars for the job, which Corinne could ill afford, having spent the proceeds from her last sale at Goodwill, buying furniture for Ian's bedroom. She'd been using the space—it was no more than twelve by eight feet—to store her finished canvases. They were now in a bin she'd rented at a storage facility, another expense.

The sea I see. The sea as sea was a brute fact, indifferent and without significance. Art and art alone could wrest meaning from it. She stood and moved to the side to change her viewpoint. The scenes had been painted en plein air—she always did her best work in daylight—and fused two perspectives. Anyone viewing the paintings couldn't be sure if they were looking down from high above or out toward the horizon or both at the same time. She liked that ambiguity, for the sea was ambiguous: now calm, now stormy; beautiful yet menacing.

In an instant, the missing element became clear. She squeezed a gob of black paint onto a piece of cardboard, mixing it with gray till she produced the shade she wanted. With a small brush, she made light strokes near the top of *Midday*, the painting completed yesterday, then stepped back and added a few more strokes, taking care not to lay on too much paint. Stepping back again, Corinne cast a critical eye at the canvas, and was satisfied that she'd captured what she'd been seeking. Depending on the viewer's perspective, the shadowy, horizontal streak could be a stormy sky or a submerged hazard, half-visible but definite enough to draw attention from the surrounding greens and blues. It suggested an ominous presence: the threat in the sea's beauty.

A banging on the door startled her. She hesitated, reluctant to leave her work; and she looked a mess besides, hair uncombed, shirt and jeans and hands spattered with paint. Whoever it was knocked again, loud and urgent. Corinne tucked in her shirt, gave her hair a quick pat, opened the door, and gulped. On the other side of the screen door stood a hulking Monroe County sheriff's deputy and a woman wearing a black T-shirt with a yellow emblem sewn above its left breast pocket. On it were the words FLORIDA DEPARTMENT OF CORRECTIONS.

"Corinne Ollerton?" the woman asked. She was average height, five-seven maybe, with brown eyes and stringy blonde hair.

"Yes. It's Co-rinn, not Co-reen."

"I'm Allison McIntyre. I've been assigned to supervise Ian Campbell's parole." Reaching into her pants pocket, she flashed a badge and a laminated ID card. "This is Officer Brown. This will be Ian's address, correct? You're his birth mother, and he'll be living with you?"

"Uh-huh."

"May we come inside? We'd like to have a look around."

Corinne unlatched the screen door, recalling what Ian's lawyer had told her months ago: she could expect unannounced visits from people wearing uniforms and badges and guns.

"Glad to be out of that sun," the parole officer said. She wasn't carrying a gun; a can of pepper spray was holstered to her belt. "But then, if you can't stand the heat, get out of Florida, am I right or am I right? You're aware that we are authorized to inspect your home without a warrant?"

"I am, yes."

Brown scanned the living room, then pointed at the tiny hallway and asked what it led to.

"The bathroom and two bedrooms."

"I'll start there," he rumbled, in what sounded like an imitation of Darth Vader.

As he clomped to the hall, Lena emerged from the kitchen and froze, transfixed by the sight of a cop who looked like he'd played nose-tackle for the Miami Dolphins. Corinne wasn't sure which country she came from, but it was most likely one where a police officer in the house meant the resident would soon have a new address in less pleasant surroundings.

"It's okay, Lena," she said, forcing an encouraging smile.

"Clean bathroom now?" Lena asked, uncertainly.

"Not just yet. This shouldn't take long."

Corinne glanced inquiringly at McIntyre, who spread the fingers of both hands. "Ten minutes."

Dragging a mop, Lena ducked back into the kitchen and closed the door behind her.

"Your maid?" McIntyre asked.

"Are you kidding? Do I look like somebody who can afford a maid? Does this?" Corinne spread her arms to take in the peeling door and window frames, the thrift-shop furniture. "I hired her for the day. To spiff things up before my . . . before Ian gets here."

"Let's sit down a minute. You seem a little . . . ah . . . tense."

Corinne motioned for McIntyre to sit in the easy chair, while she took the couch. Both pieces, upholstered in mousy-brown cloth and equally threadbare, embarrassed her; but then, her visitors hadn't come to appraise her decorating skills, only to determine if there was alcohol or drugs in the place.

McIntyre, settling into the chair, flicked a hand at the canvases beneath the skylight. "So, you're an artist?" she remarked as an ice-breaker. "I oughtta take that up, must be a relaxing hobby."

"It's not my hobby. I make my living at it."

"Got it. There's a few things I'd like to go over with you. Is this a good time?"

Corinne heard Brown opening and closing drawers in her bedroom. Christ, he was probably pawing through her underwear. She hesitated a moment, then said, "Go ahead with whatever it is."

"My job is to help Ian transition into normal society as smoothly as possible. You can help by providing a stable, sober home environment. That's your sole responsibility. The rest is my responsibility."

"The rest is . . . ?"

"To give him a hand finding a job. I've got a list of prospective employers. Next, drug counseling. I'll set that up. And I'll be checking on him, here and wherever his work place turns out to be. Ian will be meeting with me once a week, at my office. That'll be his responsibility and so will staying out of trouble, keeping his nose clean, and with all the coke that floats around here, that means literally as well as figuratively. If he commits a crime, even a minor one, or is caught with drugs on him, on go the cuffs and he goes back to jail. The parole board in Arizona made that clear to him. Questions?"

"I don't have a car, just a bike. How is he going to get to work, to make these meetings with you?"

"He can take the bus."

The sheriff's deputy, finished with the bedrooms and bathroom, went into the kitchen. A jittery Lena bustled out and scurried into the rooms Brown had vacated.

"Any other questions?" asked McIntyre.

Corinne shook her head, thinking, *Luke can drive him.* He was 50 percent responsible for Ian's existence; he could pitch in in a practical way.

Brown rummaged in the cabinets and refrigerator for a minute or two, then came out and pronounced the apartment squeaky clean.

After the representatives of the law left, Corinne struggled to get her head back into her work. It was no use.

Lena was finished by eleven and relieved to be leaving a place that had been visited by the *polizei.* She probably thought that Corinne was a troublemaker bound for an American gulag. But she'd done a job well worth the sixty dollars; the apartment had never looked so tidy. Corinne showered, brushed her hair, put on a little makeup, and changed into a clean blouse and shorts before biking to work.

The Mel Fisher Maritime Museum, named for the former chicken farmer who'd devoted years of his life to find and salvage the *Atocha* and her sister ship, the *Santa Margarita,* was housed on Greene Street, in a huge stone-block building that had once been a US Navy storehouse.

She went in the employee entrance and into a small office adjacent to the conservation lab, where an archeologist wearing a surgical mask was carefully scraping corrosion off an astrolabe. Corinne waved to her, then grabbed a sketch pad, pencils, and a stool and entered the galleries. Visitors milled about, gaping at exhibit cases filled with gold plates and salvers, gold necklaces, emeralds half as big as golf balls, doubloons, silver coins, navigation instruments, together worth tens of millions. She set the stool next to a two-ton brass cannon, sat down, and began to sketch it. The drawing would eventually go into a children's book she was illustrating. She was eager to see it in print and on the shelves in the museum store, feeling that her name on a book would further distance her from the life she'd once led.

The parole officer's visit was still affecting her ability to concentrate. Her mind skipped from one thing to another as the mind does in fits of insomnia. *A sober, stable home, your responsibility . . . he commits a crime, on go the cuffs . . .* She questioned her judgment. Maybe her daughters were right—sponsoring Ian might be more than she could, or should, take on. Of course, it was far too late to change her mind. And then there was Luke. Terry and Kate did not know about Luke. What would they say if she told them that he was here in Key West, that she'd slept with him? Their mom, hopping into the sack with an old lover who was married, who had fathered their half-brother. That was the act of the old, impetuous, reckless Corinne, whose skin she had supposedly shed. Thinking of him, remembering his weight on her, the sensation of him inside her, a tingling crawled up her thighs. *Horny! For God's sake, what is wrong with you?* Nothing and everything. Her pulse began to race, as much from fear as from desire; the recognition concealed in the back of her mind, concealed for weeks, rushed to the fore. She was still in love with him.

16

Luke parked in the covered lot at Key West International. Corinne grasped his hand as they crossed the road into the Greyhound station, in the annex to the airport terminal. She looked her best, in open-toe heels and a navy blue, ankle-length dress with a white fleur-de-lis print. It had padded shoulders, and so was slightly out of fashion, but it was her only dressy dress. Luke was wearing a straw hat, which softened the effect of her greater height, conferred by the heels. In a crisp Hawaiian shirt and creased khaki trousers, he, too, looked his best, freshly shaved, his face glowing. She wondered if they might have overdone things when they entered the station, where two unshaven guys with backpacks and ratty clothes slumped in the waiting room chairs and a scruffy young woman as tattooed as a Maori warrior stood at the ticket counter, bitching to the agent about the cost of her fare.

Corinne went to the row of molded plastic chairs and sat down opposite the dirtbags, while Luke stood behind the tattoo girl, waiting for her to finish her dispute so he could check if the bus from Miami was on time. Ian had had to change buses in Dallas and then again in Miami; he most likely would be late. One of the dirtbags stared at her, not in the way men usually did but as if to say, "Where do you think you are, lady? The first-class lounge?"

"Only fifteen, twenty minutes behind schedule," Luke said, returning.

He sat beside her, lounging with his legs extended, ankles crossed. He looked so relaxed—a little too relaxed. She reached over and again clasped his hand, giving it a squeeze. Luke squeezed back.

"It's going to be all right, you know," he assured her.

"Sure. But I've been asking myself if maybe I've bitten off more than I can chew," she said, then told him about McIntyre and Brown's social call yesterday morning. "It bothered me, I felt kind of . . ." She paused to seek the right word. "*Violated.* Like I was being burglarized in front of my eyes. They've got the right to barge in anytime they choose and turn my place inside out if they want to."

But those intrusions, if they happened, weren't the half of her insecurities.

Ian had struck his live-in girlfriend, had slammed her son into a wall and threatened to beat him up.

Fitzgerald. Bob Fitzgerald had broken her eardrum when she was five months pregnant with Terry, in the depressing third-floor flat in the Tenderloin. Grabbed her by the hair and banged her head into the headboard of the bed once, twice, and on the third smash knocked her unconscious. The divorce hearing took place in the Civic Center courthouse on McAllister. Afterward, out on the street, she saw Fitzgerald for the last time. Twisting her wedding ring off her finger, she threw it in the gutter and said, sobbing: "That's where it belongs. Why did you do this to me?"

"Because you were a green kid and I thought I could start over with you. But you're not green anymore, so maybe next time I'll toss you out of a window."

"There won't be a next time, but if you try it," she said, her Cajun temper rising, "I'll grab you by the nuts and take you with me."

She wasn't as brave—or as foolhardy—as her words. That afternoon, she packed a suitcase, emptied the shoebox in which she'd stashed her tips, and bought a rail ticket to New Orleans. She'd fled that city pregnant on a train; three years later, she went back the same way.

At five to eleven, the ticket agent announced the arrival of the Miami bus. Corinne swallowed and went out to the balcony with Luke. It rose ten feet above the airport road. Looking below, she saw passengers disembark and cluster around the baggage compartment; then a tall young man in Levi's, cowboy boots, and a red T-shirt stepped out. He put on sunglasses and joined the other passengers, waiting for the driver to offload their bags. For a fleeting moment, she did not recognize him. His hair had been long, rock-musician long, when she'd last seen him; now it was shorn like an army recruit's, and his muscular build was even more so, bulging, straining against the T-shirt. Tattoos scrambled up his bare forearms.

"Is that him?" asked Luke.

She bobbed her head. "I thought he'd be all skinny and pale. He looks like a weightlifter."

"Not much else to do in the slams except lift weights," Luke said, in the knowing way newsmen speak of things they've learned but never experienced.

Craning his head, Ian gazed up at her a second or two; then he waved and flashed his slightly rapacious smile, so like her father's. Her misgivings dissolved. She hurried down the ramp and hugged him; it was like hugging a hickory post. He threw off the scent of someone who hadn't bathed or changed clothes for three days and nights, but Corinne didn't find it offensive. The smell of the man to whom she'd given life.

Luke hung back while the two got reacquainted. To the people around them, he and Corinne must have appeared as a married couple greeting a son returning home from college, or, taking Ian's bristly haircut into account, on leave from the military. This left Luke feeling somewhat displaced: the father who wasn't a father but now had to mimic one, a double for himself. An impersonator.

"Ian, meet Luke," Corinne said, turning to face him, her arm hooked in Ian's.

Luke gave a reserved nod and held out his hand. Ian took it and, pulling Luke into him, spun the handshake into a bro-hug. It seemed a little excessive.

"Thanks, man. I mean, Luke. Thanks for everything."

Luke had paid for his bus fare and had sent an extra two hundred fifty for travel expenses. It was the amount a parolee transferring to another state was required to have in his account. "I think to make sure I don't rob anybody to eat," Ian had written in his last letter.

He slung a duffel bag over a shoulder and picked up a guitar case. It held his Strat—a Fender Limited Edition Stratocaster—his most treasured possession.

"My sister kept it for me when I went away," he said, loading his luggage into the back of Luke's Land Cruiser. "Kept it in her dorm room at nursing school. Brought it to me the day I got out. Andrea's great, she's great, man."

Luke pulled out of the lot, paid the fee, and swung west onto A1A toward town and Corrine's house. Ian slouched in the back seat, wearied from traveling two thousand miles in a Greyhound. He gazed at the ocean on the left and the long rank of coconut palm fringing the salt ponds on the right.

"Pretty here. If you've got to be on probation, better here than in Detroit."

"You've been to Detroit?" Corinne asked.

"Nope. It's just my idea of a place I wouldn't want to be in, on pro or off. They had a great music scene back in the day. Motown. Nothing there now, or so I've heard. Man, I'd love it if I could gig down here. I'd to love to play professionally again. I'd do it for free."

"What do you play?" said Luke, making the turn onto White Street.

"Heavy metal and hard rock mostly, like Van Halen, like Black Sabbath. Sometimes straight-ahead blues, Howlin' Wolf, he's my number one blues man. Can't play the blues if you ain't paid your dues. I'd say I've paid mine now. But, shit, I'd play 'Hava Nagila' at a Jewish wedding if that's what it took to be back on stage. Give it an Arizona vibe. *Hava tequila.*"

Corinne laughed, a little louder than the pun warranted. She was feeling nervous again. "The places that have live music serve liquor. I met your probation officer yesterday, and she said you can't be in any place that serves alcohol."

"The court order says any place whose *primary* purpose is to serve alcohol. A bar bar. But a place that serves food with alcohol is okay. A restaurant with a bar, that's okay."

"You'd better check with her to make sure. She's not anybody you want to get crosswise with."

"I have to see her tomorrow morning. Ten a.m. I'd better make it. Florida gave me ninety-six hours to show up from the day of my release, and I'll be cutting it close. I've got the address in my bag."

"It's on Twelfth Street," Luke said. "Behind a shopping mall. I'll drive you."

"Yo, man," Ian said. "Luke, I mean. You don't have to do that."

They were stopped by a red light at the intersection of White and Truman. Luke turned in his seat and gave Ian a grin. "Consider that I want to."

17

Sitting at her easel, Corinne penciled in finishing touches to the sketch of the bronze cannon she'd begun yesterday. Ian had showered and was now asleep. He hadn't had much sleep, crammed into a bus seat for seventy-two hours. She could hear his snores through the door. The decrepit AC in his room labored to relieve the afternoon heat, to little effect; the pedestal fan she'd bought at Home Depot took up the slack. Did she love Ian? She scarcely knew him. She was acting from obligation rather than maternal love, which would come in its time—or wouldn't. The critical thing was to do right by him.

Luke was another matter, entirely another matter. Her pencil moved more or less by rote, her mind on him. When she'd seen him in May, she'd felt exactly as she had meeting him the first time at that party in the French Quarter—drawn to him not through any girlish crush but through an instantaneous knowledge much like the inspirations that burst within her when she was painting. *This is the one, this is the man for me.* It seemed unlikely, yet she was as certain of it now as she'd been then. She'd been honest in confessing that she'd resisted the promptings of her heart throughout the weeks between their reunion and the day before yesterday, when they'd kissed. Resisted because adultery had never been among her many sins. Married men had pursued her. She'd rebuffed them, though not out of any moral scrupulousness. Scruples were no match for her carnal nature; she'd turned them down because none were worth the grief, the tension and tumult, the tedious arrangements to tryst here or there. None could give her what she craved most—love. At times she'd wondered if she deserved love. Deserving or not, Luke had loved her. She hoped he did now. Kissing her in the car, embracing her later on, she sensed as he drove into her the ardor that comes only when raw passion is tethered to love. Oh, the sweet release that tore a cry from her throat, their souls rebound by the reuniting of their bodies, two halves of a single being, separated by circumstance—and her own foolishness—made whole once more.

The Probation and Parole office was on the fourth floor in the new Professional Plaza building, a rectangle of white concrete and glass taking up close to half a city block. Parked in front, the Land Cruiser's AC blowing in his face, Luke tapped out an email to Maureen while he waited for Ian to finish with his appointment. The BlackBerry's small screen was hard to read, his fingers were too big for the tiny keypad, and he made several typographical errors before getting the terse message right.

> Hi, Maureen. I got your email. Happy to hear all going well. Same here. Will call you soon. Love, L.

He closed the phone and slipped it into his back pocket. He *was* happy to hear that all was going well for his wife; he *would* be calling her soon. Every word was true, yet the message was false, and he a fraud. Pangs of conscience aside, keeping one big secret strained the nerves; he had two in his care. Perhaps it would become less stressful as he became more practiced, though he recognized that proposition as more

hope than expectation. Pulling off the deceptions of infidelity necessi-
tated the mentality of a double agent or an undercover narc—anyone
for whom dissembling was second nature.

He gazed idly at the palm trees clumped in front of the building,
their fronds waving gracefully, softening its stark lines. Ian came out,
swaggered down the walkway, and got in the car. He was formally
dressed by Key West's ultra-casual standards: a button-down, short-
sleeve shirt in place of a T-shirt, creased trousers rather than shorts or
jeans, shoes instead of flip-flops or sandals.

"So how did it go?"

"Pretty well, I think," Ian said. He pulled a paper from his shirt
pocket, unfolded it. "She gave me a list of ex-felon-friendly employers.
Not many of 'em. Dishwasher. Motel night clerk, jobs like that."

"Did you ask her about gigs?"

"Oh, yeah, and she"—Ian snickered—"said no way in this town.
Live music here is all in bars, and I'm barred from bars. Corinne was
dead on target about that lady. Nobody to get crosswise with. Got the
feeling that one fuck-up and she'll be right there with the cuffs. If I land
a job, I'm supposed to let her know where so she can check up on me."

"Okay. Where to now?"

"Uh . . . Mind taking me to a couple of these places?" He snapped a
finger against the paper. "You don't have to. I can take a bus. McIntyre
gave me a bus schedule and a route map."

Luke glanced at the list and saw two restaurants out on Stock Island.
He switched on the ignition and put the car in gear. *I owe it to him*, he
thought.

The managers at the eateries said they weren't hiring, even though
help-wanted signs were posted on their windows. Apparently, they were
not so ex-felon-friendly. Luke headed back into town. Stopped at the
light where A1A crossed South Roosevelt, he looked sidelong at Ian's
left arm, tattooed with runic symbols above the elbow, with handwrit-
ing below.

"What's that say?" he asked, seeking some topic, any topic, that might get a conversation started. "On your forearm."

"Isaiah, sixty-one, one. Y'know, from the Bible."

"Yeah, I'm not religious, but I do know it's from the Bible."

The light flashed green, and Luke turned onto Roosevelt, making for Ian's next employment opportunity, the Southwind, a budget motel on Washington.

"I memorized it," Ian said. "'The spirit of the Lord is upon me; because the Lord has anointed me to preach good tidings to the meek; he has sent me to bind up the brokenhearted, to proclaim liberty to the captives, and the opening of the prison to them that are bound.' There was a guy who came to my unit once a week, not a minister, but kind of one, and he held worship services, and one day he read that passage, and no bullshit, chills ran right through me and I knew right then I was saved. Like that old hymn, y'know? 'I took Jesus for my savior, you take him too.'"

A jailhouse conversion, Luke thought. Like the foxhole conversions on battlefields. The question was, would it last outside the prison walls?

"So you're born again?"

"I guess so. I was saying it to myself when I was full-boarded, the Isaiah verse."

"Full-boarded?"

"The whole six parole officers on the panel. See, my request had to be approved by all six because of the intimidation charge. Domestic violence, y'know?"

"I know. What I don't know is how you wound up in the slams, how you got hooked on meth. Meth is a trailer trash drug, and from what Corinne told me, that didn't describe you. Your dad was a software engineer, your mom a hospital administrator—"

"What're you saying? That I should have been hooked on a middle-class drug, like cocaine or good old-fashioned booze?"

"No, that's not what I'm saying," Luke said, bristling. "You grew up in one world, you ended up in another. I'm curious how you made that trip."

He was driving down Reynolds toward Washington, a shady avenue of 1950s bungalows that looked like a downscale Coral Gables.

"I started using to get through playing late-night gigs, and after my dad died, I used more. It ripped me up, him dying so young. I decided I needed a vacation from reality. Then I started dealing, small-scale dealing, to support the habit."

"Here we are," Luke said, pulling to the curb alongside a two-story, pale yellow building with the words SOUTHWIND MOTEL fixed to its curving marquee.

Ian approved its appearance. "I thought, budget motel, must be a no-tell motel, but it looks real middle-class. Dogs and meth-heads prohibited."

"I think I could learn to like you, but smart-ass makes that hard."

"Sorry, Luke. Yo, I want you to know that I am definitely turning my life around. You and Corinne won't feel like you wasted your time, you won't be disappointed."

He got out of the car and went into the motel office.

After long years in the news business, skepticism had become instinctive in Luke. His first boss at AP had trained him in the ancient adage—If your mother tells you what time it is, check your watch. Had Ian been sincere, or had he mouthed what he thought Luke wanted to hear? He must have spoken similar words to the parole board; presumably they were people experienced at detecting con jobs. They believed Ian; Luke would too, unless given a reason not to.

The Southwind hired Ian as a night clerk, his hours from midnight to eight. He was to start this coming Monday, August 2.

"I could get a lot of reading done if I had something to read," he said, and forked a mouthful of Jamaican jerked chicken.

To celebrate his reentry into civil society, Luke had taken him and

Corinne to dinner at Ricky's Blue Heaven, a restaurant whose funky look belied its prices.

"There is a library in town," she said, encouragingly.

"I never did read much anyway, *Downbeat* sometimes." He rolled a finger across his forehead and flicked droplets of sweat at the sand floor. "Arizona, it cools down at night. It *stays* hot here."

"Must be the spices in the chicken," said Corinne.

"Or heredity," Luke added. "I sweat easily, and I got that from my dad. That man could go through three shirts in a day."

Earlier, in the car, he'd made quick studies of Ian's face, searching for hereditary signs. Now, he gave it a closer examination. Except for his eyes—his sexy blue-green eyes in Corrine's description—his features favored her, his nose the most obvious. His hair, shorn to a stubble, was black like hers; his skull looked as if it had been rubbed with charcoal. Luke thought he'd heard echoes of his own voice in Ian's, but he couldn't be sure. A mild disappointment crept into him. Maureen's miscarriages, and, later, his vasectomy—medically induced sterility—had denied him the pleasure of ever seeing and hearing reminders of himself in his offspring. But Ian was his regardless, his and yet a stranger whom he'd embraced simply because their genes were linked. Why was it that blood kinship was endowed with such potent magic?

"Your dad was in the army, career army, Corinne told me," Ian said.

"Thirty years. Master sergeant when he retired. Veteran of World War Two *and* Korea. A grunt—infantry—in WW2, won a Silver Star at the battle of Guadalcanal. He went into intelligence later on."

"World War Two and Korea, man. Heavy duty." The news that he was descended from an authentic war hero appeared to excite Ian. His jaw worked more rapidly, chewing the zingy chicken. "What was his name?"

"Harry. He was used to war before he went overseas, he was practically raised on it."

Luke put his elbows on the table and leaned toward Ian and told him about the Harlan County War, waged for nearly a decade in the dark hills of eastern Kentucky, where the winter sun rises at ten and sets at three. Harold Blackburn was born there in 1921, eight years old when he began to help his dad make moonshine, fourteen when he started digging coal for eighty cents a day, seventeen when he was walking a picket line with his oldest brother, Gene, and the strikers were jumped by company goons and Gene clubbed one with an axe handle, killing him. Harry had aided in his escape, but the sheriff found them and Gene ended up serving five of a ten-year sentence.

Luke then related his father's saga—hauled before a judge who, because of his youth, granted him a choice between jail or the army.

"He was under a kind of house arrest for two months, till his eighteenth birthday. That was the day he enlisted. April the fifth, 1938." Black-and-white photos from a family album flickered in Luke's mind like stills from an old film: hollow-cheeked Appalachian women in homemade dresses, men wearing miner's lamps, their faces smudged with coal dust. "After Pearl Harbor, he was transferred to the 25th Infantry Division in Hawaii, where he met my mom," Luke continued. "Rosalyn Chambers. Her father was a foreman for the Dole Foods company in Honolulu. He got shipped out to Guadalcanal, and they didn't see each other for four more years. I came along in forty-seven. So if it wasn't for a Kentucky judge giving my dad the choice between going to jail or into the army, I wouldn't be on the planet."

Ian listened attentively. Luke guessed what he was thinking—he also owed his presence on the planet to that judge. He asked, with an eagerness more appropriate to a teenager than to a thirty-year-old man, how Harry Blackburn had won the Silver Star. Luke related the tale: a buck sergeant in charge of a squad on Guadalcanal, he'd led his men in an attack on a Japanese mortar position, knocking it out of action.

"And you carried on the tradition, like by going to Vietnam."

Luke's eyes grazed Corinne's. "Let's save that for some other time."

"Cool," said Ian. "Ever since I was little, I loved war stories. I'd always read war stories. War comic books, regular books, whatever. Now I've got an idea why, like it's in my blood."

"But didn't you say you don't read much?" asked Corinne, finding a wedge into the conversation.

"I read the comics mostly. Collected 'em. From the 1950s. *Sergeant Rock, Sergeant Fury and the Howling Commandos, Combat Kelly*. I had some rare ones, like *Soldiers of Fortune* and *Frogmen*. Wish I'd kept them. They'd probably be worth something now."

"*Sergeant Rock* was my favorite in high school," Luke said, and gobbled down the last shrimp in his plate.

"Me too," Ian said, pleased to discover that they shared reading tastes, even if it was in comic books.

"I gravitated to him because his dad was a miner. *Sergeant Rock of Easy Company*."

"Nuthin's easy in Easy Company, that was his tag line."

Ian raised a fist and he and Luke exchanged a bump.

A Black guy wearing dreads and a goatee salted with gray got up on the Blue Heaven's little stage and plugged an electric guitar into a speaker propped against one of crooked posts supporting a slanting sheet metal roof that lent the stage the look of a woodshed or an oversize outhouse missing its door. He tuned up, then began to sing "I Shot the Sheriff," in a borrowed Jamaican accent.

They listened for a while without talking. A busboy came by and cleared the table, followed by the waiter, who passed out a dessert menu.

"You have to try the key lime pie," Corinne said. "They use real key limes here. That's what makes the pie sing."

Ian hooked a thumb at the would-be rasta man, now struggling through "Get Up Stand Up."

"Kinda like what this dude is trying to do? He sings the way Bob Marley would've sung if Bob Marley couldn't sing."

"Not kind, Ian. Not kind at all," she scolded. "I know the guy. Taylor Curry. He's from here."

"My bad. I'll take the pie. A dude I met on the bus in Miami told me that going to Key West and not having key lime pie was like visiting Rome and not eating pasta. My father could sing, the man could sing. In his own voice, and he did an imitation of Tony Bennett so dead-on you'd think T. B. was in the room with you. A lot better imitation than this Curry guy is doing of Bob Marley."

"Tony Bennett? Because you lived near San Francisco? Like 'I Left My Heart in San Francisco'?" Corinne said, thinking, *I lost my mind in San Francisco. Along with a few other things.*

"'One for My Baby,'" Ian said. "He could do that one, like I said, you'd think Tony Bennett was in the room with you." His eyes drifted toward the Marley impersonator, then past him to the scarred lobster pots dangling from the stockade fence enclosing the outdoor dining area. "Sometimes I'd comp him on the guitar, y'know, I'd strum the chords as soft as I could. An acoustic would have been better than a Strat, but I kept it low and cocktail loungey, and he'd croon, 'It's quarter to three, there's no one's in the place except you and me . . .'"

The waiter appeared with a quivering wedge of key lime pie. Ian waved with his fork, beckoning Luke and Corrine to take a bite. They shook their heads. He dug in with gusto.

"Yo! Sure does beat the pies we got at the Greyhound stops. I've got a little story you guys might want to know, although you probably won't believe it."

It was about his father on the day he died in a Phoenix hospital of complications from a diabetic stroke. Ian and his siblings had just arrived to visit him when the doctor gave them the news. They went up to his room to see him one last time. Ian called out to him, did not believe he was truly gone until he touched his forehead and felt the warmth leaving his body and saw his eyes slightly opened but still and his slackened jaw forming a weird half-smile, as if he were recalling some pleasant moment in the life no longer his.

"I wasn't sad, I was pissed off. It was like I'd been robbed of both parents before their time. I couldn't stay in that room. I took the elevator down to the lobby. It had big windows and sunlight was pouring through them. And I thought, 'What do you think you're doing, Mister Sun? How can you shine so pretty with my dad dead up there on the third floor?' Then I heard a piano. For a second I thought I was imagining. It was playing that Johnny Mathis tune from back in my dad's day, 'The Twelfth of Never.' The music pissed me off—how can anybody be playing music with my dad gone forever? But it wasn't anybody, it was one of those player pianos, tucked away in a corner of the lobby. I went up to it and stared at the keys, pressing down and springing up, like a ghost was on the bench, playing 'The Twelfth of Never.' Then that song stopped. This is the part you won't believe. The next tune was 'One for My Baby.' I started to shiver, like I was out in the cold in a T-shirt. My dad had passed not even half an hour before. It was a ghost on the piano bench, *his*, and I felt like he was trying to reach out to me, telling me not to be angry or grieving. Telling me that he was still around, watching me."

Corrine could scarcely breathe from the swelling in her breast. She laid her hand on Ian's forearm, the one with the tattooed Biblical verse.

"When we walked out of that hospital, each one of us felt alone. I did for sure. Like there was a hole where my insides should have been."

Luke nodded, and asked if Ian had ever seen the Huachuca Mountains, the dark green range that rises in southern Arizona, tapers down into Mexico, and looms over the city of Sierra Vista.

"When my father died—this was in 1978—and was buried in the post cemetery at Fort Huachuca, I looked at those mountains and remembered how I'd seen them every day when I was in high school. Miller Peak was the highest, almost ten thousand feet. After the burial, full military honors and all, I felt disoriented, like I would have if I'd looked up at Miller Peak and saw that it had disappeared."

"Yeah, disoriented," Ian said. "Discombobulated, not sure of anything. At sea with a busted compass. Like that?"

"Like that." Luke thought for a moment. "I didn't realize how close I was to my father until he was gone."

In recognition, Ian's head bobbed rapidly up and down, up and down. "Me, too. My dad and me, we weren't close most of the time. He had a degree in math from Cal Tech and was always on my case to do better in school, but all I ever gave a shit about was playing the guitar. He used to tell me that I had to have a backup plan, some way to pay the bills in case the music biz didn't work out. Which it didn't. After he passed, I was dealing meth to pay the bills. And I partied."

"Your vacation from reality," said Luke.

"Blew every dollar he left me. We'd had our issues, yeah, but music brought us closer, when I'd comp him when he was singing. And when we went fishing. The man loved to fish. It was his one big escape from thinking up algorithms."

Luke's pulse rate rose a notch. "Where'd you go?"

"When we lived in California, we went surf fishing at Enderts Beach, Gualala Point, for perch and stripers. After we moved to Arizona, during one spring break, my senior year, he took us to Baja, the Sea of Cortez."

"The fishing around here might just be the best in the world," Luke said, feeling that he and Ian had begun to establish a relationship founded on more solid ground than the mere braiding of their DNA— or war comics. "Does the motel give you weekends off?"

"Thursdays and Fridays are my weekend."

"Then one of these Thursdays or Fridays—you pick it—we'll go out. Sound good to you?"

"Awesome."

Corinne didn't mind being a spectator to this conversation. Luke and Ian were getting along, they appeared to like one another. That was enough for her. *It might have been like this if we'd fled to Canada and stayed*, she thought. *The three of us together, mother, father, son, enjoying a night out.* Her practical side dismissed the fairy tale. It would not have been like this, given the way they were then. Both unformed, with too much growing up to do. Most likely, they would have split up. Looking across the table at him, shifting her glance to Ian, she wanted to kiss them both, these two men who had reentered her life. Right then, another thought sprang into her mind, unbidden, and it brought a prickling to her skin: But now it could *be* like this. If that, too, was fairy tale, it was not so easily dismissed.

18

The alarm buzzed at five the next morning, a
Saturday. Luke forced himself out of bed and shuffled into the kitchen
to make coffee. While it brewed, he shook the kinks out of his joints
and muscles, then went through his exercise routine: stretches, deep
knee bends, push-ups, sit-ups. He was pleased that he and Ian had hit
it off well. For all his ex-con, ex-meth-dealer, rock-guitarist swagger, his
need shone through, like moonlight through a translucent curtain: a
place for himself in the world, a connection to a family. His adoptive
parents gone, genetics was all he had to tie him to a father and mother,
to grandfathers and grandmothers he'd never met. Luke felt that he
and Corinne were filling that gap in his life, but he also felt, acutely, the
strangeness of his own situation, its perils obvious, its outcome uncertain. And so he stuck with his daily regimen, showering and dressing after his calisthenics, then walking to Pepe's for breakfast, returning to sit
at his Olivetti and rewrite his notes. The repetition of the same actions
at the same times of day lent a familiarity to the unfamiliar, and created at least an illusion that he was in control of events. He compared
himself to a sailor adrift in uncharted waters, who nonetheless faithfully
maintains his log, takes star and sun sights at the appointed hours, and

keeps his hands on the helm, even though he doesn't know where the currents are taking him.

Following breakfast, he sat down to review the second of the four-teen notebooks covering his tour of duty, abbreviated by the rocket that lacerated his knees as he dove head first into a foxhole. The trooper running behind him took the full blast, and was blown in half, his torso tumbling into the hole with Luke, an experience that still gave him nightmares. The second notebook chronicled happenings early in his tour, along with quotes from the soldiers he'd interviewed. Names, ranks, hometowns. Facts. The reporter's hammer and nails. But facts did not convey what the war *felt* like to those who fought it. Its emotional truth. For that he turned to his journal and to the clips from the stories he'd filed for *Stars and Stripes*. But the journal was sketchy—he'd been too tired to keep it current on a daily basis—and his stories, after the editors got through sanitizing them of realities like sharing a foxhole with the upper half of a human being, read more like press releases than frontline dispatches.

He worked for two hours, sometimes holding the notebook up to the light to decipher his hurried scrawl, smudged and stained by mildew and dirt. He enjoyed the tactility of pounding a manual type-writer; enjoyed its clatter and the impressions the keys made, banging letters into paper. Reluctantly, he put the Olivetti aside, booted up his ThinkPad, and checked his office email. A page one summary from Alicia Reyes, no requests for his input; a message from Edith Buchmayr: "Incroce has lost his appeal, story to run Sunday editions. Am onto something. Flying to KW today, arriving 5 pyem. Will call when I land. Cheers, E.B." Luke smiled at Edith's use of the old telexese, "pyem" for p.m.

He replied: "I may be out in a boat, but will have my cell with me. If you can't reach me, try the landline here."

He gave the number and added that he should be back no later than six. His BlackBerry rang. He pulled it out of his back pocket and was barely able to eke out a hello before Maureen launched into an ecstatic account of her first week teaching the seminar at Trinity College. Just six students, five Irish, one from abroad, a Canadian, and all so eager. The focus was on Yeats. Took them on a wonderful trip to Yeats's birthplace in Sandymount, then on to Sligo, where he's buried, and from there to Lake Innisfree. "I recited 'The Lake Isle of Innisfree' for them. From memory!"

It was typical Maureen not to soft-step into a phone conversation with hellos and how are yous but to jump right in with whatever she had to say. Luke's finely tuned ears did not register anything amiss in her voice. He said he was glad to hear that she was enjoying herself.

"You sound like you're calling from next door," he added, unable to think of anything else.

"The globe has shrunk. They don't call the Atlantic 'the pond' for nothing. And what have you been up to?"

"Fishing, and . . . working on a book."

"A book? *You*? You once told me you had a six-hundred-word mind. What's it about?"

"I'm not actually writing it. I'm going through my notes. The notes I kept when I was in Vietnam. It'll be about the war if I ever get around to writing it."

"Bit of a shopworn subject, don't you think?"

"Which is why I'm rereading the notes. To find out if I might have anything new to say, a fresh perspective. You could be more encouraging, y'know."

"I'll try, but please don't quit your day job. Miss you, darling. Do you miss me?"

"Of course, sure," he answered, resenting himself for lying and her for forcing him to.

"You've been fishing with Mike?"

"We're going out this afternoon."

"Give him my best, and Liz, too, if you see her. Well, ta."

"Talk to you soon."

"She asked me to give you and Liz her best," Luke said as Mike idled the *Marekrishna* through the no-wake zone in Boca Chica channel. "So, from her to you through me—her best."

"And mine to her. I can't speak for Liz. She still hasn't quite gotten over it."

They passed under the Boca Chica bridge, a flood tide forming V's around the concrete pile caps; then Mike throttled up and they planed through the channel, turned hard port to cruise along the bay side of Stock Island and Key West, sped under another bridge, passing the Coast Guard station where a white cutter was moored, marijuana leaves painted on her bow to commemorate drug busts, and turning port again entered the harbor, aswarm with weekend boaters and jet skis. Mike eased off to avoid a collision. An enormous cruise ship, her upper decks towering over the buildings on Front Street, lay fast to the docks, disgorging passengers to provide the T-shirt and trinket shops on Duval with a profitable day; farther out, toward the open sea, two people floated sixty feet in the air under a parasail with the words "Get High!" splashed across its bright orange panels.

"Our once remote, funky, outlaw island has turned into a tourist carnival," Luke remarked in disgust.

"There's money in the carnival."

Mike throttled back a little more as a scow towing a barge piled high with trash crossed his bow. Plastic bottles. Rusted lawn chairs. Beer cans. Scrap lumber. Bits of junk unrecognizable as anything that might once have had a purpose.

"See all that? Collected off Astoria," he said, waving an arm at the island off to starboard. It was not an attractive piece of real estate. The slovenly live-aboard sailboats anchored all around it added to the picture of a maritime slum. "The fucking dirtbags and appies have turned it into the island of lost losers."

"Appies" was Mike's shorthand for Apathetics, a term he'd coined to describe people dazed by too much dope and sun or simply from a breakage in their mainsprings. In what way they were distinct from dirtbags wasn't clear. Both species had endeared themselves to the remnants of Key West's hippie subculture while distressing the Chamber of Commerce.

"You know that Incroce lost his appeal?" Luke asked.

"Yeah. I heard. Manny told me this morning."

"We're running the story tomorrow." Recalling what Edith had told him about the FBI probe at their lunch last month, Luke considered cautioning Mike to keep daylight between himself and the lawyer.

"Isn't it a conflict of interest for Higgs to represent the county and Incroce?" he asked, choosing an oblique approach.

Leaving the crowded harbor, Mike gunned the engines and shot up the main ship's channel at twenty-five knots.

"He's got his private practice, he can do what he wants as long as it doesn't conflict with county business, and that island isn't county business," Mike said, raising his voice over engine roar and wind rush. "Except for zoning purposes. That's the extent of our involvement."

"Can't the county find another lawyer? Higgs has got a reputation."

"He sure does. The smartest lawyer in the Keys, and one of the smartest in the state."

"Also kinky."

"Are you getting at something?"

"No. Just throwing out an idea," Luke answered, reluctant to say anything more. He trusted Mike, but a chance remark, a slip of the tongue, could jeopardize Edith's investigation, not to mention the FBI's.

They crossed the reef west of Sand Key light. The coral heads were clearly visible twenty feet below, many colorless, dead or dying due to the ocean's ever warming temperatures. A mere decade ago, they were a rainbow of oranges, reds, light greens, purple. Mike turned to starboard and the *Marekrishna* bore off toward Cosgrove Shoal. Cardenas, he said, had given him the coordinates of a spot outside the shoal, a trench two hundred feet down, a lair of huge red snapper.

"I'm talking true reds, not muttons. Gen-u-wine reds, m'boy! Monsters!" he shouted, leaning into the console, the ear and neck flaps on his long-billed cap snapping in the wind, and looking at the gauges. "Twenty-seven knots and I've got RPMs to spare. Good boat, except for the name. Gonna rechristen her. *Pangloss*."

Luke hooted. "You are shitting me."

"Voltaire. Dr. Pangloss believes we're living in the best of all possible worlds. He's the idiotic optimist, which makes him the patron saint of fishermen."

"You can't name a boat Pangloss. It sounds like a dishwashing detergent."

"I'm going to. I'll tell the world. It'll be memorable."

They motored on over a windless sea as flat as Kansas, reaching the shoals in half an hour. Mike turned south into deeper waters and began to run a search pattern, attempting to match the coordinates on the boat's GPS with the bottom shown on the depth-recorder. After ten or fifteen minutes of chugging back and forth, he exclaimed, "There it is! The coordinates are off, but that's got to be it!" The recorder's screen displayed a flat bottom at one hundred sixty feet falling forty feet into a trench, in which tiny blobs marked fish. Mike removed two sturdy rods from the rod holders, each rigged with an egg sinker, a four-aught hook, and a Penn trolling reel wound with thirty-pound test line.

"A little overgunned for snapper?" Luke said, taking a rod.

"We're not here for sport. Hook 'em up and haul 'em in fast as possible. We're meat fishing. We're providing for our families!"

As if their families would go hungry if they failed to hook 'em up and haul 'em in. It wasn't clear if Mike was kidding around or dressing a sincere sentiment in jokester exaggeration.

While he piloted the boat uptide to begin a drift, Luke netted a pilchard from the live well, hooked the baitfish through its jaws, and dropped it into the water. With the drag lever released, the line spooled off the reel until the terminal tackle touched bottom and the line went slack. He reeled in a foot so the pilchard would appear to be swimming and held his thumb to the spool to better feel a strike. One came within a minute of the downtide drift. He engaged the drag, surprised by the strength of what he assumed would be a five- or ten-pound fish, but the heavy tackle quickly brought it to the surface. It looked to be as big around as a serving platter, its scales shading from fiery red on its back and flanks to pale pink to white on its belly. A huge, beautiful specimen, huge enough to require a gaff rather than a net to bring it aboard. Luke clubbed the snapper, removed the hook, and hung it by the mouth from a brass hand-scale.

"Holy Mary," Mike said, squinting at the reading as Luke raised the fish in the air. "Twenty-six! Didn't I say monsters? Oh, you'll eat well tonight and tomorrow night and maybe the night after."

Mike caught an eighteen-pounder a few minutes later, then another of fifteen, while Luke hauled in two more, twenty and sixteen pounds. They hooked fish on almost every drift. In an hour and a half, the fish-box forward was nearly full. Dripping sweat while Mike brought the boat around to begin another drift, Luke dipped his cap into the sea and poured water over his head.

"We've got enough. Christ, you could feed a hundred people with what's in there," he said, pointing at the fish-box. "Anyhow, snapper doesn't freeze all that well."

"I'm not keeping it all. Some goes to you, some to me, I'm selling the rest. I know a wholesaler who'll pay premium for true reds."

"You've got an SPL?" The initials stood for Seafood Product License.

"Hell, no."

"You can't sell fish without one."

"A fine point," said Mike, with a theatrically comic wink. "If I can make catches like today's every weekend till the end of the year, it'll help pay for this boat."

"You can afford it without peddling the catch."

"Not the point. The point is to turn a recreational activity into a profitable one."

That wasn't really the point, Luke knew. Mike needed to think he was getting away with something. Illegal commercial fishing on a trivial scale was pretty tame as lawbreaking went, but the sheer pettiness of it was cause for a head shake. It was like watching a financier shoplift in a supermarket.

The next drift added two more snappers to the body count, and then the tide went slack and the fish quit biting.

"That's it for today. Leave some for tomorrow," Mike said in a tardy display of conservation virtue. He opened the fish-box lid, dumped two bags of ice inside, and gave the catch a satisfied gaze, as a buffalo hunter in the Old West might have looked at a wagon-load of hides. "A beer before we head in?"

Luke glanced at his watch. Three forty-five. Edith was due in at five, but he didn't expect her to call till she'd checked into her hotel. "A beer sounds good."

Mike retrieved two bottles of Hatuey from an ice chest under the forward seat. They sat drinking on the gunwales while the boat wallowed on a sea so calm it was almost as though they were on dry land. The sun beat down with what seemed like homicidal intent, its light falling into the blue water in slanted shafts.

"I wonder how this poor bastard would feel if he knew a beer was going to be named for him," Mike said. He was looking at the picture of the Taino *cacique* on the label. "The Spaniards burned Hatuey at the stake, wiped out his people, and he gets his mug on a beer bottle in exchange."

"It's the American way. Are we going in or do we discuss injustices to Native Americans?"

"Neither. You haven't told me how your reunion went. If that's confidential, I'll shut up."

"It wasn't a *re*union. More like a union," Luke said.

"How did that go? What's he like? Can't be the brightest bulb in the chandelier from what you've told me."

"Okay, he's not a genius but not a lunkhead either," said Luke, piqued. "He seems determined to stay clean. He's got a job already, night-clerking at the Southwind."

"You're going to have to fess up to Maureen sooner or later, you know that, don't you?"

"I'm not going to. I can't."

"Because?"

Luke looked into the water, at the plankton swirling and sparkling in the beveled shafts of sunlight.

"No secrets on a small island, you said. You asked me to keep one and I will, so I'll ask you to keep one."

Mike reached over and clinked Luke's bottle with his.

"I'm involved with Corinne, his mother."

"You're fucking your old girlfriend, that's what you're telling me?"

"Jesus, Mike."

"Don't mean to be crude. It's more than that?"

"Well, it is."

"You're *in love*? Gotta be a midlife crisis."

"Don't trivialize it. See, if I tell Maureen about Ian, I'm bound to tell her about Corinne. And if that doesn't shove her over the edge, it'll spell the end of my marriage. Or it'll do both."

"You're not *bound* to. Where the hell did you get that idea?" Mike said.

"It would go something like this. She'll ask me how did I find out that Ian was down here, and I'd answer that I found out from his mother, his birth mother, and then she'll ask about her, and so forth and so on."

Mike pulled out two more beers, popped them, and handed one to Luke. "Time for a marriage counseling session."

"You're qualified? Where's your license?"

"Hanging on my wall next to my promotion to colonel in the Confederate air force." He looked up, as if the counsel he intended to give were written in the sky, but nothing was up there except a lone frigatebird, soaring on the thermals. "I remember a few years ago we were shooting the shit and you said something that's stuck with me. That when you came home from Nam you felt tainted. That was the word you used. Tainted. By the war."

"Yeah, I suppose."

"And you told me that some antiwar protestor tossed a Coke in your face. And you wanted to bust him up but didn't, because you felt you deserved it."

"Hey, Mike, what's that got to do with—Listen, I've got a meet with one of my reporters in town at five."

"Bear with me, m'boy. So we jump ahead a few years. The tainted war vet meets the uppercrust Maureen. Brains like Susan Sontag, beautiful as a *Vogue* model. He's become successful. Hell, the AP has sent him to Harvard, but in his own mind, besides the taint, he's still the son of a master sergeant from hillbilly country."

Luke took a long pull from the bottle. "Where are you going with this?"

Mike cocked his chin and looked skyward again. The frigate was gone. "Luke wins her over. The taint is removed. Redemption."

"You're overthinking this, and what's the point?'

"Maureen the redeemer later on goes nuts. Maureen proves to be not everything Luke's cracked her up to be." Mike dropped his empty into the cooler. Bracing his knees under the leeward gunwale, he took a piss into the ocean. "Excuse the interruption," he said, zipping up.

"The point?"

"When you told me and Liz about this kid you had, I said I didn't have any advice for you."

"And I said I wasn't looking for any. Which is the case now."

"You're going to hear my advice whether you want it or not. Have a fling while you're here, screw the girlfriend's brains out, give this Ian a hand putting his life back on track. And *that's it*, you tell him. No more contact after you go back to Miami. Then you fess up to Maureen that you had a kid out of wedlock once upon a helluva long time ago. But don't tell her he's in Key West. Go down on your knees and beg her forgiveness for keeping it from her. Grovel if you have to. The way I see it, the only reason for you to tell her the whole truth and nothing but is if you *want* to blow up your marriage. That's how my first marriage ended. Wife had suspicions I was having an affair, wife asked me, I said yes, divorce papers served soon after. Is that what you want?"

Luke shook his head.

"Okay, that's settled. And to spare you from asking, yeah, this stays between you and me. I won't even breathe a word to Liz."

"Thanks."

Mike gripped Luke's shoulder. "Hey, what are friends for?"

"Ian likes to fish," Luke said. "I'm going to take him out on Thursday or Friday, his days off. You're free then?"

"Tied up. But you can take the boat. It'll be at the marina."

"I thought today was a test drive. You own it already?"

"Uh-uh. But I will before Thursday. Take the wheel on our way back. Get a feel for her. We've both got fish to clean and I've got fish to sell."

19

He met Edith in the rooftop bar at La Concha, at one time the tallest hotel on the island—five stories—and now that it had been rehabbed and renamed La Concha Hotel and Spa, it was among the most expensive. Dressed in Neiman Marcus resort wear, she sat in a deep wicker chair, sipping a fourteen-dollar martini while munching an eighteen-dollar crab cake salad. Her tastes in lodging, food, and drink occasioned a lecture from her managing editor, who'd ordered a beer: the grand old days were gone, the *Examiner* was trimming costs wherever possible, and he and Nick Ortega were struggling, against pressure from above, to hold onto their best staffers. Edith would do well not to submit an expense report for this excursion and absorb the costs herself.

"I did get a senior discount," she huffed. "Turned sixty-two this week."

"Happy birthday. Then it won't hurt your pocketbook too much."

"Christ, when did you become a bean-counter?"

Tired and sunburned from the day's fishing, Luke was a little irritable; it was an effort to restrain himself from telling her that the bean-counters, right up to the chief beans, the Ritters, had their parsimonious eyes on her as a prime candidate for forced retirement.

"You don't want certain people to think you're a luxury they can't afford," he said, putting the idea across in general terms. "I'm not one of them, but you get the point."

Holding her glass by the stem, Edith raised it to acknowledge that she did. "Not to intrude on your holiday, but I thought you might like an update." She turned her head slightly, appearing to take in the technicolor sunset. "Incroce losing his appeal was a setback. But the ruling was on narrow grounds, it just denied the merits of the appeal, it didn't rule on who holds title to Astoria, Incroce or the federal government. So what's his next move? He needs to clear title. How does he do it? If he's successful, full speed ahead."

"A big if."

"Maybe not too big," Edith said. She plucked a martini olive off the stick with her teeth and gulped it down. "He's got a few things going for him. His family has paid property taxes on Astoria ever since his daddy won it in the poker game, and a while back, the US paid lease fees to him to use the island for training Navy SEALs. His argument will be that the feds, in effect, relinquished their claim on that basis alone. He's got other arguments on legislation called the Submerged Lands Act, the Quiet Title Act, et cetera, et cetera. Dry stuff, if you want to hear it."

"Spare me," said Luke. "Remember I mentioned—when we had lunch at Joe's that without the money-laundering connection all you've got is a story about one more sleazy Florida land deal."

"Remember it clear as glass," she said, and lowered her voice. "I've got sources who tell me, yeah, Oceanaire scrubs dollars for the Colombians and is invested in Incroce's company. What I don't have are names and documented proof. I should get it tonight. I have to take a boat ride."

"A boat ride? Tonight?" Luke said, incredulous.

"Not a long one. A few hundred yards into the harbor. I'm being picked up in about twenty minutes. Care to walk me there?"

Luke briefly considered the invitation before accepting. The intrigue appealed to him for its own sake, but it might also take his mind off his personal life. For the past few hours, he'd been mulling Mike's suggestion that he would make a full confession only if he intended to destroy his marriage. He'd begun to question if some part of himself, a saboteur hiding just below the conscious level, was nudging him in that direction.

After weaving their way through the crowds on Duval and then through the congregants for the nightly sunset ritual loitering in Mallory Square, he and Edith walked out onto a concrete pier past snorkeling and sailing and fishing boats to an empty slip. In the harbor beyond, constellations of masthead and anchor lights sparkled in the slick, inky waters.

"He's a little late," Edith said quietly. "The guy lives on Key West time."

"You'll clue me in who this is?"

"My Deep Throat. I'd ask you to come along, but he's paranoid. With good reason. Goes by the name of Fred Finnbar, pretty sure it's a stage name. Known as Filthy Fred because he's a master of dirty jokes. A kind of downscale Lenny Bruce, minus the social satire."

Luke wiped his sweaty forehead with a handkerchief and groaned. "Your source is a low-rent comedian called Filthy Fred?"

"Not a professional comedian. He used to work the corners around Duval and Front, telling dirty jokes for pocket money. Sort of like a street artist or pass-the-hat folk singer."

"An *amateur* low-rent comedian—that makes me feel a lot better," Luke said. "How did you hook up with him? Collecting dirty jokes?"

"He called me three months back after he'd seen that exposé I did on US Sugar dumping waste water into the Everglades."

"His connection to Incroce is . . . what?"

"He hired Filthy Fred to keep tabs on the opposition to the Astoria project. Fred looks like a street person, fit right in with the groups who were protesting Incroce's plans. Tree-huggers, senior hippies who don't want to see the last of old Key West turned into one more gazillion-dollar resort for gazillionaires. He lives on that boat out there." Luke tracked her finger toward the silhouette of a two-masted vessel. "Fred comes from Philadelphia money, even though he looks like a homeless guy," Edith continued. "Studied accounting at Penn State business school and, listen to this, he used to be a bond trader in New Jersey."

"Let me guess, a white-collar crime, jail time, bought the boat with what money he had left after he got out, washed up in the Keys."

"You should be on *Jeopardy!*. Junk bonds, fraud. The tale gets better. When Incroce learned that Fred was a numbers wizard, he promoted him, put him in charge of cooking the books for the Astoria project. Fred was promised a reward commensurate with the risk. He was rewarded, but he didn't consider it commensurate and started making Xeroxes and stashing them in his boat. By that time, he and I were in touch. Last week, he and the boss had a serious falling out. He won't say over what, but assume it involved money. He'd been feeding me crumbs, now he wants to turn over the whole cake. He told me quote I want to fuck this dude, I want to butt fuck him with the threaded end of a rusty pipe unquote."

"He does have a talent for bad language," Luke observed.

The low drone of an outboard engine caught their attention.

"That would be him," Edith said. "Like I said, he's a little paranoid. That's why we're doing this"—she adopted a comically ominous tone—"under cover of darkness."

Soon, an inflatable dinghy glided into the slip six feet below. In it, illuminated by dock lights, was a man of about forty wearing cutoffs, a tank top, and flip-flops. A cigarette glowed between his lips; a brown beard, with a tobacco-yellowed patch under his mouth, dripped six inches from his chin. He held onto the side of a steel boarding ladder to steady the dinghy while Edith descended and sat herself on the middle thwart. Luke called down to her to be careful, drawing Filthy Fred to call up to him, "Who the fuck are you?" in a voice that sounded like throat cancer.

"My boyfriend," Edith answered before Luke could.

"You told me you'd be alone."

"Don't worry, he stays ashore."

"Phone me when you get back. Let me know you're okay," Luke yelled as Filthy Fred backed out of the slip, then gunned the engine. In a moment, he could no longer see the dinghy or its wake.

The schooner, fifty feet long and named *Inside Trader*, was in Bristol condition, her teak brightwork shiny, her decks swabbed, her salon tidy, the bunks made. A wind funnel in the forward hatch drew in night air to cool the interior. Edith had expected the live-aboard to be a floating dump, like all the others in the harbor. She complimented its appearance.

"Gloucester schooner, the real deal, built in 1916," Fred rumbled. His sun-browned face was as creased as a peach pit, he wore a gold earring in each ear—the required accessories for all would-be pirates—and he had the bluest eyes she had ever seen. "Took me three years and a lot of money to bring her back. The thing about a ship like this is a man and a boy can handle her, and if you know what you're doing, you can single-hand her. Have a seat."

He gestured at a banquette embracing a folding table, much like the kind found in travel trailers, then knelt and spun a combination lock on a drawer under a bunk on the starboard side, opposite his guest.

"Can't be too careful, dealing with these people," he murmured, and pulled out a large plastic chart case that did not contain charts but sheafs of paper bound with binder clips. He slapped it on the table. "Have at it."

Edith put on her glasses—a designer pair with a black, cat's-eye frame—and removed the document sets from the case, each with anywhere from twenty to over fifty pages and a Post-it note stating its contents: BANK TRANSFERS & DEPOSITS, 11/97–5/98; LOANS. 6/98–4/99; SMURFING; ROUND TRIPS; LEGAL FEES; CORRESPONDENCE, TBI/FF, 5/96–PRESENT. The thickest was labeled FAIRY TALE.

"You're very organized," said Edith, bestowing a smile on her host. "What is smurfing?"

"A laundering technique," replied Fred. He slouched on the bunk, his knees spread. "Take a big chunk of cash, break it up into small chunks, deposit them in different banks to avoid anti–money laundering regulations."

"Like this?" Edith pushed a page filled with numbers across the table. "Cash deposit, November 12, 1998, Bank of Aruba, account number blah-blah-blah, 9,500. Cash deposit, November 15, First Caribbean International Bank, Aruba, account number bloo-de-bloo, 9,500, and so forth and so on to February 17, 1999, cash deposit 9,500 RBC Royal Bank of Aruba, bringing total deposits in various Aruba banks to 114,000."

"Read on," Fred said.

She flipped through pages, tapping a manicured nail on wire transfers totaling $114,000 from the banks to the account of Blue Horizon Enterprises in the Cayman Islands Development Bank on April 6, 1999. The next page showed a payment by check in the same amount from Blue Horizon to Oceanaire Properties, Ltd, followed by a loan agreement between Oceanaire and the TBI Corporation of Miami.

"Blue Horizon is a shell company," explained Fred, slouching further against the bulkhead until he was three-fourths prone. "Mind if I smoke?" He lit up before Edith could answer. "There's three or four more shells, and you'll see that the rathole is the same dude, José Dominguez." He helpfully translated the slang, "rathole," as owner of a fictitious company. "He's got the same arrangement with Oceanaire."

"You should wear underwear or get a longer pair of shorts," Edith said, pointing between Fred's hairy, spread legs.

He craned his head and saw through the cigarette smoke a testicle peeking out from the crotch of his shorts like the head of some strange animal from its burrow. He tugged the shorts and straightened his posture.

"I didn't mean to excite you, Edith. Probably been a while since you've seen one of those."

"Not really, and the last one I saw was a lot prettier."

Bowing her head, she thumbed through the information treasure chest, muttering mmmms and uh-uhs while she tried to follow the winding, tangled filaments of financial dealings and misdealings.

"Every one of those cash deposits was cartel money?" It was more a comment than a question.

"You can bet your ass that José has a storage locker filled with stacks flown in from Colombia," Fred confirmed. "Once you go through all that stuff, you'll see that TBI, Inc. is into Oceanaire for two hundred fifty million. The secret deal is, the loans are forgiven if Oceanaire gets a 50 percent share in the project."

"And what's this one? 'Fairy Tale'?"

"The cooked edition of the raw truth."

"I'm going to need experts to interpret a lot of this—it's got my head spinning. Okay with you?"

"You're talking about your friends in law enforcement, specifically the FBI?"

Saying nothing, Edith dipped her head.

"Just so you know, the local FBI office asked me to drop by for a conversation not too long ago. It's what convinced me to unload. Some lady agent questioned me. She got zilch. That stuff is all yours, free of charge." Fred made a sweeping motion with both arms to emphasize his generosity. "I don't want or need it, but the deal is, you don't show it to anybody till I'm out of here. That should be in a day or two."

"Where to?"

Fred, having resumed his scrotum-exposing slump, popped up

straight. "I'm sailing across the big pond to France. I've researched this. France is an easy country to hide out in. I almost think they *like* harboring felons and ex-felons like me. Shit, they've wrapped their arms around a perv like Roman Polanski for twenty years."

Edith remained silent. This was information she would have to withhold from her FBI sources. It would not sit well with them if they knew she knew Fred's travel plans and did not alert them.

"Incroce and company are going down sooner or later," he went on. "The originals of what you've got in your hands are in his safe-deposit box. I signed off on the cooked version, which would put me in the feds' gunsights."

"Got the picture," she said, offended that he thought her too dumb to have figured that out.

"No, you don't. I'm not worried about going down with him. The feds will offer me immunity if I testify, and I would take it. The Colombians would be very unhappy with me. I'll be in *their* sights, and they don't just kill you, *that's* the picture."

"How do you plan to make a living in France?" Edith asked.

"Maybe go back to joke telling."

"You speak French?"

"I can learn. I've got a zillion jokes. Bond trading floors are the source of almost all the jokes on planet Earth. I've still got buddies in the business. They feed mc ncw ones nearly every day. Wonders of the internet. Wanna hear a couple?"

She gathered the documents and slipped them back into the plastic case. "No. I'm going to have to have study these in detail, preferably in my air-conditioned suite."

"I've got one that's a model of political incorrectness. Racist *and* sexist."

"I repeat, *no*. How about you ferry me back?"

20

Luke had returned to the La Concha bar to wait for Edith's call. When an hour passed with no word from her, he questioned his judgment in allowing a sixty-something female reporter to sail off in a dinghy at night with a guy who was mixed up in a money-laundering scheme with some very dangerous people, told obscene jokes as a side gig, and looked like he hadn't bathed in a week. Edith would have derided that notion as sexism in chivalry's clothing. At the same time, he was wishing he were with Corinne and Ian, the three of them together in a simulacrum of a family. At last, his phone warbled. Edith reported that she was quite safe and sound, thank you for your concern.

"I'm in the bar," he said. "Come on up."

"No. I've got some great stuff and I don't want to discuss it in a crowded bar. Meet me down at the dock where you dropped me off."

She briefed him as they strolled the waterfront near what had been Key West's Naval Station before a developer named Pritam Singh converted it into a palm-shaded, gated community for the kinds of people who could afford second, third, and fourth homes they seldom lived in. It was called Truman Annex, after the Little White House President Truman used for vacations from the big one on Pennsylvania Avenue.

"Your thoughts?" she asked when she was done.

"My thoughts are that you've got a kickass story. When do we see it?"

"Not as quick you might want. I need to go over this material, and I need to see the Feebies. They can guide me through the legal ramifications. Plus, they'll have stuff I don't have and can't get. But I've got this"—she patted her briefcase—"and they don't."

"You might be testing the limits with your Filthy Fred," remarked Luke. "He's a self-admitted crook who's going to skip town. Are you going to tell that to the feds if you go to them?"

"They deal with people like him all the time—their snitches don't sing in the Mormon Tabernacle Choir."

"I just don't want my star investigative reporter subpoenaed to testify if all this goes where it looks like it's going."

"Oh, it is. But I don't see myself being subpoenaed. There will be a quid pro quo with the feds. The old give some to get some. I give them what I've got, they give me what they've got. Indictments are what we need to keep this story from wrapping the proverbial fish the day after it runs. My thinking is, a series. But it'll take time to nail everything down. Can I count on your support?"

Luke stopped walking. They were standing by a row of shops, one of which advertised itself as an Orvis dealer. He reminded himself to outfit Ian for their fishing trip. Cowboy boots and Levi's would not be the right attire.

"Was that the point of this exercise? So I'd back you up all the way?"

"No!"

"Because if the story is solid, I would."

"I was nervous, Luke. Night. Alone on a boat with a bent guy. Nervous, I felt better with male company nearby."

"Well, I'll be damned. You and nervous don't match."

"What are you looking at?"

"Those topsiders and that quick-dry shirt in the window. You didn't have to ask if you can count on my support."

After a phone call from her elder daughter, Corinne went to her bedroom and gave herself a final inspection in the full-length mirror on the inside of the door. Trying to make himself useful, Ian had hung it the other day. Good to have a man around the house. Wearing a long-sleeved black cocktail dress with a V neckline, ankle-strap heels, and underneath, a pair of lacy tap pants, she looked at her front, turned to the right, then the left, then around, gazing over her shoulder at her backside to check for panty lines. Overall, not too bad for forty-nine. Oh, hell, why be humble? Not too bad for thirty-nine. The daily bike rides had been her figure's friend. Luke had bought her the dress this afternoon, over her protests, which were largely pro forma. She felt like a mistress and decided she didn't mind feeling that way. The outfit was perhaps too stylish for Key West. But the island's self-conscious casualness grew tiresome at times; besides, the show was being held in the Casa Marina, the classiest hotel in town. She would not look over-dressed in that grand old place.

She heard Luke's footfalls on the outside stairs and opened the door and stepped out onto the landing before he reached it. As he stood three steps below, she placed a hand on her right hip, threw out the left, and said in her playful Southern-belle voice, "Good evening, sir. Are you here to whisk me away from this hovel?"

He stared at her and said that she looked not terrific, not great, not beautiful but ravishing.

"And you're not lookin' bad yourself, honey. Those linen pants, that linen jacket, just the right amount of wrinkles. Mmmmm-um-uh. And I like that shirt. Matches my dress."

A hotel valet parked Luke's car. As they entered the lobby where mahogany pillars rose to a coffered ceiling, she heard snippets of French from two couples seated in the lounge chairs. Waiting for the elevator, she fiddled with her purse, opening it, snapping it shut.

"A little anxious, are we?" asked Luke.

"I'm thinking, What if nobody shows up? And if they do, will they like my stuff enough to buy it?"

"Listen, the way you look tonight, any man up there, gay or straight, would buy a used car from you."

The small meeting room magnified the size of the crowd—forty or fifty, Corinne estimated. Her work, seven paintings dominated by the series titled *Seascape Triptych*, hung on the back wall. Her co-exhibitors, Dennis Dunlop and Abel Martinez, had the two side walls. She was pleased that she recognized no one except them and Marissa Eaton, the gallery owner. The presence of friends and locals would have turned the gathering into a cocktail party; strangers indicated serious art lovers and, she prayed, serious buyers. She greeted Marissa, seated with a young woman at a table upon which unclaimed name tags—about twenty—were arrayed in trim rows. She took hers, pinned it to the bodice of her dress, and introduced Luke as her guest.

"Welcome, welcome," said Marissa, a sixtyish woman and one of the island's grand dames, descended from a Yankee seaman who'd made a fortune as a wrecking captain. "How do you spell your name?" she asked, her felt-tip poised over a blank tag.

"Thanks, I don't need one of those," Luke said, figuring anonymity to be the better part of discretion. "I'm not in the art world, I'm just—"

"Don't hide your light under a bushel," Corrine cooed, rubbing his sleeve. Then, to Marissa: "Luke is managing editor of the *Miami Examiner*. It's Lucas Blackburn."

The older woman wrote his name in block letters and said, "We can always use major press coverage."

"I'm not covering anything, only down here fishing, and anyway, the *Examiner* isn't the *New York Times*."

"But it is a considerable step up from the *Key West Citizen*," she said, twitching her head at a thin young man taking photographs.

As she stood and pinned the tag to Luke's lapel, like a general awarding a medal, he glanced down at table and saw four names among the remaining tags: Michael Conway, Elizabeth Conway, Manuel Higgs, Joyce Higgs. Hoping they would be no-shows, he moved off with Corinne toward the back wall.

"I wish you wouldn't have done that," he whispered. "Told that woman who I am."

"You're embarrassed to be seen with me?"

"Not embarrassed. Cautious. No secrets on a small island, like a friend of mine says. Time for you to work the room."

"I'm not real good at working rooms."

"I'll bring you a drink. Loosen you up."

"Vodka on the rocks," she said. "Tito's if they have it."

The bar, tucked into a corner near the room's only window, did not have Tito's. Luke ordered a Ketel instead, a bourbon for himself, neat. He also could use some loosening up. Otherwise, he felt on top of things. The week since his meeting with Edith had gone well enough, except for the planned fishing trip with Ian: canceled because Mike's boat needed an engine overhaul. Holding fast to his morning exercise regime, swimming half a mile every afternoon, he'd dropped five pounds; his muscles were recapturing the tone lost to his sedentary life. The swim never failed to revive him after two or three hours at his typewriter, squinting at his barely legible notes like an archeologist at an ancient scroll.

Corinne did not need to work the room; the room had come to her, a good part of it anyway. Around twenty people, mostly male— no surprise there—clustered around her or stood looking at her work. In those three-inch heels, she towered over everyone except the tallest men; the black dress and her dark maroon lipstick and nail polish finished the femme-fatale image.

He brought her the vodka. "No Tito's, hope Ketel suits you."

"It does, thanks," she said, tipping the glass to her lips. Then, bending slightly, she kissed his temple.

A flash attachment burst, blinding him for half a second. Through the spots dancing before his eyes, he recognized the skinny photographer from the *Citizen*, who then peered at their names and scribbled them in a pocket notebook. The chances that Maureen would see the photo, if it was published, were next to zero; nevertheless, Luke's skin crawled. When the photographer asked if he could get a posed shot of the two of them together, he answered, "Just her, she's the star," and stepped aside. Corinne handed Luke her drink and smiled and postured, striving to affect a celebrity's aloofness. This was in fact the first time she'd been photographed for a newspaper. No, the *Citizen* wasn't the *Examiner*, but any publicity would help. Looking around for Luke, she spotted him near the entrance, talking to some people who'd just come in. Her gaze swiveled to the wall showing Dunlop's canvases, the largest of which—it was four by three feet at least—owed a huge debt to Winslow Homer's *Northeaster*. The gallery brochures described him as a "neo-traditionalist," whatever the hell that meant. To Corinne it meant a skilled imitator. But she felt a ruffle of envy when his audience moved off and she saw the big red sticker at the bottom of the frame: sold.

Her own audience had also dispersed. Needing to move around— standing in the high heels was giving her a backache—as well as to retrieve her vodka, she'd started toward Luke when a small man nattily turned out in a salmon-pink sport coat and white duck trousers tapped her right arm.

"Ms. Terrebonne? Can I speak to you a moment?" He wasn't much taller than a thirteen-year-old, his eyes on a plane with her cleavage, which thankfully didn't seem to interest him. He motioned at the triptych.

"I find those remarkable."

"Thank you. I worked very hard at them."

"I'm certain you did, but it doesn't show. Sweat but never let the sweat show, that's the ticket. There's an ease to your brushwork, a . . . Oh, what's the word? I'm trying to avoid art-speak . . . Lightsome? A lightsome touch. And your sense of color . . ." He spoke with an accent that was almost a parody of the cultivated gentleman. "And yet, and yet . . . Forgive me. Nathan Rubin."

He plucked a business card from his breast pocket and passed it to her. It read: N. J. Rubin Galleries, 495 Broome St., NY, NY 10013. Dealers in Fine Art and gave a phone number and email address.

"You were about to say something, Mr. Rubin?"

"Nate, please."

"Corrine Terrebonne," she said, extending her hand. His grip was firm for such a small man.

"Lovely name. You're of French extraction?"

"Mostly, with a little Irish and maybe some Creole. I'm from New Orleans originally. You were saying?"

"There is something disturbing about them." Rubin flicked a hand at the triptych. "They make me feel a bit uneasy. Not in a bad way. That interests me."

"They're meant to have that effect," she said, her pulse quickening. Rubin had grasped her intention!

"I can't pinpoint how you did that, and really, I don't want to. Do you have any others in this vein?"

"No. These were my first stab at pure abstractionism. Most of my work is . . . call it semi-representational. Some are in the gallery. You can see them there."

"I will. Do you have a website?"

"A website? No, I—" Suddenly, she was feeling stupid, stupid and backward. "But the gallery has one."

"May I suggest you find someone to design one?" Rubin took a gallery program out of his inside pocket and traced a finger down the list of paintings at the show and their prices. "Do you mind me giving one more piece of advice?"

She shook her head.

"You've got a gift that isn't ordinary. Don't sell yourself short. "

Luke was trying to extricate himself from the Conways and the Higgses, who hemmed him in on three sides, his back to a wall. They'd entered the room just as he was making his way to the bar to refresh his bourbon.

"Why, Luke Blackburn, what are you doing here with the artsy-fartsy set?" Liz said. He assumed the question wasn't a tease. There were things Liz knew—the things he'd revealed to her and Mike the night of Maureen's crackup in Leenane—and things she didn't know, if Mike had been true to his promise to keep Luke's recent confession in confidence. He answered that an old, dear friend was in the show, which was true as far as it went.

Mike did him a favor, diverting attention from the reason he was at this artsy-fartsy event. "I think you know Manny Higgs," he said.

"We've met a couple of times, not for long."

"Last time was not quite two years ago," the lawyer said. "That black-tie roast in Miami. You were with a gorgeous redhead, that's how I remember."

He shook hands with Higgs, a man slightly below average height, five seven or eight, but with an athlete's physique—he was a long-distance swimmer who took part in Key West's around-the-island race every year. The feature that made the deepest impression were his large eyes, the swollen lids suggestive of Graves' disease, the pupils gunmetal gray and expressionless. Looking into them was like looking into the eyes of a crocodile.

He introduced Luke to Joyce, a blond who said she was "Manny's next ex-wife."

"Strange, running into you," Higgs said. "One of your reporters has been phoning my office all week. Edith something. I haven't had a chance to answer. Must be about losing the appeal in federal court?"

Luke shrugged. Incroce's failed appeal was old news; Edith must have uncovered something new. "I'm officially on vacation," he said. "If you answer her you can find out what it's about."

Higgs cracked a cold smile.

"If that woman is your so-called old, dear friend, I think she wants your attention," Liz said, a little sharply. She cocked her chin toward the table at the entrance, where Corinne was signaling him to come over. He excused himself and went to her.

"Guess what?" she said, a high color in her face, a color of excitement, not embarrassment. "Look at my wall. See those red stickers? I sold the seascapes. All three! To a guy from New York. A gallery owner in Soho, an art dealer. Fifteen hundred bucks, cher. And he wants to see the rest of my work. He might represent me. The major leagues!"

He kissed her quickly, chastely on the forehead—the brand of kiss you would give to an old, dear friend.

"Don't forget where you came from," quipped Marissa.

Anxious to leave, Luke suggested they have a celebratory drink outside, on the arcaded veranda that ran the length of the hotel's historic wing. They sat at one of the café tables, facing the grounds and the beach and the sea beyond, striped by a gibbous moon. Luke ordered a whiskey, this time on the rocks, and a vodka for Corinne, a Tito's if it was available. Of course it was, replied the waiter in a pronounced accent Luke couldn't characterize more definitively than East European. The Casa Marina employed a lot of Czechs, shipped over in drafts by labor contractors dangling the hope of green cards.

"Here's to you," Luke said when the drinks arrived. "The next Georgia O'Keeffe."

Georgia O'Keeffe was the only female painter he could think of.

"She painted vaginas. I mean, flowers and skulls that looked like vaginas."

"What was the idea? Sex and death?"

"I'd vote for sex, death sucks." She leaned toward him and he kissed her on the mouth. She said, "You're warming up again! Like you were uptight in there. Distant."

"Cautious, I said cautious. There were people who know me and who know Maureen."

"Those people you were with? Who are they?"

He rattled off their names.

"Conway," she said. "Wasn't he the guy who was with you when—"

"The same. The woman with the short brown hair is his wife, Liz. Manny Higgs is a lawyer and he's married to the blond."

"That guy who bought my paintings, Rubin? He told me I had a gift that wasn't ordinary. Funny way to put it."

"You mean, why didn't he come right out and say extraordinary?"

"Yeah, I guess. I don't want to be disappointed. Get my hopes up for a breakout and then be disappointed. That's usually the way. He thinks I should have a website. I don't own a computer, don't know a damn thing about them, or anyone who could develop a site. Do you?"

"Offhand, no. But I could look into it. And I could show you how to use a computer in a couple of hours with my laptop."

She stirred the ice cubes and lime wedge in her glass.

"One more?"

She answered that she didn't think so. Luke produced a credit card and called for the tab.

"I'm not ready to go home just yet," she said. "And not to your place, either."

"Which leaves us with . . . what?"

"The beach, I'd like to walk along the beach, then out to the dock."

What she truly wanted but wasn't able to put into words was to prolong the pleasure of her triumph. It deserved a magical setting like the one she was in, with the man she loved. For the moment, she didn't give a damn that he wasn't hers and never would be. The slippers would come off and midnight arrive soon enough.

Their arms around each other's waists, they went down a promenade bordered by lighted reflecting ponds and two ranks of tall royal palms. When they came to the beach, they removed their shoes, strolled in the sand to the hotel dock, and walked to its end, where they caught the flash and flicker of glass minnows swarming around the pilings.

Corrine turned to him. "I'm going to ask you a very old, very simple question," she began.

Luke pinned two fingers together and pressed them to her lips. "You don't need to."

"I need to hear you say it. I need to hear you say you do."

"I'm in love with you, Corinne. Yes, I am."

"I don't think I ever really fell out of love with you," she said.

"Complicates things. And I haven't got a clue what to do about it."

"We're not going to do anything. We're not going to think about it." She pushed against him and, taking both his wrists in her hands, placed them on the round of her ass. "'Feel those underneath? Silk."

"I'll bet you look great in them."

Every pore in her body tingled. She felt much as she had when she was young, wild and wanton.

"Let's see if I do." She quickly pulled her dress over her head, undid her bra, and stood before him wearing a wicked smile and the tap pants and nothing else.

Luke looked around in a mild panic. "Corinne—Jesus—What are you . . . ?"

"There's no one here, and it's dark. Let's go skinny-dipping."

"What? We're not kids anymore."

"I don't see any signs—Nude swimming prohibited for those over thirty."

The swamp witch. Impossible to resist. He was a little tired of being cautious anyway. He stripped in seconds, but where she had left her clothes in a heap, he folded his jacket and pants, laid them over her dress and underwear, and set both pairs of shoes on top to prevent a breeze from blowing everything off the dock. They went down a ladder, slipping into the warm water. At low tide, it came up to their necks. Corrine, who was no swimmer, half breast-stroked, half dog-paddled inshore, staying close to the dock. When they were waist deep, she embraced him and with gentle pressure on his back urged him to sit down. The limestone marl ground against his thighs and rear end as she straddled him and locked her legs around the small of his back and filled herself with him. They kissed, rocking back and forth, the marl swirling from under them in milky billows. "O yes, O Jesus yes," she moaned.

yes I said I will Yes. Maureen. Maureen was across the ocean in which he and Corinne were immersed. Maureen was three thousand miles away, and he was here, on his own vacation from reality.

21

On Friday the 13th, an inauspicious date for a fishing trip or any endeavor requiring luck, Luke and Ian waited at the marina while a forklift pulled the *Pangloss* from a rack in the shed, trundled her across an oily concrete apron, and lowered her into a slip. Dingy hull repainted a sky-blue, decks refinished, twin engines overhauled, and ridiculous new name splashed on her sides in white script, she was unrecognizable as the old *Marekrishna*. A weird name, too, but euphonic.

Luke tied the bow and stern lines to the pilings, and after stowing his fly and spinning rods, he started the engines. Ian passed him the tackle bag and dip nets and climbed aboard.

"All set? You sure do look like a saltwater angler," Luke said, noting with his hand the lightweight shirt and pants, long-billed cap and deck shoes. He'd bought the entire outfit and loaned Ian his extra pair of polarized sunglasses. "Cast us off."

"Aye-aye, sir. Where are we headed?"

"Boca Grande Key. It's eighteen miles west, give or take. We're gonna catch some blue-claw crabs for bait and then fish for permit."

Ian untied the lines and positioned himself beside Luke, gripping a stainless steel handhold on the console as they idled into the channel, marked by numbered green and red signs on stakes.

"First lesson. Outbound, red on port side. Inbound, starboard. Red right returning is the mnemonic."

"Uh-huh. And what is a permit? I thought that's what you need to park a car."

"It belongs to the pompano family. Helluva game fish and tasty. A lot of sportsman snobs look down on keeping permit—killing one is a moral outrage. But if we catch one that's, say, eight, ten pounds, we are going to kill it and eat it. The smaller ones are best."

"Whatever you cooked for Corinne and me last night, that was terrific."

"*Huachinango veracruzana.* Red snapper in Veracruz sauce. Got the recipe from a friend, the wife of the guy who owns this boat. A friend of mine. The county mayor. He was going to come with us, but he's got a meeting today."

Leaving the channel, he pushed the throttles forward. The wind blew a steady twelve out of the south-southwest, but they would be fishing on the lee side of the key, which would reduce the waves to barely more than ripples. They reached Boca Grande before nine, the sun well up but tamed by a towering cumulus, gilt with fire, as if a blacksmith were hammering molten steel on its anvil top. Luke swung into a channel on the island's north side. The depth-recorder registered ten feet, then eight, then six. In the lambent water, every detail on the sea floor was visible—tiny ridges in the white sand, seagrasses bending in the tide, juvenile snapper darting through the beds. He shut the engine, raised it to avoid damaging the prop, and let the boat drift inshore till her hull bumped bottom. He went forward, hauled the Danforth out of the anchor locker, and uncoiled about thirty feet of line; then he waded ashore, dragging the anchor up the beach, and buried its tines into the sand.

He called to Ian, "Grab those two small nets and the bait bucket in the stern and come on in."

"Aye, aye, captain sir!"

"You have my permission to stop that aye-aye sir bullshit."

Ian saluted, and with the bucket and nets in hand, he swung overboard to join Luke, who pointed out a crab facing them in the ankle-deep water—a male swatting its blue, red-tipped claws like a street fighter his fists.

"That's what we want," he said. With a swift thrust, he scooped up the crab and shook it into the bucket.

They waded slowly in the shallows. The sandy shore, striped by blackish-green tide rack, was blinding in the hard morning light. A sea-oat meadow spread inland to a wall of white and black mangrove, exhaling the pungent smell of the salt pond lying in the middle of the key. Pelicans skimmed the channel on the right, struck with violent splashes, then lofted away, bills stuffed with minnows. Except for a cat-amaran anchored off a point of land ahead and a skiff staked out on a flat half a mile away, there wasn't a sign of other people. Crowds would be here in two more weeks, on the Labor Day weekend, but for now Luke and Ian might have been beachcombers on a desert island. Luke liked it that way, the silence, the emptiness. He scooped up three more crabs. Ian wasn't having any luck, missing every time.

"Try to get the net behind them. Just stand there, keeping their attention on you, then get the net behind them and snatch it."

He attempted this, and missed again. "Son of a bitch!" he yelled and smacked the water with his net.

"Don't lose your temper," Luke admonished. "It's not attractive. Watch me." He demonstrated the technique, captured another crab, and pointed ahead. "There's one."

Ian crept up on the crustacean as if he were stalking a dangerous animal. The net darted out and came up empty. He was about to swat the water again, but Luke caught his wrist and stopped him.

"Chill, okay? You'll get the hang of it."

He succeeded on his next attempt, netting a female, distinguishable as such by her claw tips, purple rather than red. They continued on to the point, where the shoreline curved around to the ocean side, then worked their way back to the boat, snagging four more crabs between them. They had a dozen, more than enough. Luke dumped the bait bucket's contents into the live well. After retrieving the anchor, Ian shoved the boat stern first till it was deep enough for the props, when the engines were lowered, to clear the bottom. Putting his jailhouse weight-room muscles to use, he grasped the gunwale and heaved himself aboard..

Chugging up another channel that wound like an emerald river between broad tidal flats showing tan and brown through the shallow water, Luke saw fit to deliver a lesson on navigating by the sea's color. It was a rhyme he'd learned from a veteran lobsterman: Blue, blue, sail on through; green, green, you got it clean; white, white, you just might; brown, brown, run aground. He rather enjoyed this—the modern world offered few opportunities for an older man to mentor a younger in useful skills. He was the old salt imparting lore to the raw kid, although Ian was well past the kid stage and the art of navigating by color wouldn't be useful in navigating the rest of his life. "Never draw to an inside straight, never eat at a place called Mom's, and never sleep with a woman whose troubles are worse than your own" would serve him better, though possibly Luke could make a half-ass instructional metaphor out of the rhyme: learn to recognize shoal water when you see it.

The narrow channel spilled into the much larger one, five miles wide, separating Boca Grande from the Marquesas. Luke dropped anchor, netted a crab from the live well and baited one of the spinning outfits, hooking the crab through the carapace, taking care not to kill it.

"We're on a flooding tide," he said. "The fish will be swimming into it, across the flat you see there, maybe along the edge between it and this channel. You'll see their dorsal fins or tails. What you want to do is drop the crab two, three feet in front of the lead fish in a school, same distance if it's a single. Let me see you cast."

"I'm a little rusty," said Ian, taking a rod.

His first cast was short and flat, the bait smacking the surface.

"More arc, you want it to hit the water as gently as possible. Permit may be the spookiest fish in the ocean."

After several more tries, Ian's muscle memory returned, and he pitched a perfect bow more than a hundred feet. The crab, having made six or seven aerial journeys and half as many hard landings, had expired. Luke rebaited the hook and directed Ian to step up on the casting deck and lower his rod tip to keep the crab in the water. After he'd done this, he watched the blue-claw swimming in circles, segmented legs twitching, scratching, seeking purchase on a bottom that wasn't there.

"Seems kinda cruel," he said.

"It is. Give me a few minutes and I'll think of something philosophical to justify it. Otherwise, don't think about it. They're the best bait for permit. I'll probably see them first. I'll call out the distance and direction, using the clock method. Bow is twelve o'clock, stern is six, midships right is three, left is nine."

"You're giving me a lot of shit to remember. Red right returning, blue, blue sail on through, twelve, six, three, nine."

"Right now the last lesson is the only one you need to keep in mind," Luke said.

He stood behind and to one side of Ian and scanned the flat for a telltale wake, a fin breaking the surface. The wind had fallen off to a zephyr. Looking into the water, lying smooth over the whitish bottom, was like looking into a stainless steel mirror. As the incoming tide gathered force, shrimp and plankton and fish too small to fight the current tumbled through the channel; a sting ray cruised nearby with lazy flaps of its wingtips, and then a pale brown shark six feet long appeared, patrolling the edge of the flat. Luke identified it as a lemon shark, and Ian asked if it was dangerous.

"Well, they belong to a family called requiem sharks, that should tell you something."

Those were the only words they spoke for the next half hour. Luke worried that perhaps they didn't have all that much to say to each other. He wished his heart to confirm what his mind knew; wished to *feel* their genetic bond. He longed to soar beyond his present sense of obligation into the sublimity that was love.

In the past week, he hadn't seen a lot of Ian, who slept through the better part of his work days before starting his night shift at the motel. He said that he'd always been a nighthawk, playing gigs till two in the morning, getting buzzed afterward, often not sleeping at all for twenty-four hours straight. The prison regime, however, had rewound his body clock to normal diurnal rhythms; now, his job was rewinding the rewind. He spent even his days off in bed, today being an exception.

"Mind if I take a break?" he asked. Rosettes of sweat had blossomed on his shirt from collar to waist. "Feels like I'm in a microwave out here."

Eyes burning from the sunscreen dripping from his forehead, Luke signaled his okay. Setting his rod down, Ian snatched two bottles of water from the ice chest, passed one to Luke, guzzled half the other and, removing his hat, splashed the rest over his head.

"I needed that." He was still shaving his skull. The black bristles gave him a thuggish appearance, which had probably been an asset for a white guy in a prison crammed with Hispanic gangbangers. "So where are these permit fish, Luke?"

"Late to the party, but they'll show."

They stared at the glittering water for five or six minutes. Luke asked how the job was going.

"Boring," Ian answered. "Boring and minimum wage. I saw the Bitch of Buchenwald yesterday. I asked her about gigging at the place you brought me and Corrine to—the Heaven something."

"Blue Heaven."

"She said uh-uh, that would be a violation of my parole. Reminded her that mine says I can be in any place whose primary purpose is *not* serving alcohol. Never mind what it says, what counts is what she says, and what she says is no friggin' way. I can eat in a place like that but can't work there."

"Do not piss her off, Ian," Luke counseled. "You're out—"

"I know, I know. Out of jail but not a free man. But I miss playing, miss my Strat like I'd miss a lost dog. If that Bob Marley imitator can entertain a crowd, I sure as hell can. They want imitation, I can imitate Stevie Ray or Johnny Winter. I can imitate Buddy Holly singing 'Bo Diddley.' Buddy Holly was your era."

"He was, but dead by the time I started high school," said Luke. He remembered riding around Sierra Vista with his friends in a Chevy Impala, listening to "Peggy Sue" and "That'll Be the Day," which made him feel antediluvian.

"Did you ever hear him do 'Bo Diddley'?"

Luke thought that they should concentrate on what they'd come here for, but he recalled that music had been Ian's connection to his father; maybe he, the putative father, could establish one in the same way.

"He had that beat down cold," he said.

Ian began strumming an air guitar. "Keep your hand moving, wrist loose, like you're flicking water off your fingers. Down down up up down rest two three four. My guitar teacher taught me that when I was fourteen. The groove for half the rock 'n' roll tunes in the world. *Bom bom de bom bom sheh de bom bom.*"

Converting his index fingers into drum sticks, Luke tapped the syncopated rhythm on the gunwale.

"Almost," Ian said. "A little pause before the last measure."

He tried it again, hurting his fingers.

"You are down with it, yo! Let's do 'Bo Diddley.' You be the percussion." Ian, more animated than Luke had seen him yet, leapt to his feet and hit the strings on his imaginary Stratocaster and sang the first verse. Pounding with both palms *Bom bom de bom bom she de bom bom*, Luke sang the second verse in a deeper voice, deep and gravelly, like Bob Seger. Ian picked up the next, and they ran through the entire tune, sweat varnishing Ian's sunburned face as he rocked back and forth, side to side, his strum hand flashing, left hand squeezing frets.

They laughed at each other and with each other and exchanged high-fives. Ian wiped his face with his shirttail and said, "A couple of rehearsals and we can go on the road."

Luke gave a last flourish with his sore palms, *Bom bom de bom bom*, and jumped up cursing when he heard a loud splash a few yards from the boat.

"That concludes the musical interlude," he said, watching a V-shaped wake vanish into the distance. "I just spooked a whole school of permit."

After another school failed to materialize, he decided to try wading the flat, which would be only three feet deep at peak high tide, still hours away. Ian, thinking about the lemon shark, wasn't enthusiastic about leaving the boat. Luke persuaded him that the chances of a shark attacking a human being in such skinny water could be measured by a one preceded by three or four zeroes.

They stalked the flat as hunters might stalk a meadow. A thin layer of sand covered the limestone bedrock, as firm as pavement and almost the same color, though mottled in places by seagrass beds. The hard bottom and the depth, seldom past their knees, made it easy to move quietly. In honor of the boat's name, Luke had optimistically packed his mini-Minolta in his shirt pocket. Fifteen minutes into the wade, he spotted disturbed water off to the right, about a hundred yards away. It could be a sting ray or a school of bonefish or a small shark. When a black-tipped dorsal fin broke the surface, a sensation like a low voltage electric current passed through his knees—the old excitement that was as breath-catching the hundredth time you felt it as it had been the first.

"There," he said in an undertone, pointing with his rod as the school swam within casting distance. "Three feet in front of their wake . . . Okay, now."

Ian made his pitch, the crab plopped down in the middle of the school, the water boiled, and the fish streaked away.

"What the hell? I dropped it right in 'em."

"I said in front, three feet in *front*. They're not used to their prey attacking them from the air."

They moved on, taking care not to splash or stumble. Approaching the far side of the flat, where it bordered another narrow channel, Luke saw a mirror-like flash directly to his front. A single permit, and a big one, "mooning"; tilting a little as it fed on the bottom so that one wide, silvery flank caught the sunlight.

"See him?" Again pointing the rod.

Ian nodded, flipped the bail on the reel, and cast. This attempt went too far, the bait landing at least ten or twelve feet from the fish.

"Shit!"

"That's okay. Leave it in the water, reel in slow. He might see it. If you feel a solid bump, set the hook."

The hook did not need setting; the fish struck with such ferocity that it hooked itself. Instantly, line flew off the spool and through the rod guides with a sound that was part hiss, part screech.

"Holy mother!" Ian shouted, alarmed by the fish's speed and power.

"Calm, calm, calm. Stay tight to him, no slack."

A hundred yards, a hundred fifty, two hundred. Finally, the run stopped. At Luke's coaching, Ian pursued the permit on foot, reeling in as he slogged forward to regain some of the line lost to the run. He did not need coaching to fight the fish; his father had taught him well. Lowering the rod, he recovered a few yards, lifted and lowered it again, recovering a few more before the permit tore away on a second sprint.

"Holy sweet mother!"

Luke, reaching across Ian's waist, tightened the drag a quarter turn.

With twenty-pound test line, there was little danger of breaking the fish off.

Ten minutes passed before it showed any sign of flagging. Luke desperately wanted Ian to catch this fish, wanted him to experience a triumph. As the permit's runs grew shorter and slower, he threw out words of encouragement, like a cornerman to a tired fighter in the last round. "You've just about got him. Keep the pressure on, don't give him an inch of slack." At last, Ian brought it to within ten feet of his grasp, but when it saw the strange, vertical creatures standing so near, it caught a second wind and ripped another fifty yards off the reel in seconds. That was its final bid. With each pump of the rod and turn of the reel handle, it lost ground until it lay on its side, motionless except for exhausted flaps of its forked tail and sluggish pulses of its gills. Lying flat on the surface, pale gray, oval-shaped, it looked like a pewter serving tray. Luke estimated it would top twenty pounds. He made a quick grab, clutched the base of its tail, then pulled the pliers from his belt holster and worked the hook loose from its puckered mouth.

"Give me your rod," he said. "Wet your hands, hold it with one like I am, the other one under its head. I want to get your picture."

Ian struck the pose of the conquering sportsman, grinning and displaying his prize. Luke snapped three shots with the Minolta, then took the fish, and with both hands cradling it under the surface, he gently pushed and pulled to sluice seawater through its gills. The permit had fought almost to its death; reviving it took a good three or four minutes. It gave a convulsive shudder, its tail fluttered, then whipped, and it lunged from Luke's hand and swam swiftly away.

"I'm glad you did that," Ian said. "I'm glad we didn't kill it."

"Some would say it earned its freedom, but it didn't. It *won* it. Hey, congratulations. That was a fine fish and you did a helluva good job."

They shook hands.

"Thanks, Luke. Listen, when I was on the inside, y'know . . . I couldn't have dreamed of a day like this." Tugging Luke's hand, he pulled him close and hugged him. "Maybe I'm not a free man yet, but I sure as shit feel like one."

Gift enough, thought Luke. *That's gift enough.*

It was now past noon. Tired from the tussle with the fish, unaccustomed to the tropical heat, particularly out here on shadeless expanses of dazzling saltwater, Ian staggered on the quarter-mile trudge back to the boat. He dipped his cap, filled it, and slapped it back on his head, its contents pouring down his face. They reached the *Pangloss* and clambered aboard. Prior to wading, Luke had nudged her further up onto the flat and dropped a spare anchor to make sure she stayed put. Going to the stern, he hauled it in, which kedged the boat into the channel, while Ian weighed the bow anchor. The chain was up out of the water when the heavy Danforth slipped his grasp, and he stumbled off the casting deck. Luke ran forward and retrieved the anchor, coiling the rode into the locker.

"Ian, are you okay?"

"Dizzy. Feel like . . . spinning . . ." His speech was slurred.

"Sit down," Luke said, patting the storage compartment attached to the front of the console.

Ian fell into the seat. Luke got him a bottle of ice water from the chest. He tipped it to his lips, but couldn't swallow; the water dribbled down his chin. His forehead felt hot and dry—he had stopped sweating. Reaching again into the chest, Luke packed a plastic freezer bag with ice, placed it on Ian's skull, and jammed his hat over the bag to keep it in place.

"How're you feeling? Are you nauseous?"

His head lolling to one side, he looked at Luke glassy-eyed and muttered incoherently.

Alarmed because he knew the symptoms—he'd observed them in Vietnam—Luke went to the wheel, started the engines, and rammed the gear shift and throttles so hard that the boat jumped onto a plane. He raced up the channel. A few minutes later, rounding Boca Grande Key, he radioed an emergency to the marina on the VHF.

"Roger," someone answered. "What's the emergency?"

Right at that moment, Ian slid off the seat and collapsed on the deck.

"Wait one," responded Luke, then dropped the handset.

"Standing by."

He reduced speed, grabbed Ian by the ankles, and dragged him into the space between the console and the starboard side of the hull. Some shade was there. Then he dipped the bait bucket into melt water in the ice chest and doused Ian's face and chest, actions he repeated in an attempt to lower his body temperature. He was still conscious, but babbling in what sounded like a parody of a sci-fi alien's speech. *Noch! Ben sop ta Nu nu.*

"Vessel calling with emergency. Still standing by. Do you read me? Come back."

"Loud and clear," Luke answered, forcing a collected, "right stuff" tone. "I've got a passenger with heat stroke. Call 911. I'll need an ambulance to get him to the hospital. I'm off Woman Key. I should be there in half an hour. I want that ambulance waiting when I get there. Did you read all that? Over."

"Roger. Passenger with heat stroke. Need an ambulance immediately. I'm on it. Over and out."

He pushed the engines to their limit, the tachometer needle hovering just above redline. The wind created by the boat's speed, blowing over Ian's wet skin and clothes, would keep him from overheating any further. Only yesterday morning, Luke had seen an entry in his notebooks that now seemed frighteningly prophetic: "7/7/69—Op. Cedar Wing—No contact—1 casualty, non hostile—PFC John Porter—Evac w/ heat stroke—Medic sez temp 108F—not expected to live—brain damage if does."

It was under two miles from the marina to Florida Keys Memorial on Stock Island. The ambulance made the trip in minutes, Luke following in his Land Cruiser. Strapped to a gurney, a semiconscious Ian was rolled into the emergency room. A doctor quickly took his temperature with a rectal thermometer—it was 105—hooked him to an IV solution to rehydrate him, and then had him wheeled out for immersion in an ice-water bath. Luke was told to remain in the waiting room, where one of the ambulance crew handed Ian's sole ID to a woman at the admissions desk—a released offender identification card issued by the Arizona Department of Corrections. If she had any reaction to this unusual document, it didn't show as she entered his name, birthdate, and other information into a computer. Turning to Luke, she asked if the patient carried medical insurance. She was a heavyset, middle-aged woman with the manner of a matron at a girls' reformatory.

"That shouldn't make any difference," he answered. "You're required to treat emergencies."

His testy response earned a sharp look. "Yes, we are, sir. But we need to know if he has any. Does he or doesn't he?"

"He doesn't. You can bill me. Do you accept plastic?"

"What do you think? Of course we do. We charge a hundred up front, additional expenses to follow."

He gave her his American Express card while she passed him a form attached to a clipboard: an affidavit attesting that he accepted responsibility for any and all medical costs for . . . He printed Ian's name in the blank space. At the bottom, more blank spaces requested his name, contact information, etc. When he came to the line that read "Relationship to patient," he hesitated briefly, then wrote "Father." Why not? It was true, in the physiological sense anyway. After he signed the form, the woman checked to make sure the i's were dotted and the t's crossed. If she noticed the difference in surnames, she once again showed no reaction.

He sat in one of the contoured plastic chairs, phoned the museum on his cell, and asked to speak to Corinne. She was out to lunch, said the man who'd answered. Would you care to leave a message? Yes, he cared to. Please tell her to call Luke as soon as she's in, tell her it's important. He snapped the phone closed, and only then noticed that there were four other people in the waiting room: an elderly Cuban couple, a man wearing a ponytail and three bandages, one across his forehead, one under each eye, and seated next to him, the Gunny. Luke surmised that ponytail belonged to the wino squad, had either been in a scuffle or had fallen, and that Gunny, taking care of his troops, had brought him to the ER. Wishing not to be recognized because he was in no mood for talk, Luke donned the sunglasses dangling from a cord around his neck, picked up a month-old copy of *Florida Sportsman*, and pretended to read it. He felt as if loose ball bearings were rattling around in his head. *Not expected to live . . . Brain damage if he does. Please, please, not that.* A perfectly fine day had turned into a bad one, a potentially catastrophic one, in a matter of minutes. The war had taught him to expect the unexpected, but he'd forgotten its principal lesson—lives can be unalterably changed, can be ended in an instant for no transcendent reason arising from design but merely through chance. Two men under shellfire run for a foxhole; one, slightly faster, dives in as a shell bursts; the other, not far behind, also dives but is blown in half in midair. People thought of war as a unique experience, utterly divorced from the normal course of events. Luke himself thought that way, but now he questioned if the difference was one of degree rather than kind. Disasters great and small occur as isolated incidents in the placid flow of ordinary life, dulling the human capacity to anticipate them, while in war they happen all the time, suddenly and capriciously, rendering the surprising unsurprising. War could be considered nothing more than a series of pointless accidents, compressed into days, hours, or mere minutes rather than over a span of years and decades. Yet, could any real distinction be made between the man blown in half only because he could not run as fast as his buddy and the vacationing family who are wiped out when, because its driver is tired or is momentarily distracted or fails to slow down on a curve, an oncoming truck veers over the center line and smashes into their car?

Ian had had too much sun, that was his accident. It seemed a fundamental injustice that he should lose his life or suffer permanent brain damage because he'd had too much sun. *Seemed* was the operative word. There had been no injustice; the sun, like all of nature, was indifferent to the fates of the beings it shone on. At least he, Luke, had given him the sort of day he'd dared not hope for when he was in prison. Gift enough. He still did not feel the paternal love he thought he should, but maybe too much emphasis was put on one's feelings these days. One's actions counted more. What he'd done for Ian he would have done for anybody, for a stranger; nevertheless, he had sensed, racing over the seas, a desperation that would not have been there if Ian had been just anybody.

His cellphone tore him from these reflections. It was Corinne. She'd gotten his message. What is it? Is something wrong? He told her. She gasped. Was he going to be all right? Luke didn't know, he hadn't spoken to the doctor yet.

"I'll call a taxi," she said in a strained voice. "I'll be there as soon as I can."

Luke was conferring with the doctor, a short, sturdy woman with long brown hair and a gap tooth, when Corinne burst through the ER doors, pitched forward at the waist, as if walking against a strong wind. She came up to Luke, a panic glistening in her eyes, and asked, "How is he? He's going to be okay?"

"The short answer is yes," the doctor replied, taking her hand. "Hi, I'm Dr. Jones, Rona Jones."

"Corinne. Is he going to be okay? How serious is it?"

"Heat stroke is always serious. In Ian's case, not too," said Dr. Jones. " I was just telling your husband that we got his temperature down to a hundred. We've done a blood draw, and given him an MRI. It doesn't look like any major neurological damage, probably no damage at all. I'll have to look at the results more carefully to be sure. He's young, in good physical condition, and your husband did the right thing, cooling him off while he was getting him here."

Corinne glanced at him quizzically.

"I put an ice pack on him, wet him down," Luke said.

She whispered, "Not my question."

"We'll have to keep him here a day or two, make sure his organs are all functioning normally," the doctor continued. "You can see him now. He's awake, but don't be alarmed if he's not quite himself." She gave them the room number. "Go through there"—she pointed at double doors—"right at the end of the corridor to the elevators. Second floor." She turned and went off to tend another patient—the man with the bandaged face.

"Did you tell her we're married, that was my question," Corinne said as they waited for the elevator.

"An assumption on her part. All I told her is that we're Ian's parents."

Corinne considered this statement; then she said, "Well, I suppose we are, aren't we?"

Ian's room was air-conditioned to a fault, and the curtains were drawn to keep out the afternoon sun, giving it a gloomy atmosphere that the ceiling lights somehow intensified. An IV tube stuck in one arm, wires attached to his chest and one wrist to monitor his vitals, he was sitting up, munching from packet of crackers on the bed tray.

"Hey, Bo Diddley," Luke said.

"Say, Bo Diddley." Ian answered, his speech halting. "Say . . . Bo . . . Di . . . Diddley." He crunched another cracker. "Give me . . . they told me . . . It's to . . . give . . . me . . . salt."

Corinne took his hand in hers. "How do you feel, darling?"

"Not gray . . . gray-ate." His lips flapped, as if his jaws had been shot with Novocain. "But okay . . . considering."

"I've been scared sick, just sick since Luke called me. But the doctor said you're going to come through. They're going to keep you for another day or so to make sure. Did they tell you that?"

He nodded slowly. "Man, I don't know what . . . I was sitting in . . . the boat. . . . Got so dizzy, then . . . I don't know . . . Day or two? Can you call the motel? Tell them . . . can't come in . . . tomorrow. Shitty job, but . . . but . . . can't lose it."

Luke told him not to worry, he would make the call. They spoke for a while longer, the usual things that pass between visitors and a patient in a hospital. When a nurse entered to take another blood draw, they turned to go.

"Hey, Luke, thanks," Ian said. "For . . . y'know . . . If you hadn't . . . been—"

"You wouldn't have been there if I hadn't brought you. No thanks necessary."

"Make a fist," said the nurse, tapping Ian's right arm.

As he did and she inserted the needle into his vein, Luke clasped his left hand, bent down, and kissed his forehead.

"You take care now."

PART FOUR

22

North Miami Beach, crunched between the Intracoastal Waterway and I-95, felt as far from South Beach's trendy cafés and palm-fringed sugar sands as a Seminole village in the Everglades. The city did not even have a beach, its eastern limit abutting the Intracoastal. Celebrity hounds hoping to catch glimpses of Oprah or some other celebrity would search in vain in NMB, yet the city could claim a few famous native sons and daughters. Andrea Bocelli for one, and for another—Edith's favorite—Larry Kahn, MIT graduate and world tiddlywinks champion.

Edith swung off Second Avenue into the parking lot of a white concrete structure with tinted windows that had all the architectural style of a manufactured home but was considerably larger, covering close to two acres: headquarters for the Miami Field Office of the FBI, legendary in the Bureau's history for busting Al Capone and for capturing any number of interstate kidnappers, bank robbers, extortionists, most-wanted fugitives, drug kingpins, airplane hijackers, and—its most storied exploit—Nazi saboteurs who'd been landed in Florida by a German submarine during World War II.

Edith Buchmayr was one of the few Florida reporters trusted enough to have a working relationship with its investigators. Thirteen years ago, she'd won the Field Office's respect, and a Pulitzer for spot news coverage, for her firsthand reporting of a gun battle between eight special agents and two bank robbers named McEvoy and Pratt. She'd been on a routine ride-along with Metro-Dade cops when they were called to assist the agents, pinned down by semiautomatic rifle fire. A block short of the scene, the policemen ordered her out of the car—no place for a civilian and damn sure no place for a woman, they said. It was likewise no time to argue sexism. Edith got out, ran toward the gunfire, and took cover behind a tree. What she saw would remain etched in her memory forever: two agents dead in the street beside their bullet-riddled car; another car smashed against a tree (she would learn later it was the suspects' Monte Carlo); surviving FBI men, crouched behind their vehicles, exchanging shots with McEvoy and Pratt, who had jumped into the dead agents' car. A couple of rounds snapped over Edith's head, sounding like sharp handclaps. In all her years as a crime and investigative reporter, she had never once been under fire. The experience was strangely exhilarating. The shootout ended half a minute later, when an agent charged the wounded gunmen, shoved his pistol through the car window, and finished them off.

Edith's eyewitness account, which ran in the next morning's edition, extolled the lawmen's heroism, but it wasn't all that endeared her to them. In a news analysis she wrote the following day, she noted that the officers outnumbered the bank robbers four to one, yet two had been killed and five wounded, while Pratt had been hit twelve times and McEvoy six before they were taken out of action. The agents had been armed with .38 caliber service revolvers that lacked stopping power, were slow to reload under fire, and were no match for their adversaries' Ruger mini-14s. It was scandalous that federal lawmen should be outgunned by a pair of thugs, she wrote. Her article was cited in a subsequent FBI review that eventually led the Bureau to phase out revolvers and replace them with 9mm semiauto handguns.

Now, she found a visitor's parking space in the crowded lot, slung a briefcase over her shoulder, and strode into the building. In the entrance hall, decorated with the Bureau's blue-and-gold emblem, photographs of fallen agents, and framed news clips of the Field Office's more celebrated feats, she announced herself to the security desk and said that she had an appointment with Special Agent Gilbert Figueroa. The guard phoned him, then invited Edith to sit down and wait. As she did, she conducted a mental review of how she would handle the meeting, aware that she was on uncertain ground. Figueroa, head of the Field Office's organized crime and racketeering squad, was her FBI source on the Oceanaire/Astoria Island story. She'd worked with him over the years, developing a barter relationship. She would present facts she'd uncovered on a particular investigative assignment. He would either confirm or deny the accuracy of what she had, specifying that confirmations were not to be attributed to him or to the FBI but to "law enforcement sources." In exchange, he would throw her a scrap or two from Bureau investigations. Inevitably, these table leavings merely added color to a story, like a corrupt union boss's preferences in women. Once in a while, he served up more substantial fare on cases that the US Attorney declined to prosecute, such as a New Jersey mobster's reputed investment in a casino on the Seminole reservation. In a word, gossip.

What made today different was that she had solid information the Bureau did not have. No one did. It was in her briefcase—the documents Fred Finnbar had turned over to her. Filthy Fred was far out in the Atlantic by now, on course for France. She'd read and reread his photocopies for the past week, calling on a banker friend to guide her through the labyrinthine intricacies of international money laundering. Her examination finished, she phoned Figueroa last Friday with a seemingly routine request: she'd heard that a large yacht flying a Caymans flag had anchored in Key West Harbor and that this vessel was of interest to federal agents. Could he confirm that?

"Where'd you hear that?" he asked, sounding annoyed.

"From our Keys correspondent, Kristen Bernal. Can you confirm?"

"She's called the *Island Princess*. She put in on Wednesday. Word is, it's anchors aweigh first thing tomorrow morning."

"Does this yacht have anything to do with the Oceanaire investigation?"

"Sorry, Edith, we can't comment on that," he said, following a pause. "In a couple of weeks, a month maybe, but not right now."

"Okay, understood," she said. "One other thing I heard—you guys requested a warrant to search the premises of Incroce's company and it was denied. Lack of sufficient probable cause."

"Well, you know—" he began, but Edith cut him off, telling him that she had some info that might take care of the probable cause problem, then offered a teasing preview, adding that she wanted a fair trade: something from him equal in importance, like, say, why the *Island Princess* had drawn the FBI's attention.

This produced a second, longer pause, after which Figueroa promised to get back to her before the end of the day. He called at four thirty. He would meet with her on Monday, the 16th. Ten a.m.

"I gave you a look at coming attractions, can you do the same for me?"

"If you were a guy, I'd say you've got brass balls. Video and audio, very hush-hush. We'll have to establish rules of the road. Meantime, you can quiver with anticipation. Have a nice weekend."

"Edith! How are you?"

Figueroa was garbed in FBI conservative—white shirt, striped tie, a navy blue suit that his athlete's body filled out nicely. Menopause had not diminished Edith's healthy libido. She found him distractingly handsome, with the seductive good looks of a Latin movie star from a bygone era, like the guy who did the Chrysler commercials, Ricardo Montalbán. If he weren't a valued source, married, and fifteen years younger than she, she would do all in her power to waltz him into her bed.

"Just fine, Gil," she answered cheerfully. They shook hands. She could smell his after-shave. "You're looking well, as always."

"And you, too. Stylish as always." He made a wavy movement with his fingers to indicate her pinstripe pantsuit and pearl-gray blouse. "All set? The ASAC is going to sit in, and Lena Betancourt. She's our resident agent in Key West. Follow me."

Edith's spirits rose and sank in the space of half a second. The ASAC's presence confirmed that she was going to get meaty information; it also meant that she wouldn't be able to use it until he said so, and who knew how long that might be? Figueroa led her down a corridor past a communications room, then to an elevator that brought them to the second floor, and then through another corridor into a conference room as austere as an interrogation room, though it was much bigger and furnished with a long, polished table and comfortable chairs. A roll-down projection screen faced a laptop and a videocassette player at one end of the table. Edith met the Assistant Special Agent in Charge, Emmet Tisdale, a mocha-complected man in the process of losing his hair, and Lena Betancourt, a thirtyish woman with the blonde but bland attractiveness of a Fox News anchorwoman.

The introductions over, the agents sat together across from Edith, all by herself and feeling it.

"So, tell us what you've got and how you got it," Figueroa said, cocking his head to one side, two fingers joined under his perfect chin.

Edith removed the documents from her briefcase, laid them out in three tidy stacks, and pushed them across the table. "In a nutshell, records of laundered Cali cartel money, transferred through various Caribbean banks to shell companies, which in turn transferred those sums to Oceanaire Properties, Limited. Total three hundred mil, two fifty of which Oceanaire loaned to Incroce's company, TBI, with provisions that the loans will be forgiven if the Astoria Island project gets built and Oceanaire gets 50 percent of the profits. In effect, Oceanaire is Thomas Incroce's sugar daddy." Her summary sounded crisp and rehearsed. In fact, she had rehearsed it, last night and early this morning. "I assume this is what you'd hoped to find if you'd gotten the search warrant?"

"What did you do? Break into Incroce's office and crack his safe?" asked Figueroa, not entirely in jest.

"These are copies. Actually, copies of the copies that were given to me. The originals are in a safe-deposit box, or so I'm told."

"Who gave them to you and when?"

"Incroce's man Friday, accountant, gofer, whatever you want to call him. A source I'd developed. Fred Finnbar. He had them locked away on his boat. He turned them over to me last week."

Betancourt threw her a congratulatory nod. "Touché, Edith. I interviewed him and couldn't crack him."

"So he told me. Didn't mention you by name."

"We're not accustomed to reporters beating us to the punch. You ought to change careers and work for us."

It had occurred to Edith that she was now doing exactly that. A glorified snitch.

"Finnbar had a gripe with Incroce," she explained, though she hadn't been asked to. "Thought he'd been screwed financially, so exposing his patron was his way of getting revenge."

"His real name is Fred DeLeo, by the way," Betancourt said. Edith wrote the name in her notebook. "He skipped town, but we're not sure where to. Any idea?

"He told me he was sailing to France because it's difficult to extradite someone from there."

"It is, but not impossible." Figueroa sighed. "You know, Edith, we would have appreciated your cluing us in a week ago."

She responded with a half-truth: she needed the week to go through the material to assess its value; she didn't want to waste the FBI's time. The statement elicited snickers from Tisdale and Betancourt and a "Nice try" from Figueroa.

"I was referring to his sailing trip," he added. "We could have popped him before he left."

For ten uncomfortable minutes, in a silence broken solely by the rattle of shuffled papers, Edith waited while the agents studied the documents, occasionally jotting down some detail on legal pads. Looking up, she noticed two security cameras, mounted at the top of the bare white walls at either end of the room. As she expected, the conference was being recorded.

"All right, a lot here," said Figueroa, restacking his pile. "It's gonna take a while for us and our analysts to go through it all. When the time comes, we'll get a warrant and find out if there's anything more in that safe-deposit box. Thanks, Edith. You saved us a lot of time and effort."

"You're welcome."

Crossing her arms over her midriff, kicking out her legs, she signaled her readiness to hear their end of the transaction.

"Rules of the road time," said Tisdale, in a mellow voice and with a level stare. "To be clear, you've presented this—"

"I've presented the evidence to you voluntarily. You didn't ask me to gather it for you. I know the drill."

"Thank you. We're on deep background from here on in. Real deep. By real deep, I mean it's embargoed. Understood?"

"I anticipated it would be. For how long?"

"Can't give you an exact date."

"How about ballpark?"

The ASAC tapped his legal pad with a pen. "We're pretty far along. After we review the material you've shown us, search the safe-deposit box, et cetera, figure we'll make arrests by the middle of next month, end of the month at the latest."

Edith felt a letdown. "Plenty of time to spring a leak," she said.

"We're making this one as leakproof as possible."

She wriggled out of her relaxed posture and looked at Tisdale as if no one else was in the room. "Can you promise me, guarantee me, swear on your mother's grave, if she's in one—"

"She isn't."

"—that I get a heads-up first? I've worked hard on this story, and I don't want every daily, weekly, monthly, TV, and radio station between here and Jacksonville to have a piece of it. I want 'em all scrambling to play catch-up."

"Goes without saying. One good deed deserves another."

Edith didn't say that she wanted the exclusive for more reasons than those she'd given. She'd learned that Luke Blackburn had stricken her name from a roster of staffers targeted for a layoff or early retirement; she also knew that it was only a matter of time before she was again in the Ritters' crosshairs. A big story like this one might well spare her, at least for a few years. She dreaded being put out to pasture; it was a kind of death. No husband, no children, no desire to garden or volunteer for worthy causes—her work was all she had. It was she, she was it.

At about the same time and approximately 180 miles to the south, in the Big Pine Room at the Casa Marina Hotel, Luke, Corinne, and Ian stood in the crowd gathered to hear Mike Conway kick off his campaign for the state senate seat held by Addison DeMette, who was leaving office to "spend more time with my family" and to "pursue other opportunities in the private sector." In actual fact, he would be spending more time with his lawyer and pursuing opportunities to stay out of jail for using campaign funds to take vacations and buy his wife jewelry.

Ian had been released from the hospital on Sunday but was taking today off from work. To celebrate his recovery, Luke had treated him and Corinne to lunch at the Casa Marina. He'd just finished with the tab when a pair of hands dug into his shoulders from behind.

"Well, look who's here. The *managing editor* is covering my event?" Mike said. "I am indeed honored."

Luke turned in his seat. "Your . . . ?" he began, then remembered. Recent happenings had shoved the kickoff from his mind. "Oh, yeah. Kristen is covering it."

"I know, but aren't you here for it? Or do you need a formal invitation? Consider this to be one. From the horse's mouth. The kickoff kicks off in ten."

Luke began to beg off, wary about showing up at so public a venue with Corrine and Ian, but Mike insisted. Bending down, he whispered in Luke's ear, "No worries, m'boy, no worries."

"Feeling less cautious about being seen with me?" Corrine asked in an undertone as they walked to the Big Pine Room.

Luke turned to her. "I'm not sure. I know we've got to be careful, but sometimes I just want to say, the hell with it, let's give 'em something to talk about."

The room was decked out in the usual bunting and red-white-and-blue crepe ribbons. Filling it were city and county councillors, environmental activists, real estate people, assorted hangers-on, and reporters, photographers, and TV cameramen from as far away as Tallahassee. Standing on a platform, dressed in tropical formal—lightweight jacket and pants, shirt sans necktie, loafers—Mike was winding up his speech.

"Many of you know that I am an avid fisherman and diver. Seen first-hand the effects pollution has had on our beloved reef—the third largest reef in the world! Vital to the Keys' economy . . . ecotourism, commercial and sport fishing . . . As your state senator—oops! If elected your state senator—" A rustle of light laughter. "I will fight like hell to stop the polluting of our pristine waters. If you're concerned about our environment, you'll find no greater champion than Mike Conway. You won't find me spending public money on diamond bracelets. I will spend it on you and your businesses and families."

Corinne pressed her mouth to Luke's ear and whispered, "Is it my imagination? The longer he talks, the more he sounds like a Kennedy."

Luke chuckled softly. He'd noticed the same gradual shift in accent from South Boston to the plummy, not-quite-American, not-quite-British Transatlantic.

"So allow me to say in conclusion—bet you've all been waiting to hear that word—" More laughter. "—that if the people of the thirty-ninth district choose me to represent them, its future in the new century, the new millennium, will be more promising, more prosperous, more beautiful than ever."

Applause.

Tisdale glanced at Betancourt and said, "Lights."

After she'd dimmed them and fiddled with the AV equipment, footage of the *Island Princess*, which she had shot from shore, appeared on the screen.

The timestamp in a bottom corner reads "3:20 p.m. 08:11:99." The yacht is anchored at one end of Key West Harbor, near the main ship channel: all shiny white fiberglass, with raked decks in three tiers, two launches on davits port and starboard, the Caymans' ensign—a Union Jack on a scarlet field—fluttering from her rounded fantail. She looks to be about 150 feet, bow to stern. A corner of Astoria Island is visible in the background.

"We got word on the fifth from a C.I. on Grand Cayman that the yacht was scheduled to shove off on the eighth," Figueroa said. "Time enough for our team there to bug her before she sailed."

Edith scribbled notes while Betancourt darkened the screen and inserted a diskette in the computer.

The onscreen image, timestamped 1:15 p.m. on the next day, the twelfth, shows four men seated on the fantail around a mahogany table, agleam with spar varnish. They are eating lunch, served by a waiter whose very black skin contrasts sharply with his white shorts and polo shirt. The spy camera, wherever it's been installed, is in closeup mode.

"Pause it for a second," Figueroa said to Betancourt; then to Edith: "I think you recognize a couple of them."

"The guy in the green knit shirt is Manny Higgs, the guy next to him, the stocky guy on the right is Thomas Incroce," said Edith. "The other two?"

"The slick-looking dude with the black hair is José Dominguez, Oceanaire's so-called CEO and laundryman for the Cali cartel."

"Doesn't look like a photo I've seen of him."

"Probably an old one, and José has had some cosmetic work done. The fourth, that skinny guy with blond hair—it's dyed—is—"

"I recognize him now," Edith interrupted. "The dye job threw me off. Roy Stovall, all-around fixer, the Devil's Disciple."

"Right. Stovall, with a little help from his friends, namely Manny Higgs, was the matchmaker who put Incroce in the arms of Oceanaire. Those two have a history with Dominguez. I can give you details later."

The fact Edith had been trying to pin down for weeks. "You're sure about that?" she asked, restraining her excitement.

"Like the sun will set today and rise tomorrow."

Figueroa motioned to Betancourt to restart the video. "The first fifteen, twenty minutes is all guy talk. Sports bets, women, some politics. We'll fast forward to the meat, all right with you?"

She nodded and watched images rapidly flicker across the screen, accompanied by garbled conversation that sounded like an old 33 vinyl spinning at 78 rpm. When normal speed resumed, Edith saw that lunch was finished and heard Dominguez say in heavily accented English:

"Enough! Now we discuss the business, okay?"

Higgs then briefs the Colombian on the status of TBI Corporation's legal dispute over Astoria's ownership. "The next step will be to go to federal court for a final ruling on who owns the island—the government or my client. It is called a motion for summary judgment. The government will then have to file its own motion. The decision will settle the dispute one way or the other, thereby clearing title."

With a skeptical look, Dominguez asks, How confident are you this ruling will go our way? Very confident, replies Higgs, his goggle eyes fixed on Dominguez. The judge who will hear the case is politically conservative, pro-development, a great believer in private property rights. Incroce butts in: My family has paid taxes on the island for almost half a century, and the federal government has leased it from my company for Navy SEALs training. "Right there is proof the government has tacitly relinquished its claim," Higgs interjects. "You don't lease land from someone else if it's yours."

Dominguez nods, lights a cigar. So, there are no problems? he asks. Higgs again: There are, but they can be resolved, Don José. The problem is zoning. It's complicated, but to make it simple, zoning of the island falls under the county's jurisdiction. But there is a zoning law in the county that restricts new development to one structure per two acres. It is called the Comprehensive Plan. The island covers thirty acres, so only about twelve to fifteen houses could be built— Once more, Incroce interrupts: And the development calls for twice as many, plus a clubhouse with a swimming pool, plus a putting green, plus a marina.

Dominguez shakes his head, blows a plume of cigar smoke at the overhang shielding the group. "Señor Higgs, you have Cuban blood and you speak Spanish. Please tell everything to me in Spanish." Which Higgs does for the next several minutes. The Colombian thanks him, chews on the cigar and, reverting to English, says, So the problem is that this law of the zoning must be changed? Yes. And you can do this? Yes, says Higgs. I am attorney for the county, friends with the mayor of the county, Michael Conway. He is the author of the Comprehensive Plan, the *Plan Integral* I just explained to you. He is soon to announce he is running for office, the office of state senator. Here, Dominguez pitches forward in his deck chair, waving the lit cigar, and laughs. If I make *contribución* to him, he will change this law? *Quanto?* Not much, Don José, answers Higgs. Ten thousand. Don José twirls the cigar to indicate that he has no objections to such a paltry sum.

At this point, Stovall enters the conversation. There would be an additional expense, he says. Conway has a mortgage on a house in another country, Ireland. Thirty thousand dollars. It will be of great benefit if you, if Oceanaire Properties, were to pay it off. The Colombian was practically giggling. It is said, not so, that every man has his price? This one's price is *muy barato*. He is a tightfisted man, Stovall says. Dominguez asks what is the meaning of "tightfisted." Higgs translates, *apretado*. He never spends his own money, even small amounts, when he doesn't have to. Don José speaks in Spanish, then the video stops running.

"What did he say?" Edith asked.

"'Consider it done,'" Figueroa answered.

"Was it?"

"We'll show you. A video is worth a thousand words."

Betancourt ejected the disc, inserted another, and once more fast-forwarded. This footage was recorded on the thirteenth, the day Edith phoned Figueroa.

"Question. This would be day before the boat left Key West. How did you guys get the videos off of her so quickly?"

"Is that really relevant?" replied Tisdale. Which in a sense answered her—the agents had an asset on board. He delivered the diskettes. Most likely one of the crew, possibly the captain, certainly no mere deckhand.

The video began.

The scene is the same—the fantail—only now there are five men, the fifth being Michael Conway, and the time is late afternoon, cocktail hour. The waiter ferries margaritas to Don José and his guests, who are at the stern rail, conversing. Conway tells his host that the county has a cleanup campaign well underway on Astoria. He has also directed the sheriff to begin evicting the vagrants who presently occupy the island. *Excelente!* Dominguez says. What a shame for such a fine property to go to waste. The ensuing talk is inaudible; the two are speaking in undertones, and a stiff breeze further muddles their voices. The video goes blank for a second, and picks up again in the yacht's sumptuous salon, where another surveillance camera has been concealed. Oceanaire wishes to show appreciation, Dominguez declares, and hands an unsealed envelope to Conway. He opens it, peeks at the contents, and shakes hands with Don José. Your appreciation will be returned, he says. The other man offers him a cigar, which Conway sticks in his shirt pocket. *Para la buena suerte*, you know? For the good luck in your campaign.

The lights went back on. Edith sat staring at the white screen while she digested what she'd just seen: her managing editor's good friend accepting a bribe from a money launderer and narcotics trafficker.

"I'd tailed Higgs around Key West and I've got stills of him together with Conway, but no audio of him making the proposition," said Betancourt. Her golden-brown eyes sparkled. "But it's obvious he must have. We'll have Conway dead to rights if and when he shepherds that change through the zoning board."

Edith was silent. Looking back, she saw that she'd had an inkling weeks ago that the county mayor would find his way into this sleazy business. He was too close to Manny Higgs, who spread corruption like a virus and possessed an unerring ability to spot vulnerabilities in moral immune systems. He'd exploited Conway's—a small-time guy who thought of himself as a player.

There was some throat-clearing from Tisdale and Figueroa. The former said, "This investigation has a lot of moving parts. There are some sizable gaps that need filling, and the material you've turned over should go a long way to filling them. Frankly, we're a little embarrassed that we didn't discover it ourselves, but we'll take what we can get. In other words, we're grateful."

But not so grateful that you're prepared to tell me what else you're after, Edith thought.

"That judge Higgs mentioned," she said.

"Eugene Alvarez," Figueroa said.

"Anybody know why Higgs is so confident Alvarez will grant his motion and deny the government's? If he doesn't and Incroce doesn't start building, Dominguez's cronies won't be pleased with him or Higgs or anybody else in this deal, and they're not the kind of people you want to displease."

"You mean, is the judge on the payroll?" Figueroa said.

"Yeah. Or some other way Higgs has him in his back pocket. I don't think he would take a risk like this unless he had assurances beyond the judge's political views on private property rights."

"As far as we know, he's clean. Moot point anyway. None of this is ever going to end up in Alvarez's court. Let's see what happens with that zoning variance. Then we move."

She saw their play. Conway was the weak link in the conspiracy, the feds' wedge into it. If he rammed the zoning change through, consummating the bribe from Dominguez, the agents would bust him, present their evidence, and flip him.

Tisdale locked his hands behind his head. "We're keeping this investigation as watertight as a submarine," he said, swinging his chair side to side. "We'll cooperate with you if you cooperate with us. We'd appreciate it if you didn't write anything or make any more calls to Higgs's office asking for an interview. Or to anyone else involved."

She looked at Figueroa. "You didn't tap my phone. Tell me you didn't tap my phone."

"Swear on my mother's grave—and she is in hers, God bless her. We bugged Higgs's phone, heard the voicemails you left."

"He never did answer me. Nor did Stovall."

"They might suspect you're on their trail, and trying to keep their own operation watertight."

Edith placed her notebook in the briefcase. "So, we're done?"

"We are," said Tisdale.

As they filed out the door, Figueroa grasped her elbow and said quietly, "One last request. Your boss, what's his name, Lou . . ."

"It's Luke. Luke Blackburn. Way ahead of you, Gil. I didn't see what I just saw because this meeting never took place."

She felt a small, pleasant chill as his hand moved to the small of her back. "You *will* get that heads-up."

After the last camera had flashed, the last hand had been shaken and cheek kissed, and his audience dissolved like smoke in the wind, Mike Conway appeared to suffer withdrawal from the loss of the limelight. He fidgeted like a smoker who cannot remember what he did with his cigarettes. Spotting Luke about to exit with Corinne and Ian, he called to them to come have a drink with Liz and himself.

Liz frowned and said, "Oh, I'm sure they have something else they'd rather do."

"I insist," Mike declared, and he grasped Corrine's hand, all but pulling her along. "I feel like I already know you. I saw you at the exhibit the other week. I like your work."

"Thanks," Corrine said, a bit flustered. "This is . . . Ian . . . My son."

Luke had a flash of terror that Mike would say something like "Ian . . . I've heard all about you," but he confined himself to a "Pleased to meet you."

An empty table was located, drinks ordered. A southerly breeze bore opposing smells: the fresh scent of the sea, reaching out to a palisade of clouds on the horizon, and the sulfurous stench rising from the sargassum weed and bay grass rotting on the shoreline.

"So what brings you to the Keys?" Mike asked Ian after the drinks came. (Ian had ordered a Diet Coke.)

"Uh . . . Y'know, a job. Night manager at the Southwind."

"That's got to be like watching grass grow."

"Or paint dry."

"Well, you let me know if you'd like something more interesting that pays better. I'll ask around." Mike's accent had reverted to its Southy origins. "When people want something done in Monroe County, y'know who they come to? They come to me." He switched on his charming expression and his attentions to Corinne. "And you, lovely lady, you know that the Tennessee Williams Fine Arts Center is planning to hang work by local artists in the entrance?"

She answered that she did not.

"I'll put in a good word for you. Y'know who got a National Endowment grant for them?"

"I'll just bet it was you."

"I'll tell the world. I knew Tennessee back in the late seventies. I did some renovations on his house over there on Truman Avenue when I was in the business. He and I got drunk together one night. Well, Tennessee was already drunk, he was always drunk, I just caught up to him."

Luke had never seen his friend so full of himself. Liz was meanwhile sitting stiffly in total silence, pretending to show interest in the tiny paper umbrella adorning her piña colada. Whether Mike had clued her in or not was now irrelevant; she had intuited, probably at the art show, that Corinne was more than Luke's "old, dear friend." Suddenly she stood, saying she was going to the ladies'. When Corrine started to rise, as if to go with her, she displayed a chilly smile and said, "Why don't you wait here, darlin', and keep the boys company."

As she walked off and Corinne dropped back into her chair, stricken by the rebuke, Luke knew that he'd erred in relaxing his caution. While Liz's feelings toward Maureen had not improved, she identified with her as a wife. She wasn't going to legitimize infidelity and deception by politely socializing with Luke and his mistress.

Oblivious to these tensions, Mike asked if his kickoff would run in Section A of the *Examiner*, and not on its Keys News pages.

Ah! So there was the reason for the kind offers made to Ian and Corinne.

"Sure, above the fold, with the head set in banner font," Luke joked. "Like for a declaration of war."

"Far be it from me, m'boy, to take advantage of our friendship."

"Good. Because you know I can't play favorites."

23

Corrine parted with $500 of the $1,500 earned from the sale of her seascapes to buy a used Mac Powerbook. It was delivered to her door from a computer store in Miami on a late summer day when the AC, straining against the blistering heat, rattled like an old car on a steep uphill grade. She unpacked the Powerbook, placed it on a table salvaged from a yard sale, and flipped it open. Ian had helped her shop for it, advising her not to choose an older, cheaper model because the technology advanced so quickly, rendering machines obsolete in no time. A Mac, he said, was more user-friendly than a PC, less easily hacked, less frequently corrupted by something called malware. His jargon bewildered her. CD-ROM drive, RAM, Ethernet connection, megahertz and megabytes and kilobytes, hard drives and floppy drives. Considering where he'd been the past two and a half years, how had he learned all this stuff?

"There," he said. "I took a class in computer repair. They had vocational training for prisoners doing easy time."

She had so far avoided asking him about prison, figuring it to be a touchy subject, but she gave in to curiosity now.

"You said easy time. How was it easy?"

"I didn't have to live and sleep in a box the size of a closet twelve or eighteen hours a day, isolated from everybody but the guards," he said, sitting at the table, his hands clasped between his knees. "That's hard time. I got to go to Bible study and vocational classes. I got to work out in the yard. I could have books and magazines. The last three months, I was in minimum security, allowed outside the walls on a road crew twice a week. Picking up highway trash. Even that was torture, seeing the world you remembered but knowing you couldn't go into it till your time was up. Or you got paroled." There was a hardness in his voice and in his expression Corrine hadn't heard or seen before. "It was monotonous. Deadly monotonous, every day like the day before. The morning and afternoon and evening counts—that's when they make sure every inmate is accounted for. Wake up at six, lights out at eleven. And you're always on the lookout for a badass who's got it in for you for whatever reason, or no reason. Or an asshole guard who's got a hard-on for you for whatever reason, or none. There's the noise, guys yelling in Spanish and English and the smell of shit from the cell toilets and hundreds of inmates who shower maybe fifteen minutes two days a week. The hardest part was waking up. Somehow or other, when you were sleeping, your mind got wiped clean of the daily reality, and then your eyes open and you have to face it again, you have to start over, steeling yourself to face it."

"That doesn't sound easy."

"It's not, just easier than hard time. All for five grams of crystal. You know how much five grams is? One one-hundredth of a pound, a spoonful of cornflakes. But getting locked up in prison worked for me. I'll never go back inside, I'd shoot myself in the head first."

"Oh! Don't say that, Ian. Please don't say that."

"Let's drop it," he said, and stroked the Mac as if it were a pet cat. "How about I show you how to use this thing?"

She dragged a chair to the table and sat down.

"This key, the one with the semicircle with a vertical line through it? That's the on-off key. Tap it."

She did, tentatively, as if the machine contained an explosive. The screen lit up, glaring at her like a huge, square eye. Mechanical devices, even common ones like electric egg beaters and juicers, had always intimidated her. Computers took the intimidation to another level. They didn't make a sound, like egg beaters or juicers or typewriters; they didn't have a smell or taste or texture, like oil paints, canvases, turpentine, and brushes.

Ian continued his lesson. "This little arrow is called a cursor. Those little colorful doodads are icons, and this is a trackpad. . . . You mean to tell me you've never used one of these things?" The look on his face combined pity with incredulity. "Not at work or anything?"

"I waited tables and now I'm an artist. I'd like to see how well you'd do if I gave you a sketch pencil or a brush. Or a tray full of club sandwiches, this one without mayo for that guy, no bacon for the other guy, and hold the fries for the third guy."

"Why don't you practice," he said, moving his chair aside.

She sat up straight, positioned her fingers on the keyboard as best as she could remember from high school typing class, and surprised herself by producing, in a fairly short time, the well-known anagram—"The quick brown fox jumped over the lazy dog"—without an error.

"You've got it!" Ian said with a broad smile. He had a disarming smile. Meth and prison hadn't ruined his teeth. "Keep on keeping on and you'll get it all."

"Later, it's six. I'd better see to dinner. I've got red beans on the stove. That's tonight's menu—red beans and rice."

"Sounds great." He paused. "I've got a favor to ask. My parole supervisor wants to see some written proof that you're my biological mother. Have you got anything like that?"

"There's some papers in a box on my closet shelf. What does she need that for? Why didn't she ask for it earlier? Why now?"

"She didn't say and I knew better than to ask."

"You won't find a birth certificate," she said. "In those days, they destroyed the original and made a new one with the names of the adopting couple. I don't know if they still do that, but all I've got are the papers from the Registry, when I was looking for you, and some other records from then. I haven't looked at them in years. The box on the closet shelf. You can make copies if you need them."

Corinne had become a more attentive cook since Ian's arrival in her life. Re-arrival might be a better way to put it. She set the makings of the red beans and rice on simmer and the good smell followed her into the living room, where she stood in front of the AC till the sweat on her forehead dried and her skin didn't feel as if she were running a fever. The beans and the rice would be done in twenty minutes, giving Ian time to eat before he began his shift at the motel. He was getting ready; she could hear the sound, like a tea kettle's whistle, that the shower made when it had been on for longer than a minute. The lighted Mac screen was glaring at her, seemingly in challenge. She sat in front of the machine and took another stab at typing "The quick brown fox jumped over the lazy dog." Screwing up her nerve, afraid she would do something wrong, she poised her finger over the power button, then pressed it as hard as she would a doorbell. To her everlasting relief, the Mac did not explode or throw a fit. It shut down, docile as a car when you switch off the ignition.

Ian came out of his room looking buffed up and fresh in khaki pants and his work shirt, a blue knit with the word SOUTHWIND above the breast pocket. He was letting his hair grow out; that shaved skull look wasn't becoming. Corinne scooped rice into bowls and ladled the red beans over the rice; then they sat down on the living room sofa to eat from TV trays. Ian took a few bites and stared silently straight ahead, at the skylight in the angled ceiling.

"Find what you wanted?" she asked.

"Huh? . . . Oh, yeah. It's in my room."

"The papers from the Registry?"

"Uh-huh."

"They'll do?"

"Should. We'll see. I've got an appointment with her tomorrow."

He ate slowly, without any apparent pleasure and without talking. She could not account for his mood, sulky and remote, so different from what it had been less than an hour ago.

"How is it?" she asked.

"How is what?"

"Dinner. How is dinner? How is the red beans and rice?"

"Oh. Good. Guess I'm not all that hungry."

Neither of them spoke for the next three or four minutes. Finally, laying down her spoon, Corinne said, "The people I come from, when something was on their mind, you heard about it right away. Something's on your mind, cher. What is it? And don't tell me it's nothing."

Ian made a twitchy movement with his head and shoulders that might have been a shrug.

"Let me guess," she said. "Looking through those old papers reminded you. You're thinking about your parents. Feeling the grief again."

"Losing them . . . you don't get over it in a year or two or five, maybe not ever."

She stretched a hand toward him, dropping it when he didn't take it. "No one would expect you to."

"But that's not what's on my mind," he said.

She gave him a look that asked, Then what is?

"When I was going through the papers, I found one from a department, department of social services or something like that. . . . There was a date on it from before I was born, September, 1968 . . . I can get it."

"That's okay. I never told you this, but when I was expecting, the only spending money I got was from social services. Twenty dollars a month. I haven't seen that form in thirty years, but it must be the authorization to pay me. Why is that bothering you?"

Ian pushed his dinner aside and pressed his knuckles into his cheeks. "This is . . . I have to ask it. It's a hard question. Luke . . . Luke is my birth father, isn't he?"

A wave of dizziness rose, washed over her, and fell in seconds. "Of course he is! You know everything he did for me before he went to Vietnam. Do you think for one second he would have if he wasn't? Where did you get . . . ?" Remembering, Corrine stopped herself. "Oh, for God's sake. Where it asks for the father's name?"

He nodded.

"The only way I could get that miserable twenty bucks was to say I didn't know who the father was. It was a requirement, and just like you didn't ask your parole supervisor why she wants her proof, I didn't ask why I had to say that. It was totally embarrassing, made me feel trashy, but I needed the money."

Ian dipped his head.

"If you don't believe me—"

"No, I do."

"Well, in case you have any questions, you can call that department in California. I suppose it's got a different name by now, for sure a different phone number, but I'm certain you can find it and ask them if that was true then. Probably isn't anymore." She was agitated now. "Oh, hell's bells, I'll do it for you. I'll find the right department, the phone number, the name of somebody you can ask—"

He reached out to lightly touch her arm. "Corinne, yo. You've been honest with me, I'll be honest with you. I honestly believe you. That 'Father Unknown' threw me for a loop, but I honestly, hope-to-die believe you. All right? We're cool?"

"We are," she answered, though a doubt lingered.

24

After Ian left for work, she spooned leftovers into a Tupperware bowl, then washed the dishes and placed them in a drying rack. Her intention was to start a new painting in the vein of the ones Nate Rubin had bought, but the heat in the kitchen had tired her. If you can't stand it, get out, which she did. She took a cold shower, and going into her bedroom, she switched on the ceiling fan, spread a bath towel over the bed, and lay down, drying herself in the fan's breeze.

Rubin's enthusiasm for her work had aroused a hope that she might make a living, if not a life, from her art alone. A hope she declined to nurture. In the past hundred years, you could count successful female painters on the fingers of one hand. Besides, she was an anachronism, a modernist rather than a postmodernist, whatever those terms meant. Even the people who used them so freely weren't sure. She was going to have to pay rent and grocery bills somehow; her contract with the museum expired next April, the books she'd illustrated were done and scheduled to be published next month. Her share of the royalties could, with a great deal of luck, come to a thousand dollars.

The train pulling her thoughts ran her down the rails back to Ian, who probably would be gone when his probation ended. Living with his almost-fifty mother while earning his keep as a motel night manager wasn't what anyone would call stimulating. The apartment would feel empty without him; she felt an anticipatory loneliness. The train moved on, moved swiftly on to Luke. He, too, would be gone, and not in months but in a week, returning to Miami, his job, his wife. Afterward, she would see him, at most, one weekend a month, probably less. That would bring on a more acute loneliness, for she craved him as surely as she craved food or drink or breath itself. This hunger was so bound up with love that the two could not be separated. She desired him because she loved him, loved him because she desired him. The conflict in her soul was simple: she wanted him to leave Maureen and be with her, while the thought that she would steal a sick woman's husband appalled her; it stood in stark opposition to her view of herself as a fundamentally decent person, for all her early vagrancies. Practical considerations were no less daunting. Suppose he did get a divorce. Did she expect him to quit his job as well and live with her in this bizarre island city at the edge of a continent? The alternative scenario did not appeal either— her moving to Miami, where she might encounter Maureen, where she would have to meet Luke's friends and coworkers at parties or dinners and suffer their judgments, their censorious looks, for some would be sure to judge and censor her, the Jezebel, Luke's whore. She'd already tasted a sampling—that wife of Luke's friend, Liz. Liz telling her, "Why don't you wait here, darlin', and keep the boys company," with a frigid smile and in a voice that was like ground glass in a spoonful of honey, all the more cutting for its sweetness.

The thought-train shuttled her far back in time to the steamy walkup on Magazine Street where she'd lived when she was going to art school. She and Luke made love there till they were soaked in sweat. *Children, we were children playing at love*, she thought, remembering their arguments, as overheated as their sex. The worst one was over his decision to volunteer for Vietnam without speaking a word to her beforehand. "Are you fucking crazy, how can you do this?" she'd howled, and he howled back, "Afraid those hippie-dippie-yippies you run with are gonna smack you down for having a baby-killer boyfriend?" Some crap like that. She broke up with him and went for a walk on the wild side, smoking too much dope, dropping acid with those same hippie-dippie-yippies, waking up two or three times in strange apartments. If you remember the sixties, you weren't there, the saying went. And Corinne was very much there, though not for long. She sobered up, called Luke in tears, and they were soon back together.

The *thunk-thunk* of the fan overhead, wobbling on its down-rod, made her drowsy. She drifted into a state between sleep and waking, and felt a stomach-turning lurch as the bed tipped to one side and dumped her on a floor that wasn't the floor in her room. She lay on a scratchy rug in someone else's apartment; a man helped her to her feet. She vaguely recognized him, a gay guy she'd known in New Orleans. Greg? George? Gerald? He was grinning and wagging a finger at her. Spilled wine stained the rug, she could smell its sour smell. She'd been drunk or high and had passed out. Was that the reason he was scolding her?

Her eyes snapped open. She was staring up at the fan, comforted by its *thunk, thunk, thunk,* and happy to be back in her own room. Wherever her semiconscious mind had taken her, she could not have been there more than five or ten seconds, though it had seemed much longer. The vision's elements remained clear—the scratchy rug, the stench of spilled wine, the face and voice of the man, the sense that she'd embarrassed herself—and were, what's more, familiar. A memory or a dream? If the latter, then it was one she'd had before, which led her to think that she had dreamed the memory of a dream.

As the final week of his holiday from reality began, Luke retraced, and relived, his travels after he'd been wounded: by helicopter from the battlefield to the 95th Evacuation Hospital in Danang; from there across the Pacific by plane—a C130 crammed with casualties—to Travis Air Force Base, where his passage into war had started ten months earlier; and from Travis, again by helicopter, to Letterman Hospital at the Presidio.

With no written record of that period in his life, his notebooks and journal having been sent back to the States with his personal effects, he had to rely on memory, and his memory was foggy. Most of that time he'd either been in blinding pain—the rocket fragments had penetrated into bone—or in a blissful morphine haze. Hunched over his Olivetti, he recalled the C-130's cold belly, the tiered canvas cots, the soldier in the one below his dying en route; he recalled his parents' visit after he'd undergone a second round of surgery, his father hugging him and saying, "It's okay, son, it's okay," when he tried to hobble to a bathroom on crutches and broke into sobs from the pain scalding his left leg with such intensity that it felt as if it were dipped in boiling oil. He recalled the physical therapy sessions, which lasted two weeks, then graduating from crutches to a cane and outpatient status. He'd expected a medical discharge, but the US Army, like God, worked in mysterious ways and assigned him to the Public Affairs Office, where he was tasked with editing a new history of the Presidio, from its origins as a Spanish outpost to the present day. When he wasn't immersed in the activities of mounted conquistadors two centuries dead, he went into the city to search for Corinne, or word of her, a toxic compound of bitterness and loss pumping through his veins.

He pulled the typed sheet from the roller and added it to stack, which now came to one hundred and four pages, double spaced. He'd read them through yesterday, seeking but not discovering a narrative thread. At best, what he had was a series of loosely connected vignettes. Someone with a mind more acute than his might have the ability to weave them into a story and become the James Jones of Vietnam. The task was beyond him, the man with the six-hundred-word mind. Yet he was not without a sense of accomplishment; he'd set out to transcribe his scattershot notes and journal entries, and he'd done it. An inspiration had come to him last night that he could salvage something more from the effort: organize the vignettes into a narrative and present it to Ian, who was curious about his war experiences but was reluctant to ask, as Luke was reluctant to probe him for his experiences in prison. The manuscript would be a family heirloom, in a manner of speaking, like a treasured watch, or the velvet-backed case of medals Luke's father had passed on to him. Who other than Ian could he give it to?

He changed into his swimming suit, a snug, knee-length Speedo, put on his flip-flops, grabbed his goggles, and drove to the Reynolds Street Pier, feeling not loneliness but aloneness. Parents gone, no child but Ian, whom he could not truly claim as his. Still, biology did establish a connection; it also conferred a responsibility. *I should leave him something more substantial than a half-baked memoir*, he thought. Changing his will couldn't be done without involving Maureen, unless he directed his lawyer to draw up a separate document without her knowledge. But that wouldn't do either; it would weave another thread into the fabric of lies already woven.

Leaving his flip-flops in the car—left on the pier, they would be stolen—he walked barefoot over rough planks to the end of the pier, where two lovers held hands while they sunbathed. Luke stepped around them, went down a ladder into the warm water, strapped on his goggles after rubbing spit into them to prevent fogging, and pushed off toward the Casa Marina's dock. He breaststroked to loosen up before switching to a strong, smooth crawl. At low tide, the water was so quiet and limpid it was as if he were swimming through air. Four laps between the two piers equaled roughly a mile, a swim he couldn't do a month ago but now made with ease. As he finished the third lap, a school of snapper congregated around the pilings darted away in a single, coordinated movement. At first, he thought his approach had spooked them; then he threw both arms out to the side, hands backstroking to brake his forward motion. Less than two yards from him, a giant barracuda lurked in the shadows beneath the dock. Chromebright, thick as a grown man's thigh, and four feet long, it hovered over a rock pile, its long snout pointed at an opening that faced seaward, its jaws opened slightly to bare teeth like roofing nails. He knew barracuda did not attack people; yet this one communicated menace and ferocity even in repose, its black, unblinking, lifeless eyes those of an executioner who heard no appeals. Turning quickly, Luke completed the final lap in record time.

The sun was down, the lovers gone. He sat on the pier drying himself in the early evening air. He felt rather good, as he usually did after a swim, but fear lingered in his mind, like a nightmare's terror after awakening.

25

She was on the porch swing at the cottage on Catholic Lane. He hadn't expected her, which deepened his pleasure upon seeing her. She stood as he opened the front gate and gave him a wave. She'd teased her hair so that it covered her temples in tightly wound curls, and her full body was sheathed in the same caftan she'd worn at their reunion four months ago, the yellow one slit up the side to her thigh. If ever there was *une femme dangereuse*, Corinne was it, eliciting from him a crazy urge to throw himself off the cliff into a new life with her.

"This is a surprise," he said, with no attempt to hide his delight. "Been waiting long?"

"Ten or fifteen minutes." She closed the distance between them in two strides and wrapped her arms around his waist. "I knew you go swimming around five and figured you'd be back about this time if you didn't drown."

"I was going to call you as soon as I got in."

"Must have been ESP, 'cause I was going to call you before I decided to drop in. My thought is, our own private dinner dance." She turned her head to indicate the Tupperware container beneath the swing. A tape cassette was on its cover. "You'll be going soon. Carpe diem and all that."

"What's on the menu?"

"Red beans and rice. I made it for Ian last night, but he didn't have much of an appetite. It's better when it's been in the fridge for a day. All those flavors merge, cher."

While she warmed dinner, Luke went into the bedroom, got out of his damp suit, and showered off the salt water filming his skin. As he changed into shorts and a soft cotton shirt, he glanced at his BlackBerry, which he'd left on the dresser before his swim. There was the usual message from the newsroom, briefing him on the day's story budget, and an email from Maureen, sent an hour ago: "Coming home a couple days early. All is well. Arrive Friday Aer Lingus 6pm. Can't wait to see you."

He felt a deep, instantaneous letdown and was just as quickly ashamed of it, a shame doubled by a monstrous, unbidden thought—*maybe the plane will crash*. He swung his head side to side, as though to physically shake it out of his mind.

Going into the kitchen, redolent with dinner's smell, he pulled a bottle of vodka from the freezer and poured a double. Straight no chaser. Monk. No Monk, no funk—he'd presented that aphorism to Ian in one of their conversations to illustrate the jazz roots of funk-rock. Corinne was on the living room sofa, sipping a glass from his last bottle of Côte du Rhône. Luke sat next to her, his shoulders slumped, and said, "I'll be going sooner than expected." He waited for her to ask why, and when she didn't, said that Maureen was returning on Friday rather than next Monday, as planned. "That means I'll need to leave day after tomorrow."

"It couldn't wait till Thursday?"

"I'll need a day or two to . . . readjust."

"Gonna wash my pheromones right out of your hair?" She sang the question. "A woman can smell another woman on her man, and I don't mean her perfume."

"You don't seem disappointed."

"Let's have dinner. These aren't subjects for an empty stomach."

They ate at the same table with the fake porthole in its center where she'd served him gumbo, the night they'd launched their affair. Corinne had lit candles. Her lips glistened in the wavering light. Luke had an almost overwhelming urge to kiss her. He resisted, aware in a subliminal way that she was to be the choreographer in the evening's sexual dance.

The red beans and rice was as savory as promised, and when they finished, she said, "I am disappointed. More than just disappointed. But I've been preparing myself for the inevitable. It seems like you and me . . . it seems we're doomed to get ourselves into impossible situations. I never intended to—I mean that my feelings for you, they kind of ambushed me."

"You're trying to tell me something?"

"Only that I love you. I love you enough that I'm not going to make any demands. Even if Maureen wasn't . . . wasn't the way she is, I don't see how we could—I don't see how this can go anywhere."

Luke, silent, sensed what she was leading up to and dreaded hearing it.

"You told me you can't leave her. I'll take you at your word, and in case you're thinking that I want you to, I don't." Corrine went on, "I mean, I do and I don't, but more don't than do. I don't *want* you to divorce her on my account." She took a healthy swig of the Côte du Rhône and licked it off her lips. "It's because I wouldn't expect you to throw your whole friggin' life over and come down here to live with me. And because I wouldn't want to live with you up there and have to face her friends and your friends. And because I wouldn't want you to do something you'd regret later and then resent me for it. I couldn't bear it. All I want is for you to love me no matter what. There's one last because." She paused, looking for the right words. "It's like this—I heard from that art dealer today. Rubin? He's commissioning me to do some paintings for him, like the ones he bought at the show. He's positive he could sell them. He takes 40 percent of the sale price, and he'd fly me up to New York for a showing at his gallery."

"That's great, but what's it got to do with . . . ?" He stopped as it came to him. "Ah. You don't want to lose your independence."

"That sounds sort of calculating, but, yes, I suppose that's it."

"So we should end it?"

She drew back with swift, short shakes of her head like nervous tremors. "No! I couldn't bear that, either, you not being in my life. No no no no." Then she sprang up, as though she'd been startled by a noise, crossed the room to the CD/tape player, inserted the cassette, and pressed play. Fiddles, an accordion, and a triangle to keep time.

"Ian mixed this tape for me. Joel Sonnier, Sonny Landreth, Clifton Chanier. *Allons! Laissez-nous danser.*" She held out her hand, and Luke, captivated by the sudden change in her, rose and took it.

"Are you rusty?" Corrine asked.

"Sure."

"You start with your left foot, me with my right, and—"

"Long, short, short," he said.

And they began, Corrine directing him on the turnouts, he giving her a gentle assist as she stepped back on her right foot and twirled, her free hand sweeping to the small of her back. Now a double turn, the caftan's hem and wide sleeves swirling around her ankles and arms. Her movements, pure grace, bewitched Luke. He saw them in another time, dancing at Breaux Bridge and in the Jones Street apartment on their last day together.

They danced to the next tune and another and he said it *was* magic in her arms, it always had been.

"Let's go outside," she whispered when the song ended.

Two French doors opened onto a deck and the small backyard, enclosed by a stockade fence that lent a cloistered atmosphere. A light shower had fallen briefly while they were dancing, but the sky had cleared and a half moon had risen to near the zenith. The Malabar almond at the rear of the yard spread a pool of blackness, jeweled by the wet grass sparkling in the moonlight.

"You told me you get down here about once a month," Corinne said, leaning on the deck rail. "We could see each other then. You could get to know Ian a little better. I can't think of any way out for us but that. It would be enough for me. It would have to be enough for both of us. It's not right, but it's the lesser of two wrongs. Unless you have a better idea."

"It sounds like you've thought this through. You usually don't think things through." He said this affectionately.

"Guilty. But I did this time. I had to."

"I don't have a better idea," Luke said. "We'd have to be careful. No secrets on a small island, that's what Mike Conway says."

"I promise I will be. We could stay in touch with email. I have email now. I'm in the twentieth soon to be twenty-first century."

"But not to my office address. Personal emails are out of bounds. But I've got a private account. I'll give you the address."

"Does Maureen ever look at it?"

"No. She's not the kind to read other people's mail."

The greater part of him was joyful that she hadn't ended things, but another part, reflecting on the web of deceptions they would need to weave, wished she had, wished to be free of this black-haired sorceress.

"We sound like we're plotting a crime," she said. "Some people, religious people, would say that's exactly what we're doing. But love isn't a crime." She puffed her cheeks and expelled a long breath. "Kiss me, Lucas Blackburn."

Which he did. She pulled away from him and said in a half-whisper, "There, in the dark under that tree. I want to feel the grass under me."

Again, she held out her hand, again he grasped it and followed her, feeling he'd lost all powers of volition.

Luke woke up early and hungover from lovemaking: Corrine had stayed the night. He shambled into the kitchen, made coffee, and brought two cups into the bedroom. She was out of bed and dressed, anxious to get home before Ian returned from work, as if he were a ten-year-old who mustn't suspect that mommy had been naughty.

"He does know, doesn't he?" Luke asked.

"Of course. I just don't like him coming home to an empty apartment."

"Give me a sec to put some clothes on. I'll drive you."

She raised both hands to tell him that wouldn't be necessary. "I'd rather walk. It's not far. Besides, I don't want to watch you drive away. I'll never forget how it made me feel when you left, like someone was tearing my guts out."

It didn't take you long to find someone else. The thought leapt into his head, a vestigial resentment suddenly sprung back to life. Just as quickly, he squelched it and said, "I'm going to Miami, not to a war on the other side of the world. We'll be seeing each other soon."

"All the same, I'll walk it."

She kissed him and slipped out the door.

Luke threw on a pair of shorts, went outside, and watched her glide down the block till she turned a corner. Then he went back in and poured another cup of coffee and stared at the transcript of his notes on the desk. His intention, thwarted by Maureen's change of plans, had been to take the rest of the week to whip it into a narrative. Now, with an entire idle day ahead, he was seized by a compulsion to write it and present it to Ian before he left. A difficult task, but not an impossible one. He'd done stints on rewrite desks early in his career and was known for the speed with which he crafted news stories from the raw information phoned in by reporters. Sitting down at his laptop, a much faster instrument than the Olivetti, he clipped the transcript to an easel copy stand and began. He worked all morning in a caffeinated rush, took a lunch break at half past noon, then resumed. In his heyday on rewrite, he averaged fifty-five words a minute. He reckoned he was now doing forty-five, still pretty good. He wrote on automatic pilot, his fingers flying across the keyboard. Sweat trickled from his armpits, his eyes blurred, his spine felt as kinked as an old rope; but by six forty-five he was done. The computer tallied the word count at 27,458. Not bad for the man with the six-hundred-word mind.

He ran the document through spell check, made corrections, then hustled out to his car and to the Office Max in the Key Plaza mall for printing. Watching the machine spit the pages out, he marveled that he'd written so much in a little over ten hours. He thought of this whatever it was—a memoir? A reminiscence?—not only as a gift to his blood son but as his legacy. He wanted Ian and Ian's children, if he ever had any, to remember him. After the last page popped from the printer, he bought a hard-backed binder to give the manuscript a more professional appearance, printed a label, and pasted it to the cover. It read: "*Tour of Duty* by Lucas Blackburn." Not too catchy, but his word-well had been pumped dry.

Shortly after midnight, refreshed by a two-hour nap, he sat in the Southwind's utilitarian lobby while Ian checked in a couple—young travelers in faded T-shirts and shorts, carrying backpacks instead of suitcases.

"Your room is first on the left from the elevator," he said with practiced cordiality. "We serve a complimentary continental breakfast from six to nine. Enjoy your stay." Then, as the couple shuffled away: "Luke! What brings you here? Come on in." He opened the door and Luke went into the small room behind the front desk. Standing with his shoulder to a wall, he noticed two magazines on the counter, *Billboard* and *Guitar Player*, and beside them a Bible opened to the Gospel of St. Matthew.

"Those two are probably the last ones to check in," Ian said. "I won't have a damn thing to do or one damn human being to talk to for the next eight hours. But I get a lot of reading done." He pointed at the Bible and the magazines.

'Interesting combination," said Luke.

"Yeah. The Sermon on the Mount and Jerry Garcia. Funny, you

showing up. Because I was thinking of calling you. Corrine told me you're shoving off tomorrow."

Luke affirmed that he was. "Here's something for you to read."

A crease formed between Ian's eyebrows as he took the manuscript and glanced at the cover. Opening it, he read aloud, "'February 16, 1969. The first thing we noticed the instant we stepped off the plane at Ton Sa Nhut was the heat. It gave each one of us a backhanded slap in the face, and the heat shimmer rising off the tarmac was so thick it was as if a translucent curtain had dropped over the world.' What is this?"

Luke told him and added that he'd spent all day writing it, the longest piece he'd ever written in a single sitting. "It's yours to keep. It might help you to know me a little better. I know you've been curious about the war, what I did in it, and you've been decent enough not to bug me. I don't like talking about it, but I can write about it, so . . . like I said, yours. Maybe someday, if you feel like it, you could tell me what it was like for you in prison."

"Yeah, maybe. Maybe I will." Falling silent, Ian thumbed through the pages. "Man, all this in one day. Thanks. It means a lot to me, and I'm not just saying that to say it."

"I didn't write it just to write it." Luke motioned at Ian's skull. "You look better with hair, by the way."

"Oh, yeah. Sunblock, kinda, in case we go fishing again," Ian said, ruffling the short, dark strands. "Think we will?"

"Sure."

"Are you leaving right away tomorrow?"

"Not too early. What do you say we have breakfast when you get off work?"

Offering no answer, Ian closed the Bible and drummed his fingers on one of the magazines.

"Okay," Luke said. "You'll probably just want to get some sleep. I'll take a rain check."

"No, it's not that. I wasn't going to call you only to say goodbye. I've got a question."

With a movement of his head, Luke invited him to ask it.

"I go to this clinic down the road from the parole office. To get tested for drugs and alcohol. Orders from my parole supervisor. So yesterday I found out they do DNA testing there, too. I thought it would be cool if you and me took a test tomorrow before you take off."

"What the hell for?"

"It would be cool. They give you a printed report on the results. A chart, like. For me, it would be a sorta birth certificate. Corrine told me that they destroyed adopted kids' original birth certificates back in the day. It's real simple and quick. They swab your cheek with a thing like a Q-tip and you're done."

Luke studied Ian's face for a tell but saw none, which didn't necessarily mean that there wasn't more to his request than he was letting on. This young man, this son of his, a former meth dealer and an ex-con, might not always be on the level.

"And that's all? You want to have this substitute birth certificate? A chart of my DNA and yours?"

"That's it." Ian replied, spreading his hands. "I get off at eight. I could meet you there, say eight-thirty. Shouldn't take much time, you'll be on the road by nine."

"If it'll make you happy."

"It will."

"But first you've got to make me happy. You can make me happy by being straight with me."

Ian popped his lips, his eyes flitting erratically, as if tracking a house fly's sudden dips and turns. "Okay, okay. When Corrine was pregnant with me, did she collect money from the state? Sort of like a welfare payment for unwed mothers?"

Luke thought back and answered that he seemed to remember she did. Once, during the time they lived together, he went with her to the agency where she picked up the check, twenty bucks a month in his recollection.

"And she had to declare, like in writing, that she didn't know who the father was to be eligible?"

"She did, yeah, and it humiliated her," Luke said. "Is that what's behind this?"

"I was looking for some stuff and I found this old paper, like an application or something, and in the blank for father's name, it said 'unknown.' I asked her about it and she told me the same thing you just did."

"So you don't need a DNA test. You can relax."

26

Back in Miami, sitting at a staff meeting in the *Examiner*'s newsroom, Luke reflected that September might not have been the cruelest month in South Florida, but it was the hottest and the stillest, the stagnant air suffocating, the skies bleached white by a white-hot sun and the fine, pale dust borne across the Atlantic from Africa. It was the month most favorable to birthing a malign divinity, when the arid Saharan winds, mingling with the cool, wet air over the Cape Verde islands, summoned into being Hurukan, the Taino god of wind and storm.

Hurricane Andrew had greatly expanded Luke's conception of what nature could do when she set her mind to it. Homesteads had been pulverized; whole neighborhoods resembled Nagasaki after the bomb. That awesome storm was on his mind as he conferred with Nick Ortega, Alicia Reyes, and Ralph Hubbard, the photography editor. They were discussing whom to send where to cover the progress of Hurricane Floyd, almost as intense and three times as large as Andrew, on course for landfall at Cape Canaveral. Less than forty-eight hours ago, it had been forecast to make a direct hit anywhere from Palm Beach to Miami, threatening an apocalyptic disaster. Governor Bush had declared a state of emergency and ordered what turned out to be the largest evacuation in the state's history, two million people. Luke had phoned Maureen from the newsroom. When she picked up, she said, without a hello how are you, "Yes, I've heard. It's all over campus. Batten down the hatches and flee, my children!"

"Have you got your things packed?"

"I do not," she answered with an undertone of pride. "I am absolutely not going to spend a few nights in one of those dreadful shelters, like I did last time. When you get home, we'll pitch in together with the storm shutters and move the patio furniture inside and ride it out."

Luke had been too busy to argue. He'd had to cannibalize the *Examiner*'s depleted staff, pulling reporters off their assigned beats to cover the exodus on I-95 and the Turnpike, interview meteorologists, write human-interest features. Then, late last night, Floyd made an abrupt turn to the northwest, steered by a phenomenon the National Hurricane Center described as "the erosion of a subtropical ridge by an upper-tropospheric trough." It was now aimed at the Kennedy Space Center. No, *he*, Luke thought. *He* was aimed at the Space Center, for these storms had names because they had personalities, imbued with a capriciousness and a malicious intent that meteorological jargon could not dispel.

"So Mullins from sports can cover the Dolphins," Alicia was saying. The Miami Dolphins, flying home from a game against the Broncos, had been diverted to Fort Myers due to the closure of Miami International, and were now sheltered in a training camp in Davie.

"Make a great picture, wouldn't it?" said Hubbard. "Ten thousand pounds of NFL beef tucked safely into their beds. But we'll have to use wire service for art. I haven't got the people." Hubbard had lost two photographers in the latest round of staff cuts.

"Can we spare one more reporter for the Cape?" Luke asked. "Three space shuttles up there in hangars built to sustain only a Cat 2. A direct hit, say adios to NASA's whole program."

Alicia, fingers to her temples, studied the day's news budget and assignments. "The only one is Bernstein, she's closest. But we've got her on Disney World. First time ever that it's been closed because of a storm. Kind of a big deal."

"Mickey Mouse and Donald Duck aren't as big a deal as three space shuttles," Luke rejoined. "Pull her out of Orlando. I know she's a rookie. Time to get her feet wet."

Luke laughed at his inadvertent turn of phrase when Nick remarked, "Let's hope not too wet."

The special meeting of Monroe County's Board of Commissioners convened in a handsome white building with Bahama shutters that had been a middle school before it was repurposed and rechristened as the Harvey Government Center. The meeting, a raucous affair twice disrupted by angry outbursts from the crowd filling the seats and standing in the aisles, had been in session for fifteen or twenty minutes. There were enough bodies in the room—two hundred fifty, Edith guessed—to neutralize the air-conditioning. Her skirt and blouse clung to her damp skin. The five commissioners sat at the dais in front, identified by their name plates: on the right, Mr. Pinder and Mr. Carbonel, on the left, Ms. Rivera and Mr. Sawyer, and in the center, Mayor Conway, upon whose head the county seal—a ship's anchor flanked by a palm tree and a conch shell—mounted on the wall directly behind him appeared to be precariously balanced, like a large ball on a small one. Manny Higgs occupied a chair to one side of the commissioners, reacting to the crowd's unruliness sometimes with a blank expression, sometimes with a smile whose faintness did not conceal its smugness.

Normally, covering commissioners' meetings fell to the *Examiner*'s Keys correspondent, but Edith had taken this one. She needed to. The day before yesterday, after the hurricane crisis had passed, Luke and Nick Ortega had summoned her to a conference room for a private talk. Scowling, tapping a notepad with a pencil, Ortega led off: she'd been working on her investigative story since May, it was now mid-September. When could they expect to run it? Probably by the end of the month, she answered. The FBI had requested her to delay publication till they were ready to bring charges.

"You agreed?" the editor asked.

His unstated criticism registered with Edith: wouldn't it look better for the *Examiner* if a story it broke led to arrests and indictments rather than the other way around?

"They're keeping this one super-secret. They don't want to get burned."

"What guarantees that they won't burn us?"

"I made a deal. I delay to protect their investigation, they give me a heads-up well ahead of time to protect my exclusive. Ironclad."

"I'd like to think so, but do we really need them?"

"Hell, yes," she said emphatically. "For credibility and for a whole lot of other reasons I can't go into right now. I've written up a rough of B-matter. All the stuff they've uncovered so far—they've been updating me almost on a daily basis—and the stuff I dug up on my own. Announcement of the charges will be the lede. I've got enough for follow-ups, three thousand words minimum with a few hundred more for sidebars to season the stew." Edith paused. She hadn't broken her promise to Gil Figueroa not to reveal what had transpired at the meeting, but she was coming close. She went into a sales pitch to distract the editors from asking more pointed questions that might put her on the spot. "I'm on the inside, guys, and it's going to be big, big. Hundreds of millions in Colombian drug profits scrubbed clean through international banks and ultimately through Incroce's corporation. Expect him and a dozen others to be indicted for money laundering, bribery, racketeering, conspiracy."

"Who are these others?" Luke inquired.

"I don't know yet," she lied. "I should pretty soon."

Luke then asked to see the B-matter. Edith hesitated. The B-matter—journalese for background information—included an account of the surveillance video showing Michael Conway accepting a bribe from the Cali cartel's chief laundryman.

"It's all rough notes, Luke," she lied again. "It would raise more questions than it answers. Give me a few days to polish it up."

He looked briefly at his reflection in the glass-topped table, then up at her, skepticism fogging his greenish eyes. They went back a long way; he could tell when she was withholding something.

"All right," he said, letting it go. "When can I have a look at it?"

"Uh. Next week?"

"Good enough. Meantime, can you file something, *anything*? It would be good to see your byline again. For us and for *you*," he added.

She nodded to acknowledge that she understood what wasn't said. At this late stage in her career, she was where she'd been as a rookie: she had to prove her worth.

"There's a county commissioners meeting on Friday. It'll be relevant."

"Relevant how?" Ortega asked.

"They're going to discuss amending the county's Comprehensive Plan to allow zoning variances on offshore islands, including Astoria. I can cover the meeting unless Kristen objects to me horning in on her turf."

"She won't," Luke said. "Those things are usually as boring as watching test patterns."

Test patterns? Was he old enough to remember those?

"I'll bet this one won't be."

And it hadn't been. After Conway announced the sole item on the agenda, the room sounded like a rowdy ballpark. Boos, hisses, shouts. Ignorant as the protestors were of the intrigues and machinations between and among Conway, Stovall, Higgs, and Dominguez, they knew instinctively that a fix was in.

When the racket died down, Conway opened the meeting to public discussion. Hands shot up and people jostled each other as they got into line to speak into a podium microphone in the aisle between the rows of seats. A scrubbed woman belonging to an environmental group, SOK, for Save Our Keys, delivered a five-minute address on keeping the last remaining undeveloped land in Key West free from asphalt and concrete. Polite applause. A tall man, long-haired, bearded, and scarecrow thin, stepped up, gave his name as Zodiac, described his profession as "energy healer," and cried out, "This is bullshit! The county can't rezone public land!" Cheers, howls of approval, Conway calling for quiet and more decorous language. Higgs, speaking in dry, lawyerly tones, pointed out that the island's public nature was arguable, but whether it was private or public, its zoning fell under county jurisdiction. "Conflict of interest!" the man yelped, pointing a scrawny finger at Higgs. "You represent the developer and the county, that's conflict of interest!" One of his cheerleaders hollered, "Sure as hell is, but then, this is Florida!" More hoots, sarcastic laughter.

Edith recorded the exchanges in her notebook. She was sitting in the front row, reserved for the press. When she looked up, she noticed Higgs staring straight at her with his bulging eyes. It was like being stared at by a fish. She returned the stare, but with a mischievous sparkle. He shifted his gaze to a blowsy blonde who, caressing the microphone like a torch singer, accused Conway of betraying his constituents and his own legacy. "You wrote the Comprehensive Plan, you said you wanted to stop runaway growth, and now you're ramming this down our throats. Shame on you!" A band of people seated near her began to stamp their feet and chant, "Shame! Shame! Shame!" until Conway had them ejected by a sheriff's deputy.

After the pandemonium sputtered out, a vote was taken. The measure passed 4-1, Commissioner Rivera the single dissenter. Edith assumed Conway had dispensed favors to the other three to vote his way; whether he had or not, he'd voted yes, thus consummating the bribe presented by José Dominguez. She stood, tugged the skirt plastered to her rear end and thighs, and joined the procession of grumbling citizens exiting the

room. Outside, as she passed between two stately banyans standing senti-
nel on either side of the front walk, someone tapped her on the shoulder
from behind. Turning, she saw that it was Higgs.

"I saw you in the press section, but I don't think we've met," he said.
"Manny Higgs." They shook hands. He had a limp grip, but maybe
he'd relaxed it because she was a woman. "I try to get acquainted with
members of the fourth estate. You are?"

"Edith Buchmayr. With the *Examiner*."

"Oh? Where's Kristen?"

"On another assignment. I'm filling in. Pleasure to meet you, Mr.
Higgs."

"It's Manny. I recognize your name. You left me a bunch of voice
mails last month. Sorry for not answering. I was tied up."

"No problem."

"If you've still got questions, I'd be happy to answer them now.
Care to have lunch?"

She was tempted, very tempted; but instincts honed over a career
spanning nearly four decades told her to decline.

"I'm on the two o'clock shuttle to Miami," she said.

"It's only eleven forty-five," Higgs said, looking at his watch. "A
quick bite, then I could get you to the airport in plenty of time."

"I'll take a raincheck."

"Suit yourself." He took a business card out of his front pocket and
handed it to her. "In case you lost my number."

Edith taxied to the airport, checked in, grabbed a wretched sandwich in the lounge, then sat down in the waiting area with her laptop
and began to write her piece.

The Monroe County Board of Commissioners, in a special meeting often disrupted by irate citizens, voted yesterday to amend
the county's rate of growth ordinance to allow large-scale resort
and housing developments to be built on privately owned offshore

islands in the Florida Keys. The amendment's provisions will apply to Astoria Island, a controversial piece of prime real estate less than one mile from Key West.

Before a packed audience of 250, the measure passed by a vote of four to one. It changes zoning from the current one structure per two acres to one structure for every half-acre. The Commission has thus cleared one of the obstacles facing a developer who has proposed a $250 million luxury resort for Astoria. Thomas Incroce, CEO of Miami-based TBI Corporation, must however overcome another, bigger hurdle before construction can begin.

The United States government claims it owns the island, while Incroce says he does, basing his claim on, among other things, the 1955 sale of the island to a colorful Keys politician, Samuel Lowe, who in turn passed it on to Incroce's father, Thomas Sr., to settle a gambling debt. The sale to Lowe was made by the state of Florida, which the federal government contends was invalid because the state did not own Astoria.

Earlier this year, the younger Incroce appealed a decision by a federal district court that the 30-acre island is federally owned. The appeal was denied, but the appellate court's decision was made on narrow grounds applying only to the merits of Incroce's appeal. It did not settle the issue of who has clear title to Astoria.

That will be decided on October 11th, when Judge Eugene Alvarez in US district court in Miami hears motions filed by both Incroce and the federal government asking for a summary judgment on the island's ownership. Incroce's company is represented by the firm of Higgs, Albury, and Fernandez. Manuel Higgs, its senior partner, is also Monroe County attorney.

Higgs. Edith paused and fought the urge for a cigarette. She'd quit fifteen years ago, but the cravings returned every so often. *Higgs*. She'd turned down his invitation without knowing why, beyond a warning buzzer in her head that she'd learned to listen to even if she could not articulate why it was buzzing. The reason came to her now, as she watched a man and woman tow roll-aboards up to the ticket counter: Higgs had somehow gotten wind of what she was up to. Given his prominence and widespread connections from Key West to Tallahassee, that wasn't a shock. Probably he hadn't heard anything too specific, a hint here or there, a vague rumor floating in the air, yet enough to set off a buzzing in *his* head. The fish-eyed lawyer had been on a fishing expedition for firm intelligence, and who better to get it from than she? Taking his courtroom skills into account, he could have tricked her into dropping a wrong word or two that would have blown the cover on both investigations, hers and the FBI's.

27

Luke was in his office, reading Corinne's latest email. Her introduction to the digital age had made her a prolific correspondent. The mode of communication lent itself to her impulsive nature. She sent two or three a day almost every day, writing whatever popped into her mind at a given moment in short, choppy sentences that skipped from topic to topic. Her messages varied from the chatty to the tenderly romantic to the pornographic. The one he received on Friday afternoon (about the time Edith was boarding her flight) fell into the X-rated category. He deleted it, as he had all her others. They came to his personal account, which no one but he ever looked at, but he thought it prudent not to leave an electronic trail.

Later, Alicia Reyes showed him the story budget for the Keys section, which she was in charge of. Edith's account of the commission meeting led. Luke was giving it a quick look when Mike Conway phoned.

"Your ears must have been burning. I was just reading about the commission meeting," Luke said.

"Were you now?" replied Mike. He added that he and Liz had flown up to Miami that afternoon for a campaign fundraiser. Kicked off at seven at the Omni. Could Luke and Maureen make it?

"Kind of short notice," Luke said, wary of regenerating the friction between the two women, and of the chance that Liz's tongue might slip.

"I know, m'boy, but we'd love to see you there. Movers and shakers will be."

Angling for the *Examiner*'s endorsement? Luke asked himself. "Really can't do it. You know Maureen and her schedules, and besides, I've got a newspaper to put out. If you'd called earlier—"

"How about drinks before it starts?" Mike persisted. "I always run better with lubrication. Five thirty, the lobby bar?"

Luke glanced at the row of clocks on the newsroom wall showing the times in half a dozen world capitals. Conway's insistence, combined with what he'd read in Edith's piece, her reluctance to disclose the targets of the FBI's probe and to show him her background material, brought on an uncomfortable sensation. It felt like a worm crawling around inside his chest.

"Make it six and I can stay for one only," he said.

"All we'll have time for."

The Omni Hotel, a great block of concrete and glass towering over a shopping mall on Biscayne Boulevard, wasn't far from the *Examiner* building. Covering a city block, it was in decline as newer, splashier malls sucked business away, so Luke had no trouble finding a space in the parking garage. He locked his car, followed the signs to the hotel entrance, then made his way to the lobby bar, all sleek and shiny, if a bit dated. It belonged to the eighties, the decade of cocaine cowboys and *Miami Vice*. He found Mike and Liz seated at a glass table between two sofas.

Looking smart in a striped poplin jacket and tie, Mike jack-in-the-boxed out of his seat and pumped Luke's hand—"Hey! Glad you could make it!"—while Liz, rising slowly, extended hers, bent at the wrist as if to be kissed, and said, "So nice to see you again, Luke." Her hair was pinned up, its gray streak lending an appearance of graceful maturity rather than age.

Luke sat down, facing the couple.

"What're you drinking, m'boy? On me, I insist."

"Bombay martini."

"I'll join you! And you, my darling?"

"A chardonnay. And don't you drink all of that 'tini. You need to be coherent."

"It takes more than one to trip this tongue."

Mike placed the order with an auburn-haired waitress. He flirted with her a little, asking if anyone had ever told her that she was a dead ringer for Carly Simon, except for her hair color.

"You're the second one so far and my shift just started," she said, pleasantly. "I'm going to start giving autographs."

The three friends bantered while they waited for their drinks. Carly's twin delivered them and Mike congratulated her for not spilling a drop. She said the secret was not to look at them but only where you were going.

"Cheers," Luke said, hoisting his glass. "And good luck tonight. Funny coincidence, you phoning just as I was reading about the commission meeting. Sounds like you had a lot of pissed-off citizens to deal with."

"Citizens? Tree-huggers and dirtbags."

"Uh-huh." Luke swirled the olives in his martini. A line in Edith's story had been floating around the edges of his consciousness for the past couple of hours. He decided to bring it up. "Our reporter mentioned that the vote paves the way for more development, particularly on Astoria Island."

"It could. What about it?"

"A while back you told me that the county's involvement in that whole deal was peripheral. Doesn't changing the zoning sort of deepen its involvement? And doesn't it . . . uh . . . undermine the Comprehensive Plan, which you, you know, championed?"

Mike flicked droplets of gin from off his mustache—it needed a trim—and scoffed. "Undermine it? That's pretty strong. Number one, the zoning applies only to offshore islands in private hands. There aren't many of those, and ninety percent of 'em are unbuildable anyway.

Nothing but mangrove. Number two, as far as Astoria goes, no building permits can be issued until there's a ruling on who owns the damn thing. We go back a long way, so I'll level with you. I hope the judge rules for Incroce. You've seen that island—a dirtbag campground. I'd like to see it developed. It would expand the county's tax base, and we need the money."

"What I meant was—" Luke started, but Mike was on a tear.

"When I get to Tallahassee, I'm going to push for state aid for tertiary treatment plants in the middle Keys. Right now, all they've got are cesspits and all that shit."

"Be sure to say fecal material tonight," Liz cut in.

Mike chuckled. "But it's shit among us friends. All that shit is flowing out to the reef and helping to kill it. You should dive on it, Luke. I did last week with a biologist. Dead coral by the acre! Some of it from global warming, but some of it from pollution. The county can't expect the state to pay full freight, we've got to come up with our own dollars for the treatment plants, and those come from the tax base."

Luke searched for a reply besides "I'm fully aware of that." Liz looked at her watch and said that it was six twenty, they should be in the ballroom by seven forty-five. The reminder was a cue; Mike squared his shoulders, cleared his throat.

"A confession, m'boy. We didn't want to get together just for social reasons. I could use a favor."

"I had a feeling. And I've also got a favor to ask. Would you mind dropping the 'm'boy'? It sounds like I'm your son."

"I've been calling you that for years. I didn't know it bothered you."

"Mike, please," Liz said, tapping her watch with a fingertip. "Save it for later."

"All right. That reporter you had covering the meeting today."

"Edith Buchmayr."

"Her. Is she on some kind of crusade? A few months ago, she did a story about how she found a letter from Calvin Coolidge that proved

Astoria was the property of the US government. And then another story that the Florida sale of it was illegal. The Coolidge letter helped queer Incroce's appeal. It was introduced in court. Calvin Coolidge, holy Mary. Why not go back to Abraham Lincoln?"

"She's not on a crusade," Luke said as a cold tingling scampered up his arms into his neck and then into his face. "What's the favor?"

"We've known each other a long time. We've fished together, broken bread together, hell, we even helped rescue stranded refugees together."

"Mike, the favor."

"Okay. Running for the state senate, it's raised my profile quite a bit. I'm a target. The Republicans are looking to smear me, and I've heard, only heard, haven't confirmed it, that they're using this Edith person to do their oppo research for them. And the whole Astoria development and TBI are some way tied up with it. So, I'd like to know—"

"Nobody but nobody uses Edith Buchmayr for anything. If Jesus Christ wanted oppo research on the devil, she'd tell him to piss off. Good enough?"

"But what's her interest in Astoria? Seems to me it's a story for the business section."

The cold tingling burned now; it was like touching steel that had been in a freezer.

"You know I can't tell you what she's working on."

"Yeah, yeah," said Mike. He produced a mirthless grin. "Thought I'd give it shot. But if you hear of anyone dragging my name through the mud, or if the paper is going to—damn, this is awkward—to run a piece that my opponents can use to make me look bad, let me know. Forewarned is forearmed, like they say."

"Mike, if I hear anything on the street, sure," Luke said, checking his indignation. "But if it's something my reporter digs up, she'll ask for your comments, your reaction. But I can't tell you before then. You know that. I'm not a political operative."

"But you *are* his friend," Liz said, flint in her voice, the glare in her brown eyes anything but friendly. "A favor to repay one—we have been discreet, very discreet, about your indiscretions."

Mike shot her a sidelong glance; she'd gone too far.

"Liz, I'll pretend you didn't say that." Luke stood and dropped a ten on the table. "I like to pay my own way."

"Hey, hey, Liz didn't mean—"

"It's six forty. You two better hurry upstairs."

Maureen had a light schedule on Fridays, which had given her time to prepare one of her artful creations for dinner: chicken breast cordon bleu, potatoes au gratin, asparagus done in olive oil and sprinkled with parmesan. Luke was too agitated to do anything but pick at his meal. She asked if he found it not to his taste. Looking at her and the play of candlelight on her face, asking himself, *Why can't I love this woman as I should?* he replied that dinner was fine, excellent, actually.

"Well, something's the matter," she said.

He gave an abbreviated account of the conversation with Mike and Liz, redacting Corrine as well as Liz's final comment.

"Presumptuous of him, playing on your friendship like that," Maureen said. "You'd think he'd know better."

"That's more or less what I told him. I half expected him to ask me to kill any story that reflected badly on him." Luke rolled up his napkin and lay it on the table. "Something's bubbling that I ought to know about. I'm going to phone Edith. I'll do the dishes later."

"Oh, I'll get them."

He went into the den that also served as a home office, a room he was fond of, with floor-to-ceiling bookcases covering two walls, an arched window on another, and on the fourth—which Maureen had dubbed "The Wall of Fame"—awards and honors, photographs of high points in his career: a youthful Luke with Israeli soldiers on the Golan Heights, a somewhat older Luke in a sweat-mottled shirt somewhere in El Salvador, a still older Luke shaking hands with Bill Clinton at a White House reception. He sat down in the slot in his U-shaped desk and opened his laptop to retrieve Edith's home phone number from his address book. He saw a message that he'd received an email. He clicked on it. Another from Corinne, sent fifteen minutes ago.

```
Hi, baby. Missing you. a lot. Home alone.
Ian playing gig tonight. dont know about
this arrangement. My idea but dont know if
can do indefinitely. Miss you. Want you. Hope
all ok. Luv 'n lust, C.A.T.
```

The frequency and nature of these communications were beginning to trouble him. After answering—*Miss you too. I can't write much tonight. Busy with work. Love, LB*—he deleted both her email and his reply, then called Edith at her condo and said he needed to speak to her right away.

"I'm here and wish I wasn't. Do you know any age-appropriate men? Anyway, I'm listening."

"In person at my house. And bring that background we talked about. I want to have a look at it."

There was a short pause before she spoke. "I thought we'd agreed to next week. It needs fixing up."

"Bring it as is."

"I'm tired, it's been a long day. What's going on?"

"I'll tell you when you get here."

"Give me half an hour," she said.

Maureen answered the door. Luke heard her exclaim, "Hello, Edith! Don't you look marvelous! Luke's in the sanctum sanctorum." She ushered the reporter into the den, then left her and Luke alone. Edith had freshened her lipstick, brushed her hair, and had exchanged whatever she'd been wearing at home for chic white slacks and a sky-blue blouse, accessorized with a pearl necklace and a jeweled bracelet. Edith Buchmayr never failed to leave her front door without looking

her best. Luke shut the door and sank into one of two club chairs, gesturing to Edith to take the other. She sat with her knees tightly together,
a manila folder in her lap, a pinched look on her face. He then told
her about what had transpired between him and the Conways, again
deleting Liz's veiled threat.

"Mike was probing me. He knows something is going on, but not
exactly what," Luke said. "Neither do I, and I should."

"Higgs has blips on his radar screen too," Edith said. "He cornered
me after the commission meeting. I had the distinct impression he was
hoping to get me to spill something that would help him identify the
UFOs."

"And I had the distinct impression that Mike is in this mess with
both feet. Is he?"

Edith sucked in a breath and let it our slowly, her pinched, pained
expression deepening. "I really wanted to save this till next week, but—"
She removed the papers in the folder and passed them to Luke. "It
starts on page five, third graf," she said.

He shuffled through the pages and began to read her description of
the surveillance videos made aboard the yacht *Island Princess* in August.
The account continued through page seven. Finishing there, Luke lay
his head back with closed eyes. He looked like a marathoner at the end
of a race. His friend had sold himself out and compounded the grubbi-
ness of the sale by making it on the cheap.

"Son of a bitch," he murmured, feeling betrayed. He'd noticed
that the get-together on the yacht had taken place on August 13 and
recalled that Mike had begged off on the fishing trip with him and Ian
because he had a meeting that day. Some meeting that had been.

"So much for his civic-minded bullshit about treatment plants to
save the reef from pollution. And all for what? Thirty thousand bucks."

"Plus ten for campaign expenses," Edith said.

He looked at her. "You've known about this for over a month. You
kept it from me because you didn't trust me not to clue him in?"

"I did trust you and still do," she said earnestly. "But I'd promised my FBI sources not to breathe a word of it. To you or anybody."

"You work for the *Examiner*, Edith, not the Federal Bureau of Investigation."

"I'm aware of that," she retorted, a flash in her eyes. "I *was* going to show this to you. It's all coming to a head next week. The Feebies are going to bust everybody then. My guess is they're going to offer Conway a deal—immunity if he testifies against Higgs and Stovall. They've got a lot on those two, but they don't have them actually soliciting him to take the bribe."

Luke said nothing. He gazed out the window, which framed a portion of Maureen's flower garden, illuminated by the tiny lights planted the edge of the bed.

"You know him better than I do," Edith said. "Think he'll take it or will he play standup guy?"

"He might try stonewalling. Way back when I first got to know him, he told me that he'd been a juvenile delinquent in South Boston and that his ambition then had been to be a gangster. Maybe he never quite got over it. If he was dumb enough to risk everything for forty thousand, he may be dumb enough to tell the feds to take their deal and shove it."

"The zoning change. Without the quid pro quo, he probably could be charged with accepting an illegal gratuity and get two years max. With it, he'd be looking at up to fifteen. That'll be their offer—an illegal gratuity. It might change his thinking."

"You said they've got a lot on Higgs and Stovall. What?"

"It's in there." Edith pointed at the report in his lap, twenty-two double-spaced pages. "I'll summarize. Higgs and Stovall had been mixed up with Dominguez for three or four years. Stovall was scrubbing cartel money in small amounts—what that world considers small. He'd take a chunk of cash to a casino in the islands, buy chips, play the tables for a little while, then cash in the chips for a check. The check goes to a bank account registered to a fictitious person and represented as gambling winnings, Stovall takes a cut for his services. A little while later, he teams up with Higgs and they start washing bigger sums through Higgs's law firm and a kinky lawyer Higgs is partnered with on Grand Cayman. The technique is called 'round-tripping.' How it works is in the story, but I can give you the nuts and bolts now if you want."

"Later. Go ahead."

"Meanwhile, Higgs picks up TBI Corporation as a client. It runs into financial trouble; Incroce can't find anyone legit to loan him development funds. About the same time, three hundred mill arrives in Cayman from Colombia in a King Air twin. Every dollar in cash. About fifty gets laundered, but Dominguez literally doesn't know what to do with the rest. Wouldn't we all love to have a quarter of a billion we don't know what to do with? Stovall introduces Dominguez to Incroce, Higgs and his crooked pals in the other firm set up a complicated network of shell companies. The two fifty eventually is channeled through them to Oceanaire Properties and through it to the Chase Manhattan branch in Miami, and finally to TBI, disguised as loans. That's the history of the scheme in a nutshell."

Luke nodded.

"All those people in the islands are going to be indicted, in absentia, of course," Edith continued. "A couple of bank execs on Grand Cayman, another one on Aruba, and Dominguez. The Feebies would have loved to collar him when he came here on his yacht, but they needed to get those surveillance videos without alerting anyone that they were on to what was up. Oh, yeah. I'm told that at least one VP at the Chase Manhattan branch in Miami is also going down."

"So Mike is . . ."

"A minnow in a net full of sharks," Edith said.

"You told me and Nick day before yesterday that you gave some to the FBI to get some. What did you give?"

"Remember the boat ride I took to see Filthy Fred? The photocopies of transactions and communications between TBI and Oceanaire. Earlier in their investigation, the feds had tried to get a warrant to search Incroce's offices and safe-deposit box, but they lacked probable cause. The stuff I handed over gave them the probable. They'll execute the warrant, get the originals and then some, and arrest Incroce. Personally, I think the copies would have passed muster as evidence, but—"

"They don't want it known that they relied on a reporter," Luke said, completing the sentence for her.

"I'd say so, yes. So what?"

"So make sure you give yourself and the paper credit in your piece."

"Do you think for one second I wouldn't? Christ on a crutch, Luke."

His earlier, somber emotions had ebbed somewhat; a heat in his blood was rising in their place. Edith's story was going to be as big as she'd advertised, and the *Examiner* would have it exclusively. What every newsman and newswoman lived for. A scoop. And if there was any justice in the universe, this one would guarantee her job till she had a mind to quit.

"All right, when can we break it?" he asked.

"I'm told that the feds have scheduled a press conference for no later than a week from today. I'll get advance notice and have the first story and follow-ups set in type, ready to run."

"We don't set type anymore," Luke said, joking.

"An expression," she said, with the faintest of smiles.

28

**MONROE COUNTY MAYOR, ATTORNEY, MIAMI DEVELOPER
ARRESTED IN FEDERAL PROBE OF MONEY-LAUNDERING,
BRIBERY SCHEME
6 OTHERS CHARGED. ALLEGED ATTEMPT TO CLEAN $250M IN
DRUG PROFITS THROUGH KEY WEST DEVELOPMENT**

By Edith Buchmayr

In what promises to be one of the biggest political and financial scandals to strike Florida in years, FBI agents on Friday arrested Thomas B. Incroce Jr., a prominent Miami developer, Monroe County attorney Manuel Higgs, and the county mayor, Michael J. Conway, for their roles in a scheme to launder $250 million in Colombian drug cartel profits by investing the funds in a proposed upscale development on an offshore island near Key West.

Also caught up in the alleged plot were José Dominguez, described by law enforcement officials as "the chief laundryman for the Cali cartel," and a colorful lobbyist and political fixer, Roy K. Stovall, who lists himself as "the Devil's Disciple" in the phone book.

Dominguez remains free in the Cayman Islands, where he lives. The US government is seeking his extradition.

Incroce was arrested in Miami when the FBI, acting on a search warrant, raided his safety deposit box and found a trove of incriminating documents showing transactions between his company, TBI, Inc., and Oceanaire Properties. According to federal law enforcement sources, Dominguez operates the Cayman Islands firm as a front for channeling illicit cartel profits into legitimate businesses in the United States and the Caribbean.

Copies of the documents were first obtained by the *Miami Examiner* from a source close to Incroce and turned over to the FBI. The *Examiner* had been conducting a parallel investigation into TBI's plans for developing Astoria Island, a 30-acre spoil island about a mile west off Key West. It has been at the center of a dispute between Incroce, who planned to build an upscale resort on Astoria, and the federal government, each claiming ownership of it.

County attorney Higgs, 47, was seized at his home in Key West's exclusive Truman Annex and charged, along with Incroce and Stovall, with money laundering, conspiracy, and bribery under the provisions of the Racketeer Influenced and Corrupt Organization Act (RICO). The same accusations were leveled against Dominguez.

Conway, 54, who is running as a Democratic candidate for the state senate, was charged separately with accepting a bribe from Dominguez to amend the county's zoning regulations to accommodate the proposed Astoria development. Apparently, Conway was forewarned that law enforcement was closing in. He was taken into custody at Key West airport as he was attempting to flee to Ireland with his wife, Elizabeth.

In August, an FBI surveillance camera captured Conway, on board a yacht registered to Oceanaire Properties, taking $30,000 from Dominguez to satisfy a lien on a house he owns in Ireland, and an additional $10,000 contribution to his senate campaign. The list of alleged coconspirators includes Frank Sandoval, executive vice president of Chase Manhattan Bank in Miami, and four bank executives in Grand Cayman and the island of Aruba. Extradition requests have been filed to bring the four to the United States for trial. They are . . .

Luke watched the home-delivery edition—the "main sheet"—rolling off the huge offset rotary machines in the thunderous press room—60,000 papers per hour. He wasn't required or expected to be here; he'd made it a ritual to witness the press run whenever the *Examiner* broke a big story. The moment when the operators cranked the idling machines up to full speed and the enormous rolls of newsprint, each weighing as much as a rhinoceros, were fed into the webbing system thrilled him; the noise, the smells of paper and ink and an odor he couldn't quite define—it was like the interior of a vast hardware store—penetrated his skin, flowed with his blood, became a part of him.

He went into the mailroom, where the editions were stacked and bundled and sent flying down conveyor belts to the loading docks, grabbed a paper, and returned to the newsroom to show it to Edith.

Head down, she was working on tomorrow's follow-up.

"Looks good," he said. "Two columns on A-1, two more on the jump."

Pushing her chair away from her desk, she examined the front page carefully. Her story ran alongside a color photo of FBI agents perp-walking a manacled Manny Higgs out of his pastel mini-mansion in Key West. Black-and-white head shots of Stovall and Mike Conway illustrated the jump on page three.

"Kudos, Edith. You're journalism's best-dressed terrier."

She let out a quick laugh. "I like to think of myself as a bitch Rottweiler."

"What's on tap?" he asked, nodding toward the computer screen.

"Two pieces. The long one is a backgrounder on the investigation, how the paper triggered the investigation and teamed up with the feds. The other is a straight-ahead news story. Higgs, Stovall, Conway saying the usual things. Nothing to these charges, look forward to clearing my name, blah blah. All three are lawyered up. Word is Conway's open to a bargain."

Luke shook his head. "What the hell was he thinking?"

"He wasn't, that's the problem," Edith said.

The story led the nightly news on the network affiliates; it was picked up by the *Palm Beach Post*, the *St. Petersburg Times*, and the *South Florida Sun-Sentinel*, among others, all crediting the *Examiner*, all sprinting to catch up—without much success. Edith had virtually every angle covered. Her follow-ups ran for four days. The *Columbia Journalism Review* published a profile of her—the tenacious veteran who'd shown that pounding the pavement and knocking on doors still counted, that print journalism still had value in the digital age. The effect on the newsroom's slumping morale was electric; reporters and editors who'd had nothing to do with the story seemed to walk a little taller, a little straighter. They worked for Florida's biggest and best newspaper, the paper that had exposed corruption and the influence of a drug cartel on the state's politics. There was talk that Edith would win her second Pulitzer. She shrugged it off, though not from a sudden onset of humility. It was enough for her to continue practicing her craft till her hands or her eyes or her brain failed her.

Conway had taken a shovel to the hole he'd been in by lying to FBI agents the day of his arrest: he denied he'd accepted a bribe to change the zoning regulations. When the agents showed him the surveillance video, they presented their offer: The charge of making a false statement would be dropped and he would be granted limited immunity on the bribery charge if he pled guilty to a lesser offense and agreed to testify against Higgs, Stovall, and Dominguez. He copped the plea, just as Edith had predicted.

Watching footage of him leaving federal court after his arraignment had given Luke a physical pain—a stabbing sensation in his chest. Holding hands with Liz, Mike swaggered and flashed a cocky smile for the cameras. The bluff was plain to anyone who knew him as well as Luke did. Liz's tight-lipped expression was harder to read, composed as it was of equal measures of sadness, anger, and shame. It disturbed Luke more than her husband's false bravado; it was the look of a woman wronged. But by whom?

Two days later, Mike announced that he was ending his campaign; then he holed up in his house on Caroline Street.

When a TV station aired a spot calling attention to the irony of Conway being friends with the managing editor of the paper that had ruined his political career, Ortega urged Luke to write an op-ed describing the relationship. When had it begun? What kind of man was Michael Conway? It was known that he'd done a great deal of good for the Florida Keys. He'd been a conservationist, a preservationist, and polls showed him leading his opponent by eleven points. Why had he jeopardized his reputation and his future for so little? And then there was the matter of his, Luke's, own moral dilemma. Faced with a choice between betraying a friend or betraying a trusted reporter, not to mention the ethical standards of his profession, he'd chosen the former. What had that been like for him? Luke thought he could answer those questions, but he turned the assignment down; it seemed exploitative.

Mid-October brought longed-for relief from the cloying summer heat. Mild breezes drifted down from the north. Migrating harriers and broad-winged hawks appeared in the sky, and on the roads snowbirds started arriving early for the winter. The scandal was off the front pages; the scraps had been vacuumed up by media bottom feeders. José Dominguez was fighting extradition; Higgs, Stovall, and Incroce were to be tried separately, with Higgs going first in early December. Conway was expected to testify for the prosecution at all three trials. Until then, Edith had little to do. She had booked herself into a hotel on Mallorca for a vacation well and truly earned.

Three days before her scheduled departure, at a little past 6:00 p.m., her phone rang as she was collecting her things to leave the newsroom and meet some friends at a South Beach bistro. The caller ID on the tape recorder plugged into her phone displayed a number she did not recognize. For a moment or two, she considered not answering; her friends had arranged a blind date with a man who they said met specs: the right age, successful, reasonably good-looking, divorced.

But she could not resist taking the call.

"Hello. Edith Buchmayr."

"Good evening, Mrs. Buchmayr, Miami's own Lois Lane," said a male voice with a distinct Yankee accent, pronouncing Buchmayr as Buchmyah.

"Is this—?"

"Michael Conway. I'm talking to you from my car in the parking lot. The parking lot of your newspaper. I'm in a visitor's space. Wouldn't dream, oh, I'll tell the world, I wouldn't dream of stealing a reserved spot."

He sounded drunk. Edith sat down and instinctively grabbed a ballpoint and her notebook.

"What is it, Mr. Conway?"

"My story. My side of it. I want you to listen to it and to write it, Mrs. Buchmayr."

"It's Ms. Buchmayr. But Edith is fine with me."

"In that case, call me Mike."

In the five- or six-second pause that followed, she heard a clunking noise—perhaps a glove compartment opening—and then a lip-smacking sound and an expulsion of breath.

"Excuse me for asking, Mike, but are you drinking?"

"What the hell do you think? I'm Irish. Of course I'm drinking."

She almost laughed. "I'm ready to hear your side of the story."

"I don't know . . . where . . . Don't know where to begin."

"Try the beginning."

"You have a cautious, I mean a caustic tongue, Edith. But I expected it. A bitch with a caustic tongue."

She rolled her eyes in dismay, though he couldn't see the gesture. "Listen, I've got to meet some people soon. If all you want is to insult me, we can end this conversation right now."

"I do want to, but that's not all. You need to hear my side of the story, but the beginning . . . I don't know where the beginning begins. So I'll start at the end. I am at the end, where you and your rag put me. The end of my string."

A change in the pitch of his voice set off Edith's inner alarm. As always, she didn't know the reason for it, beyond the change from belligerent to plaintive. As automatically as she'd grabbed her pen and notebook, she turned the tape recorder on.

"The plea bargain," Conway was saying, "includes a fine. Not a small one, and I have legal fees to pay and the mortgage on the house in Ireland. The house my mother was born in, grew up in. She's eighty-six but all her marbles . . . She has all her marbles, and she saw the story. The *Boston Herald* picked it up, and she phoned me to tell me how disappointed she was in me. Always has been. Something of a bitch herself, my mother. And I told her, No worries, Ma, I won't disappoint you ever again—"

"Mike," Edith interrupted. "You should know that I'm—"

"Know what?" he interrupted in turn. "I should know what? That you're a bitch, too? Not an insult, Edith. A statement of fact. My wife hasn't left the house in two weeks. She's ashamed to show her face in town, plus, *plus*, we're under police protection. Word on the street is that the cartel has a contract out on me if I testify."

He rambled on in a stream of consciousness before Edith was able to dam the incoherent flow and steer him off his sorrows to the subject he'd said was the reason for the call. She asked if he knew that José Dominguez belonged to the Cali cartel, and he replied that he did not and was willing to say so under oath. Higgs and Stovall had represented the man as a Latin American real estate tycoon who'd built resorts and casinos in the Caribbean and was now seeking to expand into the United States.

That was the clearest statement she could pry out of him. He began to talk about Dominguez's yacht, which led him into a disjointed tale involving a sailboat, a yawl, he said, named the *Empress of China*. That was the beginning! The *Empress of China*. When he was seventeen, he'd helped her owner restore her, great guy, Jonas was, and he and his vessel had turned Mike's life around. Would have gone to jail otherwise, but now that's where he was going anyway, not to a seat in the state senate but to the slammer if he didn't rat on his friends. He sounded defeated, and a little unhinged.

"I doubt you'll do much time, if any," she said, trying to cheer him up and, once again, to nudge him back on track. "And if you do . . . hell, jail time is a prerequisite in Florida for holding office."

The crude attempt at humor didn't work. Conway didn't laugh. Just then, she saw Luke emerge from his office, heading for home. Standing so he could spot her above the cubicle's partition, she frantically waved to him to come over. When he did, she wrote "Conway on the line. Drunk. Babbling" in block letters on a sheet of scrap paper.

"Mike, guess—" she started to say, but the stream of consciousness had swelled into a river, braiding and branching. At a pause, she shouted, "Mike, goddamnit! Listen! Luke just stopped by. Luke Blackburn. Would you like to speak to him?"

Conway was silent for a time, then said, "Put him on."

Edith motioned Luke to a neighboring cubicle—it was empty, its former occupant having been laid off—and mouthed the words "Line two." There was a soft click as he pressed the button on the phone. She listened in.

"Hey, Mike."

"Hello, m'boy. I was just telling Lois Lane about the *Empress of China*. Remember that story? All summer fixing her up when I was seventeen. I'd been kicked out of high school, remember?"

"Sure."

"I learned to sand and varnish her brightwork and to caulk her hull, she was all wood, and that job and the guy, Jonas, turned my life around. He was the father I never had. I was going to call you right after I was done with Lois. I've got a package you should see."

"Okay. You can mail it to me here."

"Nope! Lois didn't tell you? I'm right here in your parking lot. In a visitor's space."

"So what's in the package?"

"Photos of the reef, you can tell how bad a shape it's in. And drawings, architectural drawings of the treatment plants. They won't get built now, thanks to your rag, but you should see this stuff. I'll meet you in the lobby."

He hung up.

"I'm going with you, give me a minute," Edith said to Luke. She unplugged the tape recorder, walked quickly to the news desk, and handed the machine to a rewrite man, asking him to transcribe the tape. Word for word, as spoken, and don't worry about cleaning it up to make sense.

"I've never heard him like that," Luke said as they rode the elevator to the lobby floor. "It didn't sound like him. I'm going to talk him into taking a cab to a motel to sleep it off. Don't want him behind the—"

The doors sliding open cut him off. Rounding the corner from the elevator banks into the lobby, a vast space with a twenty-foot ceiling and a marble floor, she saw Conway leaning against the security desk like a cartoon drunk against a lamppost. The guard asked him to move;

he was blocking the view of the front doors. Conway, in the same linen sport jacket he'd worn at the commission meeting, bowed comically and stepped to the side. He turned and, spotting her with Luke, called out, "There you are, m'boy." He pulled a manila envelope from under his arm and sailed it, frisbee-like, toward them. Luke snatched it in midair.

"Nice catch," Conway said, with a devilish grin. Edith barely saw the palm-size pistol he drew from his jacket pocket and jammed under his jaw, in front of one ear; she barely heard it—his flesh muffled the gunshot. The only way she was certain that he'd pulled the trigger was seeing a red mist spew from the top of his skull.

29

Shock did not half describe Luke's state of mind; he was shaken to his core. His friend's blood was still on his hands, literally—he'd given Mike CPR, though that had been obviously futile. But he was still functional. At seven thirty, while the body was on its way to the morgue and a cleaning service was scrubbing the lobby floor, he called the press room and issued the order, "Stop the presses," for the first time in his career. The early edition had been replated to run Edith's eyewitness account of the suicide, accompanied by a black-and-white photo of the body sprawled face up in what looked like a puddle of spilled oil. Ever the composed professional (she'd even included the make and model of the handgun, an H&K .40-caliber P30), she wrote the story in half an hour.

As the replate tumbled down conveyor belts onto the loading docks, Ortega summoned Luke and Edith to his office, asking her to bring the tape of her conversation with Conway. He played it back, all twenty-two minutes of it.

"I didn't hear you tell him your were recording him," he said.

"I tried, but I couldn't get a word in."

"Where did you try?"

She rewound the tape to the point where she said, "Mike, you should know that I'm—" but was then interrupted by Conway's response, "Know what? What should I know?"

"Right there," she said. "I was going to tell him right there and ask for his okay."

"But you never got it. Florida law requires consent of the person being recorded."

"I know what Florida law requires," Edith shot back, her eyes narrowed.

"We've got a potentially ugly situation here," Ortega said. His manner, normally cordial, had turned cool and formal. "A politician puts a bullet in his head in the lobby of the newspaper that exposed his misdeeds. We've run a story about it, with quotes from a tape made without his knowledge or approval."

"Look, Nick, I kept the tape running for the same reason you would a 911 call. The guy was desperate. I didn't realize how desperate, but I thought there should be a record of what he had to say. I wasn't for Christ's sake sandbagging him."

"I don't for one second think you had bad intentions," Ortega said, softening somewhat. "It was an honest oversight but still an oversight, and you know how the times are. The media has to be like Caesar's wife—above reproach. Can you guys wait next door?" He meant the adjoining office, Luke's. "I've got to make some calls."

Struggling to expel the image of the exit wound in Mike's skull imprinted in his memory, Luke went to the liquor supply stashed in a cabinet behind his desk and poured an inch of bourbon into a tumbler.

"You?" he said to Edith.

"Got any scotch?"

"I do. A single malt."

"Perfecto."

They drank without talking. Luke sat down and phoned Maureen, telling her he was going to be late, probably very late.

"I've been worried," she scolded. "Why didn't you call earlier?"

His answer elicited a brief silence followed by a gasp followed by an "O my God" followed by a string of questions.

"I can't talk right now, turn on the TV. It might be on CNN."

He hung up. Edith was on her cell, leaving a voice message for someone. *So sorry . . . Couldn't make it. . . . I'll explain later. . . .*

"Who was that?" Luke asked when she was done.

"A friend. Fixed me up on a blind date with a guy advertised as a senior woman's dreamboat. I was supposed to have dinner with them. That's where I'd be if I hadn't picked up that goddamn phone." She finished the single malt with a single swig. "Can't help but wonder where Conway would be."

"What do you mean?"

"He was leaving a suicide note. If I hadn't been there to receive it. . . . Who knows?"

"You heard him. He was going to call me. He would've left it with me." Luke felt a current of ire passing through his shock, his sadness, his regret. "Now that I think about it, I may have been his main audience. 'Some friend you've been. Look what you've done to me. Driven me to kill myself.'"

They had been waiting almost an hour when they were called to the sixth floor.

"Hope to hell I'm wrong, but I've got an idea where this is going," Edith said as they went up.

"I've got your back, all the way."

She brushed his sleeve with her fingertips. "No offense, but I don't think that'll be enough. Thanks anyway."

The elevator deposited them in a half-lit reception room where they were met by a tall, thin man with the ascetic look of an Episcopal bishop in need of some protein. His name was Joseph Barrett, attorney for Ritter Communications. He ushered them into the Ritters' wainscoted lair, which bore a closer resemblance to the boardroom of a WASPy law firm than to the headquarters of a minor media conglomerate.

Owen and Gloria sat side by side in matching leather wing chairs, like a royal couple holding an audience. Both were casually dressed—they'd been summoned from their homes and looked none too happy about it. Barrett motioned Edith and Luke to take the sofa facing the two, then sat down on their left. Ortega was on the right, a dour look on his face that exaggerated its normally mournful expression. It confirmed Edith's hunch: the proceeding was going to be like a show trial whose verdict had already been decided; nevertheless, the motions had to be gone through for appearance's sake.

Barrett led off with much the same questions Ortega had put to her. Edith, sitting up straight, attentive but relaxed (though her stomach was doing flips), gave the kind of answers expected from an experienced reporter. Crisp. Concise. The interrogation concluded with some throat-clearing and exchanges of glances between the Ritters and their lawyer.

"So my understanding is," Barrett said, turning back to Edith, "you started to tell him the recorder was on but you didn't follow through and ask his consent merely because you couldn't get a word in edgewise."

"Isn't that what I told you two minutes ago?"

"In other words, you knew you were doing the wrong thing but you went ahead regardless."

"I wasn't thinking that way," she replied. "The guy was talking like a crazy drunk. I didn't think then that he was suicidal, but I was concerned, so I let him get things off his chest without interrupting him. And I'll thank you, Mr. Barrett, not to speak to me as if I'm on trial."

"Just for your information, you could be," Gloria cut in, staring straight at Edith. "You violated a Florida law. If the state's attorney were to find out, he could file charges."

Edith stared back, steady, dry-eyed. "You're not threatening me, are you?"

"Hey! No fuckin' cat fights," Owen barked. "Here's the problem. We've got this tape. Other people besides us know about it, the rewrite desk for one. It'll be all over the newsroom by tomorrow, and it's bound to come out that you taped him without him knowing you were, and that's not just going to make you look like shit, it'll make this whole organization look like shit."

Barrett, raising a pale hand, stopped him. "Please, Owen, let's keep it clean and civil," he said in a tone more ecclesiastical than lawyerly, then again addressed Edith. "Recording him the way you did was a breach of trust, a subterfuge. The *Examiner* can't have its sources wondering if they're being taped without their knowledge or consent."

Edith got to her feet. "Let's end the dog and pony show. You're firing me, is that right?"

She was trembling, not so much from fear as from outrage, as her gaze ranged over the four people in front of her.

"Yes, that's right, that's exactly right," Gloria answered. "Check in with HR tomorrow morning."

Without another word, Edith spun on her heel and walked out. She was too proud, too dignified to beg, grovel, or plead her case any more than she already had, so Luke pled for her.

"You can't do that! After all she's done for this paper? You can't do that to her, goddamnit!"

"Cool it, Luke," Ortega said.

"You called it an honest oversight, Nick, and that's all it was. A month's leave without pay would fit the crime. We've known reporters who've done worse and kept their jobs."

"In the old damn-the-torpedoes days. It's a different environment now. We can't be ethical most of the time, we've got to be ethical all the time. C'mon, cool off."

Luke looked at Owen and his sister. "You two have been turning over rocks for an excuse to get rid of her. Get rid of her and replace her with some brat who'll work for a dime on every dollar you pay her."

"You're out of line, mister," Owen said.

Luke regarded himself as a deliberate person who weighed his options before acting. But witnessing Mike Conway's suicide, seeing him alive one instant and dead the next, bone fragments and brain matter spilling with his blood onto the bright marble floor, had done something to him, and though he could not identify what that was, he knew it was the source of an impulse about whose rightness he felt as confident as if it were the product of long consideration.

"She goes, I go with her," he said. "You'll have my resignation inside of an hour."

30

Conway's theatrical self-murder made national news; so did Edith's firing and Luke's resigning in protest. Most of the coverage was fair, but some editorialists fully took the Ritters' side. Professional integrity . . . no tolerance for reporters who broke faith with highest ethical standards. This righteous rubbish inspired Luke to write an op-ed for a rival newspaper, the *St. Petersburg Times*, that singled out the Ritters as embodying everything gone wrong with the newspaper industry. The wires picked up his polemic; the news magazines interviewed him. Barrett sent him a notice to cease and desist; he was flirting with libel.

Luke did cease and desist, but not because he'd been intimidated; interest in the story dissolved, the media moved on to other things. Soon after, he heard from Edith—she was finished in the news business, but a book publisher had given her an advance for her memoirs. She was off to Mallorca to write them—with the man who would have been her dinner date if she hadn't taken Conway's call. Luke wished her success and felt pangs of loss, a sense of things ending.

He also had job offers, one from the *Arizona Daily Star*, the paper that had given him his start; another, more attractive in terms of money and prestige, from the *LA Times*. But Maureen wasn't about to leave

Miami. She was on the ascendant at the university, one of three candidates to replace the retiring chairman of the English department. Reluctantly, he turned the offers down. She was grateful, but dismay at what she considered his rash decision to quit alloyed her gratitude. Enough of the old-fashioned girl remained in the career woman to feel some contempt for a jobless househusband, and a phone conversation with Thelma aggravated the contempt. Maureen reported Thelma's reaction to Luke—"So now you're the sole breadwinner in the family? You're supporting *him*?"—disguising her own thoughts and feelings as her mother's.

Money wasn't a problem, at least not yet. Idleness was the problem. He took a few free-lance assignments to keep occupied, went fishing in Biscayne Bay, lifted weights and swam at his gym, caught up on his reading. But he missed the newsroom, the collegiality, the sense of urgency as deadline approached, the knowledge that he was engaged in necessary work. He woke most mornings at loose ends, with an empty day yawning before him. Often he lay in bed till nine thirty or ten, not out of laziness but from exhaustion after a night's fitful sleep plagued by bad dreams; dreams about the war, from which he woke in the post-midnight black bathed in sweat. These spells were prelude to moods that toggled between anger and hopelessness, emotions he hadn't felt in years. Mike's suicide had resurrected them. Post-traumatic stress disorder. He disliked that diagnostic term for its inaccuracy. There was nothing disordered in having normal reactions to abnormal experiences, like lying wounded in a foxhole beside half a man's body, or watching your friend blow his brains out right in front of you.

Corrine had called him on his cell when she'd learned, first from Ian, later on the TV news, what had happened in the lobby; called again after she'd heard that he'd left his job to show solidarity with his reporter. A gutsy thing to do, she'd said. She was proud of him.

"Not so gutsy," he'd responded. "Maybe I did it because I felt like blowing up my life."

Character has been defined as what you do when no one is looking. Or listening. By that standard, Luke reckoned his character was flawed. One afternoon in early November, he waited till Adriana, the cleaning woman, was done for the day before phoning Corinne. He needed to see her, he said, needed to feel her long, cool body next to his, to hold her and be held by her.

"Then for God's sake come down and see me. I need you just as much."

"It can't be for more than two, three days."

"Cher, I don't care if it's for half an hour."

More practiced now in duplicity, he wove truth and lies into a plausible excuse. He wanted to get away for a while, he said to Maureen, think things over, find a new direction for himself.

"I hope you do," she said. "You moping around the house all day isn't healthy—for either of us."

Driving down the Overseas Highway, he listened to a Miami jazz station playing his favorites—Coltrane, McCoy Tyner, Coleman Hawkins. He was crossing the Seven Mile Bridge at the top of the hour—time for a five-minute news break and then the weather report, which caught Luke's attention. A late-season hurricane, named Kate, had been lurking in the Caribbean, uncertain of its direction. It had tacked south for a while, then turned north and appeared to be heading for open water when it veered west unexpectedly. It was now predicted to make landfall in the Lower Keys in the early hours of the next morning.

By the time he reached Key West, black and red warning flags were snapping from the pole at the National Weather Station on Simonton street. As cyclones went, Kate wasn't a killer—a Category 1, sustained winds of eighty-five miles an hour, not expected to strengthen. Most citizens had chosen to ride it out; shopkeepers and homeowners were taping or boarding up windows. The atmosphere on the streets reminded him, a little, of the nervous excitement preceding a combat assault.

He was distressed to see that the owner of Corrine's house had left it to his tenants to make preparations. The people in the downstairs apartment apparently had evacuated. He climbed the exterior stairs and knocked at Corrine's door. No answer, which puzzled him. He'd phoned from the road half an hour ago to tell her he would be there soon. He knocked again. This time, she called "One second" from inside. The door opened a crack, just wide enough to allow him to slip through sideways. The reason for her circumspection was immediately apparent: Corinne was naked, except for the same black tap pants she'd worn when she seduced him that night at the Casa Marina. Her brilliant eyes arrested him. She didn't speak, and didn't give him a chance to, not so much as hello, clasping the back of his neck, pulling him to her, kissing him. As extreme hunger is not felt in the belly but throughout the body, so was their need for one another not felt in the loins; it lay deeper, it was cellular. She wiggled out of the tap pants. Luke wasn't wearing much—shirt, shorts, sandals—and shed them in a minute. They kissed and embraced again and waltzed into her bedroom, where she flung herself face down on the mattress and raised her ivory hips and whispered, "Like this, I want it like this." The shutters to the room's only window were closed, and the sunlight streaming through the louvers fell on her back and rump so that she looked like some strange creature with luminescent stripes. He grasped her waist in both hands and pierced her. She felt like warm wet satin inside. Body and soul, souls united in the union of flesh. Resting on her elbows, she made some frenzied bumps and grinds, he threaded his fingers into her frizzy hair, and she groaned, "Yeah, yeah, O yeah" as he yanked her head back and exploded inside her.

In the postcoital calm, the calm *after* the storm, they lay without talking for five minutes.

"God almighty, have I missed you," she said finally.

"Same here."

"Sometimes I wonder if I'm crazy in love with you or addicted to you. It amounts to the same thing, I suppose."

"Maybe. I take it Ian isn't in his room?"

"Would it embarrass you if he was?"

"What do you think?"

"He's known that we've been . . . that we've been seeing each other almost from day one. We don't talk about it much. A part of him wishes we'd get back together somehow. Like . . . what's the word? Revive? Revive the family that would have been his if we hadn't made the choices we did."

Luke said nothing. He watched the ceiling fan's sluggish turns, the blades chopping the bars of light into segments.

"Sometimes I wish it, too," Corinne said quietly, as if frightened by her own words. "I've always felt we could have been terrific together."

"You had a strange way of showing it."

"I thought we'd gotten past that."

"We have," he said, lightly kissing her cheek, her lips, her throat. "I swear I won't bring it up again."

She sat up, and drawing her knees to her chest, rested her chin on them. "I did get some good news in the mail yesterday. From Rubin."

"The art dealer?"

"Uh-huh. I'd shipped him two canvases to see how they'd go over. And he sold both! The bigger one for—get this—twenty-two hundred, the small one for seven-fifty. Sixty percent to me equals seventeen seventy."

"That's not good news, it's great news."

"There's more. He asked me to ship the rest—there's four of them—and he'll make good on his promise to have a showing. It would be me and three other unknowns. It won't be till early next year, but he'll cover my airfare."

"The guy *is* gay, isn't he?" Luke said.

Corinne laughed. "Very. No need for jealousy." She swung out of bed and pulled clothes out of a dresser drawer. "We'd better get decent before Ian comes home."

"So where is he?"

"Him and a friend are out scrounging for plywood. He's going to board up."

She brewed coffee flavored with cardamom, New Orleans style, and served it in the living room with beignets. The room had undergone a few changes. The couch, its cushions covered in bright tropical patterns, had replaced the threadbare corduroy sofa she'd rescued from a Goodwill warehouse; the scarred dining and coffee tables were gone, deposed by a matching pair with bamboo legs and glass tops that stood on a sisal rug; and two of her paintings spruced up the pine walls, previously bare. Four more were lined up against the low wall beneath the slanted skylight. They were the four she would be shipping to New York. She described them as studies in "ambiguous perspective," viewers unsure whether they're looking down or outward, and "mixed emotions," a sense of menace secreted within the beauty.

"That's how I think of the ocean," she said. "Right now it's beautiful; by early morning it'll be scary. Hurricanes, they ought to call them horrorcanes. They scare the crap out of me."

"There'd be something wrong with you if they didn't."

Luke bit into a beignet. With her fingertip, she wiped the powdered sugar from the corners of his mouth.

"I've been in only one," she said. "Betsy. I was just starting my junior year when it whacked New Orleans. I'll never forget that wind, the sound of it." She fell into the dialect. "'Whoo-hoo-hoo,' my gramma-maw said. 'Like ten thousand ghosts all moanin' at once.'"

Remembering Andrew, Luke thought that a pretty accurate description. "This one should be nowhere near that bad," he said, and placed an arm around her.

Ian returned with his friend, Taylor Curry, the reggae singer whose Bob Marley mimicry he'd derided. Luke went outside to give them a hand unloading plywood and an extension ladder from Curry's zebra-striped van. Ian gave him a bro-hug, then introduced him as "my biological dad," which made Luke feel that he was part of some weird experiment in human reproduction.

"Guess we all got us one of those," Curry remarked. "Got to go, man. Get the ladder back to me whenever."

"I quit the motel," Ian said after Curry left. "Me and him play alternate nights at the Blue Heaven. The Bitch of Buchenwald okayed it. I make more there in tips in four nights than I made all week night-clerking. And it's not boring."

"Don't make things too interesting."

"Clean and sober. I am righteous."

He proceeded to lug a plywood sheet up the extension ladder, which Luke held steady from below, and board a window, drilling pilot holes with a power drill, banging nails into the tough Dade County pine. They finished three of the apartment's five windows in this way, then set the ladder aside and went to the upper balcony, where Luke did the last two.

The job completed, Ian fetched two beers from the fridge and brought them outside. He tipped the bottle to his lips. "Hope my parole supervisor doesn't have a spy satellite trained on me."

"She'll forgive you if she does."

"I read your story twice. That part where you got wounded and the guy behind you cut in half . . ." He shook his head to indicate he lacked the words to express the effect that episode had on him. "I was thinking of enlisting when Desert Storm broke out. It went so fast it would have been over before I got finished with basic training."

"Yeah, to a lot of vets, that wasn't a war, it was a drive-by shooting."

Ian let out a "Ha!" and said, "But I feel like I missed out on something."

"You did," said Luke. "And take it from me, it was worth missing. Sergeant Rock of Easy Company is a comic book."

"I did do my bit later on, kind of, touring with the USO. My mother got sick while I was overseas. I phoned and told her I was quitting the show to be near her, and she said no way was I to do that. So I stuck with it. I was in Italy, at the army base in Vicenza, when she died. Just a month after she was diagnosed. That cancer, it can kill you like that." Snapping his fingers.

Luke did not say anything at first, distracted by the words "my mother." A woman he'd never known, and never would know, had raised and nurtured the life he had fathered; and yet, he felt that he was slowly laying greater claim to the noun that proceeded from the verb. He had rescued his natural son from heat stroke; just now, they had worked together to accomplish a necessary task. Leaning against the balcony's gingerbread rail, he fixed his gaze on Ian's face—the eyes that duplicated his, the sharp cheekbones, prominent nose, and black hair that duplicated Corrine's (though his flowed in waves rather than spiraled in tight whorls). Hooking an elbow around Ian's neck, in the rough way men show affection for each other, he said, "I'm sorry you had to go through all that, I truly am."

Corrine changed from her paint-spattered clothes to a filmy jump-suit and made shrimp étouffée for dinner. It took two hours and would have taken longer if Luke hadn't volunteered to prep-chef, peeling shrimp, chopping onions and bell peppers, garlic and celery. With the windows blocked, the tiny kitchen was stifling. Corrine's forehead wore a corona of sweat; damp blots speckled her blouse, and her smell com-bined with the odors of the bubbling roux and the shrimp simmering in it to create a singular sensual experience. Luke could enumerate the reasons he'd married Maureen as if reading off qualifications in a resumé but could not explain why Corrine captivated him, awakening a mindless passion to possess her completely, body and soul, even as he knew that she could never be possessed.

The storm's outer bands whirled in as they ate; the wind rose, rain crackled against the tin roof. Corrine entertained Ian and Luke, and distracted herself from her own apprehensions with a tale about her grandmother when she was a child, encountering the ghost of Jean Lafitte in a swamp. After the dishes were done, they sat on the new couch to watch the Weather Channel on her portable TV. Kate was still a Category 1, though her winds had increased to a sustained ninety miles an hour and her forward speed from a leisurely five knots to ten. A graphic showed the storm's position and her course; if that didn't change, she would strike Key West before midnight, earlier than anticipated.

"We're in the crosshairs!" Luke exclaimed, feeling the giddiness engendered by an unavoidable but manageable danger.

"You sound like you're going to enjoy this," Corinne said. She scooted closer to him. "You *are* staying with us? Not at a motel?"

He hugged her in response to the plea latent in her question. "I never made reservations."

When the Weather Channel's updates grew repetitive, Ian switched to a movie on Turner Classics: *The Captain's Paradise*, about a ferry captain married to two women at the same time—a wild, hot-blooded one in Morocco and a sweet, domesticated one on Gibraltar. The parallels to Luke's present life were so uncanny he could have believed the film was being shown solely to instruct him on the perils of bigamy. The analogy wasn't perfect; for one thing, he wasn't a bigamist, merely an adulterer; for another, *The Captain's Paradise* was a romantic comedy, while his situation fell short of the comedic.

The movie ended prematurely when a transformer on a utility pole down the block exploded with a terrific bang. Corrine gasped; Luke was just able to stop himself from diving for cover. The apartment was as dark as the interior of a safe. Corinne did not keep practical items like a flashlight or a lantern on hand, so Luke braved a sortie outdoors to fetch the flashlight in his glove compartment. Howling at sixty miles an hour, the wind nearly blew him off the landing at the top of the staircase. Walking to his car was like wading waist-deep against a rushing river. The rain, whipping at a horizontal, lashed his face. A Category 1 was a small beast compared with a Cat 5 like Andrew, but a beast none-theless. He retrieved the light, struggled up the stairs, and managed to get inside without losing the door to the furious wind.

"You're soaked!" Corinne exclaimed, then brought him a bath towel.

He went into the bedroom, stripped off his clothes, toweled himself dry, and fell on the bed. She joined him there while Ian sheltered in his room.

They lay holding one another as the storm's leading edge—the northeast quadrant to meteorologists and hurricane buffs—vandalized the island city, breaking windows, ripping down phone and electrical lines, snapping tree limbs in two. Small branches fell on the roof of Corrine's house and made scratching noises as they scampered across the tin. The wind found the finest cracks in the walls, and when it gusted to over a hundred miles an hour, its pitch changed from a roar to a low, tremulous groan, much like the sound her grandmother had described as "ten thousand ghosts moaning at once."

Corrine rested her cheek on Luke's chest. "This is your idea of not so bad?"

"We'll be okay, no worries," he said, playing the hero, though the bangs and thumps and crashes outside were making the role difficult. But his anxieties floated on his emotional surface; lying there with his lover in his arms flooded him with happiness.

The eye brought a brief respite, during which Luke got back into his damp clothes—he'd felt too vulnerable with them off. Ten minutes later, the backside winds had their turn, but blew with less ferocity than the front side, and dropped to a strong breeze as Katrina whirled into the Gulf of Mexico.

Ian woke them at mid-morning, rapping on the bedroom door. "Luke, yo! It's your car."

A limb from the Spanish lime in the yard next door had been hurled like a javelin through the Land Cruiser's windshield, shattering it and mangling the steering wheel. For the next hour, he and Ian dislodged the limb—it was roughly the thickness of Luke's calf—swept the interior clean of glass fragments, and pulled jagged shards out of the windshield frame. Calls to three towing services went unanswered. When he got through the fourth he was told it would be twenty-four hours before anyone could help him. It was late in the afternoon before he reached the service manager at the Toyota dealership on Roosevelt Boulevard and described the damages.

"Hey, we're cleanin' up our own mess right now," the man replied. "Call tomorrow."

"I need a windshield and a steering wheel on a '98 Land Cruiser. How long would that take?"

"Windshield no problem. Steering wheel we'll have to order from Miami. That'll take a couple days. US 1 is blocked. A sailboat got thrown across it."

Marooned. Luke wasn't troubled.

31

While they waited for power to be restored to the neighborhood, he, Corinne, and Ian took a long walk to Pepe's for lunch. A repair crew clearing a fallen tree shunted them off course, taking them past Liz Conway's shop as she was supervising a worker removing plywood from the plate-glass windows. Luke had written her a condolence note shortly after Mike's death, to which she'd responded, "Your sympathies leave me cold. As far as I'm concerned, you and your newspaper pulled the trigger. You will not be welcome at the memorial service." Now, he thought to speak to her, but his courage withered as she shot him a venomous stare and turned her back.

"She blames you?" Corinne asked over lunch.

"She blames the paper, which is the same thing as blaming me," Luke answered, a little shaken.

"That's hardly reasonable."

"Reason's got nothing to do with it."

Key West, accustomed to hurricanes, recovered quickly. Luke's car was towed to the dealership the next morning. He phoned Maureen to assure her he was okay, and to explain why his return would be delayed. His faculty for deception both amazed and disgusted him. Three days passed before the windshield was replaced and a new steering wheel delivered and installed.

During that interlude, when Corrine wasn't sketching at the museum, Luke and she sunbathed and swam at Smathers Beach. They ate yellowtail snapper with a crisp sauvignon blanc at Saluté, a café facing the ocean, and caught Ian's performance at Blue Heaven, impressed by his mastery of some complex, jazzy riffs. One morning, he took his son (Luke now thought of him as such without any qualifiers) for a half day's fishing with Dustin Cardenas. It was an exquisite morning, very still, the gray flats joined so smoothly to the dawn-gray sky that the distant out-islands appeared to be dark clouds adrift in a horizonless world. Ian caught and released his first tarpon, and Luke shared in his excitement. Later on, eating deep-friend grouper at a canal-side place on Stock Island, they discussed Ian's future. He turned glum. Did he, an ex-felon, have a future in the conventional sense? Luke sought to boost his spirits with the tale of his uncle Gene. After serving half of his ten-year sentence, he was paroled, returned to organizing for the UMWA, rose in union ranks to become district president, and died prosperous and respected at eighty.

"I don't belong to the musicians union, so that's out for me," Ian said.

"My point is that there's always hope because you can always do something, if you work hard enough at it," Luke advised, disappointed with himself for uttering such banality.

To brighten the mood, he related a story about Uncle Gene's funeral in Hazard, Kentucky.

"I was invited to the service to represent our side of the family. Right in the middle of things, with the casket being lowered down and a bluegrass band playing hymns and a Baptist preacher preaching ashes to ashes, this old dude—he must have been ninety and looked like a cartoon hillbilly, floppy hat, long white beard and all—showed up out of nowhere and said, 'Wal, glory be, so ole Stanley Blackburn done finally gone to his ree-ward.' And somebody took him aside and told him, 'This here is Stanley's son Gene. Stanley died in nineteen and forty-eight.' And the old man just says, 'Is that a fact? I'll be . . .' and walks off."

Luke's mimic of an Appalachian twang pulled a laugh out of Ian.

"You're going to be all right," said Luke, knuckling the younger man's shoulder. "You run into any problems, I'll be there for you."

He took Corinne dancing at a downtown club off Duval on his fourth and final night in town. It was loud and crowded, with pulsing strobes that made everyone on the floor look like figures in a twitchy film.

Afterward, they strolled along the harborfront, gazing out at masthead lights swaying in the enchanted darkness. "Like torches, I should paint them," Corinne said, then nipped his lips and ears with her teeth. His hands fell from her waist to the lush curve of her ass. Two bright flashes from several yards away interrupted the embrace—a tourist trying for night shots of the harbor.

"That's a sign," Corinne said. "Let's go home."

In the morning, Ian followed him out to his car as he was about to leave for Miami.

"Do you remember, a couple months back, when I asked to take that DNA test?"

"Sure."

"Well, I'd still like for us to take it. It's been on my mind."

"You mean because of that paper you found? I told you it wasn't necessary."

"Just for the hell of it then," Ian said. "And, like the birth certificate thing."

"Did you mention this to her?"

He nodded.

"And what did she say?"

"Same thing as you. No problem. If we went now, you'd be out and on the road by nine."

"Okay, okay," Luke said, annoyed. "Just for the hell of it and the birth certificate."

He drove with Ian to the clinic—it was on Kennedy Drive, near the parole offices. A technician swabbed their cheeks, placed the samples in plastic tubes, and said that the results wouldn't be in for four to six weeks. The clinic outsourced the testing to a lab in Fort Lauderdale, which was usually backed up with high-priority, court-ordered requests.

32

He returned to Coral Gables in a cheerful mood. It was as though the happiness Corinne brought him spilled over into his life with Maureen. This allowed him to rationalize that his affair was actually good for his marriage. Maureen, too, was in high spirits. She'd been given a raise—compensation for not getting the department chairmanship—and had landed a book contract from an academic publisher for a study of Joyce's poetry collection, *Chamber Music*. She and Luke celebrated with Babowitz and other faculty at a South Beach restaurant.

They flew to Boston to spend Thanksgiving with her father, who had moved back to the city from Washington to be near his two sons, Don and Stuart. The family, minus Thelma, gathered at Don's McMansion in Newton. He was a venture capitalist in the Route 128 corridor, the Silicon Valley of the East, married to the vice president of an internet startup and the father of three teenage children, two boys and a girl, who were happy and well-behaved because they had no reason not to be. Ted Carrington, now seventy-seven, had recently been diagnosed with prostate cancer, but true to the WASP code, did not complain or mention it once. The holiday dinner went reasonably well, the only awkwardness supplied by Stuart arriving with a young man he

presented as a "friend," who flounced about outrageously as if to force
Stu to come out to his family. That night, as Luke and Maureen lay in
bed in a guest room, she said, "I wish Stu would find the right girl."
This wasn't naivety or ignorance on her part; a willful blindness, rather,
which Luke, ever wary of her mental fragility, did nothing to cure.

The job offer from PolitiWorld, an internet news site devoted to politics and nothing but politics, arrived in his inbox on the last day of
the month. With the 2000 general election season only weeks away,
the site was expanding its operations from inside the Beltway to "key"
battleground races, beginning with Florida's. It needed a seasoned
journalist with intimate knowledge of the state and also managerial
experience to oversee three reporters who would be providing coverage, two from Tallahassee, one from Miami-Dade. The job would also
entail filing a daily political newsletter, called "The Focus." Luke's
name had come up; in fact, the email stated, he led the list of candidates. If he was interested, PolitiWorld's senior editors would be
pleased to meet with him at its headquarters in Arlington, Virginia.
Luke wrote back that yes, he was interested, taking care not to sound
too eager. A date was set for the following Monday, December 6.

The news pleased Maureen—how nice it would be to have an
employed spouse once again. Luke freshened up his resumé and took
a Sunday afternoon flight to Washington, where he was given the VIP
treatment: a limo picked him up at Reagan National and whisked him
to the Westin in Arlington. The next day, he was taken to PolitiWorld's
offices, which occupied three floors midway up a twenty-story tower
with so much glass it looked like a gigantic cylindrical fish tank. He
lunched with the site's two founders, former print journalists whose
backgrounds reassured him; he could connect with them in a way he
could not with info-age whiz kids better at writing code than a good,
crisp lede. Later, he was interviewed by the executive editor, a thirtyish
woman named Amanda Valentine, who revealed, without his asking,

the reason his name led the list of candidates: Edith Buchmayr was her aunt and had recommended him. Aunt Edy, said her niece, thought him quixotic for going to the lengths he did in sticking up for her. "But she loves you for it." Valentine gave him a tour of the newsroom—sleek and bright and clean, antiseptic, actually, but not so divorced in appearance and ambience from the *Examiner*'s as to make him feel that he'd entered an alien world.

The next morning, he was summoned to another conference with the founders, who informed him that the job was his if he wanted it. Of course, he did. Their initial salary offer failed to excite him, but by cautiously demurring he got them to bump it up to a more respectable level, though it was still less than what he'd earned at the *Examiner*. That afternoon, after spending much of it learning the nuts and bolts of his new role from the editor of "The Focus" newsletter in DC, he treated himself to a massage at the Westin's spa, then phoned Maureen at home to pass on his news. There was no answer; he left a message.

He flew back from Washington the next day, concerned that she had not returned his call, nor another that he'd made before leaving for the airport. During the two-and-a-half-hour flight, he told himself that there was probably a good explanation for her silence; but the fear perpetually nested within him, sleeping like a snake in the cold, had begun to stir. Had she relapsed? He drove home from Miami International in a state swinging between eagerness and anxiety. He pulled into the garage—her car was there—and went inside and called out to her. No reply. Maybe she was taking a walk. He climbed the stairs into their bedroom and unpacked, tossing his socks and underwear into a laundry hamper in the closet.

"Welcome home," she said from behind him.

Startled, he whirled around and saw her in the doorway. She had on the green dress she'd worn at her Dublin performance and matching heels.

"My, aren't you the jumpy one."

"Going somewhere all dolled up?" he asked, wondering how she'd sneaked up on him in those shoes.

"Coming back, actually. Babowitz dropped me off. A soirée for a generous alum who wanted to meet with select faculty."

"I left you a couple of messages. Didn't you listen to them? I got the job."

Breathing easier to see her as he'd left her—that is, sane—he took a step toward her. She stopped him, both hands upraised, her eyes glaring in the way ice glares.

"I need a drink, and I think you will, too," she said, her tone as frigid as her look. "I'll be downstairs."

Changed into khakis and loafers, he joined her in the living room, where she sat stiffly in one of the wing chairs flanking the coral-rock fireplace, her legs crossed, hands folded in her lap. Two vodkas on the rocks were on the table between the chairs.

"I took the liberty of pouring you one," she said.

Luke sat down, facing her. It occurred to him that they presented a tableau of the middle-class couple enjoying cocktails at the end of the day. A *New Yorker* cartoon.

"Okay, something's going on. What is it?"

She reached for a glass. "I think that's a question you should answer," she said, stern, composed, yet with a brittleness in the composure.

And he knew. The moment he'd hoped to avoid for months had come round at last. Now that it had, he felt, more than dread, relief. But a gremlin in his brain prodded him to try buying a little time.

"I'll be PolitiWorld's Florida bureau chief—"

"Please, darling, please please don't treat me like an idiot."

Unable to meet her look, he turned his attention to the skewed rectangles the late afternoon sun, slanting through the casement windows, drew on the carpet. An Isfahan, he remembered. Her father had bought it on one of his diplomatic missions.

"Can I ask how you found out?"

"Of course!" she said with harsh laughter. "*Certainement! Certamente!*" Speaking in tongues, as she often did to aggravate him. "I found out from what people in your line of work would call an informed source. Informed but anonymous." Twisting in her seat, she pulled a manila envelope from between her back and the chair's. "This came for me in the university mail yesterday."

She passed it to him. Below the address—Dr. Maureen Carrington, English Dept., University of Miami, Coral Gables, FL 33146—the sender had written "Private & Personal" in bold, black letters. The postmark showed that it had been mailed from Key West.

Inside was a news clipping from the *Key West Citizen*. It included a black-and-white, taken at the Casa Marina art show: Corinne kissing Luke's forehead. The clipping wrapped several more recent photographs: him and Corrine walking hand in hand on Smathers Beach; entering the dance club, his arm around her waist; him and Ian playing beach volleyball, Corrine watching from the side; Luke high-fiving Ian after the game. The most damning—it proved beyond all doubt that they'd been followed by a professional—had been taken at night at the harbor, Luke and Corrine in an embrace, his hands caressing her bottom. A note printed in block letters on lined paper was attached to the photos:

"Dear Dr. Carrington: Your husband, Luke Blackburn, has been seeing another woman when he's in Key West. This is her. An old flame rekindled. She is the mother of Luke's son, who is also pictured here. She gave him up for adoption long ago, now they have been reunited. I thought you should know. Sincerely, Your Friend."

We've been discreet about your indiscretions. Not anymore, Luke thought.

"Frankly, I've wondered about your so-called fishing trips down there," Maureen said. "For a while, I thought about doing the suspicious spouse thing and hiring a private detective. I couldn't bring myself to do it. I guess I didn't want to know more than I wanted to. But here we are."

"Somebody else hired one. You know who sent this, don't you?"

"I've got a pretty good idea."

"She thinks I was disloyal to Mike, that I and the *Examiner* were responsible for what he did. This is retribution. You ruined my life, I'll mess up yours."

Maureen again lifted her glass, a mild quaking in her hands. Either the lithium shakes or the tremors of a contained rage. "I honestly don't give a damn what her motives were," she said. "Does your Queen of Tarts have a name? And this son of yours, what's his name?"

"Corinne and Ian. Corrine Terrebonne and Ian Campbell."

"To go back to your question, I want an answer. I want to hear what's been going on and for how long and why. You owe it to me, it's the least you owe me."

It took close to half an hour. Ever the newsman, he reported the facts and ducked the psychology, which left the why mostly unanswered. He halted his recitation a few times, disconcerted by Maureen's impassive expression, her stony silence. She did not once interrupt him; it was as if she were listening to a doctoral candidate defending a thesis. When he finished, he apologized for hurting her. The last thing he wanted to do was hurt her.

"But you have," she said through lips stretched taut. "Well, now I know what held you up coming home from Key West, and it wasn't to get your car fixed. That was one more lie on a pile of lies. This whole marriage was built on a lie. What hurts is that you never told me you'd had a child, and you made it impossible for us to have one—"

"You know why I did. Because—"

"Shut up! I don't want to hear that you were protecting me from myself. I pleaded with you to have it reversed, and you wouldn't do it. And all the time, you knew, you knew, Luke, that you had this boy out there somewhere and kept it from me. And then you start fucking his mother all over again and seeing him? Dear God! If it had been an affair and no kid, I think I could have gotten through it. If it had been a kid but no affair, I think I could have gotten through that, too. But both at once?"

Luke knew better than to say anything, or to beg forgiveness. He didn't deserve absolution, and what was more, didn't want it.

"What do you see in her? She looks ordinary to me, common, actually. Does she do special tricks between the sheets?"

"Maureen . . ."

"I'm going to ask a simple question," she went on, "and I expect an honest answer. Are you in love with her?"

He nodded.

"Say it, damn you!"

"Yes, I'm in love with her."

"Then get out! You can sleep on the couch tonight, but tomorrow I want you out of here." Slipping her restraints, she leaped off the chair and threw the drink in his face. "Go back down there and fuck your Queen of Tarts, and in between fucks, you can play catch with your darling boy, but do, do get the hell out of my sight."

33

She retained a divorce lawyer but relented a little, giving Luke a week to clear out his things—clothes, books, papers, CDs, CD player, laptop, etc. After that, she would change the locks. Her resolve to be speedily rid of him and all reminders of him was impressive. He wondered if she'd been as unhappy in the marriage as he but had been unwilling to admit it. The thought allowed him to let himself off the hook—but not by much.

He rented a truck from U-Haul, went to the house when he knew she was in class or otherwise out, and moved his belongings into a self-storage warehouse. It took him only two more days to find a place to live—a one-bedroom condo in Coconut Grove at a reasonable rent. Busy with practical necessities like opening a new checking account and sending change-of-address notices, he didn't dwell too much on his situation: going on fifty-two, he was launching into unknown waters as a soon to be unmarried man. For all its woes, his marriage had been familiar. The absence of its routines and rituals disoriented him.

He sent Corinne a letter detailing all that had happened. She wrote back, inviting him to join her and Ian for Christmas. Sentimental about Christmas and dreading the prospect of spending it alone in his half-furnished condo, he accepted.

How pleasant it was to go see them without devising a pretext, without feeling that he was taking part in an undercover operation.

They decorated the tree, a small artificial one perched on a chipped end table; listened to carols (no Bing Crosby, but McCoy Tyner and Herbie Hancock playing holiday songs on Luke's CD, *Jingle Bell Jazz*); exchanged presents (a new dress for Corinne to wear at the New York art show; two Hawaiian shirts for Luke; a boxed set of Jimi Hendrix CDs for Ian, who was too broke to give anything more than cards); Corinne provided what she called "a coonass yuletide dinner" (spiced pecans, crispy chicken) and entertainment by reciting the "Cajun Night Before Christmas" (*Twas de night before Christmas, an' all t'ru de house/ Dey don't a t'ing pass, not even a mouse*).

Luke had to force holiday cheer. It seemed more like a year than a month since he was with Maureen at Thanksgiving. He was feeling out of sorts and out of place, and the celebration seemed a bit like a facsimile, a simulated Christmas he was marking with his ersatz family. The mismatched, plastic glass and tableware at dinner irked him—couldn't she afford dishes that didn't resemble frisbees? The messy apartment was likewise irritating—clothes and shoes strewn in the bedroom, paint tubes and canvases cluttering the living room. Corinne's sloppiness had always got on his nerves; he attributed his heightened sensitivity to it to the drastic changes in his life. Its natural order had been upset; any disorder, however trivial, was bound to bother him more than it warranted. While she and Ian washed dishes, he straightened up the bedroom, arranging her shoes in the closet, hanging a dress she'd tossed carelessly over a chair, picking a pair of jeans from off the dusty floor. He felt that he'd won a small victory over disharmony.

In that same room, on the night *after* Christmas and after another torrid romp while Ian was gigging at the Blue Heaven, they sat up in bed, her head on his shoulder, his face buried in the warm scent of her hair.

"I'm sorry you're going through what you're going through," she said. "I did twice, I know how it feels. The end of a marriage, even a lousy one, is a little like a death. You grieve no matter what."

"I'm not grieving. Maybe a divorce is more like an operation than a death. You get over it, you stop hurting once the stitches heal."

"I want to revise what I just said. A *part* of me is sorry, the other part is . . . oh, I don't know."

"Happy?"

She raised her head and looked at him sideways. "Hopeful is a better word. What Liz did was rotten, but your wife was bound to find out sooner or later. And it, what you're going through, it opens up possibilities."

Luke didn't need to ask what those were.

"Once my contract with the museum expires, I'll be free to go or do whatever I want. I apologize if I sound like a ruthless little bitch, but if your divorce is final by then, you will be, too."

"And Ian? What about him?"

"I'm sure he won't want to stay with me. But he'll still be in my life. In yours, too, I hope. We'll have a chance to start over. The slate will be clean and we can start over."

As much as the picture of a second act appealed to Luke, practical considerations—How would they start over? Where?—stopped him from responding. Corinne's eyes drifted away from him to the window, the one with the shutters that, immobilized by their rusted hardware, could not be opened. His silence made her anxious.

"Am I being presumptuous?"

He shook his head. "Maybe rushing things a little."

He did not mind passing New Year's Eve in solitude. Its artificial gaiety bugged him. He watched the ball drop in Times Square, listened to blather about the momentous passage not only of a year but of a millennium, and went to bed confident that the human race would bumble through its next thousand years as it had the previous thousand. Near the end of the month, Maureen phoned—she was filing a "simplified" divorce petition. It was the first time they'd spoken since his eviction.

"Simplified means uncontested," she said. "It means we agree on dividing assets."

"Okay. So what do I need to do?"

"Agree!" she said with vicious glee.

"To what?"

"To give me the house."

Luke, on his condo's balcony overlooking the street (the expensive units had ocean views), dropped into a deck chair. "A lot of house for one person, don't you think?"

"It is. I intend to sell it. So you'll agree to, one, sign title over to me and then I sell, or two, we put it on the market together and you agree that the money, *all* of it, goes to me."

He sucked in a breath and said, "Florida's a no-fault state. We split things fifty-fifty."

"Fifty-fifty, schmifty-nifty. There is a fault here and it's yours. The fault is yours, my dear. It's called infidelity. You are *un mari infidèle.* You are also a liar. You married me under the false pretense that you weren't already the father of a child and you kept that from me for twenty-two years and you poured salt into that wound by seeing to it that you and I never had one together. You lied and cheated with your Queen of Tarts. That's fault in my book."

No fury in hell, he thought.

"And it would be fault in a judge's book," she stormed on. "A judge will consider infidelity and fraud when it comes to dividing assets, even in our sunny, no-fault state."

"I can tell you've been talking to your lawyer," he said.

"Damn right I have. And if you decide to contest, you'd better start talking to one yourself."

She hung up.

He took her advice, if advice it could be called, and made an appointment with one Leonard Wexler, who had handled Nick Ortega's messy divorce several years ago. Luke met with him in his Flagler Street office. He was a tanned, vigorous man in his late fifties, an avid golfer and tennis player, who wore a lugubrious expression that came from seeing too many people at their worst.

"It's depressing to watch a man and a woman who once loved each other tearing each other's throats out over who gets a favorite table lamp," he said. "But that's what butters my bread."

After Luke filled him in on Maureen's demands, and her theory that a judge would take his infidelity into account, Wexler folded his hands and lowered his chin in a meditative pose.

"Well, I've seen more than my share of extramarital affairs," he said. "I think they were invented about two hours after marriage was. But you know, I believe we're made for fidelity, even though we're so often unfaithful."

Luke looked at him, baffled by this observation.

"Sorry, waxing philosophical," the lawyer said, and opined that Maureen did not have all that strong a case. Yes, a court could take infidelity into account, but Luke's sins, in his estimation, would not be considered grave enough to justify ordering him to fork over his fair share of the house. On the other hand, Luke would be wise to weigh that probability against the certainty that a drawn-out court battle would cost a lot in terms of strain and aggravation, in addition to legal fees—"and I don't give discounts."

"There's no such thing as a friendly divorce," the lawyer continued. "It's just that some are way less friendly than others. Let me tell you, there are few things in life more stressful."

Luke replied that he would give the matter careful thought and left, his heart turned to lead. The lawyer's last statement flipped a switch in his memory, which replayed Maureen's phone call with the accuracy of a recorded message. As sensitive to her voice's pitch and modulations as a dolphin to the clicks and whistles of its companions, he detected a frangibility in her denunciations of his faithlessness and lies. That tense undertone had often, though not always, prophesied a breakdown. Might the strain of a protracted legal battle provoke one? The possibility poked the sleeping snake. *Don't do anything that could make her go crazy*, it hissed. This was what brought on the heaviness in his chest: separation from Maureen had not separated him from his role as guardian of her mental balance.

He waited a day before emailing her his decision—the house was hers. She responded with an inventory of its contents, marking an "x" after each item she claimed as hers. If he agreed, he was to sign an affidavit that her lawyer would be sending him. The inventory was very thorough, a testament to Maureen at her organized best. He read it through, and estimated that she wanted, in addition to the house, at least three-fourths of the stuff in it. He had the impression that she was trying to provoke an objection from him and thus, unmindful of the strain, drag the process out as long as she could. When Nick had been going through his divorce, he and his ex-wife had fought for weeks over every chair and table. They engaged in this pointless warfare to wound each other, but also because neither was quite ready to let go; they maintained their relationship by, perversely enough, feeding on its poisons. Thinking about this, Luke came to another decision—he would not take Maureen's bait, if she was trying to bait him—and wrote a two-word reply: "I agree."

She filed her petition on Valentine's Day.

He called Corinne almost every day; they would talk and talk, like lovestruck adolescents. He was able to see her only once before the end of January, when she phoned from Miami International to say that her connecting flight to New York had been delayed two hours due to bad weather in the north. How about he come by for a drink and see her off? He rushed over and met her in a concourse bar. She was joyful as well as worried that she would flop and Rubin never again exhibit her work. Luke's encouragements were anodyne and had little effect on her apprehensions. Their goodbye kiss at the security checkpoint, like their long phone conversations, was inappropriate for people their age.

PolitiWorld had given him a title, State Bureau Chief. It sounded impressive, though it represented a significant comedown. He who had once commanded a newsroom staff of five hundred was now in charge of three reporters not long out of journalism school. They were, he begrudgingly admitted, pretty good, proving that info-age whiz kids could write a crisp lede after all. The best of the three was a twenty-seven-year-old with a Hollywood name—Mandolit Cervantes. She required almost no direction, her stories only light editing. The daily newsletter had to be posted to subscribers by 6:30 a.m., and that included Saturdays and Sundays. Luke was usually out of bed and at his laptop by five, worked till eleven, then grabbed a nap before he checked the wire services and the major Florida papers for news trends and made assignments to his tiny staff. He'd yet to meet them face to face, perhaps the weirdest aspect of a weird job with weird hours. All the work was done remotely, by computer or phone. It made him miss the newsroom's camaraderie even more, and watching a fresh edition roll off the presses, a product that could be folded and cut, touched and smelled.

34

He was in his dining room/office, finishing edits on a story Cervantes had filed in advance of the Democratic primary between Al Gore and Bill Bradley, the former forward for the New York Knicks. Cervantes's piece was a "thumbsucker"—in the archaic parlance for a news feature—reflecting on Florida's aging core Democrats, the retired dockhands and garment workers and other blue-collar types who'd moved to the state twenty-five years ago but whose Flatbush and Brooklyn accents had not faded in the Florida sun, though they themselves were fading as a political force a candidate ignored at his peril. Luke scrolled through the story, made a few corrections, and pressed SEND, feeling as the feature flew through cyberspace like a defector from his former ink-stained tribe but pleased to be back in the game and earning a salary. Can't beat 'em, join 'em.

He stretched his arms overhead, cracked his knuckles, then went down to the condo's mailboxes to collect his mail. The usual junk: catalogs, credit card come-ons, ads for handymen and window washers, an electric bill. One piece was addressed to him rather than to "occupant"—a thick, oversize envelope bearing the return address of Island Testing Services, 1901 Kennedy Blvd., Key West, FL 33040. The DNA test he'd taken with Ian! When was it? At least two months ago. He'd forgotten about it.

Back in his apartment, he tossed the junk, opened the envelope, and found another inside it, sealed, along with a letter and a three-page "Guide to Reading a DNA Paternity Test."

In the letter, the director of ITS reminded him that the tests had been outsourced to a Lauderdale laboratory, Veri-Genetics Labs, and apologized for the extraordinary delay in reporting the results. Veri-Genetics had been swamped with court-ordered tests, which had taken priority over those requested by private individuals. The guide explained the terminology: "STR locus" indicated genetic markers; "Alleles" referred to the DNA segments of the markers; the "Combined Paternity Index," expressed as a number, stated if the tested male was or was not the biological father. Luke slit open the second envelope, which contained a chart with three columns of bewildering figures. They meant nothing to him. He turned to the second page and scanned down to the "Statement of Results" at the bottom.

His first thought was that he'd misread it, so he reread it, moving his lips as if he were semi-literate.

"The alleged father is excluded as the biological father of the tested child. This finding is based on the non-matching alleles observed at the STR loci with a CDI equal to zero. The probability of paternity is zero percent."

On the right side of the statement, reinforcing its devastating conclusion, were two white squares, one atop the other:

Combined Paternity Index

0

Probability of Paternity

0%

And so to his second thought: *This can't be right! There's been a mistake!* The samples had been in the lab for so long they must have gotten mixed up with someone else's. Short of breath, as if he'd run up a flight of stairs, he pulled a Lauderdale Yellow Pages from his desk drawer, but found no listing for Veri-Genetics. Directory assistance gave him the number. The technician he spoke to, a woman with a British or Australian accent, asked for the case ID code on the report, then told him to hold. When she came back on the line, she confirmed the findings.

"Not possible," Luke snapped. "You people must have screwed up."

"Excuse me, sir," she replied, icily. "We do all tests twice, to make sure they're correct, and we've done thousands without once being in error."

"How much would it cost to have it redone?"

"Two hundred dollars. We'll need fresh samples from both parties. The wait could also be a long one. Do you want to make an appointment?"

"No."

"Then good day, sir."

Luke slammed the receiver down. For a long while, he sat at the dining room table, staring at nothing, thinking nothing. If he'd been struck by lightning on a sunny day, he could not have been more dazed, more confused.

Then, after reading the report a third time, a firestorm of outrage burned through him. Corinne had betrayed him twice; twice and more—every day in the past seven months, from their reunion onward, had been a betrayal. It sickened him to realize he'd been right to mistrust her; sickened him physically. He stumbled into the bathroom and dry heaved, the spasms in his gut and throat turning to sobs as he thought of Ian. A true bond had been forged between them. Now it had been severed by three words and a single digit: Probability of Paternity—0%.

If he wasn't the father, then who was? She'd had plenty of opportunity to sleep with someone else during the times he'd been absent at Fort Polk. Maybe there'd been more than one. Collecting himself, he looked at his watch. Two p.m. Ian would be waking up after a late-night gig. He called Corinne's number. The answering machine picked up.

"Ian, if you're there, come to the phone." Luke began to count to five by thousands. At thousand-four, Ian responded in a voice distant and listless.

"What is it?

"I'm calling because—"

"I know why."

"You've seen the test results?" Luke asked.

"Came in yesterday's mail."

"In mine today. I don't know what to say."

"Me neither," Ian said.

"I can't believe it. I even called the lab to make sure they didn't make a mistake. They didn't."

"Uh-huh."

"Have you talked to her about it?"

"She's in New York."

"I know that. I meant did you phone her?"

"Uh-uh."

"This is tough on me. It's got to be tougher on you."

"Yeah." There was a long silence; then Ian, dropping the monosyllabic responses, poured out his hurt: "It makes me feel almost like I did the day my dad died. It's close to that. It's like you died. It's like I lost two fathers. When Corinne told me you were getting a divorce, I thought . . . I was hoping you two would get back together, and then the three of us . . .we'd be like, you know . . ."

Luke wished the phone would do to him as it did to his voice— convert him into an electric impulse, speed him through the lines, and reconvert him to his physical self at Ian's side. He would hug him, as if he really were his son. "When is she due back?" he asked.

"Tomorrow. Four o'clock."

"I'm going to come down there. I've got to talk to her. You can be there when I do. Or not. Whatever you're comfortable with."

"I'll think about it. The way I feel right now, I don't want to look at her lying face."

"Listen, one other thing. You told me you told her we were taking the tests, right?"

"Uh-huh. The same day we took 'em."

"Remind me. How did she act?"

"Kind of normal," Ian replied. "She didn't get nervous or any-thing. I remember she said she thought it wasn't necessary, like you did, but that if it made me feel better to take it, she was cool with that."

Luke left late the next morning, his nerves raw after a night of fragmented sleep. He felt that he was the victim of a shameful deception, yet he could not fathom what Corrine's motives might be. Money? She'd never asked for any, and what little he'd spent on her and Ian he'd spent voluntarily. On the drive down US 1, admiring, as he always did, the shimmering Atlantic on one side, the Gulf on the other, he was teased by her reaction to Ian's declaration. If she'd known, or even half believed, that Luke wasn't the father, wouldn't she have been upset? Wouldn't she have tried to talk him out of taking the test? Maybe she was a better actress than he'd given her credit for—dissimulation was the grifter's fundamental art. But again, what was the grift if it wasn't money? Was she capable of such deceit for some other, unknown reason? This was a woman who had enticed a man into her bed, rifled his wallet while he slept, and flew off to have an abortion. This was a woman who'd thrown Luke over to marry that same man, and then vanished. He vividly relived the days he'd wandered through San Francisco in search of her, and those mem-ories overwhelmed any impulse he might have had to give her the benefit of the doubt.

He pulled into the airport parking lot at ten past two, checked the arrivals board in the terminal—the Miami shuttle was on time—then bought a *Time* magazine and this month's issue of *Salt Water Sportsman* and sat down to wait. It was hard to focus through his jumbled thoughts. He was rereading a paragraph about marlin fishing for the second time when the cellphone in his pocket vibrated. It was Ian.

"I'm hanging out with Taylor," he said. "Where are you?"

Luke told him.

"I've decided to sit it out. I'm afraid I'd say something that can't be taken back. Besides, it's between you two. And what's between me and her, I'll deal with that later."

"That sounds best. I'll let you know what she says," Luke said. "Listen, you might feel like getting drunk or high. Don't."

"I'm cool."

The shuttle landed at a quarter past four. As he watched it taxiing to a stop, he felt an incipient panic, an urge to bolt back to his car, but then, seemingly of its own will, a picture of Mr. Hayakawa appeared in his memory; the tranquil, meticulous Mr. Hayakawa, whose image reached across distance and time to quiet his nerves.

Key West's small airport did not have jetways. By standing near the baggage claim carousel and looking through the open entrance door, he was able to watch Corinne disembark with the other passengers. She was wearing an outfit he hadn't seen before—white pants, a patterned peach blouse, white open-toe shoes. A winter coat was thrown over one arm. He would have been struck by her if he'd never met her—her height, her walk, at once sinuous and regal, her sable hair. Even at a distance, she exerted a power over him. He could imagine himself losing all resolve, losing himself in her, carrying on as if nothing had changed.

Her tired traveler's expression brightened when she spotted him. She called, "Luke! What a surprise!" and with a quick little run came up to him and kissed him. He returned the kiss—his marriage had made him proficient in the art of faking affection—and gallantly took her bag off the belt and carried it to the car.

"How did you know when I was coming in?" she asked, clicking the seat belt.

"Ian told me."

It was no more than a fifteen-minute drive to her place—time enough for her to relate her smashing success in New York. One of her paintings had taken an honorable mention at the show; it and another had sold for a total of . . . Dipping into her purse, she pulled out a check for $3,000, her net after Rubin's 40 percent fee.

"So I splurged. Bought this outfit at Saks. On sale. What do you think?"

"Looks good," he said, mechanically.

"I'm trying to keep things in perspective," she carried on. "But after all, a Soho gallery. I wasn't competing against the second string, and I got an honorable mention. That counts for something, besides the money."

"It does."

Buoyed by her triumph, she didn't notice the indifference in his responses. He pulled up in front of the Ashe Street house, reached into the back seat for the folder containing the DNA report, and, tucking it under his arm, toted her suitcase up the stairs. Inside, he flopped down on the couch while she went to the bathroom, then into the kitchen, emerging with two glasses of white wine.

"So let's celebrate," she said, sitting next to him, her knee touching his. "To Mister Rubin and an honorable mention and three grand."

Luke scooted away from her, the folder in his lap, arms crossed tightly across his chest.

Corrine looked at him askance. "Did I say something?"

"No."

"What's the matter, then?"

"I need to talk to you. I drove down here because I need to talk to you."

"Sounds ominous."

"About this," he said, handing her the report. "I need you to explain it."

Corrine, scowling, glanced at the columns of figures: D31358 - 0.000; D135137-0.768; D 251338 - 0.000 . . .

"Explain what? What do these numbers mean?"

"They mean that my DNA and Ian's don't match. They mean that I'm not his father."

Her head jerked back, as if she were dodging a blow, and her eyes fluttered with quick, irregular blinks.

"Read what it says on the second page," he said.

This she did, softly but aloud. "Probability of paternity, zero percent. What the hell is this? Where did you get this?"

"The results of the paternity test I took with Ian. He told you about it. Where did I get it? In the mail. The lab mailed the results to me—and him."

"You mean to tell me he thinks you're not his father?"

"He knows I'm not, just like I know it."

"Bullshit!" she yelled. "It's bullshit! These people fucked up some way. There's no way in hell—"

"I thought the same thing," he interrupted with studied calm. "But they run the test twice to make sure they get it right. Verified. I guess that's what the 'veri' means in Veri-Genetics. Verified. Veritas. Truth. It's what I'd like to hear from you. Why have you lied to me all this time?" he implored. Almost the exact words Maureen had thrown at him. The symmetry between what had passed between his wife and him and what was happening now struck him as karmic: he'd been wronged as punishment for the wrongs he'd done. "Why did you lie to me then and now? What did you expect to get out of it?"

"I haven't lied to you. Not then, not now, not ever. This is the lie!" She rolled up the report and swung, intending to swat the air; instead, she struck her wine glass, knocking it to the floor, its contents spilling onto her practically new sisal rug.

"Goddamnit!"

When a petty mishap occurs in the midst of a calamity they cannot manage, people tend to magnify the former into a disaster that must be dealt with immediately simply because they're capable of dealing with it. Corinne ran into the kitchen, wet a dish towel, and knelt on the rug to sop up the spill. *Blot, don't rub,* she reminded herself, feeling the sisal prick her knees through the thin pants. In her distant, careless youth, she would not have gone to the trouble; she might have regarded the resultant stain as a mark of her contempt for bourgeois tidiness. Returning to the kitchen, she wrung the towel out in the sink. The cheap wine's vinegary smell rose into her nostrils, and suddenly her head swam, her chest tightened, making her almost breathless. *Gerald.* That was the name of her gay friend in New Orleans; his apartment where, half-dressed, she'd woken up on the scratchy rug after passing out at an all-night party, had been on Chartres Street. Now, she knew what had happened there. She also knew that she'd always known but hadn't been able to face it. So her mind had played tricks on her, deceiving her into thinking it had been an hallucination or something she'd dreamed. Gerald, finger wagging. Naughty girl.

She gripped the edge of the sink to steady herself and took deep breaths. She began to cry, quietly, but loud enough to bring Luke to the kitchen door. Turning, she waved him back into the living room, then dried her eyes with the back of her hand, collected herself, and followed him.

"It happened that time we broke up," she said, and leaned against a wall for support.

Luke did not say anything. He sank onto the couch.

"It was during that month. I partied a lot. I was at a party. A gay guy I knew threw it. I hung with gays, because I thought they'd be safe. But there were straight guys at the party, and—"

She stopped. Luke looked at her, quizzically. "And what?"

"It must've been one of them."

"*Must have been?* You don't know?"

"No."

"You're at a party, and some guy . . . and you don't have any idea who?"

"I'd had a lot to drink, and somebody passed me a tab of acid. I was high, tripping, couldn't tell what was real, what I was imagining. I remember going with him into another room, the bedroom, and I saw his face above me . . . but I must've thought I was hallucinating or something."

Luke took ten or fifteen seconds to absorb this; then he asked, "And all of it is just now coming back to you? Like some kind of recovered memory?"

"It's come back to me, yes. I don't know about recovered memory."

He stared at her as if she'd broken out in sores. All the misgivings he'd ever had about her, all the doubts he'd suppressed, bubbled to the surface. "You never said one single goddamn word to me. You let me believe I was Ian's father for all this time. All this time. Jesus Christ, Corinne. Jesus loving Christ."

"Because I believed it!" she said. "All those times we'd been together . . . I never would have thought I could have gotten pregnant from that one time. One guy, *one time.* I never lied to you. Not deliberately. Do you believe me?"

"The trouble is, I do. You lied to yourself, and that's how you lied to me and Ian." Luke shifted his gaze to the skylight, to the square of blue it framed. "I told Ian that I'd let him know what you had to say, but I'm going to leave that to you. You'll have to tell him that his father was some guy you can't remember because you were too stoned. You'll have to tell him exactly that."

She swallowed and nodded, then floated across the room, sat beside him, and reached for his hand. It did not disturb her when he pulled his away. She expected him to. "Can you still love me? Can you forgive me?"

He continued to hear echoes of his confrontation with Maureen. He considered his answer, aware that the slightest ambiguity could doom him. "I closed my forgiveness account when I forgave you for disappearing on me. You used me, just like you used your first husband when you pinched his wallet to pay for an abortion."

"That is not true, Luke. That is absolutely not fucking true!"

"I don't trust you. I'd like to, but I can't. No trust, no love." He stood and looked down at her, torn between an urge to kiss her and another to slap her, giving back hurt for hurt. Then a cold wave surged through him and swept both away. "We're done, Corrine. I'd say we're done."

She flinched, as if he *had* struck her. "You don't mean that, you can't possibly mean that."

"Yeah, I do."

"No, you don't. We can get through this, Luke."

"I don't see how. It's all right there, plain as can be." He motioned at the report lying on the floor. "Probability of paternity—zero."

"You're going to throw away everything we've been to each other, throw it all away because of this?" She picked up the papers and flapped them in the air and flung them back to the floor. "This DNA crap? Ian is as much a son to you as he is to me, DNA or no DNA."

"That's something else you can tell him."

"He needs you. I need you. And you need us. Yeah, you do."

He turned toward the door. Corrine stood, raising a hand to stop him. "Know what? I think you're still pissed off at me for jilting you way back then. And this is revenge. For a mistake I made when I was a kid. That's all it is. Go ahead, then. Walk out. Go back to your nutty professor if she'll have you."

Luke would later feel grateful for the cheap shot; it stiffened his wavering resolve. He left. She flew to the door. "We would have been terrific together!" she cried out as he started down the stairs. "I still think so!"

"I don't," he said, not looking at her as he continued down.

Corrine shut the door. Going into the bathroom, she contemplated herself in the vanity mirror. Had she been feeling more sorrow than anger, she would have been in tears. "Stupid!" she said to her reflection, then slapped herself on the cheek, slapped hard enough to make it sting. "Stupid!" She struck the opposite cheek. "Stupid!" And then the other again. "Stupid! Stupid! Stupid!"

35

In the future, Luke would look upon the period in his life between the autumn of 1999 and the winter of 2000 as the season of shocks. In four months, he'd lost his best friend, his job, his wife, his lover, and (if the discovery of Ian's true paternity counted as a loss) a son. A profound sense of isolation and disconnection, aggravated by his barren apartment, overtook him. The rootless army brat, parents deceased, no family to speak of except for distant cousins back in Kentucky whom he'd not seen since his uncle's funeral. He was a planet dislodged from its orbit, wandering in a frigid vacuum. As an antidote to self-pity, he reminded himself that much of his situation had been his own doing.

He went on a buying spree for furniture and artwork to warm his place up or at a minimum make it look less like a model apartment. That occupied his spare time for about two weeks. Even so, he had too many idle hours on his hands, during which Corinne stalked his mind, stirring up an internal free-for-all between yearning and repugnance. Gradually, though he knew he would never go back to her, he began to think that he'd been too harsh in his judgments. And he was in no moral position to judge anyone for withholding a painful truth.

In late March, he sent a birthday card to Ian in St. Petersburg, where he had moved after serving out his term of parole. In an email, he wrote to Luke that he'd landed a job as an apprentice in computer repair and was playing with a band that had a steady weekend gig at a beachside club. He and Corinne were struggling to reconcile the reality of his paternity with the incontrovertible fact that she was the only mother he had. "Sometimes I wish to hell we'd never taken those tests," he said. "But I guess it's better to know than not know. I think of you as my almost-dad."

Those words inspired Luke to do some research. When it was done, he flew to St. Petersburg first chance he got, met Ian at his rundown apartment complex, and treated him to dinner at his hotel downtown. They took a table at the poolside restaurant, the height of luxury to Ian. He ordered a steak. Luke appreciated that he asked first if a steak would be all right, price-wise. After they'd caught up, Luke got around to the purpose of his visit.

"I've been thinking what it means to be an 'almost-dad,'" he said.

Ian chortled. "That was something that just came to me. I don't know that it means anything."

"Well, it could. Are we only bags full of DNA, genes, chromosomes, or do we have souls? As a bag of DNA, there's no way I could be your father. As a soul, maybe."

"What d'you mean? A soul-father, like a soul-brother?"

"I hadn't thought of it like that, but yeah. I like 'soul-father' better than 'almost-dad.' I've been looking into adult adoptions. They're legal in Florida as long as both parties agree to it."

Ian's eyebrows arched up and down, like furry black caterpillars trying to crawl. "You're saying you want to adopt me?"

"If you consented to it."

"Hard to know what to say. I'm thirty-one. Weird to be thirty-one and adopted. But it wouldn't be the first time: I'm an experienced adoptee." He momentarily looked away, tracking with the hungry eyes of a healthy young male a woman in a bikini as she walked past, stood at the pool's edge, and dove in. In the ripples she made, the submerged lights wavered, as if they had turned into water. "Would I have to change my name? I wouldn't do it if I have to change my name. That'd be like betraying my dad."

"I looked into that, too. You wouldn't have to if you don't want to. Adoption would give us a legal connection, Ian, it would be like the difference between a man and a woman living together or getting married. You're like a son to me. I want to make it official. Not your almost-dad, your dad."

"Yo, man." Ian was close to choking up. "It's a lot. I've got to think about it."

Forty-eight hours later, he emailed his approval, writing that for the first time since his parents' deaths he felt anchored in the world. Luke was buoyant. Corrine had been right: He needed Ian, Ian him. Attending to the legal details required another visit to Wexler, who helped him fill out the petition for adoption. A consent form was mailed to Ian for his signature. The process was going to take some time. Copies of death certificates for Winslow and Justine Campbell had to be obtained to verify that they were deceased, and the birth mother had to give her consent in writing. That worried Luke. Corinne might refuse, to spite him. She did not; there was a generosity in her nature, and it came through. The signed form arrived at Wexler's office with a note to Luke attached:

> I'm doing this for Ian's sake. I think it will be good for him to have a connection to you. He and I are working to settle things between us. I understand why you were (are?) so angry with me. I'm angry with myself. But I want to say something I said before. This could have worked out if you'd been able to forgive me and love me and marry me. Ian is now as much your son as he would be if you shared the same blood. Then

we could have been a real family. But I guess this will have to do for second best. I'm leaving K.W. in a week or so. Going back to N.O. Got a job with a graphic design firm there, and Rubin gave me a hand establishing a contact with a gallery in the Quarter. So long, Luke, and love. C.A.T.

He looked at the familiar backhand, pierced through his core, and had a fleeting vision of them living together as man and wife, getting together with Ian on weekends or holidays. A real family. A tide of love rose swiftly in him and as swiftly ebbed when he reflected on their affair and saw that theirs had not been a love resurrected but desire arising from desire remembered—a kind of nostalgia. Latent within it had been a fanciful, and futile, longing to recapture the past and somehow make it turn out differently, as if the unalterable past were clay, to be remolded to suit one's wishes.

He plunged himself into his work, grateful to have it. A job to do, a place to go. He deployed his trio of reporters to cover local races and the contest for the US Senate between the "two Bills"—Nelson the Democrat, McCollum the Republican. To see what his people looked like and get a sense of their personalities unobtainable in online conversations, he flew to Tallahassee to meet with his state capitol staffers, a Black guy, Darrin Jones, and a white guy named Jay Cesnik. For the same reasons, he lunched with the Miami correspondent, she of the dramatic name, Mandolit Cervantes, a daughter of Venezuelan immigrants (Black, white, Hispanic—PolitiWorld had the diversity boxes checked).

Some five months had elapsed since Maureen kicked him out of the house, nearly three since she'd filed for divorce; but she had yet to serve him the divorce papers—the "Petition for Dissolution of Marriage," as it was termed in legalese. Nor had he heard from her, leading him to wonder if she was having second thoughts or if she was dissatisfied with their settlement agreement and contemplating additional demands. He should have contacted her weeks ago, but inertia had overtaken him; he'd been content to let things play out in their own time. Clearly, the time for that had passed. He sent her an email asking what was the holdup.

She responded almost immediately, as if she'd been waiting patiently for word from him.

> Caro Luke—In answer to your query, one, I have been busy with my classes and with my book. You may recall that I have a contract for a book about Joyce's poetry. *Chamber Music*, remember? I have a deadline. You of all people should understand what that means. I've been under a lot of pressure, and pressure isn't good for me and I'll thank you not to add to it. But if you're so eager to dissolve our marriage—isn't that sweet, dissolve, like a marriage is a substance easily liquified—perhaps you should file your own petition. Are you eager, and if so, is it to marry your Queen of Tarts? Ciao, ciao, M.

The term of endearment, *Caro*, the breezy sign off, *Ciao*, clashed with the message's tone and threw him off balance. He allowed himself a day before writing back.

> Maureen—I thought I'd asked a simple question. When can I expect to be served the divorce papers? I assume your lawyer told you that you have 120 days or case dismissed. Close to 90 have gone by already. As for my eagerness, all I want is to get this

over with and move on. It's not to marry
Corinne. It's over between her and me. All
Best, Luke.

Her reply came three days later.

Caro Luke—So, so sorry that your rekindled
affair has been extinguished (not really
sorry, of course, the Queen of Tarts broke
my heart). How is your darling baby boy, by
the way? Reason for the delay—I had asked
my lawyer to give me a few weeks to review
things. I called him this morning, you'll
have the papers anon. Ciao, M.

A process server delivered them to him on the last day of
April. Because the divorce was uncontested, Luke would not be
required to appear in court for the final hearing, set for May 10, a
Wednesday. Almost exactly a year from the day he and Mike and
Dustin had rescued the refugees marooned on the Marquesas Keys.
There wasn't much point in thinking about what might have happened if that had not.

He phoned Dustin and chartered him for the 10th—he did not
want to be in Miami on his D-for-divorce day. They fished the flats for
tarpon and told stories about Mike Conway, Dustin still in disbelief that
he had done what he had done. Didn't seem the kind of guy who'd put
a pistol to his own head.

Luke missed a few casts to cruising fish before hooking one on a
black and purple streamer, beautifully tied by Emilio Cortazar. He was
selling them to charter captains for half what they cost in tackle stores,
in addition to his after-school job cleaning the *Marekrishna*.

"The kid's doing okay," Dustin said. "Learning English fast. Whenever anybody asks him how he got here, he tells them that he drove from Cuba in a '59 Mercury."

Key West felt haunted to Luke. On his way to Pepe's for breakfast the next morning, he learned that Singleton's packing plant would close within a year; the shrimp beds had been netted clean, the boats were heading elsewhere in quest of pink gold, the docks where they had berthed were going to be converted into a marina, their rough captains and deckhands replaced by yachtsmen.

The squad of winos occupied their usual place in front of Garland's grocery, but Gunny wasn't among them. Luke asked after him.

"He's gone," answered one of the men in a pack-a-day voice.

"Where to?"

The man's shoulders slowly rose, giving him the crouched look of a night heron, then slowly fell. "I mean the man is *gone*, as in no longer on the planet."

"How?"

"Tired, I guess. I could use a buck for a cup of coffee."

Maureen's next email arrived in his inbox on the 12th.

> Caro—So now it's done. We have been dis-
> solved as a married couple, like soap powder
> in a laundromat. You haven't told me yet how
> your darling baby boy is doing.

Luke considered replying at length, but chose to keep it short.

> M. Ian is not my son by birth. We took DNA
> tests and they proved we're not related.
> He's doing fine.

> Carissimo—Ha! So the Queen of Tarts tarted

you! The fact that you're not related to Ian
is irrelevant. All those years you believed
you were and you kept it from me and you had
that procedure making it impossible for us
to have children. I may still have some love
left for you, but you really truly honest
to God make me sick. I wish you would stop
communicating with me.

It was futile to point out that in her last two messages it was she
communicating with him. He did not hear from her again until the
Memorial Day weekend.

My dear ex-husband: If I have a chance to
marry again, and pray that I do, I wish to
marry in the church. Therefore, I have been
in touch with my parish priest about setting
the wheels in motion, destination—An annulment! You will have to answer some questions
that will be put to you by the Marriage
Tribunal. M.

Tribunal? It sounded like something out of the Inquisition.
In the middle of June he received a flurry of emails over the course
of ten days. They began to take an ominous turn, and the pathological
notes in the final one could not have been clearer.

My Ex—The Tribunal meets in my used to be
our house Friday night be there! Annulment
prefer annul to dissolve don't you? No longer binding Maureen unbound!! You haven't
answered previous msgs. Perche non mi hai

```
riposto? Hard to concentrate but must must
deadlines approach and you not making it any
easier who betrayed me for a common slut.
The Tribunal will unbind me in the eyes of
Holy Mother the Church. Seven pm. Be there
to answer for yourself, ciao mi carissimo.
```

He formed a mental picture of her as she typed these chaotic lines—lips tight, fingers racing to keep up with her racing thoughts.

Today was Friday.

He called Dr. Pearle's office and asked, all but pleaded, to speak to him immediately. The receptionist was unyielding. The doctor was with a patient, he would phone Luke as soon as he was free.

It was close to five before he did, apologizing for the delay. Crowded schedule. Luke asked if he had seen Maureen lately. Two weeks ago to check her lithium levels and to see how she was handling the stress of divorce. And how was she handling it? Fairly well, all things considered.

"Maybe not so well now," Luke said and read the email to him.

There was a long pause on the line before Dr. Pearle voiced his agreement. "She should come in first thing in the morning. Are you going to see her tonight?"

"I am, and I'd appreciate it if you could go with me. A house call, sort of."

"I would if I could. But I'm the keynote speaker at a hospital fundraiser. It kicks off at six thirty. I should be wrapped up by nine. If there's an emergency, call me at home. You have the number?"

Luke replied that he did.

"It's damn good of you to be concerned for her. It's not really your responsibility any longer."

"Oh, it is, Nathan," said Luke, wearily. "It will be until I drop dead or she does."

36

The dormant snake was fully awake, fully aroused, coiling around his heart as he rang the front doorbell. The window blinds were closed upstairs and down. Through the cracks, he could see a flickering light, as from faulty bulbs. Receiving no answer, he tried a loud knock, waited five or ten seconds, then turned the handle. The door swung open. He stepped through the entry hall into the living room and gaped in wonderment at candles burning everywhere. There must have been twenty—tapered candles in single and double holders, squat candles burning in glass jars while a chant mass played on the CD. *Sanctus sanctus sanctus . . . Dominus Deus sabaoth . . .* But that scene was merely curious compared with the one that greeted him when he entered the dining room, where more candles, in menorah-like candelabras placed at either end of the table, illuminated four figures seated facing one another, two on each side. They were composed of bed and throw pillows covered in black, hooded cloaks, such as kids might wear on Halloween.

"Maureen!" he called, moving into the kitchen, into the den, into the Florida room, and back into the living room. "Maureen! Where are you?"

"Right here," she answered from the top of the stairs. In a sheer white nightgown that showed the outline of her body, she was holding a duplicate of the candelabras on the table. In the guttering light, she looked at once beautiful and terrifying, a dazed smile on her lips. "I am so pleased you could make it for your examination," she said, drifting down the stairs, like a ghost in a Gothic novel. She swept past him into the dining room.

"Come here. The Tribunal has questions for you."

The normality in her voice made the bizarre scene all the more bizarre.

"Maureen, get hold of yourself!"

"Come here, Luke."

He moved toward her, uncertain what else to do. He'd never seen her this delusional, but how far gone could she be? She must have planned this, thought it out like a set designer; must have gone out to buy the candles and holders and hooded cloaks; must have shaped and arrayed the pillows on the chairs to resemble human figures and put the CD in the player and drawn the curtains, closed the blinds, turned off the lights. The orderly arrangements of a disordered mind. This encouraged him—there had to be a part of her, still sane, that he could reach.

"Listen to me now," he said, soothingly. "This is crazy, and I know you know it is, deep down you know it."

"Quiet! Don't tell me this is crazy. Satan was in the house, and now he's gone. That is what I know."

Looking at the twitching circles of light the candles cast on the walls, listening to the chant wafting in from the adjoining room, *Agnus Dei, qui tollis pecatta mundi*, he almost believed that a supernatural presence had been here and might still be in residence.

"Please put those candles down, go upstairs and get dressed."

"The Tribunal wishes to know. Did you commit adultery and did you knowingly withhold from me that you were the father of a bastard? Answer those questions that I may be Maureen unbound."

"You have got to get hold of yourself, damnit!"

He reached out to her. With her free hand, she slapped his aside.

"Don't you touch me!" she hissed through gritted teeth. "Those fingers have been in the filthy cunt of your Queen of Tarts and I will not have them touch me!"

In seconds, her rage swung to manic laughter, which in seconds more changed to tears and then back to rage.

"Blazes Boylan and his big red brute of a thing that was stuck up her filthy cunt, was it not? Tell them"—flinging an arm at the dummies—"how you cheated on me and lied by your silences a sin of omission was what it was Blazes you son of a bitch!"

Luke knew from a past conversation with Dr. Pearle that there was a clinical term for these rapid transitions in mood—cyclothymia. Like "psychotic episode," the word did nothing to dispel the effect the phenomenon had on anyone witnessing it. He pulled his cellphone out of his back pocket.

"What are you doing who are you calling?" Maureen shrieked.

"An ambulance. You're very sick," he said, as if speaking to a child. "You need to go to the hospital."

"Oh, no not that do not send me to that dreadful place please—"

"Then get control of yourself."

The sound she made, half scream, half sob, froze him where he stood. She threw the candelabra at him, and as he dodged aside, she fled the room. Flung from their holders, the candles fell on the floor and on the dummy closest to him, setting the cloak on fire. It must have been made of some highly flammable synthetic material, because in seconds it was blazing like a torch while smaller flames licked the carpet under the table. Luke ran into the kitchen, remembering the fire extinguisher kept there, yanked it off the wall beside the rear door, then ran back into the dining room, where the dummy and the chair were now both ablaze. Following the instructions on the bottle—PULL HANDLE DEPRESS LEVER SPRAY BOTTOM OF FLAME WITH SIDE

TO SIDE MOTION—he snuffed the fires. A few embers continued to burn on the carpet. He hurried into the kitchen again, filled a mop bucket with water from the sink, and dumped it on the floor, the chair, and the charred remains of the make-believe tribunal judge. The ashes hissed and smoked and the stench of scorched wood and carpet seared his nostrils. He was dismayed to see that he'd dropped his cellphone in the panic of the moment; it, too, was burned, its screen melted.

Afraid that Maureen had run out of the house, he started toward the front door but stopped when he heard a thump directly above. He flew up the stairs to the master bedroom, flicked the light switch, and saw a vodka bottle tipped over on a night stand and a light slithering through the bottom crack in the bathroom door. He tried it; it was locked from the inside. He banged on it, calling to her. There was no response except for what sounded like attempts at speech that came out as moans and grunts.

Standing well back, he drove a foot into the door just below the handle. It did not budge; nor did it move on a second kick. A third, which sent a shock up his leg into his knee and from there into his gut, dislodged it. Taking another step backward, he lunged into it shoulder first and broke it open, ripping off the molding inside.

Maureen lay semiconscious on the floor, in an undignified sprawl that would have shamed her if she could have seen herself. A prescription bottle was on the bath rug beside her, along with a few scattered tablets. Ambien.

"Jesus Christ, what have you done to yourself?" he cried, then knelt and pressed two fingers to her carotid artery. Her pulse felt weak.

"What have you done to yourself, Maureen?" he cried again, his hand moving from her neck to her cheek, stroking it gently.

She made more unintelligible sounds, slow, quavering hums.

"Shhh," he whispered. "Quiet now."

Ambien mixed with alcohol was a lethal combination that could kill in minutes. He knew that, but not what to do about it. CPR? Induce

vomiting? Placing his hands under her armpits, he lifted her partway
off the floor and dragged her into the bedroom; then, raising first her
torso and next her legs, he swung her onto the bed.

What the hell did you do for an Ambien overdose? He had to call
911, tell the dispatcher: drug overdose, send ambulance immediately.
But as he reached for the phone on the night table, his arm felt as
though he were trying to move it through mud or wet concrete. An
immense weariness overtook him, an exhaustion more spiritual than
physical. This was never going to end. The ambulance would speed
her to the ER, the doctors would stabilize her; then Dr. Pearle would
examine her and commit her for a week or two weeks or however long
it took to restore her to herself. Maureen would be Maureen again. Mr.
Finnegan is fine again. And then, in six months or a year or five years,
the demon would afflict her once more, and he, Luke, would be there
to see her through, husband or not-husband, it made no difference. No
end to it. Unless—

The thought burst fully blown in his mind—*Unless he just let her go.*
He need do nothing but wait till life left her and released him from
her, she from the monster that tormented her. No one would see, no
one would know.

Then Wexler spoke in his memory—*We are made for fidelity, even
though we're so often unfaithful*—as Maureen made the humming sound
again, steady, with hardly a change in pitch.

"Shhh, quiet, shhh," he said, and picked up the phone.

About the Author

Philip Caputo was born in Chicago in 1941 and educated at Purdue and Loyola Universities. After graduating in 1964, he served in the US Marine Corps for three years, including a sixteen-month tour of duty in Vietnam. He has written seventeen books, among them three memoirs, ten works of fiction, and four of general nonfiction. His first book, *A Rumor of War*, is considered a classic of war literature. It has been published in fifteen languages and has sold more than 1.5 million copies. A Pulitzer Prize–winning journalist, Caputo has written dozens of articles in major magazines, op-ed pieces, and reviews for publications across the United States, including the *New York Times*, *National Geographic*, and the *Chicago Tribune*. He lives in Norwalk, Connecticut, and Patagonia, Arizona.